C000302173

Extreme Expectations of the Exiled

Through the Treeline: Book Three

Tuesday Simon

Copyright © 2022 Tuesday Simon

All rights reserved

The characters and events portrayed in this book are fictitious. Any similarity to real persons, living or dead, is coincidental and not intended by the author.

No part of this book may be reproduced, or stored in a retrieval system, or transmitted in any form or by any means, electronic, mechanical, photocopying, recording, or otherwise, without express written permission of the publisher.

ISBN-13: 9798795623481
ISBN-10: 1477123456

Cover design by: Candice Puga
Library of Congress Control Number: 2018675309
Printed in the United States of America

To my parents, because they raised three wild daughters and deserve recognition for that. And also because they were my first example of what it means to love your best friend.
They've always supported every aspect of my creativity and for that I am so thankful.
And to the toad that jumped out at me that fateful night... I toad-ally still loathe you.

Contents

Title Page

Copyright

Dedication

Pronunciations

Chapter 1	1
Chapter 2	13
Chapter 3	21
Chapter 4	26
Chapter 5	39
Chapter 6	53
Chapter 7	61
Chapter 8	69
Chapter 9	76
Chapter 10	81
Chapter 11	90
Chapter 12	96
Chapter 13	101
Chapter 14	114
Chapter 15	121
Chapter 16	128

Chapter 17   134

Chapter 18   139

Chapter 19   148

Chapter 20   153

Chapter 21   158

Chapter 22   165

Chapter 23   169

Chapter 24   176

Chapter 25   183

Chapter 26   188

Chapter 27   200

Chapter 28   206

Chapter 29   211

Chapter 30   216

Chapter 31   226

Chapter 32   233

Chapter 33   237

Chapter 34   246

Chapter 35   252

Chapter 36   258

Chapter 37   268

Chapter 38   273

Chapter 39   282

Chapter 40   290

Chapter 41   302

Chapter 42   308

Chapter 43   317

Chapter 44   328

Chapter 45   334

Chapter 46   343

Chapter 47   352

Chapter 48   368

Chapter 49   377

Chapter 50   383

Chapter 51   393

Chapter 52   400

Chapter 53   415

Chapter 54   425

Chapter 55   434

Chapter 56   442

Chapter 57   449

Chapter 58   461

Chapter 59   467

Chapter 60   471

Chapter 61   481

Chapter 62   488

Chapter 63   495

Chapter 64   503

Chapter 65   513

Chapter 66   523

Chapter 67   531

Chapter 68   540

Chapter 69   546

Chapter 70   552

The End   555

The saga will conclude with"Through the Treeline"   557

Book Four

The history is finally told in the Through the Treeline   559
prequel

About The Author   561

Pronunciations

A quick list on how the author suggests you say
some of the names mentioned in this story
Rilonck= rye-lonck
Farein= fair-ine
Keilon= key-lon
Sorner= sore-ner
Teyle= tay-lee
Dylah= die-luh
Kunor= koo-ner
Kremon= crim-min
Delin= dell-in
Verinas= vair-in-us
Gomdea= gom-dee-ah
Nevely= nev-uh-lee

Chapter 1

300 years ago...

"I demand an audience with the king!" The slender blonde man spoke as calmly as he could to the two guards posted outside the Fellowrock castle doors.

"We can't allow you inside," a guard replied in monotone.

"He's my brother!" he huffed. "Don't you have the slightest clue telling you who I am? Must I shout about the qualities that flow in my veins?"

"I'm sorry, Sorner, but King Keilon has banned you from the castle."

"Under what grounds?" Sorner clenched his teeth. "Is it because I'm actually sane? Hm? Is that it? Has logical thought been banned as well? You all might be under his tricky spells but not me!" He shook his head. "Absolutely maddening. Prepare yourselves, I will begin to shout soon."

The castle doors creaked open, a strong frame stood in the doorway as a low chuckle echoed forth.

"Little brother, you just can't take the hint, can you?" Keilon took a step out of the castle, shutting the doors behind him.

"What are you hiding in there, Keilon?" Sorner's dark green eyes met Keilon's electric irises. "Women? Murder? Another one of our siblings that you've escorted to an early demise?"

"Perhaps all of that and more." Keilon flashed a smile. "And none of your concern, I should have you arrested for treason."

"Treason? Oh what a glorious word to throw around!" Sorner laughed. "As if I'm the one who sent Fellowrock into ruin?!"

"We are not in ruin!" Keilon pushed Sorner back. "We are in a state of planning!"

"We can't leave the border, Keilon!"

"Temporary," the king growled.

"I warned you that something like this would happen, I never imagined it would be this extreme, but I knew you'd be the one behind it."

"It's been a year, Sorner, I'm sorry you were frightened by tall blades of grass." Keilon chuckled. "You always were a soft one."

"Do you have any idea what repercussions have already begun to unfold?" Sorner grabbed his brother's arms. "Don't you see beyond the courtyard walls at all?"

"We are strong."

"We are suffering!"

"In what way are you suffering, prized child of Fellowrock?"

"Of course you think I'm being selfish!" Sorner seethed. "We can no longer transport lumber for trading, we will need to start burning our dead because we can no longer expand our land for burials, children have wandered and have never come back, we have always relied on being able to leave, and now we can't! We are stuck, we are failing, our people are declining, and you are doing nothing!"

"I'm listening to this pointless conversation."

Sorner stared speechless, he narrowed his eyes and peered into the image of chaotic power. "You worry."

"I do not!" Keilon shouted as he covered his eyes. "Don't do your little party trick on me!"

"You worry there is no way out of this curse, you feel guilty, and of course you miss Teyle."

"Stop!"

"You fill that void with women and beer and violent sport but it will never go away, Keilon. You should feel guilty."

"Sorner! Enough!"

"Let me help you!" Sorner pleaded. "It's what I'm meant to do! You and I have always been close, don't let your guilt and this dreadful curse push us apart. Maybe we can solve this if we combine our strengths." He sighed. "Can't you sense how unbalanced this all feels? It's absolutely annoying, Keilon."

Sorner watched with quiet anxiety as the flames smoldered in his brother's eyes.

"You're a thorn in my side, you know that?" A smirk spread on the king's face.

"And yet you still don't pluck me out." Sorner laughed as he wrapped an arm around his brother.

On a still night, Sorner escaped into the trees and breathed a sigh of relief when the familiar figure stood at the treeline.

"Brennit!" Sorner ran towards the figure and met him in an embrace. "I'm so glad you received my message!"

"Sorner, I have missed you so much!" Brennit, the younger brother of Teyle, clung to Sorner before grasping his face and forcing their lips together. "My love, I have thought of you constantly." He patted Sorner's face, the tendrils of perfect curls that hung around his ears, and the immaculate blonde bun that rested at the curve of his skull, just to be sure that he was actually in front of him.

"It's too dangerous here." Sorner's voice dropped to a whisper. "Follow me to my house."

"But, your wife." Brennit gulped.

"A marriage by chance is all." Sorner flashed a smile. "We are simply two great friends who have started a family, but I must warn you, our children are frighteningly adorable."

Sorner and Brennit snuck between the trees until they reached a modest house on the outskirts of the main city. When the way was clear, they ran to the door and bolted into the house.

"Aye, is this the lover?" a chipper voice said with a laugh.

Brennit's eyes went wide as he settled on the small red-headed woman with a baby in her arms.

"This is my wife, Jelina, and our son, Rone, our daughter is asleep, her name is Brenna."

"Br-Brenna?" Brennit's hazel eyes lit up in the dim candle light of the house.

"Yes," Jelina chuckled. "After you! Rone is named after my own lover, Varonee, I miss her dearly."

"Brennit, I cannot begin to put into words the joy my heart holds to see you standing in front of me once again." Sorner sighed. "But I'm afraid that this meeting is more than just a happy reunion."

"Is it Keilon?" Brennit held Sorner's hands. "Has he gotten worse?"

"So much worse." Sorner's eyes were filled with fear and regret.

"He's a bastard!" Jelina cackled.

"I've been playing a dangerous game, Brennit." Sorner began to take quick deep breaths. "I've been part of his court, I've seen him do incredibly heinous things. He has no remorse for the situation he's left us in, he has killed our father, two of our brothers, and many others. Our kingdom is not adjusting well to this curse, children have gone missing-" his voice trembled. "So many children."

"What can I do to help?" Brennit squeezed his hands. "Anything for you."

"I've recruited a few others who are willing to stand up to him." A brief smile grew on his face. "I've taught them how to avoid his gaze, we are ready to make a stand. Would the Fareins be willing to help? If we take him out will your sister take back the curse? If I am forced to kill my beloved yet crazed brother, will it end our unjust confinement?" Tears began to stream down his face. "This is not the way life is meant to go! So much chaos, Brennit, I no longer sleep! Where is the order? Where is the justice? My kingdom is dying because of the amorous gluttony of my brother! Damn the havoc that spills forth from him! And damn those that allowed it!"

"Sorner, my love!" Brennit pulled the tall man down to rest his head on his shoulder. "I know how much you strive for harmony, we will get through this. I will organize my forces. I will talk to my sister, I promise I will do whatever you need to get you back to me."

"How soon can you be ready?" Jelina butted in. "The sooner the better. We can't take much more of this tyranny."

"Give me a week and I can have reinforcements."

"We need a signal." Sorner stood up straight, his green eyes dark with worry. "In case things take a turn. I would never want to endanger you, my love."

Brennit thought over the request. He smiled when an idea came to him, he pulled the corner of his emerald cape and tore a strip of it off. "Tie this to a tree on the edge of the treeline, and I will come for you."

"No, the signal would be to keep you away from the danger!"

"If I'm away from the danger that means I'm leaving you at the mercy of it. I could never do that. I will always come back for you."

"I'm a bit stronger than you, my prince." Sorner laughed. "Although, I do admire the way you can stab people from a great distance."

"You're just jealous because you're a terrible shot."

"I am not! Always hitting the mark is in my nature!"

"Why don't you two just retire for the night?" Jelina cut in.

Six days later Sorner was busying himself in the Fellowrock castle, trying to keep up the charade that he was Keilon's ally. It hadn't been an entirely fruitless effort, there were some days where he could see a sparkle of Keilon's old self, he hoped it would be enough to bring him back. But when Sorner saw Keilon approaching along with an armed guard, he knew that his ruse was over.

"Little brother," Keilon growled. "We need to talk." He grabbed Sorner's arm and pushed him up the steps up to a room on the fifth floor, with a set of grand wooden doors and three slender windows.

"What seems to be the problem?" Sorner stammered in a panic.

Keilon pushed his brother into a chair and shut the doors. He sat down on the other side of the desk. "People are plotting against me."

"Really? How worrisome! Who?"

Keilon shut his eyes tightly. His fists clenched on the desktop and he sunk into himself through the force of a calculating sigh.

"Keilon?" Sorner whispered.

"You." Keilon's glare met his brother's shocked expression.

"I think you are terribly mistaken!"

"Jelina and the children are already in holding." Keilon's eyes were full of storm clouds.

"How dare you!"

"I trusted you, Sorner." Keilon seemed to be fiddling with something beneath the table. "And you plan to overthrow me? How? Were you going to kill me? Barter my life for an end to this unbreakable curse?" He took a ragged breath as the clouds in his eyes warped to an ominous black. He set a scrap of green fabric on the table. "I was growing suspicious of your actions. You were just a little too cooperative, that's not like you at all. So I had the guards search your home, they brought me this."

"A swatch of fabric?! That's why you've locked up my wife, my infant son, and my barely walking daughter?!"

"Just a swatch of fabric? You have time for hobbies and crafts? No, this isn't just a scrap." Keilon was looking away from his brother as he continued running his fingers over the emerald fabric. "This is from Brennit's cape. I'd recognize this green anywhere. You're colluding with Teyle's brother!"

"You misunderstand! Purely a memento from a love lost." Sorner's face fell into his hands. "You weren't the only one in love with a Farein."

"I know. Did you think none of us noticed how often the two of you were missing from those stupid family dinners?"

"And yet it's your boring love story that will probably be echoed for the remainder of history." Sorner smiled with relief.

Keilon smirked. "Us Riloncks sure are charmers, huh?"

"Perhaps the Fareins are just very, um, gullible."

Keilon slid the scrap across the table. "Keep your memento, I'll have your family released. You're honestly one of the few people I can still trust, I'm sorry for jumping to a rash decision. I'm really trying to calm down."

"It's not your nature to be calm, Keilon." Sorner smiled. "It's mine."

Keilon's smile fell and in a rare occurrence he looked at his brother with the bluest eyes. "I don't need you to agree with everything I do, Sorner. I need you to be my balance. I feel it all so strongly, it's almost like it takes over me. I can't handle this on my own." His voice caught in his throat. "I'm drowning."

"If only the one who preceded you could give you some advice." Sorner shrugged. "You're right, your gift has always been so much different than mine, you needed a teacher who understood the weight your eyes put on your shoulders." He shook his head. "I'm sorry that we were never given the best mentors."

Keilon's eyes faded to green. "Do you think there's a way I could be that person for whoever comes after me?"

"Perhaps!"

Keilon tried to swallow his worry, but he vocalized it instead. "Do you think there's a way to ensure that I'm the last one with this terrible gift?"

"Brother, I don't think so. There is so much unknown about chaos and harmony and everything that lies between. Who would we be if we were to disrupt that?"

"I guess." Keilon looked unnaturally weak. "You may go. Jelina was being kept in a bedroom, and we took them gently."

"I appreciate that." Sorner stood slowly. "I can stay if you need me to."

Keilon forced purple into his irises as he shook his head and gestured for his brother to leave.

That night Sorner was torn between continuing his plan, or formulating a new one that would oust Keilon calmly. He needed advice, so he snuck to the treeline and tied the swatch of fabric, hoping Brennit would know what to do.

Instead, at the first light of day a Hightree army marched through the trees. They surrounded the castle and filled the courtyard. Brennit stood at the front with arms crossed, he shouted at the castle doors demanding Keilon's attention.

Keilon had already sent guards to gather his brother. He met Brennit in the courtyard and threw a battered Sorner at his feet.

"Take him," Keilon growled.

"I can't do that!" Brennit clenched his teeth. "Because of you!"

"Because of your sister!" Keilon stepped closer to the Farein, his eyes a mix of night and fire. "You turned my brother against me, you might as well just keep him."

"Keilon-"

"I am a king, Prince Brennit, you will address me as such."

"And how did you get that title, your majesty? Through tricky magic and breach of trust." Brennit smirked. "Or was it the buckets of blood constantly dripping from your shiny sil-"

"Withdraw your forces now, you know my army is stronger, you will be sacrificing your men and that would make you no better than me."

Brennit narrowed his hazel eyes and forced himself to stare into the consuming onyx of Keilon's irises. "What will you do with Sorner?"

"I already told you!" Keilon chuckled. "You can take him."

"What?"

Keilon took a few steps back, and in a booming voice announced, "At sunset tonight I hereby sentence my brother, Sorner Rilonck, his wife, Jelina Rilonck, their children Brenna and Rone, along with the families he conspired with, to be exiled."

A gasp floated over the crowd of both Fellowrock citizens and Hightree soldiers.

"Keilon!" Sorner whimpered from the ground. "Please!"

Keilon glanced briefly down to his brother with eyes like oceans. "Sunset."

Brennit was reeling from the sentence, he stared blankly at Keilon. He wanted to thrust a dagger into his heart, he wanted to gouge his eyes out, he wanted to inflict so much injury to this evil man, but then Keilon met his stare. It seemed unnatural that Keilon's eyes would be such a steady green in the heated moment, even moreso, they seemed to be pleading. Brennit felt a pull on his own soul looking into the dreadful image.

"Withdraw your forces, say goodbye to Sorner, you may never see him again." Keilon's eyes grew wider. "For at sunset he will be exiled."

The day followed with one awful event after another. The families found to be colluding with Sorner were corralled, one hundred people total, including many young children. Keilon was seen pacing for most of the day, he never stopped to eat or drink, he only mumbled orders and kept his eyes to the ground. There were sounds of crying constantly drifting through the air from those about to lose their loved ones, from those who were heartbroken over the realization of their tyranny, and those who were slowly accepting their fate.

An hour before sunset, Sorner was escorted into a room with a still pacing Keilon. The guards latched the door and within a heartbeat Keilon's arms were around his brother.

"Keilon?" Sorner whispered.

"You have to understand!" Keilon's hold tightened. "This is the only way I can keep you safe."

"You're damning me to a life of constant danger."

"No! You'll be protected, Brennit will protect you all."

"Keilon, you sentenced me!" Sorner pushed himself away. "How dare you be concerned about my safety now! If that's truly how you feel then you'll have no trouble taking back this evil sentence."

"You don't understand." Keilon's eyes once again shone blue. "It's not safe for you here. It's only going to get worse, it's going to grow and soon your balance won't be enough."

"It could be!"

"No! And the day that happens I just know I would succumb to what the soul wants, and it always craves violence."

Keilon swallowed. "I can't do that to you, little brother. Not after everything we've been through together."

"I don't believe you!" Sorner shouted.

"You want me to be the villain?" Keilon lightly laughed. "Will that make this easier for you?"

"You are the villain. You always were." Sorner gritted his teeth. "There is no helping you."

"Fine."

"You say you can't let me succumb to your violence." Sorner laughed through his anger. "Did you feel that way about our father? Our brothers? Did you notice that your downfall led our mother to her doom? What makes me so special, and not them?"

"I can't wait to have you gone," Keilon seethed.

"Nevik, Hekar, Endast, Calidy, and oh so many more," Sorner sneered. "Don't forget to add my name to your list of lamentations."

As the sun was sinking, the traitors were forced over the treeline with swords drawn on them. Some went silently in saddening disbelief at the fate in front of them, others wailed in agony.

The last one to cross was Sorner.

"This is goodbye, brother." Keilon stood in front of him.

"Do me one last favor and finally let your true colors shine." His tight stare was unbreaking. "Don't force that blue color for my own entertainment."

"Sorner, I'm not," Keilon said in a nearly pleading tone.

"Let me see that glorious pink lightning! Let me see the eyes of chaos one last time before I am forced to roam this land as a pest!" He leaned closer to his brother. "Come on, Keilon! Let me remember you as the monster you are!"

Keilon's face was flat for a moment, then he met Sorner's glare with the color he so wanted to see. "I'll remember your eyes too, Sorner."

Sorner spat at Keilon's feet. "The havoc within your eyes will be the visual that remains as so many take their last breaths."

Keilon pointed a sword at his brother and walked forward until Sorner had seemed to disappear.

Finally, with no one left in Fellowrock to keep him in check, the chaotic soul was free to do as it pleased. The first Keilon's reign was filled with blood, lust, and power.

Although the facts diluted overtime, it was a stain on Fellowrock's strong history. The return of the chaotic soul was a cloud hanging over Hightree and Fellowrock for three centuries, until it was given to Dylah Rilonck who became a Farein in name, through war and death she set forth to use her gifts to foster peace. It was ultimately her decision to have the curse placed on her own soul to keep her kingdom safe. But her chaos would always differ from her predecessor's and the curse that once trapped them became her weapon to wield.

Chapter 2

Aged Redundancy

As blissful breezes whipped through the rusty leaves of the Fellowrock forest, tension built within the courtyard of the stone castle. At a table, Kunor gripped the bridge of his nose and sighed before looking back up hoping any strategy would come to mind. With a cautious hand he slowly moved a game piece up and over one square.

"Beat that!" he exclaimed, feeling victorious.

He watched in disbelief as another piece moved in front of his and knocked it over, the move was only coupled with the sound of a light giggle.

"You're cheating!" Kunor sighed.

"No!" the young boy across from him shouted back. "Just better than you!"

"How dare you talk to me like that!" Kunor began to laugh at the child's tenacity. "My father is the king here!"

"Yeah." The boy rolled his eyes with a natural swiftness. "And my father is the king over there!" He pointed towards the neighboring kingdom.

"That's a fair point," Kunor groaned before moving a game piece with obvious reluctance.

Thunderous laughter rose from the young boy before he outmaneuvered Kunor once again.

"Uncle Kunor, you are not good at this game," the boy said as he covered his mouth trying to calm his laughter.

"Well it's not fair." Kunor laughed. "I'm twenty-two and I'm getting beat by a four year old."

"It's okay!" The boy smiled with all of his teeth. "I am really smart!"

"I know you are!" Kunor began thinking about his next move. "Just like your father."

"You can move that piece, but I'll just knock it down when it's my turn." The boy stuck his tongue out at his uncle.

"But you act just like your mother," Kunor mumbled.

Suddenly, a woman in a navy hooded cape appeared as if from thin air. She removed her hood releasing her long blonde waves and stood behind the child while casting a smoldering stare on Kunor.

"What did he say about your mother?" she spoke slowly with a raised eyebrow.

"You're in trouble now." The boy giggled.

"I thought you would be hung up in my father's office for longer, Dylah."

"I escaped." Dylah laughed as her eyes faded to a soft lavender and she sat next to her son. "He was boring me."

"Can I escape?" the kid asked, looking up at her. "He's boring too."

"Sorry, kiddo." Dylah ruffled his soft brown hair. "You're going to hang out with your Uncle Kunor for a little while longer until he takes you over to Hightree later, okay?"

"Why can't I go to the castle now?" Cav sighed.

"Because your father is very busy." She forced a smile. "But he can't wait to see you later."

"Why can't I go where you're going?" Cav looked up at

her with pleading eyes, one hazel, one lavender.

"Well, my son, that's an easy one." Dylah laughed. "You're just too big!"

"Your mama does some crazy stuff, Cav!"

"Aunt Dylah!" A teenage boy ran up to the table nearly out of breath.

"Kane!" Cav shouted.

"Oh no, he's here, huh?" Dylah's eyes darted around her surroundings.

"Yes!" Kane, Bahn's younger son, spoke in an exasperated voice. "Just crossed the treeline, I heard him ask a guard where you were."

"Okay, Cav, mama has to go!" Dylah held her son tightly and kissed the top of his head. "Behave for Uncle Cousin Kunor, and if your father or Uncle Grandpa Keilon asks, I was never here."

"You can't hide from it forever," Kunor said calmly with a slight smile, "Queen Dylah."

After an ignited eye roll, Dylah ran into the trees and seemed to disappear.

"My wife." Axen sighed angrily as he stood in front of a Fellowrock soldier. "Your commander, have you seen her?"

"Describe her again, your majesty."

"Are you serious?" Axen sighed even louder. "Dylah. Everyone knows Dylah. She's your Second in Command, wears a navy and lavender cape, navy leggings with green and orange stripes, not very tall. Come on!"

"Could you give me more specifics?" the soldier replied flatly. "Like, what color are her eyes?"

"Are you kidding?!" Axen nearly shouted.

"It's no use." Keilon appeared by his brother-in-law's side. "They're all being just as secretive." He laid a hand on Axen's shoulder and led him toward the courtyard. "Cav is with Kunor."

"Well I knew that." Axen reluctantly followed. "But

where's Dylah? I checked the house, the field, the range." He shook his head. "Why is she being so flighty lately?"

"Would it make you feel better to know that at our meeting today she was suddenly gone?" Keilon laughed. "She just needs time to adjust."

"I know." Axen glanced at the surrounding trees still looking for her. "But Arkon has been asleep for nearly four months now, I know we only got the titles a few weeks ago, I just thought she was expecting it."

"She'll come around," Keilon said in a proud voice. "But you're doing especially well!"

"I'm really trying." Axen looked around again. "It will be easier when we move to the castle. But I am dreading convincing Dylah to leave our house."

"Let me know if you need backup." Keilon slapped Axen's shoulder. "I will always enjoy telling my little sister what to do."

"Not as much as she enjoys telling you what to do." Axen slapped his shoulder in return.

The two kings arrived at the courtyard just as Kunor was about to lose patience with his young nephew who was giggling unceasingly.

"You can't do a move like that!" Kunor tried not to shout.

"I just did," Cav replied calmly.

"Are you losing to a four year old?" Keilon asked, looking down at the many knocked over pieces on the table.

"Yes." Kunor sighed and gripped the bridge of his nose.

"Daddy!" Cav jumped from his seat into Axen's arms.

"Hey buddy!" Axen laughed as he spun around holding his son tightly.

"Should I be greeting you like that?" Kunor asked, looking up at Keilon. "Ya know, make up for lost time?"

"No."

"Hi, Uncle Grandpa Keilon!" Cav wrapped his arms around Keilon's leg.

Keilon put a flat hand on top of Cav's head. "Just Uncle

Keilon."

"That's not what mama says." Cav giggled as he stared up at him.

Keilon's heart sank looking into the child's wide eyes over an insistent grin. As much as Cav was a mix of his parents, all Keilon could see was a young Dylah.

"You're lucky you remind me of your mama when she was your height, kiddo." Keilon sighed then smiled. "Which I guess was only a few years ago."

"Speaking of." Axen knelt down to be at Cav's level. "Have you seen your mama today?"

"She was never here," Cav replied quickly.

Keilon sighed as he looked at his son. "What about you? What's your answer?"

"She was never here," Kunor said softly.

"How long ago?" Axen asked with a stern stare on Kunor.

"She ran away when she heard you were looking for her," Kunor answered with a quickly diminishing volume.

"Damnit." Axen sighed as he stood. "Any idea where she went?"

"Mama said I was too big to go with her," Cav happily added. "But she's bigger than me! She's funny."

"Great." Keilon looked to the sky. "That does the opposite of narrowing it down."

Axen laughed lightly. "I think I know." He ruffled Cav's hair. "Beat Kunor for a little longer then mama and I will take you to the castle."

"Want me to come with you?" Keilon asked.

"No thanks." Axen smirked. "I know how to handle her."

After a quick walk to the border of Fellowrock and Hightree, Axen slowly opened the lavender front door of their home. He walked on quiet feet into their kitchen while carefully kicking Cav's scattered toys to the side. He smiled seeing her cape draped over a chair at the kitchen table, he unhooked his own green cape and laid it over hers.

Analyzing the kitchen, he could tell that she didn't make coffee, which ruled out her hiding in their room, or the living room. With the same level of continued stealth, he stepped over a faded white line on the floor of the kitchen and made his way to his office.

Opening the door sent a rush of guilt, the past few months had been so busy for him that he hadn't had time to work on new inventions or even scribble down a quick equation. The room seemed unnaturally stale, but he knew she was nearby. The chair skidded across the floor as he sat down with a hopeful sigh noticing the slightly opened top drawer of his desk.

Axen pulled the handle and was thrown back to a treasonous deal he had made years ago. There she was, on the tiny bed, a book in one hand, and a mug of coffee in the other.

"Damnit." Dylah didn't even look up. "You found me."

"Your son sold you out." Axen laughed.

"I think you mean your son," she said as she crashed against the pillows on the bed. "No child of mine would snitch on his mother."

"Come on, Dylah." He sighed. "We need to talk."

"Are you breaking up with me?" Dylah laughed. "Well at least we had some good years, enemy prince. But please be prepared, because my kingdom will be promptly attacking your kingdom to carry on the breakup traditions of our ancestors."

"You're a nightmare." He fought the urge to laugh. "Can you come out, please?"

"I don't know, I have a pretty good set up." She shrugged. "I could probably survive a few months here."

"You would get lonely, princess." He rolled his eyes feeling the aged redundancy of the subject.

"You can go ahead and close it," she said before taking another sip of her coffee.

Axen took a deep breath trying to rationalize his next action but muscle memory took over and he reached into the drawer, scooped her up, and set her on the desk.

"Not fair," Dylah groaned as she walked off the edge of the desk returning to her normal size before she hit the ground. She faced her husband with tightly crossed arms and a raised eyebrow.

He wanted to be mad, he wanted to call her out on her distance, he wanted to blame her for the worry she had caused him. Instead, he took quick steps towards her, wrapped his arms around her and rested his chin on top of her head.

"Calm down." She laughed against his chest. "You really need to get a hold on all of this anger."

"Shush." He held her tighter. "This is the most I've seen you all week."

"Sorry." Her voice fell to a whisper. "Trying to stay busy."

He tilted her chin up and felt his stomach sink as he looked into her stormy eyes.

"I know you're not thrilled about being a queen."

"I just never thought I would be."

"Okay, well, you had to have known there was a possibility when you married a second in line prince." He smirked.

"We shouldn't be ruling in Arkon's place." Her blue eyes quickly changed to a forced green as they filled with tears.

"Stop." He laid a hand against her face. "You don't have to force your eyes around me, I know you're not handling this situation very well."

Dylah looked away as soon as she felt the tears building. "If I had gotten to him faster he would still be with us." She looked up at him again, her eyes a dark navy. "I can't be the queen knowing that I only have the title because of my own failure."

"No no no." Axen pushed her against him and began to run his fingers through her hair. "We got separated, your battalions were ambushed, none of that is your fault."

Dylah pushed away from him and wiped her eyes. "I think we'll just have to continue to see things differently."

Axen grabbed her hand. "How about we go get our son and let him watch the clouds in the field?"

Dylah had a small smile as green and lavender broke apart the dark blue of her eyes. "That sounds lovely."

"Great!" He pulled her out into the forest before she could offer any objections. "He's with Kunor and Keilon."

"I'll meet you at the field then." Dylah slipped away from his hold. "I can't deal with Keilon right now."

"And how do I know that you'll actually meet me there and not just hide again?"

"Because." She offered a weak grin. "You already found my hiding spot."

Chapter 3

Certain Events

Dylah reveled in the stillness of the lilac field, her legs outstretched, one arm supporting her, and the other hand gently twirling her sleeping son's hair. The sun was casting a kaleidoscope of hues over the already bright flowers as it sank into the horizon.

"We should probably wake him up or he's not going to sleep at all tonight," Axen whispered.

"No." Dylah smiled down at her peaceful son. "He's just recovering from having to deal with Kunor all day."

"So you're saying you don't want to wake him up?" Axen asked cautiously. "Not at all?"

"How could I wake him up when he looks so perfect?"

Axen took a deep breath. "We need to move to the Hightree castle." He held his breath waiting for Dylah's reaction.

"No," she whispered with subdued ferocity.

"We have to, I need to be there." Axen sighed. "And I don't want our family living in two different places."

"You went through so much to build that house! That's where Cav was born!" Dylah continued to whisper through grinding teeth. "We are staying there!"

"Dylah, I'm sorry, but this is part of our job now as king and queen." He watched the anger grow on her face and quickly pointed to their sleeping child. "Kings and queens live in castles."

"This isn't a suggestion, is it?"

"I'm sorry." He began to reason. "But Cav will be there with four of his cousins, and all of his Farein aunts and uncles. He'll love it. You're still close to your trees. It's not permanent."

"Not permanent?" Her expression softened.

"Well yeah, Arkon has to wake up at some point." He flashed a quick hopeful smile.

"Okay."

"Really?" Axen was taken aback by her sudden agreement.

"Yeah." She looked at him with serious green eyes. "It's what we have to do."

"I can move my desk to the castle too." He smirked. "If that would make you more comfortable, my queen."

Within a blink her eyes sparkled like amethyst. "That's very considerate of you, enemy king."

"Should we head back?" Axen asked, feeling relieved after the conversation he had been dreading. "I can carry the kid."

"I would rather not," Dylah groaned. "If we go back I'll have to talk to Keilon and he'll lecture me about skipping out on the meeting and give me a whole new metaphor about leadership. I can't do it."

"Well." Axen held back a laugh as he gently scooped Cav up. "I already told him where we would be." He slowly gestured to the nearby clearing where a figure stood.

"Seriously?!" Dylah clenched her teeth. "I can't shrink here! It's the lilac field!"

"I know." Axen laughed quietly as he took steps away while the figure simultaneously grew closer. "Have fun."

"Little sister," Keilon spoke in a low voice as he stood casting a shadow over her. "Is now a good time to finish our meeting?"

"Did we even need to have a meeting?" she asked. "The world is calm! There's no more wars left to fight! How boring!"

"We were talking about a trek to visit Derck and Molix." He kept a flat expression. "A meeting doesn't always have to be about impending doom."

"Sure, but those meetings are always more fun." She smiled widely. "But is that the smartest decision for all of us to go to the sand countries?"

"That was precisely what the meeting was about." Keilon rolled his eyes. "But apparently that was too boring."

"The last time we all went somewhere, it shattered these kingdoms." Dylah stood with her arms crossed. "You were injured, Kunor was injured, Delin, Kremon, and Brig also hurt." She sighed. "And more importantly, what happened to Arkon."

"I know it's heavy, but you need to try to move past that." Keilon put a hand on her shoulder, both for comfort and to make sure she couldn't run away. "Sometimes the enemy has the upper hand and there's nothing we can do about it. They surprised us, it could have been much worse."

"I know."

"No injuries even compared to a spear through the side, little sister." He smiled. "So don't worry about the small scars some of us have from that incident."

"Sure." Dylah half smiled "Did you forget that about six years ago Zether sent a spear into your side too?"

"Please, that was barely a scratch."

"What makes you want to visit Derck anyway?" She asked after rolling her eyes.

"It's been two years and he is our brother." Keilon

laughed. "I think that should justify a visit."

"I am curious to see how our very quiet brother is handling leading those tribes." Dylah held back a laugh. "Who would have thought that half of the Rilonck children would end up being kings?"

"Actually, only one Rilonck child became a king," Keilon said as he led her to the trees. "You're a queen and I don't even know what title Derck is holding."

"Close enough." Dylah laughed loudly. "Speaking of queens, how are things with Teyle?"

"I would rather you not ask me that," he said sternly as they walked toward the courtyard.

"If you're happy then I'm happy for you."

"Go ahead and say it."

"But if you're unhappy then I am livid." She grinned. "So, how are things with Teyle?" she repeated.

Keilon waited for a moment before answering, "She is distant right now, but give it a few weeks and she'll be right back at it."

"Off and on for some time now, huh?" Dylah snickered. "What a love story."

"Sometimes I wish you'd just do that little disappearing act." Keilon sighed. "You never do it when it's the most convenient for me."

"And I never will." She lightly smacked his face, when he turned to her in shock ready to hit her back she had vanished, but quickly reappeared out of arm's reach. "Too slow."

"When will you let your son know about the special abilities you have?" Keilon asked. "And when will you explain to him that I am only his uncle?"

"At some point we will have to explain to him the curse that separated the kingdoms, and the war that brought his parents together." There was worry in her voice. "He is just so smart and I know it will have to be soon. I'm fully expecting him to be afraid of the curse, and then I'll have to show him that I'm the one who kept it. He's seen me reappear but he doesn't understand how I do it just yet."

"What about your eyes?" Keilon asked, hoping to steer her away from her spiraling thoughts.

"He doesn't know the full power of them, no," she answered. "He's only ever seen them change to purple, I don't let him see the other colors. And I'm not sure they would work on him, not that I'm going to try it. Although it would be very convenient at bedtime, using my power against my own son is a step too close to the old guy." Dylah raised an eyebrow up to her brother. "You already know these things, why are you asking me now?"

"He's getting to the age where he'll be mixed in with other kids, his mother is a legend, he will start hearing things." Keilon tried to mask his concern. "You may need to start thinking out your explanations for certain events."

"Right." Dylah rolled her eyes as a fire grew within them. "How should I explain to him my brief stint in the afterlife? Should I also go into detail on how it feels to shove a dagger into a man's heart? Do you think my four year old son would benefit from those discussions?"

"I'm just saying, you might want to start planting those seeds so he's not blindsided by the truth." Keilon sighed. "Think of how much better things would have gone if I didn't lie to you for so long about not being cured?"

Dylah stared up at him unblinking. "That's a solid point." Her lips curled up into a smirk. "See that's what makes you such a good grandfather."

"You're lucky you managed to make the cutest kid." Keilon rolled his eyes as they walked into the castle.

"Excuse me?" Dylah scoffed. "I thought I was the cutest kid?!"

"Not as cute as Cav."

Chapter 4

Little by Little

Within a week, Axen, Dylah, and Cav had moved into the grand Hightree castle. Their suite of rooms was situated in the middle of the structure, just below the third deck. They had a large master bedroom with walk-in closets and a spa-like washroom, with an adjoining door to Cav's bedroom, another door opened up into a hallway that led to a seating area with a kitchenette.

Dylah stared out the large window studying the way the fresh new sunlight bounced off the slowly yellowing leaves of her homeland. She sipped her coffee, readying herself for the day.

"You're up early." Axen laughed as he walked into the living room.

"Cav was sleepwalking again." She turned to him and yawned. "But I think he's almost used to the new place."

"It still confuses me why he never did that before we moved." Axen poured himself a cup of coffee with the little that remained in the pot.

"Your son is half Rilonck." She laughed and raised an eyebrow over electric pink eyes. "He will always be drawn to the trees."

"My son's mother is a nightmare," Axen said with a smirk, "and he's becoming more and more like her everyday."

"And that's a bad thing?" she huffed. "He's like you too."

"Well I remember this castle having a very similar effect on his mother twice before." His smile grew wider. "Did he bite you?"

"I'm sure he'll put me in a glass someday." Dylah narrowed her eyes at him. "This castle seems to have that effect on his father."

"And I will be proud." He raised his mug as if he was making a toast.

"I'm taking him to the drills today," Dylah said with reserved caution.

"Avalia doesn't mind watching him."

"Cav said that he doesn't like Frenia, and that the twins are mean." Dylah sighed. "I don't want him to hate this place."

"I don't blame him, the twins are hellions," Axen said with a kind smile. "Take the boy to the trees."

"What do you have planned for the day?" she asked, taking another drink of her coffee. "Your majesty."

"Lots and lots of meetings."

"Delin said he could stop by later this evening," Dylah added. "He's going to try another dose on Arkon, then he's going to run some tests on me." She stared into the coffee hoping he wouldn't notice the swirl of blue in her gray eyes.

"Do you think more tests are a good idea right now?" He spoke softly. "You're under a lot of stress to begin with and it's only been a few months since-"

"It's not in my nature to take a break." She looked up at him as her eyes shone with hints of pink.

"Okay, more tests can't hurt." Axen forced a smile.

"Mama?" Cav's quiet voice came from the hallway.

"You look like you need some coffee, kiddo!" Dylah smiled.

"Absolutely not." Axen sighed.

"I want coffee." Cav laughed. "Mama likes coffee."

"Two nightmares." Axen laughed as he ruffled his son's hair. "You're going with your mama today."

"Yeah! We're going to go beat up Uncle Bahn!" Dylah held up her fists.

"Why?" Cav tilted his head.

"I'm not sure." Dylah seemed to be pondering. "We'll figure it out on the way."

"Can I wear my cape?!" He giggled.

"Wearing your cape is a requirement, soldier." Dylah crossed her arms and looked at him sternly.

"I know you're just kidding, mama." Cav laughed as he walked away. "Your eyes are purple and that means you're happy, they'd be a different color if you were mad."

Axen and Dylah looked at each other in disbelief as their son skipped away.

"Damnit, Keilon was right," Dylah growled to herself. "He's going to catch on sooner than we're prepared for."

"Come on, that's not as concerning as it seems." Axen tried to lend his support. "He's always known what the purple eyes mean."

"He's only known what the purple eyes mean." She shook her head. "Even when he's in trouble I force my eyes to be green. Can you imagine how scary it would be for a kid to see their mother with fiery eyes?"

"Then who told him there were other colors?" Axen asked softly. "And what else have they been telling him?"

"Maybe I shouldn't take him today," she said looking down. "I need to think of some age appropriate answers on how to describe to a child that their mother is chaos reborn."

"Slow down." Axen held her shoulders. "You went nearly twenty-five years without the full truth about yourself, he doesn't need to know everything right away." He smiled. "Eye color equals mood is just about all he should know."

She nodded. "I'm going to need more coffee for this day."

"How about you brush it off like nothing happened, then tonight we can break it to him together?" He took her hands. "We can finally tell him the story about the girl who helped the enemy prince and how he thought about her lavender eyes for ten years until she finally showed up again."

"I don't really come off spectacularly well in that part of our story." Dylah rolled amethyst eyes. "But yes, I'd like some back up for this."

"I will bring wine." Axen quickly kissed her forehead. "Lots of wine."

"We were just a few years older than him when we first learned about the curse." Dylah sighed. "I guess this isn't too terrible."

"Oh we're saying everything now?" He laughed nervously.

"Might as well." She crossed her arms. "He's your kid, he's too smart, we give him a piece and he'll just dive deeper and deeper until he knows everything."

"Okay, well, we can't exactly tell him the story we were told." He took a deep breath to steady himself. "We both know the first Keilon wasn't the best person, seeing as how he killed you. Plus, Cav loves Aunt Teyle."

"I'm ready!" Cav yelled as he jumped into the room donning his navy and green cape.

"Excellent, soldier," Dylah said quickly in a commanding tone. "Wait for your commander in the hall."

"Wait!" Axen held up a halting hand. "First, what is your chant?"

"For the height of Hightree!" Cav exclaimed with a laugh as he ran out of the room.

"If you don't wipe that smirk off your face, I'm keeping our son in the trees." Dylah glared at him with eyes of fire and lilacs.

"I'll see you later for wine and condensed honesty?" He smiled wider. "Or will you be hiding out in furniture?"

"I guess you'll find out later," she said before a set of parting kisses.

Dylah and Cav spent the day jumping from field to field overseeing various training sessions. Dylah was no longer the archery commander, because of her special skills she often led smaller scouting groups or jumped in wherever Keilon needed her. She was a proud and respected Second in Command, no soldier could deny the person who had fought death and won.

"Oh good, I needed to speak to my Second and Third in Command." Keilon laughed as he walked up to the edge of a training field.

"What do you need, Uncle Keilon?" Cav asked happily. "I'll do it."

"So today I'm just your uncle?"

"Yeah." Cav shrugged. "My grandpas are dead."

Dylah's eyes grew wide as she looked from her son then up to her oldest brother.

"Who told you that?!" She quickly knelt by him.

"Hey Cav, I really need my Third to run and touch that tree all the way over there." Keilon thought fast. "Twice!"

Without a word Cav bolted off on his fruitless mission.

"Who is telling him these things?!" Dylah's face fell into her hands.

"What other things?"

"He knows about my eyes, he mentioned something about them this morning," she groaned. "Was it you? Did you let it slip? Is that why you were asking me the other day?"

"No, of course not." Keilon quickly offered his defense. "Kids just sense things."

"Are you saying that my four year old son just sensed that his grandfathers were dead? The ghosts of Tarok and Fren just tapped him on the shoulder and said 'Hey kid, wow you look like our kids!'" Dylah rolled gray and orange eyes.

"You're spiraling, but that's an entertaining thought." Keilon chuckled. "Papa would've explained it better though."

She offered him a quick smile of agreement. "We are already preparing to tell him the truth tonight now I guess we'll just roll in a quick spiel about his dead grandparents."

"Has he been around anyone new since moving to the castle?" Keilon began to think out loud. "Maybe the truth spilling wasn't malicious, maybe they assumed he knew certain things about his mother."

"No, not really." Dylah sighed. "Just Kremon's kids." Her voice caught in her throat. "He told me he didn't like Frenia and the twins. Damnit!" Her fist clenched at her sides. "Why didn't I see that?!"

"How fast was that?!" Cav yelled as he ran back.

"Really fast!" Keilon smiled and clapped his hands. "One more time, Cav!"

Cav ran away as fast as he could.

"How did you do it?" Dylah asked quietly.

"Do what?" Keilon asked hesitantly. "I've done quite a few things."

"How did you break so many terrible things to me?" Dylah sighed. "You told me our parents had died, you explained why they could never come back, you told me about the curse, you taught me so many harsh truths." She exhaled forcefully. "When I think about doing that for Cav, I just can't. I want him to stay blissfully clueless."

"I wanted you to stay clueless." Keilon sighed. "But that's not how life works, kiddo."

"But I could just keep it to myself, right?" She stared off at nothing in particular. "You kept things from me, I turned out fine!"

"Most of that was to protect you." He took a slow breath. "I'm not going to tell you what you should and should not explain to your kid, all I know is that it hurt like hell to tell you the truth and it hurt just the same to leave you in the dark."

"I hate this."

"I find it entertaining." He grinned.

That evening Dylah canceled her tests with Delin, she only wanted to focus on her son and the first taste of harsh reality he was about to face.

After the small family had eaten dinner, and Dylah had inhaled one glass of wine, they sat on the couch.

"Cav, we're going to let you in on something," Dylah spoke in a happy voice. "We're going to explain why you have a lavender eye, and why I sometimes have the same eyes."

"And sometimes she has different eyes," Axen added. "Your mama has a special gift."

"I know," Cav said quietly. "Frenia told me."

"I knew it." Dylah mouthed to Axen over Cav's head.

"She did?" Axen asked. "Well, she doesn't know everything."

"So you know that my purple eyes mean I'm happy, right?"

"Yes!" Cav laughed.

"And you have one eye like mine because you make us so happy, and that's even what your name means." Dylah held his small hands. "Cav means joy, and you are our joy, Cav."

"I know, mama!"

"Well sometimes, my eyes aren't green, and sometimes they aren't purple. Look at me Cav." She took a deep breath and closed her eyes. "My eyes change based on how I'm feeling." She opened her eyes to a deep blue. "When I'm sad, they're this blue color. When your father first saw this color it made him sad too."

"It's true, it did," Axen said quietly. "They still make me sad."

Dylah closed her eyes again. "When I'm angry they look like fire." She opened them showing an inferno.

"That's so cool!" Cav said in amazement.

"Not very cool when they're pinned on you, kid." Axen

nudged his son.

Again, Dylah closed her eyes. "When I'm really set on doing something they change to a very bright pink." She smiled as her eyes electrified. "One time your dad really wanted to help me because I was sick, but I looked at him with these eyes because I wanted to do it myself."

"I carried her anyway," Axen added with a proud laugh.

"What other colors?" Cav asked with wide eyes.

"Well." Dylah took another deep breath. "When I'm confused about something, or thinking things through, or even processing how I feel, they turn gray." Her eyes clouded over. "Like this."

"They look like storm clouds!" Cav yelled.

"I know!" Axen smirked.

"And there's one last color, Cav," she said seriously. "But I'm going to warn you, it might scare you."

His expression matched his father's. "I'm brave."

Without a word, Dylah changed her eyes to an ominous black.

"W-w-what does that mean, mama?" Cav said in a panicked whisper.

"Those are her war eyes," Axen said quickly, noticing the fear on their son's face. "Those rarely happen."

"Sometimes they happen when you don't put your toys away." Dylah smiled as her eyes returned to green.

"Dylah!" Axen whispered loudly.

"Now you know that mama has some weird eyes." Dylah sighed with relief. "Any questions?"

"Yes." Cav stared at the ground. "Why?"

"Because," Dylah said with a hint of reluctance, "I was given a very important job and in exchange for doing that job, I was given these special eyes." Dylah quickly looked to Axen for reassurance.

"Yeah!" Axen added in a happy tone to support her answer. "She didn't always have them. Sometimes she would get so sad that her eyes would stay green for a long time."

"Why?" Cav asked.

"Your father and I met when we were just kids, but we couldn't be together." Dylah spoke slowly, thinking out her words.

"Why?" he asked again as children do.

"He wanted me to go with him, but I couldn't, and that made mama very sad, my eyes stayed green for ten years after that. Until I found your dad again, and he fixed them."

"That's silly." Cav giggled. "Why couldn't you go with him?"

Dylah and Axen shared an intense stare trying to decide who would explain the implications of their budding relationship.

"Okay, Cav." Axen sighed. "A long time ago Hightree was very afraid of Fellowrock. They were stronger and we didn't want to lose. So Hightree put a curse on Fellowrock, and for three hundred years your mama's kingdom couldn't leave their border."

"What?" Cav asked with wide eyes. "But you can leave now!"

"Your Uncle Delin found a cure." Dylah smiled.

"But it didn't work on everyone," Axen explained. "It didn't work for your mama."

"Why not?" Cav asked sadly.

"Because of my eyes," Dylah said slowly. "But because your dad and I love each other so much, we broke the curse."

"Wow!" Cav yelled.

"I know!" Dylah laughed back.

"What was the curse?" Cav asked with a grand smile.

Axen and Dylah stared at each other once more.

"Are you ready for bed?" Axen blurted when he noticed his wife trying to form a reply.

"Okay." Cav sighed as he walked towards the hallway.

"That went better than I thought." Axen collapsed against the couch after returning from Cav's room.

"We didn't tell him everything." Dylah sighed. "He still

has questions."

"Little by little, you nightmare." Axen laughed as he stood, kissed her forehead, and walked to the kitchenette to replenish their glasses of wine. "And maybe it's okay that he doesn't know absolutely everything yet. I don't want him to be afraid for you, for his uncles, for Fellowrock, or anything else for that matter."

"I just don't want him to feel like we're hiding things from him."

"And that's what makes you such a good parent."

"I'm going to punch Kremon in the face," Dylah growled into her wine glass. "Cav would still be my clueless little baby if it wasn't for my brother's spawns."

"Frenia is just like Avalia," Axen added. "And the twins are worse than demons."

"I'm going to punch him in the face," she repeated quietly.

"Whatever makes you feel better, princess."

"I'm actually the queen now." Dylah raised her eyebrow. "Enemy prince."

When Axen excused himself to tend to some paperwork, Dylah snuck into Cav's room and laid in his bed.

"Mama?" he asked as his eyes blinked slowly while she stroked his hair.

"There are some things I want you to know, kiddo." She smiled.

"Curse?" He yawned.

"Yes," she whispered.

"What was it?" He smiled in the darkness.

"Do you know how Uncle Keilon, and all the other uncles are really tall and strong?"

Cav nodded as he slowly fought through his residual sleepiness.

"Hightree was afraid of us because we were so big and strong." She smiled. "So they cursed us to be the opposite."

"Small?" he asked as his worry grew.

"Tiny." She smiled. "Itty bitty."

"Oh!" A mix of emotion flooded his small face. "You were tiny, mama?"

"That's how I met your dad the second time." She nodded. "I lived in his desk drawer, and I slept on his pillow every night until one day I had to leave."

"Am I going to be cursed?" Cav asked with growing concern.

"No!" Dylah kissed his forehead. "I made sure of that."

"You did?"

"Well, instead of the whole kingdom being cursed, I asked if it could just be me," she said, trying to keep her composure.

"You're cursed, mama?" Cav seemed to be on the verge of tears.

"Yes!" Dylah laughed. "But it's not as bad as you think, I control it. Wanna see?"

"Yes!"

"If I do it, you have to promise to fall right back asleep okay?" Dylah said with sparkling lavender eyes.

"Yes." He smiled widely.

She smiled back, kissed his cheek and whispered some words into his ear.

"I know, mama," he replied.

With a deep breath, Dylah enacted the power of her curse and laid on her son's pillow.

"Goodnight," Cav said with a smile as he closed his eyes.

Dylah was surprised he had fallen asleep so quickly, she was soon lost in watching him sleep peacefully, like the truths they had told him made him lighter. She was thrown back to when he was such a small baby and she spent her nights pacing his crib as he slept. Soon enough she had succumbed to the lullaby of sweet memories.

Axen finished his paperwork and knew that Dylah wouldn't be where he had left her. He knew the plan she already had in her head as he walked softly to their son's room.

Though he wasn't sure if Cav should know the full truth, he understood why Dylah felt the need to tell him. Their son was adventurous yet calculated, the drive he had was challenging to slow down, and Axen had to agree that drive fueled by truth was better than fear.

He smiled seeing her on their son's pillow as Cav slept so soundly. Axen tiptoed across the room and knelt by the bed to carefully move Dylah to his hands.

"What are you doing?" Cav asked as his eyes flickered open.

"Shhh go back to sleep, Cav."

"Why are you taking mama?" Cav sat up.

"Let me tell you something, son," Axen said with a smile and a sigh. "Your mama might be the one who can be really tiny sometimes, but I'm the one who takes care of her when she's so small."

"You are?" Cav laughed.

"Yes." Axen smiled. "I protect her, I make sure she's happy and safe. Sometimes I put her in my pocket. And when she falls asleep in places she shouldn't be falling asleep I move her."

"Can I do that too?"

"Maybe when you're a little bit older." Axen whispered back. "She is actually kind of hard to handle when she's like this. Sometimes she bites."

"Bites?!"

"Why do you think I call your mama a nightmare?" Axen held back a laugh. "Go back to sleep, okay?"

"Okay," Cav said with a quick yawn. "Make sure mama is happy and safe."

"Always."

Axen quietly closed the adjoining door as he held a still sleeping Dylah. He was impressed and full of pride that their son had taken all of the information so well, he wondered why they had been so secretive to begin with. After stepping quietly across the room, he placed Dylah on her pillow before he laid down on his side.

His mind was racing with the list of things he needed to do in the morning, coupled with planning out how he would confront his sister about her chatty children, but then the weight of Dylah's head on his chest quieted his mind.

"You moved me," she mumbled with her eyes still tightly closed.

"That's part of my job, princess," he answered with a smile as he ran his fingers through her waves.

Chapter 5

Cautionary Tale

The next morning Dylah sat in the Fellowrock castle kitchen gripping a mug of coffee so tightly it was only seconds away from crumbling. Keilon was breezing through their weekly family meeting. Dylah would have skipped out by now but she was staring daggers at Kremon, waiting for any opportunity to call him out.

"Any other business?" Keilon asked cautiously, noticing his sister's expression.

"Yes." She stood up. "I need to punch Kremon in the face."

"Why is it always me?" Kremon laughed as he looked at his two other brothers and oldest nephew.

"I have been very clear about what I wanted my son to know about me," Dylah spoke slowly to contain the rattle in her voice.

"Yeah?" Kremon leaned across the table towards her. "What's your issue?"

"Your children told him things about me that he shouldn't have known just yet." She sighed loudly. "He knew about my eyes and he knew that his grandfathers were dead."

"I'm sorry he had to find out that Keilon wasn't his grandpa, you had to have known that that little joke wasn't going to last forever." Kremon rolled his eyes. "And I don't feel bad about him finding out about your eyes. I always thought it was a stupid thing to keep from your own kid."

"Hey, maybe we should calm down," Keilon suggested.

"You thought we were the absolute worst brothers in the world for not letting you know about your curse." Kremon laughed loudly. "But now you're the parent keeping big secrets from your son. You're supposed to do better for your kids, Dylah, not worse."

"Excuse me?" Dylah clenched her fists at her sides as her eyes turned to black within one blink. "Your kids run around without any rules and you're judging my parenting?"

"Yeah, well have a few more and we'll see how well you cope." Kremon reared his head back and laughed loudly. "Or would you just continue to lie to make yourself look better?"

"Stop!" Delin hit the table after watching his sister's face turn solemn hearing the words.

"Is that why you've only had one?" Kremon continued to snicker. "Easier to control, right?"

"I agree, stop," Bahn added with a groan.

"I get it, Aunt Dylah," Kunor spoke softly. "The way my mother lied to me was malicious, the way you lied to Cav was a form of protection."

Dylah sat back down in her chair speechless. She stared into her mug as she forced green to cover her irises, if only to hide the blue she knew was trying to show through.

"Dismissed," Keilon quickly ordered.

"Really?" Kremon sighed. "I thought I was supposed to get punched in the face?"

"Leave!" Delin almost shouted.

Shocked that his calmest brother was growing angry,

Kremon slowly left, along with Bahn.

"Are you okay?" Kunor asked with caution.

"Yeah," Dylah's answer rattled out in a hushed tone.

"If he knew he wouldn't have said those things." Delin slid his hand over to hold hers.

"It's okay to cry." Keilon moved his chair closer to her and put an arm around her shoulders. "You don't have to be tough right now if you can't be."

"Wait, what's going on?" Kunor whispered to his father.

"Kunor, why don't you meet us outside?" Keilon whispered back after a quick glance back to his distraught sister.

"I can't have any more children," Dylah said softly as tears fell from her eyes and crashed against the table. "We've been trying for years, it just won't happen. And when it does happen I lose the baby very early on."

"I'm so sorry," Kunor spoke slowly. "Excuse me." He slid his chair out and calmly left the kitchen, and the castle altogether.

"You didn't have to tell him," Keilon said, holding her a little tighter.

"Sometimes it's freeing to say it out loud." She took a deep breath and sat up straight wiping the tears from her eyes before shrugging away her doting brothers. "I'm really okay." She stood and walked to the coffee pot to refill her mug. "He just sucker punched me, I'm fine."

"His children are awful," Keilon added with a kind smile.

"I avoid them at all costs," Delin said seriously.

"Can I just be superficially mad that he somehow got four hellions and I can't seem to have just one more perfect little baby?" Dylah forced a laugh.

"Cav is pretty perfect." Keilon laughed.

"I know." Dylah smiled. "I'm so confused about how I got him so easily." Her smile fell as she leaned against the kitchen countertop. "By all accounts I shouldn't have gotten him at all. I'm pretty sure I died very early on in my pregnancy with him, how did I get him? If I can't hold the others for longer than a handful of weeks, how did I feel him move and grow for all of those long months? How did he get my eye?"

"What if it has something to do with the curse?" Keilon asked with caution.

"We already went down that route." Delin sighed. "It makes no sense."

"We don't have to talk about this anymore." Dylah smiled and took another drink. "Really, I'm fine."

"What the hell, Dylah?!" Kremon yelled as he ran into the kitchen, a bloody hand clasped over his nose as Bahn followed closely behind. "And what the hell, Keilon?!"

"What are you talking about, what did I do?" Dylah asked with a genuine laugh. "What happened to you?"

"Don't act dumb!" Kremon leaned over the sink. "You sent Kunor to hit me!"

"We most certainly did not!" Keilon said in defense.

"I did it myself." Kunor laughed loudly from behind the group. "I tapped him on the nose just like Aunt Dylah taught me!"

Dylah quickly clasped her hands over her mouth to stifle her laughter.

"You broke my nose!" Kremon's yell echoed against the walls of the sink.

"Your kid is pretty perfect too, Keilon." Dylah laughed as she left the castle mouthing 'thank you' to Kunor before slipping behind the grand castle doors.

Dylah walked through the courtyard, jumped into the trees, and bounced from branch to branch until she ran out of limbs to land on. She took quick steps through the streets of Hightree, kindly waving to the citizens that were now under her rule. Soon she found herself ascending the endless steps in a trance that was only broken by Avalia answering her knock.

"Dylah," Avalia said nervously. "I wasn't expecting you so early."

Dylah stepped around her and entered a suite similar to

her own. "Where's Cav?" she asked calmly. "I'll be taking him for the day."

"It's no trouble for me to watch him," Avalia said happily. "He blends right in with my own."

"You know what this is about, Avalia." Dylah sighed. "I'll be taking my son now."

"I already told Axen how sorry I am." Avalia began to panic. "I didn't think Frenia would tell him everything."

"Don't worry about it." Dylah smiled widely with flaming eyes. "Your husband has a broken nose by the way."

"Mama!" Cav exclaimed as soon as he saw her. "With your fire eyes!"

"Mama had her war eyes on earlier, Cav!" Dylah knelt down and held him. "Wanna come with me for the rest of the day?"

"Yes," Cav replied shyly, looking away from his aunt.

"Who was mean to you today?" Dylah asked as she looked up at Avalia.

"Taron and Terner," Cav said quietly.

"And what did they say?" Black streaked through her eyes as her glare stayed pinned on her sister-in-law.

"They told him that his mama died and was just a ghost." Avalia swallowed the words. "I tried to explain it to him."

Dylah quickly scooped Cav up into her arms and held his head against her shoulder. "I can't believe this," she muttered.

"Don't hit me," Avalia said softly as tears welled in her eyes. "I'm pregnant."

"Of course you are." Dylah groaned and took a deep breath. "I'm sorry. Congratulations, really. I'm excited for you." Her eyes clouded over. "And c'mon, I wouldn't hit you."

Dylah stomped away as Avalia followed her.

"I'm sorry, I didn't know they would tell him!"

Dylah paused to stop herself from saying anything from the list of awful things she wanted to throw at her sister-in-law. "I would like to speak to you and Kremon in private later tonight."

Avalia seemed shocked that she was speaking so calmly while her eyes screamed violence.

"Sure." Avalia gulped. "When he gets home the kids can play and we can talk."

"No, I don't need your children to do any more damage," Dylah spoke through clenched teeth. "For the time being your services concerning my son are no longer needed."

She didn't let Avalia answer, she quickly began her descent towards Axen's office, still holding Cav tightly.

"I can walk, mama." Cav laughed as he bounced in her arms with each step.

"You're right," Dylah said with a laugh as she set him down. "You're getting big, kiddo. Maybe you'll be taller than your uncles."

"I'm already a lot taller than you sometimes." He laughed as he took steps down.

"Well then that makes you the world's shortest giant."

"That's amazing!" He giggled.

They walked hand in hand until they arrived in front of Axen's door.

Cav opened the door and ran in towards his father's desk.

"I was kind of expecting you to be here an hour ago," Axen said slowly as his wife walked into the room.

"It's been a morning." She sighed.

"Yeah." Axen gestured to a corner of the room where Kunor was sitting. "I've been made aware."

"My father sent me here for as he put it." Kunor cleared his throat and spoke in a low mocking tone. "It was in my best interest if I left the kingdom for the day."

"Kremon's still mad?" Dylah laughed.

"I would assume so." Kunor shrugged. "I broke his nose."

"That's not very nice of you, Uncle Kunor," Cav said with a scowl.

"I did it for your mama!" Kunor said in defense. "He was being mean to her."

"But that doesn't mean you should hit everyone when they're mean to you," Axen added quickly. "Just so we're clear."

"Kunor, could you take Cav to the gardens?" Dylah asked with a smile. "I'll meet you out there in a bit."

Kunor quickly threw a giggling Cav over his shoulder as he left the room with a wave.

"What happened, Dylah?" Axen asked from the stately desk. "All Kunor said was that Kremon upset you and he felt like he needed to hit him for you."

"Yeah." Dylah seemed to deflate as she fell into the chair across from him. "I confronted Kremon about his unruly children, and he told me that I should have a few more so I could understand." She sighed loudly. "It just caught me off guard, is all."

"You want me to hit him too?" Axen asked with a straight face. "He's not under my command anymore, I could hit him. Nose is broken? I could punch him in the stomach."

"Perhaps you've been around Riloncks for too long."

"What a terrible observation to make about the king of Hightree." He smirked.

"It's all really okay." Dylah laughed lightly. "He doesn't know our situation."

"And he doesn't need to," Axen added. "I talked with Avalia earlier, she was very remorseful."

"Yeah, well prepare yourself to talk with both of them again." Dylah rolled her eyes. "The twins told Cav that I'm a ghost, because I died."

"You're kidding." Axen's face fell into his hands. "How do we explain that one?"

"I have no idea." She groaned. "But I already told Avalia that I don't need her watching Cav anymore."

"I bet she didn't take that very well." He laughed nervously. "What are we going to do instead?"

"We have a big family, someone will be able to watch him when he's not with me." Dylah added. "Chany has told me many times that she would love to have him since Brig and Kane are older. He loves Teyle, Aloria is also great with him."

"Okay, we'll figure something out." He seemed to deflate a little. "But maybe we should take a few days just to calm down."

"Actually-"

A loud knock echoed through the room followed by an uninvited twist of the doorknob.

Kremon stomped into the office, bruises hung under his eyes like shadows, his nose had one solid stripe and leaned towards the left.

"I hear we have a discussion ahead of us." Kremon calmly sat in the chair next to Dylah.

"Your kids told my son that I'm a ghost." Dylah raised an eyebrow over her fiery eyes.

"Well, aren't you?" He laughed. "I went to your wake, Dylah."

"Kids don't need to know that!" Dylah smacked the top of the desk.

"How about we wait for my sister to get here," Axen quickly added. "Then we can go to our suite and approach this discussion calmly."

"I'm going to punch Dylah back, I hope that's understood."

"I keep multiple daggers on me at all times, I think you should rethink your threats."

"Okay!" Axen clapped his hands together. "Let's head to the suite now and I'll open a bottle of wine so we can all just calm down."

"Fine." Dylah stood. "I'll take Cav to Fellowrock."

"You hate my children so much that you're sending your kid to the opposite kingdom?" Kremon laughed loudly.

"No actually, I'm going to give my son a little tour."

Dylah smiled kindly. "Yeah, in the streets of Hightree I'll show him where his father almost died because of his mother, then before the treeline I'll point out where his parents nearly killed a tyrant, and then when we get to the courtyard I'll show him the spot where I landed after being thrown from a balcony."

"Great idea." Kremon rolled his eyes.

Dylah held Cav's hand tightly as she grazed over his knuckles with her thumb. She was trying with all of her might to hold on to his innocence, and somehow that felt encapsulated in the softness of his small hands.

"Mama do you know that there are lilacs in the castle gardens?" Cav giggled.

"I do!" Dylah smiled. "Your dad took me to them a few times."

"They're not as nice as the ones in the field," Cav added. "I like the field a lot better."

"Me too, kiddo." She squeezed his hand.

Dylah slowly opened the door to Keilon's office and smiled nervously when he looked at her with obvious confusion.

"Do you mind spending some quality time with your nephew?"

"Mama fired Aunt Avalia." Cav hopped into one of the chairs at the desk.

"Well," Keilon sighed. "Your mama went through quite a few nannies herself, so it seems only fitting that you would too, Cav."

"Except my sweet child isn't the problem." Dylah smiled widely. "No worms or jumping out of windows for this one."

"You disappeared today." Keilon looked at her with subtle signs of worry. "Concerning after a certain discussion."

"She doesn't disappear." Cav laughed. "She gets really small. It just looks like she disappears."

"Is that right?" Keilon looked at Cav with artificial amazement. "That's impressive!"

"Yes." Dylah rolled her eyes. "Maybe you two can discuss other very impressive things."

"Did my mama die?" Cav asked with a straight face.

Keilon's eyes grew wide as they drifted over to Dylah.

"See, I felt like you were better equipped to handle that conversation." Dylah laughed. "I can come get him later tonight, I have no idea how long this discussion with Kremon will last."

"Sure." Keilon tried to breeze past the subject. "We can go for a walk around the pond."

"If my son brings home another toad, I swear you will regret it." Dylah spoke through grinding teeth.

"But he likes toads." Keilon laughed loudly. "Don't you, Cav?"

"I bet I can catch five this time!"

Dylah quickly kissed her son's forehead and thanked her brother, she rested against the closed door and began to make a script of the things she needed to say.

"Dylah?"

She turned her head towards the voice. "Hey, Chany." A forced smile curled on her face as her sister-in-law approached.

"Take it off, I know it's fake after the morning you've had." Chany crossed her arms. "Bahn told me everything. Let's get away from Keilon's door, I may start shouting."

Dylah followed quietly. "It just surprised me, it's no big deal." She sighed. "He didn't know."

"Yes, some things can be looked over for the sake of ignorance." Chany put an arm around her. "But that doesn't mean that everything said out of ignorance should be excused. Sometimes people need to know that certain subjects are not okay to thrust on others."

"Yeah."

"He should be thankful that he's never had to experience

that heavy loss." Chany shook her head. "Being blessed with all healthy babies is certainly a rarity."

"That's not something he'll ever understand." She stared at her feet. "It's not like losing someone you knew." Dylah swallowed the words.

"Because it's losing someone you never truly knew but wanted to hold and love for the rest of your life." Chany squeezed Dylah's shoulders. "I'm sorry it has happened to you so frequently. One left a piece of my heart forever shattered."

"You'd think that after getting my hopes obliterated so many times I'd learn to stop giving them names and picturing their sweet smiles." Her eyes seemed fixed to the floor. "Instead I build a mountain of hopes and future memories only to watch it come crashing down every damn time."

"Hope is a good thing to keep a hold on." Chany released her embrace and gripped Dylah's hand. "I hate believing that pain is just a part of our destinies, that never truly made sense to me. But if anything, the pain you feel now will strengthen the beauty you'll finally see."

"It's still going to be a perfect life if Cav is our only." She looked down the hallway full of bedroom doors. "But I loved growing up with such close siblings, I really wish I could give him that."

"I know, I wanted my boys to be closer in age." Chany's expression fell. "Brig was almost two when I miscarried."

"I'll be leaving Cav with you more often if you don't mind." Dylah smiled for the sake of lessening the burdens on their shoulders. "The list of people I trust to watch my miracle child is quickly dwindling."

"Of course, I've always been his favorite aunt." Chany gave Dylah a quick hug. "You're doing better than you think, dear."

"That's good to know." She lightly laughed. "Because it feels like I'm drowning."

The king and queen's suite was so deadly silent that a

mere exhale seemed to cut through the tension that hung between the two couples. The Farein siblings looked at each other with heavy disappointment, while the Rilonck siblings glared with a practiced ferocity.

They had been here for at least an hour. The only words spoken so far belonged to Axen as he handed out glasses of wine. But when his sister declined the offer due to her pregnancy, the silence began immediately after Axen's words of congratulations. Avalia and Kremon seemed to not know how to start, while Axen and Dylah gripped the other's hand to convey the hurt and jealousy they were feeling.

But this conversation wasn't about what they didn't have, it was about the giggly four year old they wanted to protect, and the adults who they thought they could trust to do that.

"We use you as a cautionary tale," Avalia finally said with her eyes pointed to the floor.

"You what?!" Dylah made a fist around the stem of her wine glass.

"It's not like we can threaten them with the curse like when we were kids!" Kremon said in his wife's defense.

"So you use their aunt as an example?" Axen glared at his sister.

"How do I come off in these cautionary tales?" Dylah was almost intrigued. "Am I the villain? Am I like the first Keilon?"

"No no no." Kremon shook his head. "It's more like if you don't clean up the toys right now you'll die just like your Aunt Dylah."

"You're kidding," Dylah said with a flat voice and expression to match.

"Yeah." Avalia forced a half smile. "Or if you don't stop making faces at your brother he'll get scary eyes like your Aunt Dylah."

"That doesn't seem like a viable threat." Axen rolled his eyes. "And why would you want to desensitize them to something as harsh as death?"

"I said it one day on accident when they were being especially energetic and-" Avalia glanced at her husband.

"Well it really worked so we just kept doing it." Kremon flashed a smile.

"So sure, it's easy to make those kinds of warnings to kids." Dylah huffed. "Keilon basically told me everything would kill me when I was little." She straightened up her posture. "But I don't need my nieces and nephews and especially my son thinking I'm some evil magical entity."

"We don't paint you out to be that great." Kremon chuckled. "Evil magical entity, really? You think pretty highly of yourself, huh?"

"Okay, calm down," Axen said, watching the agitation grow on his wife's face. "Come on, you two have always gotten along."

"Yeah well, his children are corrupting our son." Dylah said before taking a quick drink from her glass.

"Corrupting?" Avalia asked with a worried tone.

"Dylah, when you were only two years older than him you dealt with a lot worse." Kremon glared at her. "You turned out okay, right?"

"Apparently not!" She held her glass in the air. "I'm a cautionary tale!"

"You're a commander, a queen, a mother," Kremon added. "You're doing well."

"Thank you?" Dylah tilted her head.

"Our kids see that." Avalia smiled. "We like that they see how in control you are after everything you've been through."

"I'm sorry, let me get this straight." Axen laughed. "You're trying to compliment her?"

"In a way." Kremon grinned. "We kind of also want them to know that if they fight with someone so much bigger than them they could get thrown to their death."

"Not that we've given them those details," Avalia said in

a panic.

"It's all a little odd to me, but I do understand," Dylah said slowly. "I still don't want him around your kids for the time being. I'm not saying your kids are bad or that you're bad parents, we're just approaching these things differently and I need time for this to buff out. What he learned so far left him a little confused and quite frankly, we don't know how to explain those things to him just yet."

"I understand." Avalia sighed. "I'm sorry, I love having him around, he's such a good kid."

"Yeah." Kremon winked. "Considering who his mother is."

"It's comforting to know you think he takes after me." Axen smiled. "So is this resolved?"

"I think so, your majesty," Kremon said with an exaggerated volume and inflection.

"Delin can probably reset your nose." Dylah held back a laugh.

"I gotta say," Kremon said as he and Avalia began walking towards the door. "I didn't think Keilon's kid took after him until today."

"I didn't realize how late it had gotten." Dylah looked out the window at the dark sky. "I should go get the kid."

"I'll go with you." Axen grabbed her hand. "Scary dark forest for a dainty little thing like you."

"I think you mean evil magical entity." She winked.

Chapter 6

Dream Ridden

Dylah and Axen walked through the still halls of the Fellowrock castle. When they reached the fourth floor a small scream echoed around them. Recognizing the cry of her child Dylah began to run with Axen close behind. She threw open the door of her old bedroom to see Keilon holding Cav closely and rocking from side to side.

"He was sleepwalking," Keilon whispered. "He's still trying to move but I think he's calmed down."

Without a word, Dylah reached her arms up as Keilon handed over the small child. She cradled his head against her shoulder and sat on the bed whispering inaudible phrases into his ear.

"Does he do this often?" Keilon asked.

"Just recently," Axen whispered back with a sigh. "We thought it was the move that was prompting it, but now I don't know what to think."

Dylah watched as Cav's wide yet sleeping eyes flickered

into consciousness.

"Hey, kiddo." She smiled. "What were you dreaming about that made you want to run away?"

Cav's eyes darted around as he checked his surroundings, Dylah couldn't help but notice that his lavender eye seemed to twinkle.

"He was here, mama."

"Yeah, I was here." Keilon knelt by the bed. "Did I scare you?"

"No," Cav said as he continued to look around in a panic. "He looks like you though."

"Was it one of the other uncles?" Axen sat by Dylah on the bed. "Bahn? Or maybe Delin?"

"No." Cav seemed to cling to his mother even tighter.

Dylah and Keilon shared a look of concern.

"Have you been seeing this man at the castle too?" She held her breath as she waited for the answer.

"Yes," Cav whimpered. "I see him a lot."

"Has he been talking to you?" Keilon asked.

Cav nodded. "Tonight he was walking back and forth and saying the same thing over and over again." He sighed. "I thought he was mad, it was scary."

Dylah tried to steady her breathing.

"What was he saying, Cav?" Axen asked, noticing how frozen the others were.

"He was just saying youngblood." Cav yawned. "What does that mean?"

"It's just a dream, kiddo." Dylah kissed the top of his head. "Mama and your Uncle Keilon had the same dreams when we were younger."

"Really?" Cav said through another yawn as he nestled against his mother's shoulder.

"I'm going to stay here tonight," Dylah whispered. "What if he comes back?"

"He can't come back," Keilon added. "And if he does I'll kill him."

Dylah gestured for them to leave as she laid Cav down on the bed.

Out in the hallway they seemed to be a swirl of thoughts and panic.

"How is he even speaking to Cav?" Axen asked.

"He's my son." Dylah began to pace.

"I know that." Axen rolled his eyes. "But I thought he only showed up to the two of you because you had pieces of the soul."

"Do you think Cav has a piece?" Keilon whispered loudly.

"No, that's impossible." Dylah shook her head. "I hold it in my eyes, that's why draining my blood didn't take it away."

The three seemed to reach the same conclusion simultaneously.

"Cav has my piece?" Keilon asked with wide eyes.

"That could be a very strong possibility," Axen spoke slowly as he tried to piece it all together.

"I'm going in there and falling asleep so I can give that ghost a piece of my mind." Dylah's eyes shone pink. "How dare he terrorize my kid." She disappeared behind the closed door.

"I have whiskey in my office," Keilon said, looking at Axen.

"Perfect." Axen sighed with a smirk.

Dylah laid rigid in the bed holding her son closely. She tried to sleep but her heart was pounding and flashes of terrible memories filled her head. Her mind played a loop of falling through the sky and crashing against the pavement until exhaustion finally took her.

The floor creaked and Dylah awoke in the dream.

"Hey there, youngblood," a low voice rumbled in the darkness.

She turned her head to the corner of the room where a familiar figure stood.

"What do you want, old man?" she asked as she stood

between him and Cav.

"I see you had a child. Odd course of action for someone like you." He laughed as he took a step towards her. "Cav, is it? Named after our predecessor I'm assuming."

"What do you want?" Dylah asked again with grit in her voice.

"Never one for conversation, huh?" Old Keilon sighed as he took another step. "I forgot how small you were. How did you ever beat me?"

"Dagger in the heart."

"Right." He grinned. "I've been trying to reach you for a while now."

"You've been trying to get to me?" Her breathing quickened. "Not my son?"

"You know how sensitive kids can be to these other-worldly things." He glanced past her to the bed. "Yes, I have no need for the child."

"Just tell me why." Dylah began to grow impatient. "We didn't exactly leave each other on good terms, so please just get to the point."

"That's right, you died too. That explains why I can see you when I couldn't in previous dreams, we're both ghosts!" His smile fell. "Your mother has been giving me lots of grief over that situation."

"Keilon! Focus!"

"There's something coming," he finally said. "Slowly, but they're coming."

"They?" Dylah's mind began to turn. "A war?"

"Maybe." A half smile grew on his face. "I can tell you that they want revenge."

"Why should I trust you?" She crossed her arms.

"Look, I get it," Old Keilon said with a laugh. "You killed me I killed you, as far as I see it, we're even. You're the reigning chaotic soul and I felt as if I should give you a heads up. It's fine that you got taken down by someone that is your equal, but I'm not going to let you die again by someone weaker than me."

"That is oddly nice of you to say." Dylah thought through his warning. "This has something to do with you doesn't it?" She arched an eyebrow over pink and orange eyes.

"Barely."

"I have a question," Dylah said quietly. "Did I give any piece of the soul to my son?"

"I am intrigued by that eye of his," Old Keilon answered slowly. "But not that I can tell, and it rarely works that way."

"Okay." Dylah breathed a sigh of relief. "I just thought that since I was given Keilon's piece from his blood that maybe it transferred to Cav somehow."

"Keilon still has his piece." The ghost smiled with a wink as he began to disappear. "Until next time, youngblood."

"What?!" Dylah took quick steps towards the now vanished figure.

She shook herself out of her waking dream, gently carried her son up to the fifth floor office where her husband and brother were waiting.

"It was definitely him," she said with a sigh. "He came to warn me."

"Warn you?" Keilon laughed. "What does the man who killed you need to warn you about?"

"People are coming and they want revenge," Dylah replied in a hushed tone. "So I think we should be on our guard."

"No." Axen sighed. "The last time we trusted this guy things didn't end particularly well."

"But his warnings have always been legitimate," Dylah fired back with glowing pink eyes. "We can't deny that."

"How about we all just get some sleep and reassess in the morning?" Keilon began to smile. "You informed both kings so you're already a step ahead."

Axen carried a still sleeping Cav while Dylah followed,

lost in thought. She seemed to check behind every tree and her eyes shifted in the direction of the slightest sound. When they finally reached their suite she walked right to one of the windows and gazed out on the kingdoms below.

"I don't think he meant they were coming right this second, princess." Axen laughed as he wrapped his arms around her. "You should get some unhaunted sleep."

"He doesn't think that Cav has a piece of the soul," Dylah said quietly as if entranced by the view below. "But he said Keilon still has a portion." Her shoulders slumped. "What am I supposed to do with that information? Does that mean there's still a part of me that will go haywire? Did I somehow give it back? What's coming for us?"

"Hey, stop." Axen turned her to face him and held her head against his chest as he rested his chin on her messy waves. "Everything is going to be alright. We don't have to trust the murderous ghost a hundred percent this time around."

"It's been a very long day." She sighed with a laugh.

"Let's go to sleep and tomorrow I'll push a few things back and we can just relax with the kid all day." He held her tighter as he smiled. "You can read and I can build something. Life has gotten a little hectic for us, maybe we just need to take a day."

"That sounds very tempting." She laughed. "I'm not sure I can swing it though."

"Well too bad." He held her out in front of him. "It's a royal decree."

"Oh is it?" Her amethyst eyes twinkled up to him.

"Of course, my queen." He smirked.

There was a sudden pounding on the door, it shook the suite and Cav immediately began to yell in fear. Dylah went towards the cries while Axen went to the door.

Dylah held Cav and coaxed him back to sleep with the usual whispered words. She sat on the bed running her fingers through his hair until she heard the sound of Axen's footsteps approaching. With practiced stealth she exited the room towards the omen she knew had been approaching.

Axen's face was solemn and he was gripping a piece of paper in one hand.

"I've received a letter from your brother in the sand countries." He took a deep breath. "It's a warning."

"Derck?" Dylah asked in disbelief. "A warning against what?"

Axen calmly laid down on their bed and gestured for her to lay next to him. Dylah complied with confusion. They laid staring up at the ceiling, their hands tightly clasped.

"He said that a group of wanderers happened upon the sand countries, they caused a few fights." Axen paused, readying himself for the next bit of information. "He said that when they finally found him they said they were looking for Riloncks, but after only finding one they left in search of more."

"Why Riloncks?" she said only above a whisper.

"He said their leader is a woman and they seemed to be prepared for war," Axen spoke slowly. "He also mentioned that under extreme duress, Molix sent them in our direction."

"What?!" Dylah squeezed his hand almost too tight.

"The letter was only sent to me, he said he worried that it would get intercepted by one of them if he sent it to Fellowrock," Axen said with a bit of hopefulness. "He did add that it seems these people are under the impression that there is no peace between our kingdoms."

"So they could come here first hoping to gain an ally." Dylah smiled. "And that will be our opportunity to take them out."

"I'll fill Keilon in on the information tomorrow morning, and we'll just keep an eye out." Axen sighed. "We really should get some sleep. This has been a very interesting day."

"What could they want with us?" Dylah seemed to be thinking out loud. "Why just the Riloncks?"

She looked to Axen for any answers but saw that he could no longer fight the exhaustion the day had brought him. Seeing him at peace gave her a sense of relief and she too collapsed against him into a dream ridden sleep.

"See, youngblood." Old Keilon's voice interrupted the war planning in her dreams. "I wasn't lying."

Chapter 7

The Five

A week had passed since Derck's warning letter first arrived at the Hightree castle. The Riloncks had quickly devised many plans for whatever was coming for them. Delin scoured the scarce history books and any documentations of an event that would warrant a revenge, but he came up empty. The few facts they knew about the vengeful wanderers weren't adding up and it only made their worries grow.

Dylah stood on the ledge of the third deck, the wind whipped her navy and lavender cape around as she peered across the open landscape. Her hand rested against the dagger on her thigh as if she were prepared for an enemy to leap at her from the skies.

"Remember when you wanted me to fall from this ledge?" a familiar voice laughed from behind her.

"Remember when I immediately took that back?" she spoke with a growl in her voice. "Enemy prince."

"Nightmare," Axen said as he stepped up onto the ledge next to her. "I can lift you a little higher if you want me to."

"Six years," Dylah groaned. "It's been about six years since I was a helpless little fugitive princess."

"Fine, I'll drop it." He laughed, staring at her eyes of amethyst on fire.

"Thank you," she huffed and continued to stare at the horizon.

"Buttons," he whispered.

"I will push you," she threatened, trying not to laugh.

"Why are you always out here lately?" he asked with caution. "We have scouts posted at every corner of both kingdoms, we'll know if something is coming for us."

"I know." She sighed. "But as someone who has taken out a few scouts in my day, I'd like to be a bit more vigilant."

"Not every army has a lush for chaos."

"What if it is someone like me?" she said quietly. "Their leader is a woman and they are seeking revenge. I might be meeting my match here."

"Has the old guy shown back up?"

"No," she answered, seemingly lost in thought. "And Cav hasn't been sleepwalking."

"I do notice how our child sleeps," Axen said with an annoyed laugh. "I'm not oblivious to that."

"You sure were during those night terrors when he was two." She looked at him with a smirk before jumping back to the deck. "I'm going to go check in with Keilon."

"When are you going to tell him that he still has a piece?" Axen caught up to her. "He deserves to know."

"I'm trying to figure it all out." She sighed and turned to him so fast he caught the breeze from her cape. "I had to have all of it or else the first Keilon wouldn't have been able to come back, right?"

"Yes, I do believe that was the stipulation."

"Because he came back the same night they gave me Keilon's blood." She shook her head. "It happened almost instantly."

"I remember the storm."

"Then how was the piece taken back?" She masked her confusion with anger. "Did someone take it from me, and more importantly, how?"

"The way I see it is you have a choice of two people to consult about this." Axen's face fell. "One lives on the very edge of Hightree, and the other one is Delin."

"I don't want to see Atta any more than I have to," she huffed. "I'll talk to Delin."

"And then Keilon." Axen grabbed her hand. "You have to tell him."

"I will." She rolled green and gray eyes but when she looked up at him, the gray intensified.

"What is it?" he asked in a hushed panic.

Dylah pushed by him and stood on the ledge.

"Hightree scouts are returning." Her fists clenched at her sides. "And they're riding extremely fast."

The Fareins and the Riloncks gathered in the council room of the Hightree castle.

"There's no need to worry, we've laid out many plans of action already," Axen spoke loudly reassuring the group. "The scouts said the approaching camp is still a day's march away at the earliest."

"We're just going to wait for them to come to us?!" Bahn growled.

"Remember, they will probably come to Hightree first seeking an alliance against Fellowrock," Keilon added. "But I agree with Bahn, I don't like the idea of sitting around waiting for them to attack us."

"So we go to them," Dylah said in a stern voice.

"No," Axen added quickly.

"Yes," she said with her pink eyes pointed at him.

"Let me get this straight, what you're saying is," Kremon paused to laugh, "we meet them with both armies, and we're like 'hey, heard you wanted to fight us' then we skip on home?"

"Because something so careless is usually the way I plan these things." Dylah rolled her eyes. "No. Honestly it could just be the five of us."

"Five?" Axen asked, looking around the table and counting seven, including Kunor.

"The Riloncks." Keilon nodded to her. "I like that idea."

"I don't." Axen sighed.

"I'm a Rilonck," Kunor said quietly. "Dylah technically isn't."

"You and Axen need to stay behind," Keilon demanded.

"If Dylah goes, I go," Axen said loudly.

"So let's say you go and something happens." Keilon leaned towards him. "How well do you think Hightree will do with a four year old king?"

"So why can't I go?" Kunor asked with sudden worry.

"Let's say something happens." Keilon solemnly glanced at his son.

"The last time we went into danger like this we suffered a great loss." Dylah sighed. "We can't let that happen again. It'll be just us five."

"We can handle it!" Bahn hit the table with a crazed smile.

"Yeah! I'll shoot 'em!" Kremon hit the table in a similar fashion. "Bahn can stab 'em, Keilon will punch 'em, Delin will bore them to death with facts, and Dylah will scare the hell out of 'em!"

"I'll bore them?" Delin sighed. "I have weapons, no one ever talks about my weapons."

"I like your weapons," Axen added as he fought off a laugh.

"Are we leaving now?" Bahn asked, looking at Dylah.

"No," Keilon answered quickly, reading the sudden worry in her eyes. "First light of day."

"First light." She nodded to him with a smile.

With a plan in place the room cleared out, except for Axen and Dylah.

"I can't say that I'm a fan of this plan." Axen sighed. "I think I'll tag along just in case."

"You can't." Dylah forced the words out. "I'll be fine, I promise, we always come back to each other."

"Yes, I know." He smirked. "But?"

"But what if we don't." Dylah closed her eyes tightly. "I was only a little older than Cav's age when I lost my parents, I don't want history to repeat itself. At least this way he'll have you for sure."

"Don't talk like that." Axen pulled her in. "We're going to be around to annoy Cav until he's married his twelfth wife and has fathered his thirty fifth child."

"I told you I don't like that joke." Dylah laughed lightly.

"Your family has its traditions, and so does mine." He held her a little tighter. "What are you going to tell him?"

"I have no idea," she whispered. "When we left the last time he still didn't quite understand, but he saw the shape his uncles were in when we came back, and now he knows so much."

"I'll keep him distracted while you're gone." Axen rested his chin on her head as she seemed to sink into him. "It feels wrong having a conversation of this caliber outside the lilac field."

"The lilac field was not planted for cathartic moments, enemy prince," Dylah said with a muffled laugh.

"Still feels wrong." He laughed with her.

They spent the rest of the day carrying on like normal with Cav, although Dylah worked in some special moments. She played a game of tag with him around the gardens, slyly shrinking to hide within the flowers as he ran by. They took him to the range and let him pick out which arrow tips Axen would use, Dylah made a game out of guessing which ones he had picked. Then later that night, Dylah sat on his bed as he laid down for the night.

"Kiddo, I have a special job for you." She forced a happy tone. "Are you up for it, soldier?"

"What is it?" he asked in a sleepy voice.

"I need you to watch out for your dad the next couple of days, okay?" She willed her eyes to stay a happy amethyst. "Can you do that?"

"You usually do that, mama."

"You're right, Cav." Dylah smiled. "But, mama has to go help your uncles with something."

"You're leaving?" Cav asked as his smile faded. "Where are you going?"

"You remember earlier today when your dad shot that arrow way past the target?" She grabbed his hand. "Well it was a really important arrow, he was very sad that he lost it, so I told him that I would go find it for him."

"Why can't dad go find it?" Cav asked. "Or I could help."

"Hmmm let me think." Dylah put a finger to her face as if she was in deep thought. "Do you know how everytime we need to go somewhere it seems that you and your dad can't find your shoes?"

"Yes!" He giggled.

"Who always ends up finding them for you?" She smirked.

"You!" Cav giggled louder.

"See that's why I have to go find it." She started tickling him. "You two would just keep walking right past it, oblivious!"

Cav's giggling was interrupted with a long yawn.

"Okay, bedtime kiddo." Dylah sighed.

"Can you lay with me until dad comes to get you?" Cav asked shyly with another yawn. "That's his job, right?"

"Correct." Dylah laughed as she nestled into the bed holding her son close.

As Cav's breathing slowed she leaned in closer to him and whispered the words she had said to him every night since he was an infant.

"I know, mama," he mumbled as he drifted off to sleep.

When he was sleeping soundly she slowly rolled away from him and walked towards the door, turning every half step to check on him one last time. She shut the door behind herself and fell against it with her eyes shut tightly hoping to barricade the tears.

"You're coming back, Dylah," Axen whispered from across the room.

"I know," she said in a broken inhale.

"Come lay down with me until first light, my favorite nightmare." His smile could be heard in his voice.

"You're perfect." She sighed as she fell on the bed next to him. She rolled to her side and grabbed his face. "You are so damn handsome. You're my best friend. I love you so much."

"You're coming back, Dylah," Axen repeated himself. "So stop your last words."

"I just wish I knew what these people wanted." She closed her eyes tightly. "What revenge could they want on a kingdom that has only been free for such a short amount of time?"

"I think you will figure that out tomorrow, my dear," Axen said with a hopeful smile. "And you'll show them those scary eyes and they'll go back to wherever they came from."

"What if my eyes aren't that special to them?" Dylah's eyes opened wide as clouds swirled in her irises. "What if they all have eyes like this? What if my mother made some crooked deal to get me and they're coming back to retrieve me?"

"Keilon was a witness to your birth." Axen sighed. "You're spiraling."

"I'm just trying to prepare myself." Dylah smiled. "Anything is possible, we know this to be true."

"What you really need to do to prepare is sleep." He yawned.

"Not really." She laughed. "I can sleep on the way there."

"You're going to sleep while riding a horse?" Axen chuckled. "Now that's impressive."

"I'm not riding a horse." She smiled widely as her eyes shone pink. "It's a tactic. They'll see four coming, but there will be five."

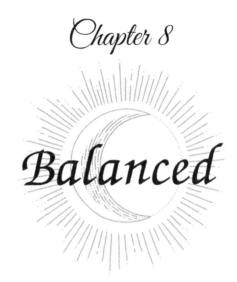

Chapter 8

Balanced

"Well this is lovely, right?" Kremon laughed from the back of his horse. "Just like we're kids again."

"When we were kids we couldn't leave the trees," Bahn grumbled.

"You know what I mean." Kremon reached to his right and smacked his twin brother's arm. "We're out doing some reckless things, no spouses, no children. No rules, right, Keilon?"

"Just don't die," Keilon answered with a laugh, remembering the games of their youth.

"Exactly!" Kremon took a deep breath. "No worries when it's just the Riloncks."

"Derck isn't here and Dylah is a Farein." Delin laughed. "Remember?"

"Maybe by name, but she's still a Rilonck. I am no less a Rilonck just because I married a Farein, and neither is she," Kremon said in a proud voice. "Probably the most Rilonck of us all."

"I wouldn't say that too loud," Keilon whispered. "She doesn't need the ego boost."

"I'm pretty sure she's asleep." Delin pointed to a box strapped to the side of his horse. "And if she's not, she's trapped in this box."

"Her curse has brought us so much peace." Kremon chuckled loudly.

"Shh!" Keilon abruptly pulled the reins, halting his horse. "There's a camp up ahead."

The four horses stopped in a staunch line as they gazed at the horizon and the answers it would give them.

"The camp seems to be mostly families," Bahn said, returning to the small wooded area from his scouting. "But there is a very obvious royal tent in the center of the camp, it is surrounded by heavily armored guards."

"No problem." Dylah laughed. "Lead them here."

"What?" Kremon crossed his arms with a silly grin. "There's only five of us, remember? That was your master plan."

"I think she's thought this through," Keilon pointed strong eyes at Kremon. "Listen to her."

"Why are you two more twinly than me and my actual twin?" Kremon pointed to Bahn who was naturally scowling. "I will never understand that."

Dylah knew exactly why her and her brother were so similar, it wasn't just that he raised her, but that they still shared a soul somehow. "Okay, so this is the plan," she said to ignore the truth she couldn't put into words yet.

After a brief explanation Keilon, Kremon, and Delin, hid behind trees. Dylah sat perched high on a branch nearly invisible, wearing dark green leggings, a gray shirt, and a black hooded cloak.

Just as everyone was getting restless, Bahn ran back into the shadows of the trees and disappeared with his brothers as two guards chased after him. When the guards in simple armor with pale green embellishments caught up they began to look around in confusion. Suddenly a figure landed on the back of one of the guards shoving a sharp tip into his neck, she jumped off of him as he collapsed against the ground. The other guard watched in disbelief, his grip tightened on his sword as he charged her, but was shocked to have not hit her. The guard's head whipped from side to side trying to locate the assailant, when he couldn't see her he sheathed his sword and headed back towards the camp. He had only taken two steps when a right hook slammed against his jaw, he swung back, but only hit the still air. Again, she appeared in front of him with a sudden knee to his stomach, he doubled over in pain giving her the perfect advantage to stab him in the neck with another tip.

"That was quick!" Keilon laughed as he and Delin dragged the comatosed guards into the shadow of the trees.

"Three more coming!" Dylah said before she jumped into the branches.

"He ran this way!" a guard yelled to the two following him. "Wait. Where are the first soldiers?" The guard turned to the others and found them lying motionless on the ground.

"They're all sleeping," Dylah smiled beneath the shadow of her hood. "Would you like to join them?"

Before he could answer he was met with a punch, a stab, and instant dreams.

Four more guards ran into the wooded area and stared around in disbelief finding it empty. They split off into different directions, but that was the wrong decision. Keilon discreetly tackled one, Kremon shot a sleep tip into another, and Dylah used her power to sneak up on the remaining two. Watching their faces flatten as she appeared in front of them gave her great entertainment.

Five more arrived.

Followed by eight more.

Then four more.

Finally two scared guards arrived on shaking legs.

While her brothers grew tired, Dylah was energized by the fight, fueled by the chaos she was living.

"How many more of you are running into certain failure?" she asked the last remaining guard while pointing a dagger and her pink and black eyes at him.

"We were the last two she sent out," the teenage boy stammered. "We- we're the only ones left!"

"Are you lying to me?" She took a step closer.

"No!" He fell to his knees. "We're a small moving community, our defenses are few."

"Well that's not very smart!" Dylah laughed. "What revenge are you seeking on the Riloncks?"

"You're a Rilonck, too?" the boy asked with wide eyes on her, but his next blink seemed permanent as he fell to the ground.

"What the hell, Kremon?!" Dylah growled. "I had him!"

"You're taking too much time," Keilon whispered loudly. "Go to the tent."

"Fine." Dylah pulled a navy scrap of fabric from her shirt pocket, placed it on the ground, quickly shrank, and returned to her normal size donning her usual cape. She picked up a smaller scrap of black fabric and casually dropped it into her shirt pocket. Noticing the confused faces of her brothers she laughed loudly. "You're just jealous that I can pack so lightly."

At the camp, Dylah casually darted behind tents, when anyone approached she simply shrank to remain undetected. She stood hidden outside the royal tent watching until she knew only one person remained inside.

"We need to have a discussion," Dylah said, suddenly appearing in front of the doorway inside the tent.

A woman looking to be in her late thirties with ringlets of golden strawberry hair framing her face, looked up from her desk in shock. She stood with her fists clenched at her sides and dark green eyes pinned on the stranger approaching her.

"Leave!" the woman barked. "My guards will take you away!"

"I already took care of your guards." Dylah laughed.

"You what?" The woman stepped in front of her desk, she wore a long loose white dress with pale green details and periwinkle gems. She stood only slightly taller than Dylah.

"They're fine, but they'll be asleep for a bit longer." Dylah crossed her arms. "So we have plenty of time to chat."

"Would you like to have a seat?" The woman gestured to a chair by her desk.

"As long as you sit first." Dylah smiled coyly with forced green eyes.

The woman returned to her seat. She rested her interlaced fingers on the table as she sat with well practiced posture waiting for Dylah to take a seat. Dylah complied.

"I am Nevely," the woman said with a light but proud voice. "My people have traveled a very long way and we still have a bit more to go."

"Until you reach Fellowrock?" Dylah asked with a raised eyebrow.

"Yes," Nevely replied calmly. "Now introduce yourself."

"I'm Dylah." A smirk formed on her face. "I am Second in Command to the Fellowrock armies."

"I see."

"Yeah, you guessed it." Dylah leaned towards her and whispered, "I'm a Rilonck."

The green in Nevely's eyes seemed to dim.

"Tell me, Dylah Rilonck." Nevely smiled. "Is your family still reigning the kingdom?"

"You already met my brother, Derck." She smiled watching Nevely's eyes darken. "We have an older brother too, he's the king of Fellowrock, his name is Keilon. Along with three other brothers, each carrying all of the Rilonck features and strength you'd expect."

"Keilon?!" Nevely's delicate fingers twisted into tight fists. "Your family still carries the name of that tyrant?!"

"That's not the only thing we carry." Dylah laughed as she allowed her eyes to show through, shining pink in the dim tent.

"It's you." Nevely's eyes brightened. "You're the soul of chaos."

"You've heard of me?" Dylah said in shock as her eyes faded to gray. "Where did you say you're from?"

"Fellowrock." Nevely smiled. "Well, my family's lineage is from Fellowrock, but we haven't been able to return for over three hundred years."

"That doesn't make any sense, we were cursed for so long." Dylah shook her head.

"Does the name Sorner Rilonck ring a bell to you?" Nevely asked. "He's my ancestor."

"You're a Rilonck?!"

"Distantly, yes." She laughed. "I imagined we would be closer in age, being what we are."

"What are you talking about?" Dylah stood preparing to escape. "What do I have to do with you?"

"I am the Sorner to your Keilon." Nevely smiled widely as she stood taking slow steps towards Dylah.

"Sorner was Keilon's younger brother, right?" Dylah began to think out loud. "And they had a falling out, which led Keilon to-" Dylah looked to Nevely with a blank stare. "How?"

"How did we survive being exiled?" Nevely crossed her arms and laughed loudly. "It wasn't easy, and that's why I wanted revenge."

"Oh," Dylah replied softly.

"But that's more your style, right?" Nevely smiled kindly. "Dycavlon, Keilon, Dylah, all three of you thrive so heavily on chaos, so much so that too much of it would leave the world out of balance."

"It feels pretty well balanced to me." Dylah clenched her

fists at her sides.

"That's because of me," Nevely answered smugly.

Dylah tried to slow her panicked breathing as she watched Nevely's eyes change various different shades of green, from nearly white to almost black, but always a shade of green.

"You see, little Rilonck princess." Nevely laughed, taking another step towards Dylah. "I bring balance to the chaos that unceasingly ripples forth from you. Where you find joy in war and havoc, I spread order. You may be the soul of chaos, but I am something even more important."

"I don't understand." Dylah forced the words out.

"It's simple." Nevely pinned her bright green eyes on Dylah. "I am the soul of harmony."

Chapter 9

Best Friend

At the Hightree castle, Axen paced the living area of their suite, occasionally looking out the window hoping to see four approaching horses. Dylah left just a few hours ago, the day was still new, and yet he felt like she had been gone too long.

"Is mama back yet?" Cav shuffled into the room.

"Not yet, buddy," Axen answered with a smile as he ruffled his still messy hair.

"Why did you shoot that arrow so far away?" Cav looked up to him with wide sad eyes. "It's going to take her days trying to find it!"

Axen was confused by the question, then he thought to the day before when Dylah ran up to him at the range and asked him to shoot an arrow as far away as he could. She didn't explain her request, but he now understood the need she had.

"Sometimes my aim just isn't very good, Cav." Axen

shrugged. "But your mama is going to find that arrow as fast as she can and she'll come right back."

Cav smiled and jumped on the couch. "Let's wait for her."

"We could do so many fun things today!" Axen said as he collapsed on the couch next to his son. "All the things that mama doesn't like us to do."

"Like catch toads?!" Cav giggled.

"Yes!" Axen smiled. "We can catch all the toads you want!"

"Uncle Keilon can help us too, he likes toads!"

"Actually, Uncle Keilon is helping your mama." Axen tried to keep his upbeat tone.

"Oh," Cav said with obvious disappointment. "Why did she take Uncle Keilon with her?"

"Well she needed lots of help, so she took Uncle Delin, Uncle Kremon, and Uncle Bahn too."

"Why couldn't she take me?" he asked looking down. "Or you?"

Axen thought fast, hoping he could come up with an answer that would satisfy the wonderings of his young son.

"Your mama and her brothers are very close." Axen smiled. "She's the youngest, and you might have noticed that your uncles are a lot taller than her."

"Yeah they are." Cav giggled.

"Well, they worry about her a lot!" Axen over exaggerated. "So even though you and I know how strong she is, her brothers still see her as a little kid and try to go with her everywhere."

"If they're helping her, maybe she'll find the arrow faster!"

"Exactly! But the more important question here is," Axen stood up and began walking backwards towards the hallway door. "Who can get changed and ready to go faster? You or me?"

After a series of races getting ready, eating breakfast,

and running down the many Hightree steps, Axen and Cav walked on soft feet around one of the Fellowrock ponds.

"There's so many jumping today!" Cav giggled. "Last time there weren't very many, and Uncle Keilon was sad."

"Well maybe we should catch one for him and you can give it to him when they come back," Axen suggested.

"No!" Cav objected. "He'll chase mama with it."

"You're right." Axen laughed as he watched Cav attempt to sneak up on a toad that quickly jumped into the water.

"Why is mama so afraid of toads?" Cav shook off his disappointment and walked towards another toad. He lurched forward quickly and held the squirming amphibian in his hands. "They look so silly!" He laughed loudly making the toad dance.

"That's something you'll have to ask your Uncle Keilon." Axen smiled thinking back to a conversation he had with his brother-in-law years ago in a foreign land.

"He told me not to ask him any more hard questions for a while," Cav said after letting the toad jump away.

"Why would he say something like that?" Axen asked as he knelt against the damp soil targeting his own toad.

"He didn't like that I asked him how mama died." Cav quickly jumped after another toad.

"And what was his answer?" Axen asked with caution disguised in a happy tone.

"He told me that mama really wanted to save everyone," Cav spoke as if the story was incredibly normal. "He said that she did save everyone, and it made her so tired that she fell asleep. She couldn't wake up and everybody was sad." Cav gave up his chasing and looked to his father. "But she came back because she missed you too much."

"That's exactly what happened!" Axen laughed, feeling a sense of relief. "That's the thing about your mama and I, we always come back to each other."

Axen kept Cav distracted all day, but mostly for the sake of keeping himself distracted as well. He didn't think Dylah would be gone for a full day but night had come and he put their son to bed by himself. He laid in bed that night staring up at the ceiling trying to ignore the empty space next to him. Sleep finally began to take over when soft footsteps crept towards him.

"I can't sleep," Cav mumbled, standing on Axen's side of the bed.

"Me neither, buddy." Axen pulled Cav to the bed and sat him on Dylah's side.

"You miss mama, too?" Cav said, his one amethyst eye glittering in the dark.

"I do," Axen answered with a sigh and a smile.

"Does she say the same thing to you that she says to me?" Cav asked.

"I know she whispers something to you every night but she doesn't do that for me, bud." Axen lightly laughed. "I think that's just for you, Cav."

"No." Cav shook his head. "She told me she said it to you before and you've said it back."

"Really?" Axen asked with slight confusion. "I can't think of what that would be."

Cav yawned and he blinked slowly. Axen pulled the blanket over his shoulders and tucked him in tightly.

"You've always been my best friend," Cav whispered.

"I have?" Axen brushed a stray strand of light brown hair from Cav's face.

"And you always will be." Cav yawned again with his eyes closed.

"Hmm, well let's see how things go when you're a teenager."

"I loved you then and I love you still." Cav's voice trailed off.

Axen smiled to himself remembering the words he had heard while recovering from an injury and the words he reciprocated the night he finally got Dylah back. He had seen her whisper something to their son every night as Cav began to fall asleep but never asked her what she said after all this time. Now, knowing that she had been repeating some of the most important words of their relationship, he finally found peace and fell asleep.

Chapter 10

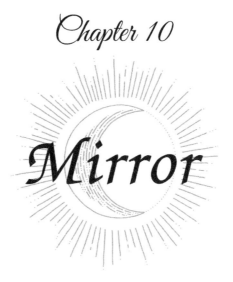

Mirror

Dylah sat across from Nevely in the strange tent while the light outside slowly began to waver. Silence hung between them as their thoughts buzzed overhead.

"Is harmony really the opposite of chaos?" Dylah finally asked, staring off at nothing and slightly shaking her head.

"Yes," Nevely answered shortly. "You could also call it order, organization, balance, symmetry, or peace."

"Peace?" Dylah laughed. "I've brought peace as the chaotic soul just fine. That job doesn't solely fall to you."

"I am confused about something." Nevely sat up straight in her chair. "Why are you younger than me?"

"Is that a serious question?" Dylah scoffed and crossed her arms. "It seems that I was born a few years later than you, does that clear things up?"

"No." Nevely's face fell flat as her eyes began to darken. "The chaotic soul always comes first, then the soul of harmony." She leaned closer. "Dycavlon was older than Allinay,

Keilon was older than Sorner, and you should be older than me."

"I don't think that's a written rule." Dylah's smirk was amplified by her amethyst and orange eyes. "It seems to be just a coincidence to me."

"It is completely obvious to me that you have gone so long without a source of balance."

"I have many sources of balance." Dylah smiled widely. "You've already met one of them."

A look of confusion spread over Nevely's face, she was forming the words when the canvas parted and a tall, broad, and blonde man barged in.

"I didn't need you to come." Dylah rolled her eyes, she didn't even need to turn around to know who had entered. "We're just talking."

"You were taking too long and her soldiers are waking up." Keilon sighed as he sheathed his drawn dagger.

"This is Nevely." Dylah smiled as she gestured to the strawberry blonde woman across from her. "She is also a Rilonck."

"No." Keilon laughed loudly as he took steps toward the desk. "That's impossible, I know every Rilonck down to the third removed cousins."

"Her lineage goes back a little further," Dylah said nervously.

"I come from Sorner's line," Nevely replied with magnified pride.

"Who?!"

"The first Keilon's younger brother," Dylah answered before Nevely could. "The one he exiled."

"So what you're saying is that this woman is a liar." Keilon chuckled. "Because that would be impossible. You seriously claim that your family lived for three hundred years with the curse?"

"Yes." Nevely looked up at him with soft green eyes. "And may I have your name?"

"I am Keilon Rilonck." He smiled proudly below a slight glare. "King of Fellowrock."

"Please have a seat." Nevely gestured to the empty chair next to Dylah.

After a look of approval from his sister, Keilon sat with rigid posture.

Dylah and Keilon looked at each other as if they were communicating with their thoughts.

"What a special bond the two of you have," Nevely said, breaking up the silence.

"I raised her," Keilon snapped back.

Dylah watched the smile of realization grow on Nevely's face. She feared that the mysterious woman had figured out the secret she was keeping from her brother.

"Dylah," Nevely's voice rose in a melodic manner. "Do your eyes work on your brothers?"

"Yes," Dylah answered quickly. "Though I haven't used it on them in a very long time."

"Really?" Nevely smiled widely. "Even Keilon?"

"Yes," Keilon growled. "It's a memory we don't talk about."

"Do you mind demonstrating, Dylah?" Nevely asked as her irises brightened. "I'd love to see it."

"She will not!" Keilon barked.

"Oh come on." Nevely laughed. "I'm sure she won't make you do anything terrible. Her power is just so different than mine, I'm interested in seeing it."

"Your power?" Keilon asked in a suddenly calm voice.

"Nevely is the soul of harmony." Dylah sighed. "She is meant to balance out the chaos that comes from me."

"Is that really a thing?" Keilon's glance darted from his sister to the stranger.

"Look at her eyes."

Nevely smiled as her eyes transitioned through every subtle shade of green.

"Oh." Keilon slyly leaned away from the stranger across

from him.

"Dylah, please." Nevely batted her eyes. "I'd love to see your power."

"It's fine." Keilon nodded. "You can show her, I trust you."

Dylah's fingers twisted into a nervous fist when she saw Nevely's haughty expression. She gulped and looked at her brother with intentional purple eyes.

"Laugh with me, big brother," Dylah ordered with a smile.

"No," Keilon said, his mood unchanged.

"I knew it!" Nevely clasped her hands together.

"Knew what?!" Keilon was growing angry through his confusion. "Why didn't it work, Dylah?"

"The chaotic soul cannot be used against itself," Nevely said flatly.

"What does that even mean?" Keilon asked with growing volume but seemed to freeze when he saw his sister slumped with swirling gray eyes. "Dylah? What did you do?"

"It makes so much sense now." Nevely laughed. "I'm older than you because he came first! I knew there was no exception to the rule."

"That doesn't explain why my sister's power isn't working on me," Keilon huffed. "In fact, everything you're saying sounds like complete nonsense to me."

"The power doesn't work on you because, as I said, the chaotic soul cannot be used against itself." Nevely sighed. "A lesson that Sorner learned the hard way when he tried to make Keilon use his own power in a mirror. It did not work."

"So Dylah is looking into a mirror?" Keilon asked.

"In a way." Nevely laughed. "I can't believe you don't know."

"No," Keilon whispered to himself as he looked at Dylah. "How?"

"I don't know," she replied shyly. "We'll have to talk to Delin."

"But you knew?" Keilon pinched the bridge of his nose. "How long?"

"Since the night I talked to the old guy." Dylah sighed. "There was never a good time to tell you."

"What old guy?" Nevely interrupted.

"The First Keilon," Dylah said with glowing pink eyes. "He visits my dreams from time to time and sometimes gets resurrected and kills me."

"Is that a joke?" Nevely asked as she grimaced.

"Yes!" Keilon answered quickly. "So much chaos with this one."

"And with you too though, right?" Nevely slowly smiled. "We'll be in touch."

"Could you be more specific?" Dylah asked.

"We'll see you soon." Nevely's smile curled into a malicious grin. "Please return to Fellowrock."

"You're coming to Fellowrock?" Keilon asked.

"We'll see you soon," Nevely repeated.

Keilon was growing angry but Dylah quickly grabbed him by the arm and led him out into the dark camp.

"We have to get more information from her!" Keilon pulled away from Dylah.

"No, we need to get back to Fellowrock and prepare for an attack!" Dylah gritted her teeth.

The siblings were locked in an angry stare down when those in the camp began to grow curious.

Dylah casually turned to one with intentional blue eyes and a smile.

"How are we feeling tonight?" she asked, testing her power.

The innocent bystander looked back at her with wide eyes slowly filling with tears before they ran off.

"Well that's good to know!" She laughed until she focused back on her scowling brother. "Okay, fine, let's go."

When they returned to their waiting brothers, they

wasted no time in releasing the tied up guards. Then immediately shot them again with sleep tips to ensure that they would not know which direction they would ride off in.

Fellowrock was only half a day's ride away, but well into their return as the sun was slowly rising Keilon halted the four horses.

"Why are we stopped?" Bahn groaned. "We're only a few hours from the treeline."

"We need to have a discussion in a neutral environment." Keilon's words were full of gravel as he dismounted from his horse. "Let Dylah out."

"What did she do?" Kremon asked with a laugh. "Did she kill someone again?"

"Surprisingly, Dylah is not the problem here," Keilon answered gruffly.

Delin held the box that housed their sister with a firm grip.

"Delin, let her out," Keilon demanded.

"What do we need to talk about?" Delin asked. "Does Dylah really need to take part? I imagine she's sleeping off the day."

"Wait." Kremon's eyes grew wide. "Is Delin the one in trouble? That rarely happens!"

"Let her out," Keilon nearly shouted. "This involves all of us."

"Come on," Bahn growled. "I'm ready to get home."

"Yeah!" Kremon added. "I wanna see my kids too."

Delin sighed and opened the box letting a still tired Dylah walk onto his hand, but just as she was about to jump off and return to her normal size he let the box fall to the ground as he covered her with his other hand.

"HEY!" Dylah's muffled voice yelled.

"What are you doing?!" Keilon took slow steps toward him.

"Let her go!" Kremon pushed himself to stand between Delin and Keilon. "What's wrong with you?!"

"I will," Delin said near panic. "I just want you to promise that you're going to listen to my reasoning."

"Are you really so afraid of getting hit that you're holding our little sister hostage?" Bahn rolled his eyes. "Pathetic."

"We just want answers, Delin." Keilon sighed. "I think that's fair."

Delin finally opened his hand, Dylah soon appeared in front of them with her arms crossed and her eyes on fire.

"Are you kidding me?!" she snarled glaring at Delin. "What the hell was that?! Face or stomach? Where would you prefer to be punched first?"

"We are approaching this calmly." Keilon put a hand on her shoulder. "So fix your eyes, little sister."

"Can someone please explain what is going on?" Kremon sighed loudly.

"Keilon still has a piece of the soul," Dylah said, still glaring at Delin. "And since I had to have all of it to resurrect the first Keilon, we are a bit confused on how he got it back."

"Oh," Kremon said quietly. "Good luck, little brother."

"Let me explain." Delin held his hands up as if to show that he was holding no secrets. "After that whole terrible ordeal, after we thought we lost Dylah, after we finally got our kingdom back, when Dylah took control of the curse, after Cav was born, when we were all finally back to normal. I noticed something."

"Explain faster," Dylah growled.

"You two just weren't clicking like you used to." Delin looked from Keilon to Dylah. "You still got along, sure, but it wasn't the same. I even held a meeting with the brothers about it."

"Right," Bahn added, "he did."

"Then I realized what it was that gave you two your solidarity." Delin sighed.

"And you couldn't have come to us about this?" Dylah asked, trying to remain calm.

"Don't you remember how reckless Dylah was without

the full soul?!" Keilon gritted his teeth. "You would chance that again?"

"It's been about four years and she seems fine, maybe even better," Delin said calmly.

"He's not wrong." Dylah laughed. "I've been killing it."

"I consulted Atta," Delin added quickly.

"You what?!" Keilon took a strong step towards him.

Dylah stepped in front of Keilon. "How dare you bring her into this without our knowledge!"

"Yeah, that crosses a big line, Delin." Kremon shook his head.

"She helped me figure out just how much to take from Dylah so that she'd stay the same." Delin looked to the ground. "Dylah is holding the majority still, yes, but Keilon, you have more than what you had originally."

"So Dylah has less than she did before Arizmia?" Kremon asked loudly. "I don't understand."

"It is a bit complicated." Delin looked at his oldest brother. "It's not a full split."

"Explain better." Dylah's anger returned.

"So, I extracted parts of the soul." Delin half smiled. "Dylah kept the power in her eyes, obviously, Keilon got the pride but he basically already had that. I split the tenacity, drive, strength, whatever you want to call it. And everything else I divided evenly. You didn't notice a thing."

"Still." Dylah raised an eyebrow. "It wasn't your place to meddle."

"I have noticed that you two seem to know what the other is thinking," Kremon added. "I thought it was just years of Keilon's torture finally breaking ground."

"It's fine if you're mad, I get it." Delin looked almost remorseful. "But just know that you went a very long time without realizing it. And under no circumstance am I giving one of you total control. It's better that it's split."

Dylah and Keilon looked at each other in silence.

"Just think about everything great that has happened,"

Delin continued. "Fellowrock is thriving. We lost a battle but won a war. We are stronger than ever and it's because we're being led by two halves of the same soul."

Keilon and Dylah glanced at each other once again in silent conversation.

"It might seem like Keilon getting a partial soul initially was an accident, but for some reason, I think our mother did it on purpose," Delin spoke quietly. "She could see the future, she knew what was going to happen. She knew you two would need each other." His eyes locked with his oldest brother. "She knew that Dylah would need you a lot in life, Keilon."

"We can drop this," Keilon said quickly as his mother's words began to echo in his head. "We should keep moving."

"If I get back in that box, can I be sure that you'll let me out later?" Dylah asked, staring up at Delin with fire in her eyes.

"Yes." Delin chuckled. "No hard feelings, it was only a tactic."

"Next time I'll bite," Dylah muttered before using her curse to return to her box.

Chapter 11

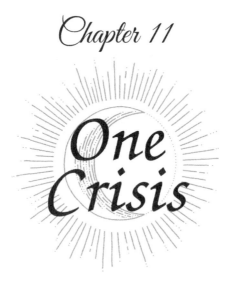

One Crisis

Dylah and Kremon walked through the Hightree castle three hours after the sun had risen and parted ways a few stories up the seemingly endless steps.

Dylah was frozen for a moment outside the office door, she paused to listen to the muffled back and forth laughter of her husband and son. She calmly held an arrow in her hand as she turned the knob with the other.

"Did someone lose an arrow?" Dylah said with a laugh in her voice as three hazel eyes locked on her, along with one amethyst.

"You found it!" Cav giggled before running into her arms.

"I told you I would!" Dylah smiled as she held him in her arms and quickly spun around.

Axen walked towards her, frantically assessing her physical state and feeling relieved that she seemed to return completely untouched.

"Was it where you thought it was?" he asked with a concerned smile.

"Even closer." Dylah smiled back with slowly graying eyes.

"Can we go see Uncle Keilon?" Cav asked. "I want to tell him how many toads I caught yesterday without him!"

"Toads?!" Dylah gasped dramatically as she dropped her arms to let Cav dangle upside down. "Where?!"

Cav giggled as his head hovered only slightly above the floor. "Not here, mama!"

"Yes, we can go see your uncle," Dylah said as she propped him back up. "We may even stay there for a few days!" She smiled widely at her son but glanced with knowing eyes at her husband.

"That will be so fun!" Cav clapped his hands. "Can we stay at the old house?"

"Cav, why don't you run up to your room and start packing some clothes, Aunt Aloria is just across the hall waiting to take you," Axen suggested. "And we'll get going as soon as we can!"

Cav's face lit up before he ran out the door.

"So they're coming pretty fast then?" Axen asked as he wrapped his arms around Dylah.

"Yes," she whispered. "I'm still not too sure what they want."

"And you think they'll come here first?"

"I talked to their leader, I introduced myself as a Rilonck." Dylah sighed. "She didn't seem to know there was peace between our kingdoms."

"And you're hiding Cav in Fellowrock because of his eye?" Axen took a deep breath. "Did they notice your eyes?"

"Yes," Dylah answered shortly. "I think we should sit for this discussion."

Axen's arms fell to his side as he looked into her vibrant pink eyes. He watched as she slowly noticed his expression and quickly changed her eyes to the calm lavender he knew and loved.

"You don't have to do that, princess." He smiled and returned to his chair.

"I just want you to come up with your own reactions without immediately knowing mine." Dylah sighed as she fell into the chair across from him. "I feel like that's how normal relationships work."

"We will never know." He smirked. "Let me have it, what information has you reigning in the full visible reaction of your ancient chaotic soul?"

Dylah took a deep breath and let the words spill out. She told him about Nevely, her lineage, the soul she possessed, and the difference in her eyes. She filled him in about how Nevely picked apart the fact that Keilon still had a piece of the soul, then delved into the conversation about Delin's reasoning. After she had divulged every ounce of information she had accrued in a little over a day, she sunk back into the chair.

"Well that is a lot." Axen sighed. "Who knew there were more Riloncks?"

"Nobody knew." Dylah's face fell into her hands. "I don't know where they were living, or even how they were living."

"I can't begin to imagine the efforts that went into sustaining so many lives under those conditions." Axen shook his head in disbelief. "And to think that the curse came back after less than two years of it being broken. What do you think they did?"

"I'm sure we will find out soon enough." Dylah looked up. "I can't fathom the drive they have after a history like that. We might not win this one."

"Or maybe they just want to know their family."

Shortly after arriving home, Dylah was once again packing her things and heading back through the trees gripping her son's hand tightly. Kremon also decided to stay in his home country for the time being, bringing along his blondest children.

Once the former Fellowrock siblings were situated in their old rooms, a meeting was called to discuss the approaching conflict. Scenarios were laid out, solutions were made, backup plans, and worst case decisions were also brought up. Scouts from either side were sent to watch for any movement. For two days the kingdoms waited. Families were again separated, but that didn't stop the two whose love had brought the kingdoms together.

When the night was at its darkest, Dylah slipped out of the bed she was sharing with her son and crept towards the door. She carefully pulled the door shut and breathed a sigh of relief feeling proud of her stealth.

"What are you doing?" a voice whispered behind her.

Dylah turned quickly. "I'm going to the tunnel to see my husband," she huffed. "What are you doing?"

"I don't know," Keilon whispered. "I just suddenly woke up and felt like walking."

Dylah's expression fell. Since Delin had explained to them his medical trickery, the two had been noticing their similarities more and more.

"You've always been a night owl." Dylah sighed trying to side step what she knew they were both thinking. "And everyone seems to be a little anxious."

"Yeah." Keilon laughed lightly. "Everyone." He rolled his eyes. "Nice try."

"I won't be gone long." Dylah flipped her navy hood over her head. "Then we can discuss how we're the same damn person over lots and lots of coffee."

"No, not yet." Keilon's usual proud voice slightly wavered with panic. "One crisis at a time."

"Yes." Dylah smiled widely. "It is a crisis."

Axen paced in the torchlit tunnel, he began to worry about every dangerous reason why Dylah wasn't there yet.

"Haven't I warned you about meeting me in Fellowrock?" Dylah's voice echoed down the tunnel as her shadow approached.

Soon she was in front of him, her purple eyes pointing up to him. He was taken back to when they were nothing more than two people thrown into the drama of war and double sided treason.

"Why are you looking at me like that?" Dylah laughed.

"You're really pretty." Axen smiled widely.

"Oh it's my eyes, isn't it?" Dylah fell against him and laughed. "I promise you I am definitely not the person you think I am." Her laughing grew. "You see, my eyes are only like this because I descended from a long line of pixies."

"You're a nightmare." Axen laughed as he held her tightly. "And I've missed you so much."

"It will all be over tomorrow." Dylah smiled against his chest. "Until then you're once again, the enemy prince."

"Enemy king." Axen squeezed her tighter.

Dylah pushed herself out of his hold and put her hands on the sides of his face.

"I love you." She smiled up at him.

"I love you too." He smirked back. "How's the kid?"

"Kunor is fine." Dylah laughed loudly. "He definitely misses you."

"Well that is great to know, please tell him the feeling is mutual." Axen rolled his eyes. "And our son?"

"He's been very well distracted, but he misses you a lot." Dylah sighed with a half smile. "How did we get such a sweet kid?"

"I think he gets it from his mama." Axen pulled her back in and rested his chin on top of her head. "He told me what you tell him every night."

"Four years." She shook her head. "Kind of impressed that he kept the secret that long, but I'm also concerned that I've raised such a snitch."

"Did you just call our son a snitch?"

"Your son," Dylah huffed. "No son of mine is a snitch."

"I can't wait to have you both home." He laughed lightly.

"It's too quiet."

"It might surprise you to hear this." Dylah took a deep breath. "But I wish we were home with you too, in Hightree."

"If I'm being entirely honest, I wish we were in the house I built for us." Axen's voice seemed to trail off.

"One crisis at a time," Dylah said looking up at him with a kind smile below twinkling amethyst eyes.

Axen kissed her forehead, then her cheek, and everything after was a whirlwind of a dream.

"And tomorrow night we will have a bed." Dylah laughed as she positioned her hood to cover her eyes.

"Among other things, but I like where your priorities lie." Axen smirked. "I guess I'll see you tomorrow at some point?"

"Yes you will, enemy prince." Dylah quickly kissed him. "I love you to a ludacris extent."

"That much, huh?" He kissed her forehead. "I love you too, and the extent has been proven by trial." Axen squeezed her hand just before she turned to leave.

A few steps back towards the darkness Dylah turned around.

"Please be safe!" she yelled, containing her laugh and waiting for the response she had heard thousands of times but still so desperately wanted to hear.

"Of course, princess."

Chapter 12

Immense Amount of Hate

The beginning chills of fall swept through an already brisk early afternoon and they seemed to carry in a mass of unknown people to the streets of Hightree.

Axen was ready, he met them at the gates donning his green cape, a sword sheathed at his hip, and a smirk on his face as he watched the woman with rose-gold hair walk gracefully towards him. Her dress was a shimmering pale pink nearly matching her hair with a light green sash tied around her waist. Tight curls hung evenly on either side of her face and she smiled kindly below calm green eyes.

"My people come seeking an alliance," Nevely spoke proudly a few steps away from Axen. "I believe you and I have a common enemy."

"My only enemy is those wretched Riloncks on the other side of those hideous trees," Axen answered in a gravelly voice. "If your grievance is against Fellowrock, then my king-dom is definitely in support."

Nevely smiled sweetly and her eyes seemed to brighten. "I am Nevely, my people and I have come a long way ready to obtain justice for the wrongs that were done against us so long ago." Her eyelashes batted as she looked up at him and took a step closer. "And who would you be?"

Axen was taken aback by her obvious advancements but forced himself to remain in the character they all had agreed upon.

"I am King Axen Farein." He calmly crossed his arms. "I can have a war council ready within the hour."

"I appreciate and greatly admire your haste." Nevely reached out and laid a hand against his folded arms. "Is there a place we can wait?"

Axen's arms fell to his side, he turned to a nearby soldier and opted to shout his simple request, successfully making Nevely jump and take a step back.

"Give me a few minutes and I'll have a written warning sent to those heathens." He smiled widely. "I'll call for a meeting with them."

"That isn't necessary." Nevely's gaze darkened.

"The Fareins and the Riloncks have long hated each other, we have battled many times, each time we have held a meeting prior to any fighting." Axen scowled. "I run my kingdom with the utmost respect to every citizen and their safety. An unwarranted attack would tarnish that and risk the lives of many innocent people." The corner of his mouth turned in a slight questioning smile. "I consider that to be common courtesy, but if that's not a practice of yours then maybe we should reassess our partnership."

"I understand." Nevely grinned. "I admire your morals."

Axen mindlessly reached into his pants pocket and fidgeted with the ring he was hiding. He smiled back at her. "I'm glad to have an ally in you."

Just as he expected, Nevely and several of her guardsmen followed Axen everywhere he went.

"I noticed that you aren't married," Nevely nearly sang.

"Any reason why?"

Axen turned to her and smiled. "Well, some women are just nightmares."

"I'm surprised your family hasn't tried to unite with the Riloncks through marriage." Nevely sighed. "Have you met their princess, Dylah?"

"Like I said." Axen smirked. "Some women are just nightmares."

"I'm glad we agree." Nevely laughed lightly. "But no other attempts, even with your sister and one of those princes? Maybe even with Keilon?"

"You think I'd let my sister marry someone so beneath her?" Axen seemed to be annoyed. "I thought you hated them as much as I do?"

"I do!" Nevely said quickly. "You'll see the hate I have soon enough, when will we be meeting them?"

"As soon as my sister joins us we will walk to the trees," Axen answered flatly. "And you will see the immense amount of hate I have."

The five Rilonck siblings, along with Kunor, Brig, and Kane, walked through the treeline to meet a line consisting of two Hightree soldiers, Avalia, Axen, Nevely, and two of her own guardsmen.

"I'm happy you could make it, Riloncks," Axen said with a smirk. "I believe a few of you know Nevely."

"I do." Dylah stood with her arms crossed tightly next to Keilon, her navy and lavender cape cascading over her shoulders, wearing leggings without any stripes. "I see you found the despicable Fareins, Nevely."

"A great ally to have in times like these." Nevely calmly linked her arm with Axen. "The king and I have discussed many plans."

Dylah's eyes lit up with a black inferno. "Do tell."

Axen dropped his arm and took a step forward, as if to be intimidating, but also to distance himself from Nevely's advances.

"Her people have been waiting for an opportunity to get their revenge, and Nevely believes we can help her get that," Axen said with a slight nod to Keilon.

"Really?" Keilon laughed. "And does she know just how deep our hatred for each other goes?" Keilon quickly shifted his eyes to Avalia.

"Such hatred." Avalia sighed and took a step forward. "Nevely, I would like to introduce you to someone you may find very important."

"Really?" Nevely asked with obvious annoyance. "Is now really a great time?"

"Yeah!" Kremon added. "Is now really a great time?"

"Nevely, this is my husband." Avalia stepped forward and linked her arm with his. "Prince Kremon Rilonck."

"What?!" Nevely snarled.

"It's true." Kremon grinned from ear to ear. "We just can't get enough of each other, we have four children."

"And one on the way," Avalia added with a proud smile and a hand on her belly.

"Axen." Nevely whipped her head to look at him. "You said these families were never united in marriage."

"Did I say that?" Axen offered a coy smile. "I'd also like you to meet our half brother, Kunor."

"You mean my son, Prince Kunor?" Keilon said with a loud laugh.

Kunor stepped forward and waved at an overly flustered Nevely. "It was a shock to me too a few years back."

"So your families have come together despite the conflict," Nevely groaned and shifted her nearly black eyes to Dylah. "Even with the madness that comes from this one?"

"Especially with the madness that comes from that one," Axen fired back.

"What is that supposed to mean?" Nevely's eyes widened and she grabbed Axen's arm above the elbow. "I believe that you've been mesmerized by what she is."

"You are definitely right about that." Axen smirked and shrugged away from her. "You asked me if I was married, and the truth is, I have a very beautiful queen, and she is a damn nightmare."

"No." Nevely snapped to meet Dylah's grin. "You said you were a Rilonck!"

"I am!" Dylah's wide grin fell the moment her eyes went black. "But my last name is actually Farein, and if you could stop touching my husband, the man whose love for me broke the curse, that would be lovely."

Nevely watched in horror as Axen linked arms with Dylah between the two sides.

"I'm not sure what your objective is exactly," Axen spoke up. "But I should warn you, our kingdoms have been a strong alliance for a while now. Our victories greatly outweigh our losses, and honestly, I don't like the way you speak about my wife." He grinned. "I would suggest you reassess your goals here, Nevely."

Chapter 13

The Pull

Dylah sat across from her brother in his office, a scene that was all too familiar for both of them. Their bond had spanned decades in a variety of forms. They were born as siblings, became parent and child through tragedy, they leaned on each other through every twist life threw at them, and oftentimes they were each other's greatest rivals. It was all beginning to make sense to them why they had always felt so connected to the other. Their eyes narrowed as they stared into the other's soul, the soul they shared.

"What am I thinking?" Dylah broke the silence.

"Coffee," Keilon said with a light laugh.

"Come on!" She sighed. "We really need to figure out how closely we're affected by this."

"Does that really matter?" Keilon leaned back in his chair. "We didn't notice for years."

"But now it's hard to ignore." She raised an eyebrow.

"Fine," Keilon huffed as he opened a drawer and pulled

out a blank piece of paper before promptly ripping it in half. "This way you won't cheat."

"You think I want to discover how much of a soul I share with my brother?" Dylah rolled fiery emerald eyes.

"The feeling is mutual." Keilon grinned. "Think of any two words, write them down. I will think for a bit then write down what words I think you wrote down." He paused. "Then we'll switch papers."

Dylah nodded in agreement before scribbling down a few words.

Keilon stared at her for a few seconds before writing down his own words.

Without any discussion the siblings exchanged slips of paper, and flipped them over at nearly the same time before again looking at each other with wide eyes.

"You wrote sunlight and pen," Keilon said above a whisper.

"And you wrote bright and ink," Dylah muttered as gray and pink began to speckle her irises.

"But, obviously, we're next to windows with bright sunlight pouring in and we were using pens with ink." He nodded his head as if to agree with his own logic. "We should try it again."

"Agreed. Absolutely inconclusive." Dylah nodded back as Keilon handed her another blank slip of paper.

She stared at the white page trying to come up with the most outlandish words she could muster. Finally, she wrote down her thoughts knowing that they would provide her a sure answer. She covered the paper with her hand and felt relieved that her brother wasn't noticing that she was writing more than two words.

Keilon stared at her for a few seconds before quickly jotting down a single word. They slid the papers across to each other.

"I only wrote one word," Keilon said with a half sigh.

"I wrote more than two," Dylah replied with a nervous

smile.

They simultaneously flipped the papers over and stared at the papers in near silence.

"Oh," Keilon said through a hefty exhale.

"Yeah." Dylah stared at his response.

"You wrote, 'I've been your second since I was...' you didn't finish the thought." He shook his head.

"But you wrote 'six.'" Dylah shifted her pink eyes up to him. "You completed the thought."

"Fix your eyes." Keilon began to pinch the bridge of his nose. "You're reading too much into this."

"Am I?"

"Yes." He leaned back in his chair and looked to the ceiling. "You and I have been pretty close for a while now, of course we can guess certain things about each other."

"I wish my eyes worked on you," Dylah said with an angry sigh. "I could stop you from being so damn difficult."

"I want to hit you," he grumbled back.

"You'd throw a right hook first, right?"

A knock shook the still surroundings before Axen walked in, followed by Kunor. They walked slowly into the room as if the tension between the siblings had stiffened the air.

"Everything okay here?" Axen asked with a slow step towards the desk.

"Yes, we're done with our discussion." Keilon glared at Dylah.

"Right." Axen shifted his eyes between the siblings. "The other Riloncks have not budged their camp on the outskirts of Hightree."

"They will." Dylah sighed. "But we both know that, right, Keilon?"

Keilon and Dylah stared at each other from across the desk moving their eyes ever so slightly as if communicating.

"I've never understood how the two of you can do that," Kunor said, breaking through the silence.

"Do what?" Keilon and Dylah seemed to ask in unison.

"I think we should give them a minute." Axen pulled Kunor's shoulder towards the door.

The door clicked shut and Dylah was ready to spill the thoughts building in her mind, but Keilon held up a halting finger.

"No," his voice rumbled. "We are not diving into this right now."

"Yes, we are!"

"Why?" Keilon sighed. "Why now?"

"What if there's a power we aren't using because we've been ignoring our connection for too long? What if that power is what we need to keep Nevely at bay? Come on, Keilon, you and I both know we are a lot closer than typical siblings."

"I know, but that's only because-"

"You raised me, yeah, yeah, yeah." Dylah rolled burning eyes. "Let's think back to those happy times shall we?"

"I don't like where this is going."

"You knew where to find me so many times."

"But I didn't know about your time in Hightree."

"I think you did." Dylah smirked. "Remember you were trying so hard to leave the camp to visit me, I think you knew I wasn't there."

"Fine," Keilon huffed. "But I didn't know about Axen."

"And yet you still gave him your blessing before he even asked for it."

"Well, I didn't run to your side when Atta tried to kill you, there were so many dangerous things I should've picked up on."

"We also have to think of the maturity of the soul at those times," Dylah added. "Think of after the soul matured, and after you got your piece back, the past five years just think about it."

Keilon's scowl fell as memories came to him.

"When Cav tumbled down the stairs and had that cut on

the back of his head, do you remember that?" Dylah asked.

"Yes, that was awful."

"What did you say when you walked in the back door and saw Axen and I on the floor holding our two year old bleeding son?"

"I said that I knew something bad had happened," Keilon whispered.

"And how many other times have you just popped by when I was in distress?" Dylah exhaled. "How many times have I done that for you?"

"Dylah, no, it's just all coincidence."

"I know we're both thinking of the same incident." She arched an eyebrow as black and blue streaked through her eyes. "Neither of us should have left that battle alive."

"That man in the woods." Keilon's eyes went wide. "The second I saw him aiming at me you put an arrow in him."

"And more notably, when Arkon and I got separated from the rest of you."

"We don't have to talk about this." Keilon reached across the desk and grabbed her hand. "I know it's still a very deep wound for you."

"Of course you do." Her icy eyes met his.

Dylah gulped as they began to recall the events of the battle that left their allied forces so torn.

Four months prior, the allied armies of Fellowrock and Hightree were trekking through a snow filled mountain pass. Their allies in Arizmia had called for backup as they fought against the mountaintop kingdom of Gomdea, the forces were stopped within a day's march of their destination.

Keilon and Dylah were huddled with other commanders around a wagon staring down at a makeshift battle map.

"We're getting close," Arkon said in a monotone. "We should be on the lookout for their scouts, they will be well camouflaged without a doubt."

"You got that, Second?" Keilon shifted his eyes to Dylah.

"On it." Dylah smirked below electric pink eyes as she adjusted her fur lined hood over her brows.

After a quick goodbye with Axen, she made her way into the surrounding pine trees. She shrank at any given sound but found no threats. She returned to the camp with a head full of swirling worries.

Dylah approached Keilon to give him the unsettling news that she had found nothing. Mid-sentence Keilon became abruptly quiet, he turned his head to a formation of boulders on his left and met the shrouded eyes of a man wielding a blow dart. But then, the would-be assailant fell to the ground with an arrow in his neck.

As blood poured from the enemy and coated the surrounding snow, Keilon was pulled by Dylah away from the open area.

"How did you-" Keilon began to ask.

"You need to be on your guard, big brother!"

"How did you see him so fast?!"

"I don't know! I just knew!"

"That can't be their only scout," Axen interrupted. "We should fan out our camp."

"I agree." Keilon cleared his throat. "You and Arkon should move your battalions to one side, Dylah and I will be on the other, and we will disperse the other groups evenly."

"That's not very well thought out." Axen sighed. "We need to separate. Think about it."

"No," Keilon growled. "If there is an impending attack I need my Second."

"I'll be your Second," Axen suggested. "Dylah and Arkon need to team up and you and I should be a group." He sighed. "That way if they successfully sneak up on one of us the commanders of an entire army are not wiped out."

"It's morbid but I understand." Dylah nodded to her husband then to her brother. "We should move our camps fast, it looks like there's a storm moving in."

The allied forces split off into five camps spaced out

sporadically at their designated commanders' discretion. Where the other commanders knew of a loose location for the surrounding camps, the precise placement was decided too hastily to map out.

The night passed in stillness, but morning came with howling winds and clumping heavy snowfall. Dylah was preparing the mixed encampment to pack up and meet at the designated regrouping location. But as the snow stacked winds howled through, a burst of black dust rose from the outskirts of the camp.

Dylah was mesmerized by the floating dust as it coated the stark white snow. Out of everything she knew about chaos, the most blatant truth was that it always started with a beautiful display of welcoming distraction.

Arkon and Dylah quickly armored up and began slinging commands to their troops. Archers shot fire tipped arrows along the perimeter hoping the heat would help dissipate the surrounding blizzard, but more bursts of black dust rose closer and closer to their groupings.

"Come on, Legend!" Arkon laughed proudly over the oncoming commotion. "Let's go give them hell, help will arrive shortly!"

Dylah looked back at him as pink lightning burst through the clouds in her eyes. "Give them hell, your majesty."

The two split directions followed by various men wielding a mixture of needed weapons.

Dylah held a bow horizontally in front of her while also ready to grab a dagger from her leather wrists cuffs at any given second. As they pushed closer to the edge of camp a horde of light gray clad soldiers descended upon them while even more bursts of black dust rose from the camp. Clanking of weapons joined the symphony of explosions and war cries.

After plunging a dagger into the neck of a persistent enemy swordsmen, Dylah took a breath and saw the sight of even more camouflaged enemies charging to Arkon's side of camp. With a whistle she withdrew her able men and progressed to his aid, but before they arrived she watched in horror as the sight of a flowing orange cape was swallowed up in a cloud of black dust.

Dylah charged into the mass of enemies along with her following men, bursts erupted all around her as men donning the allied army colors fell to the red and black stained snow. No matter which way she tried to turn she was blocked by a blade, a burst, or a falling soldier.

The enemy again grew in size as Dylah's army shrank, her eyes darted along the body scattered ground searching for Arkon but the enemy began to circle what little men were left.

Dylah met the gaze of the advancing Gomdean soldiers, her eyes more blue than black. Though her soul was screaming at her to act, she thought of Cav's wide smile and mismatched eyes, she heard her husband's voice in her head and it gave her the strength to ready her bow. When the enemy began to chant in foreign scattered syllables she remembered her lilacs, her trees, her brothers, her family, then the thought of her waiting mother in the forest of perpetual twilight.

As the enemy marched even closer Dylah felt a pull around her waist.

"Retreat!" Keilon yelled.

Dylah found her footing and began sending shock arrows into the mass of enemies.

"Dylah, go!" Keilon demanded.

"Arkon!" She struggled to get the words out. "I couldn't find Arkon!"

Keilon looked down into her gray and blue eyes only amplified against her shocked and pale complexion. She quickly shook her head and continued firing into the oncoming danger.

"Axen is forming lines just over there, go to him!" Keilon gripped her shoulders. "You've done enough here!" He held her against himself as a scuffle passed them. "I can't lose you again, please go!" He didn't give her the chance to argue, he pushed her in the opposite direction and let a wall of charging soldiers separate them.

Dylah tried to push through the commotion but reluctantly left the unknowns of battle to join her husband. Axen and his archers formed lines flanking the enemy who had again grown in size.

Axen pulled her in close and pressed her head into his chest.

"Arkon," Dylah said weakly. "I couldn't get to him in time, I don't know if he's okay!"

"We can't worry about that right now," Axen said, pushing his own growing worries down. "Let's hit them with everything we have."

Axen finally looked at her, black dust clung around her eyes, snowflakes plastered themselves into her hair, the edges of her navy cape were torn and the footprints she had left in the snow were outlined in red.

"I'm going back in." Dylah's eyes bolted up to him the color of power.

"Absolutely not!"

"Keilon, Kunor, Kremon, Delin, Brig, and Bahn!" Tears began to fall. "They're all in that mess!"

"Defend them from here, you've already done enough!"

"They are getting hit with everything, and I'm here doing nothing!" She gritted her teeth. "That's not nearly enough!"

"I know you have a voice in your head right now screaming at you, telling you to run into that havoc and take care of it yourself." Axen sighed. "But there's another voice, another soul, who calls you mama. Listen to that one."

Dylah spent the rest of the battle on the edges slowly taking out the enemy, while her brothers and other assorted kin fought at close range. Her eyes strained from constantly trying to make out the blur of clashing figures in the distance.

The blizzard subsided. The thunderous sounds of war grew still. The enemy had retreated leaving the allied armies standing few but strong.

Dylah finally exhaled the anxious breath she had been holding. Her boots crunched against the muddled black and red snow. She scanned each fallen face hoping to find her brothers and nephews alive and well.

First she happened to find Kunor, kneeling against the snow as blood soaked through the layers of fabric on his arm and leg. Then she found Delin, he had a deep gash down his thigh and blood streaked so thickly over his left eye it was nearly impossible to determine where the injury was. Kremon found her, he limped over the scattered bodies, his face was unnaturally solemn as he carried a snapped bow and various slashes were seen on his clothing. Dylah fell to the ground next to Bahn when she saw her nephew, Brig, barely seventeen years old lying unconscious. She gripped Bahn's hand as they watched Brig's chest slowly rise and fall, a blood covered lump on his forehead.

After more panicking she walked forward through the settling commotion, her feet froze to the ground and as if she had heard the call of her own name, she turned to her right. She pushed through a crowd slowly forming and without a thought ripped a strip of fabric from her cape to fashion a tourniquet beneath Keilon's left knee. His shin bone was exposed, most of his clothing was ripped, and his usual golden hair was stained with blood.

Dylah slapped at his face until he lightly blinked his eyes open, Delin soon arrived to administer pain medication and to further tend to the wounds Keilon had sustained.

In the corner of her eye she saw the tattered green cape flow in the unnervingly calm breeze, attached to a still figure. Dylah ran to her husband's side as he stared down in disbelief at Arkon's badly battered body.

Axen's knees finally went numb as he crashed to

the ground holding his brother's pale unmoving face. He smacked against the sticky blood covered tufts of Arkon's beard hoping to trigger any reaction but the only movement was the spaced out subtle puffs of breaths from his nose.

The armies regrouped the best they could. They mended those who were broken and buried those who had fallen all while trying to believe it was just a terrible dream. With each passing breath the reality set in that many of their men had been cut down and so many more would bear permanent scars.

Dylah walked through the camp with fists clenched, her mind raced with regrets as she replayed running towards the orange cape over and over again. She walked in circles until she stopped outside of a tent surrounded by rows of somber soldiers watching for any movement from the canvas doors.

"You really should be resting," Dylah said as she stood next to Keilon standing with a crutch.

"Now is not the time for rest." He sighed. "Now is the time for waiting, hoping, and planning."

"So no news on Arkon?"

"None."

"If I was only a little bit faster I could have saved him." She stared at the tent.

"Or you'd both be approaching death." Keilon's voice fell to a whisper. "You're here, little sister, remember that."

Keilon and Dylah stared down at the desk after digging through the events they both wanted so badly to forget.

"How did you know to come for me?" Dylah shook her head. "That blizzard was so thick and we were on opposite sides, we were so far apart, how did you know we were in trouble?"

"I don't know, Dylah!" Keilon pinched the bridge of his nose. "I just knew."

"If you hadn't shown up we could have lost both of those battalions." She sighed with a slight growl. "Did you not hear the voice? Did you not feel the pull? The force that told you to go when you knew you should stop, the feeling that you must conquer everything on your own?" She gritted her teeth at his avoidance. "You can't ignore it anymore, Keilon! Your soul is full of chaos and so much power, and now would be a great time to really hone it in, big brother!"

Dylah didn't let him answer, instead she stomped towards the office doors and slammed them shut.

Keilon took a long deep inhale and as he finally exhaled he rested his head against the well worn desk. His mind raced with his sister's words, of the battle that went poorly, and then of the last conversation he had had with Arkon before he fell into an endless sleep.

Night had fallen on that dreadful day, the soldiers walked around the camp in pained silence, but there was hope on the horizon. Keilon, Dylah, and Axen stood around Arkon's bed, he was awake and making weakened conversation.

Arkon was badly injured, a shattered leg, multiple broken ribs, slashes on his stomach, and an odd puncture wound on his neck.

"It's nice to see you acting like yourself," Axen said with a forced laugh. "You really had us worried."

"Come on, Axen," Arkon said with a rattle to his strained voice. "You know that Hightree kings live well past their prime."

"And you haven't even hit yours yet!" Axen joked as the surrounding Riloncks laughed.

Time passed with light conversation and avoidance of the previous events of the day, then Axen and Dylah decided to go to their own tent for some sleep.

Keilon was also about to leave when Arkon called for him.

"Keilon," Arkon coughed and winced in pain. "You are the friend I never expected to make, and the one I could never see being without."

"I think you're just saying that because of our very extensive peace treaty." Keilon laughed as he hobbled closer to the bed.

"You wretched Rilonck."

"You damn Farein."

The friends chuckled until Arkon used every ounce of his reserved strength to loosely grab Keilon's wrist.

"Keilon, listen to me," Arkon whispered. "You are strong, you are driven, and you are powerful. Look at me."

"I think you've been given a bit too much pain medicine, my friend." Keilon laughed nervously.

"Listen. Look." Arkon raised his voice the best he could. "The strength, the drive, the power, I can see it in your eyes, Keilon."

Keilon shook the memory out of his head and looked around his office for reassurance that he was away from the painful past. After he left Arkon that night he never saw him as his normal self again. In the night Arkon took a turn for the worse, the puncture on his neck turned a deep black, and even to this day he remained in a place of nearly barren existence. The words of his friend circled his mind and they soon mixed with Dylah's accusations. He began to worry what a culmination of their observations could mean for him and the soul he possessed only a fraction of. Keilon pulled a silver dagger from the sheath on his hip and stared at his reflection. He breathed a sigh of relief when jade green eyes looked back at him.

Chapter 14

Havoc Within

"Nevely would like a council," Keilon seemed to growl as he entered Axen's office.

"And she went to you and not me?" Axen laughed. "I'm a little hurt."

Dylah rolled her eyes sitting across from Axen. "Are you starting to regret your choice in Riloncks?"

"I just really thought she and I had a nice thing going there," Axen said with a half grin. "I guess I only attract one type of woman."

"Those with an ancient soul?" Dylah laughed before her face fell and her eyes drifted over to Keilon. "So when would she like to meet?"

"Now." Keilon crossed his arms. "Kremon and Delin are keeping her company in Fellowrock."

"You're the king, why didn't you send someone to come get us?" Axen stood from his desk and began tidying the assortment of papers.

"That woman creeps me out." Keilon shook with a fake shiver.

Soon enough Dylah was bursting into the meeting room at the Fellowrock castle, her navy and lavender cape flowing behind her as if to catch up. She sat at the opposite end of Nevely and stared at her with stoney irises paired with a raised eyebrow.

The rest of the Riloncks and Fareins took their seats, all pointing a similar expression at their strawberry blonde adversary.

"Thank you all for coming." Nevely's voice drifted over the table as two guards stood stoically behind her. "I am not meaning any harm to either of your kingdoms."

"That's not what you were saying a few days ago." Axen rolled his eyes.

"I also seem to remember a war council being held." Kunor laughed.

"My plans have changed." Nevely's eyes darkened. "As a few of you know my only goal is to bring peace and order to the world. I am the opposite of Dylah and Keilon, I am the light to their darkness, I am their balance."

"I'm sorry, what?" Kremon shook his head. "You think you're their balance?"

"I am their balance," Nevely repeated in a monotone voice.

"You are the most arrogant person I have ever met." Kremon chuckled.

"Kremon," Keilon whispered fiercely.

"No, big brother, I got this." Kremon shifted his eyes back to Nevely. "You think you can walk in here and just declare that whatever soul they were given has led us down a dark path?" He pointed at Keilon. "Keilon has led this kingdom since he was seventeen. While we were all mourning he was seeking freedom for his people. After Delin found a cure, Keilon was the one who organized it's distribution, he was the one who planned our revenge, he even withdrew from that war and took the loss for the sake and safety of our little sister. And you think he needs balance?!"

"Well," Nevely started.

"And speaking of that little sister." Kremon gained volume and pointed at Dylah. "She fought for our enemy to keep one person safe, she risked her life to take down a ghost and ended up dying anyway! Her soul has only brought our kingdoms together, it has helped us obtain victories and growth, she saved a kingdom from a tyrant, she established peace! How dare you say that she needs a source of balance. Look around this table, every green and brown eyed person here is their balance. We always have been, long before your existence was ever known or cared about." Kremon slumped in his chair and took a deep breath to steady himself.

"I have a question." Nevely smiled as her eyes brightened.

"No!" Bahn growled. "What more do you need to know? As you can see we have been handling things very well without whatever the hell you are."

"I just want to know what he meant when he said she died anyway." Nevely's gaze rested on Dylah across the table.

A tense silence filled the room as the Riloncks and Fareins exchanged glances, especially Dylah and Keilon who seemed to sigh in unison.

"My wife was killed about five years ago," Axen's voice broke through the stillness. "Through some helpful magic and an ongoing purpose in life she was brought back."

"Who killed her?" The words could barely leave Nevely's lips as her shocked eyes shone almost white.

Dylah smirked across the table. "After I stabbed the resurrected first Keilon in the heart his last waking action was to throw me from a fourth story balcony." She watched joyfully as Nevely's face fell. "I was dead for a day, I joined my mother in a forest with endless time, I met Dycavlon, then I came back."

"Dycavlon?" Nevely whispered.

"Yes, helluva guy!" Dylah laughed loudly. "As you can probably tell, two of us are named after that ancestor to an extent."

"Adequately named, little sister." Keilon laughed.

"You too," Dylah replied before winking across the table at Nevely.

"I would like to get to know you more, Dylah." Nevely forced the volume of her voice. "You seem to have done interesting things with the soul you were given."

"You think we're leaving our sister alone with you?" Delin jumped in. "No."

"You may want to rethink your request, lady," Bahn mumbled. "That feral badger could claw your eyes out."

"It's fine." Dylah smiled and forced her eyes to be green. "It'll be a friendly chat."

After some time only Nevely and Dylah remained at the table, though many remained outside the closed door.

"You didn't use your eyes on any of them," Nevely spoke as if she was asking a question. "That's peculiar."

"I rarely use my power on my brothers, and I've found that I never really need it with my soldiers." Her green eyes slowly filled with bright blush. "I think that speaks to their loyalty and my ability to command them."

"You have quite the loyal fan base, I have noticed that."

"And what about you?" Dylah leaned forward as the pink overpowered the green in her eyes. "Do you subject those who trust you to the power within your eyes?" Dylah softened and gray swallowed the amaranth. "What is the power in your eyes?"

"Yes, I use my power on my followers quite often." Nevely smiled. "But it's not as invasive as your power, because my soul strives for order and control. My power is geared towards erasing the chaos that lives within people."

"Explain better."

"I can read the deepest worries of someone's mind." Nevely smiled widely. "Then I can help them fix those worries. It's one of the ways I bring order to the world."

"Oh." Dylah relaxed. "That's kind of nice."

"I can do it to you if you'd like."

"Do my -"

"Your eyes don't work on me, but mine will work on you." Nevely leaned a little closer. "Like I said, my power is less invasive, I can't make you do anything you don't want to do. It will only take a few seconds for me to retrieve what plagues your worries."

"I don't think that-"

"Dylah." Her smile fell. "This is what I meant by balance. I know it can't be easy holding the weight of your soul, part of my purpose is to lessen the load for you."

"Fine." Dylah forced herself to lock eyes with her.

Nevely's eyes brightened and darkened then she sighed. "Of course that worries you."

"What?"

"Your inability to have children." Nevely sighed again. "So much pain for you to not bear a life you so desperately want. You worry your husband is also growing weary of the waiting."

"Yes." Dylah swallowed the words she couldn't articulate.

"I'm sorry no one must have told you," Nevely spoke slowly. "It was specifically detailed in Sorner's old writings, though I suppose you never had the chance to read those. It's a harsh truth, but the chaotic soul can never bear a child."

"Really?" Dylah calmly arched an eyebrow. "What about my brother's son? Or the first Keilon's children?"

"They're men, you and I both know that that is different as far as reproducing goes." Nevely laughed lightly. "Men give what they can and carry on with their lives until there is a tangible child to hold." She sighed with an airy breath. "But women, we grow the life, it takes so much of us, we feel it, we sacrifice our bodies, we go through so much pain." She stopped and her eyes darkened. "I'm sorry, I don't mean to go into so much detail of what you'll never have."

"Never?" Dylah forced a frown. "And what makes you say that being what I am makes me unable to create a life?"

"For another life to live within you for so long, absorbing what you are, the havoc within your heart, and then to be raised by such an unsteady parent." Nevely shook her head. "Nature always knows what's best."

"I guess you're right." Dylah smiled. "And you? Are you able to have children?"

"Of course." Nevely nodded. "I have a son and a daughter."

"I see," Dylah said with a chuckle, "one of each. How perfect."

"Well I could never produce something so unnervingly lopsided as having five sons and only one daughter."

Dylah turned to hide her quickly rolled her eyes. "Would you like a tour of Fellowrock? Now that you aren't planning a war against us?"

"I would cherish seeing the land where Sorner lived." Nevely sighed with relief. "Really, I would like to be a source of balance for you in the best way possible. If we could be friends or even just civil with each other I would love that."

"Well I am nicer among the trees, so let's give it a shot." Dylah laughed as she stood from her seat. "I knew the first Keilon, he taught me a lot, but what I learned most from him was how to not repeat the past he built."

"I'm glad to hear that." Nevely walked towards the door.

In the courtyard Dylah pointed out the different corners and how the area would be decorated for their upcoming fall festival, but soon a small force landed against her.

"Hi, Cav," she said as she picked him up and intentionally faced him away from Nevely. "What trouble are you getting into today? I thought your father was keeping you busy."

"I escaped!" Cav giggled.

"Well you did learn from the best." Dylah laughed with him.

"Your nephew?" Nevely asked.

"No." Dylah smiled. "My son." She held Cav tighter.

"Oh, oh I see." Nevely sighed. "Your heart wanted to love so badly you acquired what you couldn't make. Was he one of Avalia's perhaps? She seems to have had too many."

"No," Dylah replied sharply.

"Okay, I understand." Nevely nodded. "I apologize if I overstepped any secrecy you have kept with the child."

"Who are you?" Cav turned his head to Nevely.

"His eye." Nevely gaped. "Why does he have an eye like that?"

"Like I said." Dylah smirked. "This is my son."

"Your true son?!" Nevely asked with wide and dark eyes. "That's impossible!"

"Yes." Dylah smiled widely. "Nature knew what was best when it gave me my child."

Chapter 15

Lucky Magic

For three days Nevely was seen pacing the courtyard, her perfectly curled ringlets of strawberry blonde were even slightly frazzled. The Riloncks were careful to stay away from her, since she met Cav she seemed to be overly stressed. Although it was great entertainment for Dylah, the mysteriously lovely woman mumbling to herself as her eyes went from seafoam to the deepest emerald was beginning to worry her.

Dylah was walking hand in hand with Cav through the autumn glow of the forest.

"I have questions." Nevely's voice bounced off the surrounding bark of the trees.

The moment Nevely walked into view Dylah scooped Cav up and pressed his head against her shoulder all while her mind listed off every possible route to escape when necessary.

"What hexes did you use to conceive him?" Nevely's eyes

were dark and brooding. "Who helped you achieve such an impossible thing?"

"My husband." Dylah smirked.

"I was unaware Axen used such abilities."

"Oh you poor dear, I see you have been missing out on one very joyous part of life." Dylah laughed and turned to walk away from the agitation radiating from Nevely.

"Must everything be a joke to you?" Nevely took quick steps after Dylah. "I understand the soul itself makes you a bit off-putting, but still."

Dylah spun on her heels and faced Nevely with blackened irises rimmed in bright magenta. "I will remind you that this is my son, he came from my flesh and blood, he is the perfect mix of myself and Axen. You will not talk badly about his mother in front of him, understand?"

"Does he not know what you are?" Her eyes brightened slightly and a smile began to form. "Does he know the things you've done? The battles, the trickery, the blood?"

Dylah gritted her teeth and again began walking away without offering up a single reply.

Nevely smiled as Dylah stomped away, but Cav lifted his head and stuck his tongue out at her, which prompted Nevely to return to her pacing.

A few more days passed with little incident, a premature sprinkling of snow had fallen, but the ice was yet to come.

"Any idea what this meeting is about?" Dylah asked as she walked through the dimly lit halls of the Fellowrock castle with Keilon.

"No idea." He sighed. "And I'm a little offended that she called it through Axen but is having it in my castle. That's just so impolite."

"I have a feeling we're going to be finding out more about why you and I are the worst people in all of the kingdoms."

"Ah yes, for we are the most chaotic, how dare we be

born with a soul neither of us asked for."

Dylah stopped in front of the meeting room doors. "You said we." Her pink eyes looked up at him as she quickly smirked before opening the door.

"When are the others getting here?" Keilon looked around the nearly empty meeting room. Nevely at one end, Axen at the other, along with Kunor and Delin on either side.

"No, we're all here." Nevely smiled below calm green eyes.

"I'm not entirely sure why I'm here," Kunor whispered as his father sat next to him. "I don't like this at all."

Axen promptly grabbed Dylah's hand and squeezed as soon as she was next to him.

"I've called you here to discuss Cav." Nevely's smile widened.

"Excuse me?!" Dylah's eyes were black within one blink. "What quarrel do you have with our son?!"

"He shouldn't be your son." Nevely's eyes nearly matched Dylah's.

"I would love to hear your justifications on that theory," Axen snarled as he squeezed Dylah's hand even tighter.

"Trust me, I've done my research." Nevely calmly arched an eyebrow. "As you know, when the chaotic soul is given to a female it renders her barren, this is why it typically goes to a man. I've called the prince here as an example." She gestured towards Kunor. "See how quiet and reserved he is despite the influence of his father's nature?" Her posture seemed to straighten. "But Cav is not so lucky, a child growing within the embodiment of chaos is cruel and unnatural."

"Yes, because my son does exhibit traits of a cruel gestation." Axen rolled his eyes.

"It has riddled me that he was given to you in the first place, but I now understand that it was simply just very helpful coincidences that led to his birth." Nevely continued, "Thanks to the magic of a few, the traits of your soul were bypassed and you were given your abomination."

"Abomination?!" Keilon growled. "Be careful how you speak about my nephew."

"Of course you don't think of him that way," Nevely narrowed her eyes at Keilon. "He stems from your wretched soul too."

"Nevely, you will speak of my son, my wife, and my brother in a respectful manner." Axen's voice rattled. "Or this discussion is over."

"I'll get to the point then." Nevely sighed loudly. "Let me explain just how lucky you were."

"Please do," Dylah's voice rattled.

"I was made aware of the events prior to Cav's brith, here is my conclusion." Nevely locked eyes with Dylah. "Your son was conceived in the lilac field where you are free from your curses, he grew within you, and died, but before you fully lost the pregnancy, you yourself perished. Then, through more magic, you were brought back to life, along with the child that was within you. Do you follow?"

"I guess that is awfully lucky." Dylah glared back at Nevely.

"How can you think that a life that went through so much just to be born doesn't deserve to thrive?" Kunor mumbled to himself as he stared down at his fidgeting fingers.

"Wait." Axen shook his head. "How do you know about the lilac field? And how do you know about the timing of her death?" His eyes darted around the table and landed on one person. "Who offered up such personal information?"

"I did have a very welcoming Rilonck help me reach this conclusion, actually, it was mostly him." Nevely laughed lightly.

Dylah's eyes faded to blue as she looked down the table. Her voice caught in her throat and came out like a whisper. "Delin?"

"I know what you're thinking, but this isn't a betrayal," Delin spoke calmly. "Who are we to deny the truths of an ancient soul? I needed to find the fluke that led to Cav's birth.

Nevely is right. He shouldn't be yours."

"Get out!" Keilon hit the table.

"We're not done yet," Nevely replied, her demeanor unchanged.

"Are you going to expand on how you brainwashed my brother?" Dylah pinned onyx embers on Delin. "Because the Delin I grew up with wouldn't abandon his family like this."

"I looked into his eyes and saw that his biggest worry was the two of you going haywire and destroying the kingdoms." Nevely ignored the anger in the room. "I told him there was a way to figure out that knot, and the knot is you, Dylah, you shouldn't be a mother."

"And what about me?" Axen blurted. "I possess no ancient soul, do I not deserve to have my son?"

"No." Nevely slowly shook her head. "It was something you agreed to when you fell for the bearer of the soul."

"You're wrong." Axen furrowed his brows. "I saw Cav the night Dylah died. Doesn't that line up with the timeline of him being dead within her? If he was never supposed to live then why did I know we would have him?"

Nevely's face fell flat. "What do you mean you saw your son that night?"

"You're right, I did fall for the bearer of the soul, I fell for her when I was only twelve years old, isn't that something?" Axen laughed lightly, happy to have shaken Nevely's smug expression. "And when angry people like yourself appeared and badgered her about the soul she has and threw so many obstacles in front of her such as curses and ghosts, they threw one in front of me too." He smirked below an unwavering glare. "You see, they wanted to make sure that I could handle her soul and everything that could come out of it."

"Handle me?" Dylah laughed.

"And how did they determine you were a fit partner for her?" Nevely's voice was low and dark.

"They gave me three trials. Did Delin not offer up this information?" Axen shifted his eyes to Delin. "Odd that you would leave out such an important detail." Axen laughed and looked back to Nevely. "I had to disarm, diffuse, and calm my wife in three different emotional states. I met a Dylah that had never met me at all, she was cursed, she was belligerent, and she was really easy to flirt with." Axen calmly winked at his wife. "Then I met a Dylah who had lost my love, she was angry, she was charged by sadness, she was still partially cursed, she had a really strong punch, but again, I promised to love her. I feel like I'm always promising to love her to people that don't understand how much I actually love her."

"And what was the third trial?" Nevely asked as her anger grew.

"Right, the third trial sent me to my own house, I walked into a room and saw a crib. I saw Dylah sitting in that crib staring in awe at the baby, we talked about how perfect he was, I told her how perfect she was, then he began to stir and I held him as Dylah wrapped her arms around both of us. It was a perfect vision that I was soon thrown out of. I was so confused about it, Dylah and I had only just been on the same page about having children and here was this display of what that life would be like. I told her about seeing our son just minutes before she was thrown to her death. I was mourning her and the life I knew I could have had with her. When she came back I threw all of that pain out, I erased it the second I saw those lavender eyes again." Axen sighed to align his many emotions. "Months later I walked up our stairs and I knew I was in that vision. I walked into that room, I saw Dylah in that crib, we talked about how perfect Cav was, then he began to stir and we held each other. Our family is perfect, and I knew I would have it long before you came here telling us that my son is an abomination and a result of lucky magic. Damn you, Nevely! Keilon and I will have no issue banishing you from these kingdoms."

"So maybe you did deserve to have Cav." Delin cleared his throat. "But that still doesn't mean that Dylah should have him. "

"Think about your next words very carefully, Delin," Dylah spoke through clenched teeth.

"I'm sorry that it is such a bitter truth, but Dylah, Cav was never supposed to be yours, there's a reason why you've had so many failed pregnancies after him. It was a mystery that saddened me for so long. I felt your pain, I really did, but now I understand that you just can't be a fit mother to a child."

"Delin!" Keilon hit the table again.

"I don't care if you're mad at me, it is the truth." Delin shook his head.

"We will be taking your child away from you," Nevely said in a slow monotone. "Not now, we'll wait, just know that we are righting the wrongs that magic allowed."

"You are not taking my son!" Dylah stood and leaned towards Nevely. "I am stronger than you, my power is stronger than yours, I have more allies than you, and I will not hold myself back."

"Precisely the reaction I needed to justify this decision." Nevely smiled.

"Dylah," Delin spoke quietly. "This isn't something you'll be able to punch yourself out of."

Dylah quickly pulled the dagger out of her leather wrist cuff and pointed the tip at Delin. "I don't always punch."

"I'm sorry, but you have to know how strongly I feel about this to be siding against you."

"You're siding against all of us!" Keilon stood. "Get out! You will not be allowed back in this castle until you renounce any allegiances you have with this outsider."

Nevely and Delin calmly stood after a nod and headed towards the door.

After a quick breath Dylah was at the door, she grabbed a fistful of Delin's collar and snarled up at him.

"Just to be clear, if I am forced to choose between my son and my brother, I will not hesitate to end your life."

Chapter 16

What Chaos Demands

Dylah laid awake, her eyes scanned every corner of the dark room as she tightly held her sleeping son. Her mind raced with the places she could hide her sweet child, and ways she could slowly kill the evil Nevely, which only reminded her of her heartbreak over Delin's blatant betrayal.

"My dear, you must sleep," Axen said in a groggy voice as he sat up in bed. "If I hold on to the kid for dear life will you sleep?"

"I'm not letting her take him," Dylah whispered.

"And neither am I." Axen fell back against the pillows. "And where have we landed on Delin?"

"We hate him."

"That's where I was landing as well." Axen sighed. "It's going to be okay, we'll keep the kid safe, and I'll keep you safe, just like I've always promised."

With no answer, Axen looked over with relief to finally see Dylah sleeping, but now he was wide awake, keeping guard with his own darting eyes.

His mind filled with plans to protect his wife and child, and he smiled at the thought of finding a glass big enough to fit a four year old. As the sun began to rise he arrived at a solid yet heartbreaking plan.

Keilon had come to gather Cav, knowing that his sister would need a break but wouldn't trust anyone else with the protection of her child. Axen took the alone time as an opportunity to finally lay out his plan.

"The sand countries?" Dylah's face fell into her hands as she stared into her cup of coffee.

"Yes," Axen said matter of factly. "We sneak him onto the next shipment of lumber and he gets delivered to Derck and Molix for safe keeping until we get rid of Nevely."

"And I'm guessing your plan entails that neither of us would accompany him?"

"I'm sorry, that would only draw suspicions." Axen sighed. "I can figure out who to send with him."

"That is better than any other plan I thought of."

"I'm very confident that my plan requires far less stabbing than yours does, you nightmare."

"You are right about that." Dylah grinned.

Axen's plan was immediately set into motion. Calendars were looked at, a shipment was picked for next week to sneak their son away. Guards were interviewed, Aloria was chosen to accompany her nephew on the trip along with five trusted guards.

Fellowrock's fall festival was canceled for fear that Nevely would use the jubilee as a ruse to take her prize. An unease was felt over both kingdoms, but also a sense of preparedness as the pieces of their fight fell into place.

Dylah sat waiting in Keilon's office as Cav happily sat in the prominent leather chair across from her. She watched as his hands drifted over markings on the desk made by a past king she had barely known.

"Uncle Keilon is mad," Cav said with a laugh.

"And why would your uncle be mad?" She laughed through her own confusion.

"People aren't listening to him." He shrugged.

Dylah raised an eyebrow, and deep within her she could sense the anger coming towards them. The door opened as stomps shook the floor.

"I can't believe her!" Keilon nearly shouted. His eyes glanced at his young nephew in his seat and he opted to sit in the chair next to his sister. "I caught four of her guards just walking around our forest!"

"Was she with them?" Dylah asked with wide gray eyes.

"No," Keilon answered quickly, sensing her panic. "But they wouldn't leave! They just kept saying how they were ordered to patrol, they wouldn't listen to me!"

Dylah flashed a glance over to Cav who seemed to be entranced by the markings on the desk, she began to wonder how he knew the worries his uncle had before they were even voiced.

"Your real grandpa made those marks, Cav." Keilon reached over the desk and pointed to where Cav's fingers fidgeted. "His name was Fren."

"And your grandma's name was Junia," Dylah added.

Cav seemed to ponder the information, instead he tilted his head towards his uncle. "Do your eyes change too?"

"No," Keilon answered slowly.

"Oh." Cav grinned.

After discussing a few matters, Dylah held Cav's hand through the long torchlit tunnel, hoping to keep him out of sight from those who wanted to steal him away. Emerging from the tunnel she noticed a sense of urgency in the Hightree streets.

Dylah held Cav closely while discretely gripping a dagger in her free hand. Soldiers ran past, but none of them wore a green cape. Her heart raced until loving arms wrapped around both of them and pushed them into the safety of the castle.

"She's here," Axen whispered into Dylah's ear.

Four guards led them up the endless steps while six guards followed. All ten guards waited in a line outside of the room with a seemingly secret hallway to another room. That's where fourteen year old Aloria and two strong guards were waiting to protect the young prince of Hightree.

Dylah held Cav as tight as she could, she kissed his forehead over and over again. She repeated her usual words, while Axen listed several instructions to his teenage sister and the guards. Soon the parents traded places as Axen offered his son jokes and funny faces along with a tight hug while Dylah voiced the instructions only a mother could explain.

They shut the door to the secret hallway, exited the room, and nodded at the ten guards before descending down the steps, walking towards the unknown threat that called herself harmony.

Of all the times Dylah and Axen had gone to battle together this particular walk into danger felt heavier. The battle of Hightree almost took Axen from Dylah, the first battle in Arizmia almost stole Dylah from Axen, and even though death took Dylah in a fight with an ancestor, nothing felt quite as serious as the life and well being of their son. A son that was so perfectly formed from pieces of both of his parents. A happy, tenacious, smart, swirl of hazel and amethyst wrapped up into the silly grin of a four year old. The grin that was driving the stomping of boots towards an adversary with pale pink hair.

They met on the outskirts of the town, in the empty space before the treeline.

Standing in front of Nevely, Dylah's grip tightened on Axen's hand.

"Where's your son, Dylah?" Nevely's eyes and words arrived with darkness.

Axen and Dylah offered no words in response to her wicked question, instead Axen squeezed Dylah's hand twice.

She took the signal and stared at the guard on Nevely's right with intentional gray eyes. The guardsman looked at Dylah in the familiar trance the gray-eyed mind control prompted.

"Run away," Dylah commanded with a smirk.

As the guard was sprinting away as fast as he could, Nevely turned to warn her other guard of the danger Dylah's eyes possessed, but it was too late, he was already lying in the dirt stiff as can be with an arrow sticking out of his arm.

"You're left defenseless, Nevely." Dylah crossed her arms. "The soldiers you have charging our castle have been shot with tips that will render them paralyzed for hours, giving us a grand opportunity to hold them captive." She pointed a grin at the dark green eyes staring back at her. "How is your plan going?"

"Chaos." Nevely grinded her teeth. "Don't you see the chaos that is demanded to undo the unjust result of your child?"

"Chaos you started!" Axen shouted.

"There must be balance!" Nevely's eyes watered as if she were pleading with the stars.

"Do you want to know what chaos demands?" Dylah pointed to the trees behind them where the Fellowrock army was lined up with weapons drawn. "It demands you leave us alone."

"I made sure you wouldn't be able to call for reinforcements!" Nevely's fingers fidgeted as she tried to maintain the fists at her sides. "All routes were strategically blocked!"

"And did Delin offer that information?" Axen smiled.

"He forgot to mention a very important route. A hidden one made by a severed soul." Dylah pointed electric pink eyes at Nevely. "Which is odd seeing as how he made it. You may want to rethink your alliances."

"This isn't over!" Nevely shouted.

"Yes, it is." Axen pointed an arrow at her and whistled.

Hightree archers, along with Kremon, led corralled enemy soldiers towards Dylah.

Once again, Dylah turned her eyes to a commanding gray.

"Carry your wretched leader away from these kingdoms, walk for two days straight."

The soldiers slowly nodded before they lifted Nevely up on their shoulders and marched away with her into the night.

Scouts were sent after them, battalions were strategically placed around the borders of Hightree and Fellowrock.

The Fareins and the Riloncks knew their troubles were nowhere close to being over, but at least now they had time to prepare for a final solution.

Chapter 17

Unnervingly Furious

Days had passed with no reports of a new threat from Nevely's forces. Axen and Dylah were still set in their plan to hide Cav away, this time reluctantly adding Atta to the plan, who would be able to use her magic to warp Cav away at a moment's notice. Cav, along with Aloria, twenty guards, and Atta were set to leave for the sand countries in two days. Discretion was their main goal, magic was their backup plan.

Axen and Dylah strived to keep daily life feeling completely normal for their son, despite the threat aimed at him. They had a fun couple of days, and Cav never caught on to the extra daggers his mother had stashed in her boots, or the lethal tipped arrows his father had made in response to the promise made by dark green eyes.

Dylah tucked Cav into bed, she kissed his forehead and whispered the words she told him every night, then she herself nestled into bed waiting for Axen to return from posting guards around Hightree.

Axen slid into bed with a sigh seeing that his wife was already asleep, he pulled her close and ran his fingers through her hair. With the ever changing events around them he reveled in the peaceful rising and falling of her breath. He pushed a few rogue waves away from her face and kissed her forehead but froze when she started to stir.

"Hello, my enemy prince," Dylah muttered with eyes still closed.

"Go back to sleep, my favorite nightmare," Axen whispered back.

Her eyes flickered until sparkling amethyst shone in the dark room. "But you're here."

"And you're difficult."

"How's it looking out there?" Dylah asked with growing worry.

"It's surprisingly still." Axen sighed. "No movement, but don't worry, we'll know if they try something."

"Maybe they finally realized who they're dealing with and decided to stay away for good." She smiled and closed her eyes returning to her restful sleep.

In the dead of night Dylah's eyes flew open and her feet pressed into the cool wooden floors. She could hear her heart beating in her ears and was overwhelmed with panic. An unexplainable force pushed her to the window that faced her home kingdom.

Her hands gripped her face as she tried to muffle a scream.

Fellowrock was burning.

She shut her eyes tightly hoping it was all some terrible dream, but in the depths of her mind she heard the sounds of crackling wood, hustling men, and her oldest brother barking orders. She willed her eyes to open again. It wasn't a dream.

Fellowrock was burning.

Dylah dressed with panicked haste, she screamed her worries at Axen who also hustled to ready himself.

After gathering Kremon they ran towards the ever growing flames surrounding their beloved homeland.

Closer to the forest they saw Keilon and Kunor lining up rows of archers, then watched as ice arrows penetrated the brightly burning trees.

Bahn and his scouts returned with no information on the arsonists or their pastel clad leader.

Dylah ran through the forest to make sure the flames didn't reach her lilac field, in the terror of the night she was relieved to find the purple flowers untouched.

Keilon stomped around the burning trunks slinging orders to the soldiers trying their best to extinguish the offensive flames that carried a scorching message.

Efforts were proving successful, flames shrank quickly as if they had received their own curse, ash floated with an unwelcome grace from the sky. Darting green eyes searched the darkness for what was to come next.

The Riloncks stood in a statuesque line watching the steam rise into the starry night sky as the last tendrils of flames subsided.

"I'm going to kill her," Dylah whispered.

"How much is lost?" Kremon asked.

"Do you think she burned with it?" Bahn scowled.

"Some Rilonck she is, burning trees, it's like she doesn't even get it." Kunor sighed, pinching his nose.

"Order soldiers to take care of what is smoldering," Keilon said with grizzly calmness. "You all need to stay in Fellowrock tonight." The volume of his voice rose, as did the rattle of each syllable. "We are at war."

The Riloncks and a few Fareins funneled into a meeting room in the Fellowrock castle.

Dylah was pacing until Axen walked into the room and she crashed against his chest.

"Where's Cav?" she asked in a panic.

"Sleeping in your old room, Aloria is with him." Axen

smiled. "And four guards are posted outside the door."

"Now that the other king is here can we get started?" Keilon's voice was more commanding than usual.

They sat quietly at a long table. Keilon and Dylah at one end, Axen and Kunor at the other, Kremon, Bahn, Brig, and Kane, on the sides.

"Burning the trees of Fellowrock is an offense punishable by death!" Bahn started.

"Agreed," Dylah snarled.

"How do we go about righting this wrong?" Kunor asked.

"We need to be smart about this." Axen sighed. "It's very obvious that she has a knack for tactics, we can't be too hasty and let her outsmart us again." He began to nervously tap the table. "We need to figure out how she snuck up on us when we were so vigilant."

"Can't we have Dylah use her special gift to sneak up on her?" Kremon looked at his sister. "She's the sneakiest thing we have."

"I'm okay with that plan." Dylah met Kremon's gaze with a proud smirk.

"No," Keilon interrupted. "Remember, she has Delin in her grasp, and I'm sure he's divulged the power that Dylah has and don't you think Nevely will anticipate that? And what could she do to Dylah if she traps her like that? We aren't doing that."

"Then what's our plan?" Kunor asked, staring at his father from the other end of the table.

"I didn't call you here to make a specific plan." Keilon sighed. "We are all reeling, I am shaken, I can see that each of you are too. What a cruel injustice against our kingdom! We are lucky that we stopped the flames before they spread, her plan only destroyed a portion of our trees and for that I am grateful, but still, I am unnervingly furious." He smacked the table and stood. "I called you here to help you prepare for the fact that we will be going to war. That woman has wronged us and we will bring her a war. She strives for order and harmony yet set the most harmonious place aflame, she will get a war." He closed his eyes tightly feeling them throb from overwhelming emotional exhaustion. He opened them and looked around the table. "I hope you all are ready to bring her a war."

Where he thought he would be answered with excited agreement, they stared back at him in silence. Except Dylah, who was smirking.

"What's wrong with all of you?" Keilon asked with slight agitation and confusion. "We are going to war!"

"Brother, look at me," Dylah said. "Look at me and tell me what color my eyes are."

"Is now the time, Dylah?" Keilon turned his head to look at her with an angry sigh. "Your eyes are pink, as they should be in a time like this."

"Good, as you know my pink eyes mean I am channeling the full power of the chaotic soul. They're triggering me to act, to fight, to keep going."

"Yes, Dylah, I know that."

"Keilon?" Dylah raised an eyebrow over electrified pink eyes.

"What?!"

"Your eyes are the same color."

Chapter 18

Regretfully

The meeting quickly fizzled, Keilon retreated to his office to confront the truth he knew had been coming. He stared at his reflection in the gleam of his dagger, all while trying to tell himself that the stormy eyes staring back were his.

"Weird, isn't it?" Dylah asked after appearing as if from nowhere and taking a seat across from him.

"I locked the door." He raised an eyebrow.

"And it's still locked." She smiled widely. "Hey maybe you'll be able to do that fun trick too!"

"I don't think I want that ability."

"They fit you, ya know?" Dylah said quietly. "On the old guy they looked like a tool, sometimes I see them on me and think it's just another wild aspect of myself I can never hide, but on you, they fit." She gulped. "I've always admired you, you never needed the eyes, but they were meant for you."

"They fit you too." He was almost shocked to hear her

words. "You're driven and powerful but you still spread joy and you own every one of your actions. These eyes were meant for you."

"And who do you think I learned that from?"

"Why now?" He laughed nervously. "I am nearing forty, I am not a young man anymore, this doesn't seem right."

"We have to remember certain magical and medical meddling that took place."

"Do you think he knew this would be a result of his intrusion?" Keilon stared at the worn down grooves of his desk. "Do you think it's part of the plan he's helping them formulate against us?"

"Of course not! He may have made a poor decision but I don't think he'd ever betray us like that!"

"He burned the trees, Dylah."

"Okay, sure, but why would both of us being powerful work against us?" Their cloudy eyes met.

"Think about the events that followed your eyes turning pink."

"Okay, well, you've always made better choices than me, you should be fine." She rolled her eyes.

Keilon was again lost in thought, trying to piece together a truth that had taken so long to enter his life.

"I'm a little confused about something," Dylah finally said. "My eyes never just turned pink, first they were a wild color, purple pupils fading to pink irises, then the changes happened."

Keilon raised an eyebrow. "I would have remembered seeing your eyes like that."

"Right, the Fareins could only see them at first and you couldn't see that color until they were mature and I got the full power."

Keilon let out a sigh as the last words from a fallen Farein echoed in his head.

"Arkon saw them," he muttered. "Before he fell asleep he must have seen them. He knew."

"That doesn't seem right." Dylah shook her head. "That was months ago, why is it all finally visible?"

"What makes you think I would understand this any more than you do?" He sighed. "I didn't even put it together in time to ask him before we lost him."

Dylah was mesmerized by the revelation and the look of swirling oceans in her brother's eyes.

The dark night seemed to dull even more as storm clouds rolled in outside, the rain began to pour, and the wind shifted every few minutes.

"Good, rain will help dull the smoldering." Keilon nodded to himself.

Dylah began to breathe frantically and the color drained from her face. "We need to hide."

"Hide?" Keilon laughed. "Why would we need to hide?"

Lightning flashed close by and illuminated the office.

"Think about the events that followed my eyes turning pink."

A shattering thunder shook the room, and once again the Rilonck siblings were blinded by lightning. Then everything was still, as if the storm hadn't even happened at all.

"Lock the castle doors!" Dylah urged.

"It's too late for that." Keilon's eyes lit up like fire as he pointed to the corner of his office where a grand silhouette was leaning against a wall.

"Hey there, youngblood." Old Keilon smiled with all of his teeth. "What lovely eyes you have, Keilon."

Dylah turned to her brother and met his black as night eyes. "Oh wow, those really are scary!"

Old Keilon took a step closer which prompted both Keilon and Dylah to quickly point a dagger at him.

"Quick on the draw." His low laughter rolled forward along with his steps. "Quite the welcome."

"Stop right where you are!" Keilon ordered.

"I mean no ill will." The living ghost held up his hands. "Trust me, I never expected to be brought back twice, this task was supposed to go to Dylah, but since she is still alive, here I am."

"She wasn't alive at one point," Keilon growled. "Do you remember how that happened?"

"She came right back!" Old Keilon chuckled. "Catch me up, someone has burned the trees, I'm on your side here. And to you, my newest prodigy, I'll let you kill me this time around."

"How about right now?" Keilon took another step closer.

Dylah seemed to vanish and reappear with her hands up in front of the first Keilon. "Let's see how we can use him first."

"How did you do that, youngblood?"

Dylah turned with a smirk. "I kept the damn thing you caused."

"Brilliant!" Old Keilon said with a toothy grin. "Though I was never aware that that was an option."

"I'm still not seeing his usefulness." Keilon's grip twisted around his dagger.

"Three chaotic souls in one room!" the first Keilon boasted. "How unheard of!"

"And a soul of harmony somewhere nearby." Dylah sighed.

"No." Old Keilon's eyes went wide and gray. "Sorner?" he whispered as indigo flooded his irises.

"Yeah, you really ticked off his entire bloodline!" Keilon gritted his teeth below smoldering eyes.

Dylah was at a loss looking at her ancestor's depressing demeanor. "Sorner isn't here, it's his own prodigy, her name is Nevely and she is the one who burned the trees."

Old Keilon clasped a hand over his mouth and began shaking his head. "No, that doesn't make any sense. Why would a soul that craves peace create so much panic and destruction?"

"I think she's trying to balance the world." Dylah's proud posture fell ever so slightly. "She says that I wasn't supposed to be able to have Cav, so I feel as if she is trying to correct the impossible."

"You did achieve the impossible with him, Dylah." The first Keion looked to the ground. "I was so confused about his existence."

"So is she!" Dylah crossed her arms. "Her plan is to take him from me, and she is going to some horrendous lengths to fulfill that goal."

"There's a reason why I exiled Sorner," he paused as the memory engulfed him. "Combatting the souls of harmony and chaos is a rather tricky business."

"Wait." Keilon sat back down at his desk. "You don't seem too surprised that Sorner was able to survive his sentence."

"Ah, yes." Old Keilon scratched his head. "That is a bit of my past that was never quite understood, but let me explain. It all started with a damn Farein named-"

The office doors swung open and in a flash of emerald green, yet another dagger was pointed at the ancient Rilonck.

"What the hell are you doing here?!" Axen seethed, pressing the blade against Old Keilon's throat.

Dylah calmly pulled her husband away. "I know it's strange, but I believe he can actually be useful."

Old Keilon remained silent. He stood there frozen with wide green eyes as he studied Axen. "Do you know why your cape is green?"

"Are you kidding me?!" Axen sheathed his dagger and pocketed the key he was still clutching. "Are we really getting into history right now?"

Old Keilon gestured for Dylah and Axen to have a seat across from Keilon, while he leaned against a dark corner. "Hightree's colors weren't always orange and green, those colors were picked early on in King Tovin's reign. I might add that Tovin was made king at just seven years old." He paused to look around the room. "Wait, Tovin is dead, right?" A grin spread on his face as he watched his small audience nod.

"Choked on his own self adoration I'm assuming. That's how he went the first time I'm pretty sure. I loathed that man but it sure was fun to constantly threaten him the last time around, he cooperated so well, don't you think?"

"I believe you were giving us an unwanted history lesson." Keilon narrowed his eyes.

"Right." He laughed before continuing. "Tovin's cape was always orange, the man was obsessed." He paused to roll his eyes. "And when his son became of age, that boy began wearing a green cape."

"And why is this important?" Keilon huffed.

"His son's name was Brennit. A good man, very honorable, a solid friend at one time." Old Keilon slouched. "You see, while I fell for Teyle, my younger brother Sorner fell for Brennit."

"Oh." Dylah smiled.

"Yes." Old Keilon smirked. "Us Riloncks have always been quite the charmers, and the Fareins have always been especially gullible to our advances."

"I guess," Axen muttered.

"After the curse was placed Sorner began to worry about the state of the kingdom, and of myself. The actions he took against those repercussions were unceasing because that was what his nature called for, harmony. I distanced myself from him, kept him away, but that's the thing about havoc and peace, they're always drawn together." Old Keilon shook his head at the thought. "About a year after our forced isolation, he pushed himself into my reign and I allowed it. He really did bring balance to the chaos that came off of me, things were looking up for us. But, he had convinced Brennit to help in overthrowing me. I caught on to this plan, I didn't want to believe it, but soon enough a green cape and his archers were in my courtyard."

Axen froze hearing the similarities, he tried to speak but was stopped before a word could form.

"Yes, it appears your family traits are quite strong, Farein." The first Keilon's proud grin fell as he prepared himself to put the rest of the story into words. "That's when I sentenced Sorner and the other families that had plotted against me. Yes, it was an evil thing to do, but I didn't completely abandon my brother. I could never do that!" He shut his eyes tightly. "I needed him to be safe, and the safest place for him was far away from me."

"But the curse!" Dylah blurted.

"I had a plan, okay?" Old Keilon pointed blue eyes lined with pink at her. "I met Brennit in the trees just hours before the exiling. I begged him to keep my people and my brother safe, I told him where we would be making them step out of the border, I told him an exact time, I shook his hand and pleaded." He sighed. "Sorner was the last to cross the line, of all the evil things I've done in both of my prior lives, that was the worst. We corralled them at sword point and made them succumb to the curse, mothers clutched their children, so much wailing. And the way Sorner looked at me-" The ghost seemed to hold his breath. "But soon after I saw Brennit's figure arrive in the trees, he had two large baskets. He saved my brother."

"Do you know where he took them?" Axen asked.

"Brennit quickly became king, and in our old age a letter was sent to me informing me of my brother's death. He said that he had lived a happy life with his wife and their four children, two of which were born under exile." Old Keilon focused on his tightly clasped hands. "That's all I ever knew. I never allowed anyone to tell me their exact location. Chaos will always seek power over its balance. Even trapped in the forest I knew that knowing where Sorner was would only be a death sentence for him."

Silence hung in the room for a while, the chaotic souls reeling from the events caused by their nature, the Farein piecing together the likenesses of him and his own ancestor.

"So!" Old Keilon clapped his hands together to dissipate the clouds that hung in irises and over their heads. "How have you been, Hightree Prince?"

Axen grimaced in his direction. "I'm the king."

"So you're saying that little youngblood here is the queen of Hightree?" He slapped his knee. "Never thought I'd live to see the day!"

"I think you've lived quite enough days," Axen grumbled.

"Yes, I surely have!" Old Keilon chuckled. "But I have once again, regretfully, been revived!"

"What a realization," Keilon mumbled as he rolled his eyes.

"How are you here again?" Axen asked like a complaint. "I thought you only came back last time because Dylah had the full soul."

"Yeah, that's true." Dylah raised an eyebrow. "Now it's split, what's going on, old man?"

"I think you overthink things." Old Keilon grinned. "The full soul is here even if it's split, and it has once again reached maturity in this spry fellow."

"I believe you are quite a bit older than me," the current Keilon growled.

"Maybe in years but once again I came back young, sir." Old Keilon's smile grew. "I think I'm even younger than youngblood this time around! I just might need to rethink that little nickname."

A collective annoyed sigh filled the room from three different agitated sources.

"Dear?" a sweet voice said from behind the door.

"This should be funny!" Dylah nearly shouted. "Come in!"

"Oh, Dylah!" Teyle said as she stepped into the office. "I thought Keilon was alone, I apologize." She took a look around the room and immediately clasped her hands to her mouth to silence the bloodcurdling scream she knew would come without certain avoidances.

"Who were you calling 'dear?'" Old Keilon asked with

arms crossed. His eyes went wide and black as he looked to the man with his same name. Within a blink his eyes changed to amethyst above a wide smile. "You're more like me than you realize, your majesty."

"I greatly resent that." Keilon glared back.

"We'll let you all hash this out." Axen wrapped an arm around Dylah as he walked them towards the door. "We're going to check on our son."

"Good luck, big brother." Dylah winked as she exited the office.

Chapter 19

Incredibly Even

"Do we trust that guy?" Axen asked as they walked hand in hand towards Dylah's old room.

"I know it's all very strange," Dylah started, "but I feel like we can."

"If you start wearing all black again or you even think about smoothing those lovely waves, I'll be sending him to the ground."

"I believe there is already a line." She smiled widely before offering a quick peck, excusing the guards and opening the door.

"I am so sorry he's not asleep yet." Aloria stood at the sound of the door. "He was for a little bit then woke right back up full of energy!"

"That's okay." Axen smiled. "Lots of excitement tonight."

"And I'm not even tired!" Cav grinned back.

"Aloria, how about you go relax for a bit while we see if

we can calm this little nightmare down," Axen said calmly, ignoring his son jumping on the bed behind him as his wife cheered him on. "Correction, while I calm both of these nightmares down."

After Aloria left with a light giggle towards her brother, Axen quickly caught Cav mid-jump and fell onto the bed with him. Cav struggled to be free but to no avail.

"I know, kiddo." Dylah shrugged watching her child struggle. "He has a pretty strong hold."

"Fine." Cav finally gave up. "Maybe I am a little tired."

"I knew it." Axen loosened his hold and closed his eyes. "Me too, buddy."

Dylah laid next to them. "Me too."

A moment of peace hung in the room as the small family finally caught a breath.

"Are the trees okay?" Cav asked quietly.

"They will be." Dylah forced a reassuring tone. "Don't you remember our creed?"

"Unmatched!" Cav paused to yawn. "Unbroken!"

"You Riloncks sure are scary." Axen laughed.

Cav's eyes were heavy as Dylah leaned in to whisper the words she said to him every night, but she was stopped.

"So that man is here?" Cav mumbled.

"What man?" Axen asked with caution.

"The man you've seen in your dreams?" Dylah swallowed the lump in her throat.

"Yeah." Cav sighed. "I was asleep, but he was pacing the room shaking his head."

"Did he say anything to you?" Axen stared wide unblinking eyes at his wife with a similar expression.

"He just kept asking why they would burn the trees, I tried to tell him we would be okay but I don't think he could hear me." Cav's eyes had closed. "Then he said 'oh not again' and told me he'd see me soon."

"Go to sleep, kiddo." Dylah kissed his forehead. "We'll be here when you wake up."

Time slowly passed while Axen and Dylah made sure their son was sound asleep. Axen carefully dislodged his trapped arm and stood.

"I'll go get Aloria so we can get back to the Keilons." He smirked. "Hopefully there are still two of them." Then he left the room.

Dylah gently stroked Cav's fawn colored hair in the dull predawn darkness of the room.

"Mama," Cav mumbled with eyes still closed.

"Shh." She pressed her forehead against his. "Sleep, Cav."

"Mama, help his sister first."

"Whose sister?"

"Mama, help his sister first," Cav repeated. "It'll be okay."

Cav's head lulled to the side and he was peaceful once more.

Dylah was at a loss for words when Axen arrived and Aloria sat with Cav. She nodded to the posted guards then walked down the hall and up the staircase in a fog.

"What's going on?" Axen finally asked.

"Just thinking." Dylah sighed. "I need to find out exactly what that old guy has been saying to our son."

They opened the office door to see Keilon in his usual leather chair scowling at the ancestor sitting across from him.

"I see you worked through things." Axen forced a laugh.

Before either could voice their grievances, Dylah was at the other seat facing Old Keilon.

"Did you have a sister?" she asked.

"Yes, two. Though one died pretty young." Old Keilon answered with gray confused eyes pointed at her. "But Makray lived a good long life, very sweet, my reign made her a little wild."

"Did she need saving?" Dylah pressed.

"Once, a terrible first husband." He shrugged. "Quite the bleeder." He added a wink.

"Anything else? Any other dangers, or tendencies, or

anything really?"

"Despite the havoc I caused, she managed pretty well." Old Keilon seemed to sit uncomfortably. "Why do you ask?"

"Could she come back too?" Dylah sunk into the chair lost in thought. "Is she somehow connected to all of this? Could she be the answer to solving this ordeal?"

"I know you've seen your fair share of revivals but not everyone can just come back, youngblood."

"I know." Her voice was uncharacteristically quiet. "It just didn't make sense."

"How often do you keep our son company while he sleeps?" Axen finally got his question in.

"Often." The ghost grinned. "I like that kid, never imagined a child could have the best of both worlds, but he's neither a Farein or a Rilonck, he is incredibly even on both sides."

"I know." Dylah smiled.

"And the fact that he even made it into this world is a marvel in itself because of what you are." Old Keilon met her eyes with a bright amethyst that seemed too soft for him to wear. "You named him well."

Clunking sounds echoed down the hallway.

"What was that?" Keilon stood and walked to his door with a hand on his sheathed dagger.

Again it sounded even closer, like armored footsteps.

Axen and Dylah shared a look before bolting out the door to return to their son.

Fellowrock guards were swarming the hallways, shouts were heard outside and within. A panic stifled the air.

At the end of the fourth story hallway, surrounded by four other unmoving guards, they saw her.

Dylah broke into a sprint and crashed onto the floor taking a heavily bleeding Aloria into her arms. Axen ran into the opened door of the empty room.

Dylah pressed a hand over the gash that was bleeding the heaviest on Aloria's stomach.

"D-Dylah. I I I tried to stop them," Aloria stammered through the pain. "They- they took him!" she wailed.

Axen appeared again in the doorway, his eyes wide, stressed sweat glittering his brows, and fists clenched at his sides. He took three steps down the hallway walking with a mission.

"Where are you going?!" Dylah shouted through her own panicked tears.

"I'm getting our son back!"

"We don't even know where to start!" Dylah pressed harder as Aloria groaned in pain, gashes oozing over her arms and stomach.

"Help my sister first!" Axen shouted before disappearing into the havoc within the castle.

Dylah collapsed onto Aloria. She was the sister she was told to help. Questions began to swirl in her mind over how her young son could have known such a thing would be happening.

Chapter 20

Immeasurable Severity

Axen didn't even feel his boots meet the stone floor of the castle as he searched for his son, nor did he hear the crunch of twigs, shouting, or anything except the intense volume of his worries and racing broken heart. The Rilonck brothers and nephews banded with him to search, but he never noticed their unceasing comradery at his side. He had never felt so helplessly alone.

Meanwhile, Dylah still clutched Aloria who grew paler by each passing moment.

"You need to stay awake," she choked on the words.

"I-I can't, Dylah." Aloria winced. "I'm so sorry."

"Come on, just think. Let's think of our first day to-gether. You need to stay awake." Dylah gulped. "Remember when I didn't want to wear that pink dress?" She squeezed her shoulder with a hand still pressed to her deepest wound. "What did you say to me that finally scared me enough to wear that thing? Think."

"I can't."

"Try," Dylah begged. "Stay awake."

"I was going to," Aloria paused as a groan of agony rose from her.

"Whisper."

"I was going to throw you down the stairs." The words only barely lifted from the teenager's lips.

"How many steps do you think are in the Hightree castle, Aloria?" Dylah squeezed her shoulder once more. "Think. Stay awake."

Aloria's head lulled against Dylah.

Dylah began to yell for help, but Aloria wasn't the only one injured in the quick attack.

Soon the Hightree princess was taken away, painfully still, dress soaked in crimson, and breath barely coming. After ensuring her sister-in-law was in good hands, Dylah bolted towards the trees.

She ran among the bark, the calming breeze through the leaves sounded like the shrillest of screams, her place of calm was now the sharp realization of her worst fear. She ran numb to the burning in her legs and her blood soaked clothing cooling in the crisp air. The ache of her lungs and the friction in her throat from shouting his name on repeat began to feel like the simplest breath.

Crying out the name that meant 'joy' felt hypocritical, his name was never meant to be said with anything other than a smile. Cav, the sweet name she gave to him the moment she looked into his beautiful mismatched eyes. Without his presence there was no joy, only panic. Dylah continued running, searching every haunting shadow hoping to find the purest part of herself. The only force that stopped her was a hand practiced at grabbing her shoulder.

"Let me go, Keilon!" she yelled up at her oldest brother.

"Just stop for a few moments, please." Keilon wrapped his arms around her. "Breathe."

Dylah fought against his hold with a fury he had never

seen in all their years together.

"NO!"

Keilon grabbed her shoulders and their navy eyes met each other.

"I know you feel absolutely helpless right now." The points of his fingers dug into her skin. "I know you think there is no one you can turn to, but you are not alone. We will bring him home, we will not stop until Cav is back with you." He stared at her as her face was blank but her mind was a flurry.

"You don't know," she managed to whimper. "My child was taken from me. My sweet, perfect, beautiful son. How can I ever forgive myself for finding that room empty?"

Keilon pulled her in as she began to sob with weighted guilt.

"I found that same room empty about seven years ago," he whispered. "A helpless feeling to know you weren't there at such a scary moment for your child."

Dylah pushed away from him. "This isn't treason and war games! This isn't rightful revenge and a meticulous plan! This is worse than every pain I've ever felt combined." Her hands clasped her face. "This is a thousand spears to the side, this is crashing against the pavement over and over again." She began to shake. "This is a heartbreak of immeasurable severity."

The sun rose through the trees, illuminating the dew and glittering the ground, but the shine did nothing to mend the scorched trees and broken hearts.

After wandering mindlessly, Dylah and Axen finally crossed paths for the first time since discovering Cav was missing. There were no words between them, only quiet stares from heavy eyes until finally an embrace.

Keilon scanned the crowd that had been following Axen for hours, Kremon, Bahn, Brig, Kane, and Kunor. Each man a strong soldier, each man visibly broken.

"What do we do?" Dylah whimpered. "Where is he?"

"I don't know." The words escaped through Axen's heavy sigh.

"We're not stopping." Keilon pointed strong pink eyes to the others.

"That witch will pay!" Bahn growled.

"We'll bring him home," Kunor added.

Kremon raised a fist to add his own encouraging words, but a rustle in the leaves startled them.

"I scoured all the hidden trails," Old Keilon sighed, walking into view. "I'm sorry, youngblood, I couldn't find him."

Instantly, five daggers were pointed at the ghost they were all so surprised to see.

"It's actually okay," Dylah managed to say.

"He killed you!" Kunor shouted.

"And this time I'll kill him." Keilon furrowed his brow. "But for now, I believe we can use him."

"Having three chaotic souls against one soul of harmony should be helpful." Dylah nodded.

"We need a plan of attack." Old Keilon walked closer to the group.

"I agree." Dylah sighed.

The group began to align their guilt with their vengeance as they stood in the glow of the rising sun concocting multiple plans.

A twig broke in the distance. A mix of green, hazel, pink, fire, and black eyes snapped towards the sound.

Delin stood in a clearing. "I come unarmed."

Dylah pulled a dagger out and took two strong steps towards him. "You're smarter than that." She took another step. "Tell me where Cav is!"

"He's safe, Dylah."

"Tell us where!" Axen was soon at Dylah's side, hand gripped on the hilt of the sword at his hip.

"I can't do that." Delin's face was still. "I will tell you that he is being looked after and will live happily."

"He was already living a happy life!" Keilon shouted, joining his sister's side.

"Keilon, your eyes." A look of wonder spread on Delin's calm demeanor.

Dylah returned her dagger to it's sheath on her forearm. She walked until she was standing toe to toe with the man who was once her trusting and understanding brother.

"It seems you didn't do the best job separating that soul." She pointed irises swirling with power and war up to him but he was avoiding her gaze. "Take a look at who was able to join us thanks to your meddling." Delin's mouth gaped when he noticed the return of the first Keilon. "You see, your master may claim her spur of violence was in the name of peace and harmony," Dylah spoke through bared teeth. "But we come bearing the name of chaos, violence is our given nature. You can run back to wherever you are keeping my son, but tell that mockery of peace to keep in mind that it is three against one and we want blood."

Chapter 21

Deepest Hatred

After the frantic searching, the meeting with Delin, and Aloria's injuries, the Riloncks and Fareins were finally channeling their panic into organized rage. While the others sat at the table, Axen leaned against a corner with his face in his hands, and Dylah paced the length of the room sharpening her daggers against themselves producing an ominous yet fitting noise.

"Sister, please sit." Keilon forced the words.

"We shouldn't be sitting at all when my son is in the hands of a crazy witch!" Dylah slid the blades together for one last deafening screech.

"I know this is awful, but at least he's with Delin, we know that he would never hurt a child." Keilon tried.

"Delin burned the trees," Bahn growled.

"We don't know that," Kremon quickly added.

Kunor stood in Dylah's path to make her pacing come to a halt. "We're going to get him back, but first we need a really solid plan."

"You think we can even fathom a plan right now?" Axen finally said in a rattling voice. "After seeing how brainwashed Delin is? After all the searching?" He shook his head. "We knew exactly what was coming and we still failed. Do you think we can see past our anger and guilt?"

"No, I don't," Keilon answered, his blue eyes locked on his distraught sister. "We just need you to know that we're not stopping until a solution is reached."

A knock came to the door, all heads turned with hopeful anticipation as the handle twisted and the door opened.

"I had no luck in tracking that brother of yours or any remnants of her soldiers." Old Keilon sighed. "But these two were waiting in the courtyard, they said they would like to offer their services."

A young man and a woman shuffled in, donning pale green vestments and strawberry blonde curly hair. The woman had a rapier hanging from her hip.

"Hello, Riloncks and Fareins!" The man stepped towards the table, his curls fell like a mop over his ears. "Allow me to introduce ourselves! I am Navent and this is my older sister, Sentry."

"Sentry?" Kunor asked with a disclosed chuckle.

"Yes," the woman snapped back. "My true name is Navaly, but given who our mother is you may see why I chose to distance myself from that name."

"Your mother is Nevely?" Dylah took a small step towards the strangers.

"Yes!" Navent grinned. "And we hate her!"

"So do we," Bahn growled.

"We know she took your son," Sentry said as she gripped the handle of her sword. "I swear we will do everything in our power to return him to you."

"And how can we begin to trust you when your company has caused so much damage?" Keilon asked with crossed arms. "Our trees have been burned, an innocent child has been kidnapped, a teenaged girl is recovering from many deep cuts, all at the hands of your kind."

"We had nothing to do with any of that, I promise you." Navent met Keilon's burning eyes. "Please, you can trust us. Truly, we have the deepest hatred for our mother."

"She's the personification of mud on silk." Sentry's teeth grinded behind her tight scowl.

Dylah soon stood in front of them, her tear strained eyes a deep shade of blue with streaks of black. She pointed a dagger at the strangers. "If what you're saying is true, then I would appreciate your help in locating our son." Dylah slammed the dagger into the table as her eyes ignited with fire and pink lightning. "But if this is some kind of elaborate ruse from that disgusting pastel demon, you should know I turn to violence very easily." She allowed her eyes to turn every mind numbing shade. "And it's something I could force you to do to each other."

"Oh you are perfect!" Navent clasped a hand to his mouth. "Please, kill our mother!"

"Here, please inspect my sword!" Sentry loosened her belt and handed the sheathed rapier to Dylah. "You have our utmost respect."

"Seems genuine to me, youngblood." Old Keilon shrugged.

"What information can you offer us?" Axen asked, still staring at the ground.

"All of it!" Navent grinned from ear to ear.

Within minutes chairs were pointed to a corner where Navent and Sentry were seated. They looked to be young, Navent in his late teens and Sentry in her early twenties. They carried their mother's fair and lovely features but there was an air about them that screamed rebellion.

"Well, who would like to introduce themselves first?" Navent grinned.

Kunor leaned forward, eyes pinned on the lovely new-comer. "My name is Kunor," he paused to clear his throat. "I mean Prince Kunor Rilonck heir to the throne of Fellowrock."

Sentry raised a single unimpressed eyebrow.

"This is not some meet and greet," Dylah stood in front of them leaning almost too close. "I need to know absolutely every little detail that will help me in taking down your wretched mother. Her likes, her dislikes, her wants, her fears." A half smirk formed under onyx eyes. "The center of her worst nightmares, any deadly allergies, a bone she might have broken as a child that could be a potential weak spot, is there anything she is particularly attached to?"

"I for one would like to know just where you all came from," Keilon spoke over his sister's crazed ramblings. "No one has divulged that just yet."

"Introductions first." Sentry met the king's stony gaze.

"I'd love to know who we're spilling our juicy family secrets to." Navent flashed a smile. "We of course know the very sweet Dylah. Your eyes gave you away, all the nights we spied on our mother's camp we heard your name quite a bit!" He paused. "But this peculiar fellow also has eyes that change various colors." Navent gestured towards Keilon.

"Yes, just him." Dylah nodded. "We're both the reigning chaotic soul, he's my brother and the king of Fellowrock. His name is Keilon."

"OH!" Navent's face fell. "Like THE Keilon, the traitorous bastard who sent generations of people to a damned life of miniscule stature and embarrassing servitude?"

Many sets of eyes shifted towards the living ghost who was sitting casually.

"Yes," Keilon responded. "These are our brothers, Kremon and Bahn, our other brother Derck lives far away, and another brother has fallen under your mother's spell. You've already been introduced to my son, Kunor, and these other two are my nephews Brig and Kane, they are Bahn's sons."

"And I am Axen Farein." His tired hazel eyes finally looked away from the floor. "I am the king of Hightree, Dylah is my wife and the queen."

Navent turned to his sister and nodded with approval.

"Just one question before we can proceed." Navent turned his head to the broad bystander. "Who is this fellow? No one bothered to introduce him."

Stares, nods, and various expressions were met among the Riloncks and Fareins trying to silently figure out how to introduce the twice resurrected embodiment of chaos.

"I'm Keilon." The ancestor grinned. "The first Keilon. The traitorous bastard, to be clear."

"Odd time to make jokes, my friend." Navent's smile fell. "What is your true name?"

"He is actually telling the truth." Dylah snapped her fingers to regain their focus. "Spill it."

Navent met her surging pink eyes and smiled. "We are from the land called Verinas, our family first arrived there three hundred years ago during the reign of Queen Varonee."

"We are Riloncks by heritage but our family name is Glavit, our mother's maiden name is Sorner, a name her family took in honor of her supposed predecessor."

A sigh was heard from the corner of the room.

"And does she hold a title?" Dylah pressed. "A queen? Princess?"

"Verinas no longer practices the worship of royalty, no one is special because of their blood." Sentry rolled her eyes.

"Many people in this room would disagree," Keilon muttered.

"So how does she wield so much power without a royal title?" Dylah asked.

"The eyes." Navent shook his head. "People trust her advice in respect to their deep down worries. Her power may seem helpful and harmless but it is manipulative, some go to her many times a week just for her calming presence."

"She gives them vague answers, leaves them wanting more." Sentry's proud frame slouched. "That's how she gains their allegiance, they always want more from her."

"And did the supposed queen of conception just will you both into existence or have you got a father?" Dylah's eyes burned on them.

"We had a father," Sentry started, "he was a great man. Respected military leader with a grand army."

"We lost him not too long ago." Navent looked to the ground. "He was who we grew up with, our mother never approved of us."

"What do you mean she never approved of you?" Keilon asked with a sudden parental fury.

"I'm older." Sentry sighed. "Which would have been fine if I were her only, but when Navent was born a year later she had very little to do with us."

"She believed that a proper set of siblings was an older brother and younger sister." Navent shrugged. "So our father raised us."

"I hate your mother." Dylah grabbed each of their hands. "You're taken care of here."

The young siblings shared a look.

"Most of us have lost our parents," Kremon said.

"Some of us had awful parents," Kunor said with a nod to Axen.

"Some of us became the parent to a child that wasn't ours." Keilon sighed.

"Some of us have a perfect child that was taken," Axen muttered.

"And some of us killed our parents!" Old Keilon chuckled. "Maybe just me."

"Back to the point," Keilon took a step towards them. "We understand your pain, even after taking advantage of your help you are welcome to stay here."

"Back to the point, indeed." Dylah's eye ignited with pink lightning. "Does your mother know you're lending your help to her enemies?"

"We haven't seen our mother in years." Navent smiled. "Six nearly blissful years."

"After the curse was broken our father was called to war and took the opportunity to steal us away." Sentry paused to gather her words. "His death was brought about by an action set forth by our mother, since then we have been discreetly following her camp, gathering any information we could, and waiting for the right time." She laid a hand on the handle of her rapier. "My sword is made from what was left of his own sword."

Navent tapped his hip. "And I'm armed with his dagger, a dagger that has a history of killing tyrants."

"Perfect." Dylah grinned. "Let's start making our plans."

"Let's get our son back."

Chapter 22

Game of Unknowns

No matter what time of day it was, after a night of devastation even high noon felt like pitch black darkness.

Scouts had been sent out to assess the location of Nevely and Delin, for with them would be Cav.

Aloria was badly injured but holding on.

Keilon and Kunor were still gathering information and preparing for what was to come with Navent and Sentry.

Fellowrockians banded together with Hightreeans to repair, to heal, and to mourn what was lost.

So much was being done to pull together the shards of a broken family and kingdom, but for those feeling the most pain, an escape was needed.

Dylah walked slowly through the scorched area at the start of the treeline. Her boots rolled against the ashen ground and as she studied the cracked black bark she felt jealous that the trees were holding themselves together better than she was.

She should have never left her son's side. She should

have posted a hundred guards. She should have questioned the odd advice he left her with. She should have whispered those words to him again instead of leaving in confusion. Her mind couldn't stop listing the things she should have done.

"Dylah?"

She was oblivious to her name, a part of her felt unworthy of a labeled existence.

"Dear!" the voice drew closer.

As she finally turned she was wrapped into the arms of her husband.

"You shouldn't be wandering around by yourself, Dylah." He pressed her head against his chest. "I know this is hard, but we have to stay together. I couldn't lose you too. We're going to get him back, and it's going to be under a well thought out plan with a team of people who would do anything for our son."

Dylah began to shake in his hold, breathing slow shallow breaths, all signs pointing towards a fracture within herself.

"It's my fault," she finally said. "All of it."

"No." Axen held her tighter. "Don't go down that road. There is an endless amount of what ifs and it will not serve us one bit to decipher this heartbreak. All that's left to do is to fix it."

"I failed him." Dylah pushed away shaking her head. "I should've never left his side, this is all my fault!"

"Stop."

"Delin's betrayal, the trees, Aloria, the guards we lost, all of it is on me and this damned soul!"

"It's not your soul doing the damage!" Axen grabbed her wrist and pulled her back in.

"Sure, in my younger years I could justify the amount of chaos that spilled forth because of what I am." Her pink eyes shone up to him. "Not being able to be cured? Understandable. Throwing myself into fight after fight? Yes, I could accept that drive. Allowing myself to be oblivious to every injury? Fitting. But this? No." She squeezed her eyes shut. "Our child being taken, sitting somewhere unknown to us, alone and scared. I can never allow myself to clear that, to say it was demanded of the ancient thing I never asked to be."

"So demand something else!" Axen pleaded. "Now is not the time to let the havoc that stems from you run loose, grab it, channel it, use it." He sighed slowly to calm himself. "You have always made it answer to you, don't stop now."

Dylah stared into the burnt forest. "There's truth to this, you know, that a balance is needed."

"Sometimes what we see as truths are only a string of similar occurrences."

"Come on, it's a truth that chaos will always demand harmony and vice versa." She took a deep breath and looked up into the broken canopy. "Hundreds of years ago when they caged us here because they thought it would bring peace, all it did was ignite a tyrant. When Atta tried so desperately to undo her actions and get her friend back she severed my family. When the love between us grew at such a young age and you promised me safety, the soul within me thought the worst and sent you away." She shut her eyes tightly. "And when I thought I finally had a hold on this constant game of unknowns, when I took the curse as my own, when I knew I was giving us a son, I thought I had won, but look what it caused!" Dylah turned to the scorched forest. "Burnt shelter and shattered hearts." She turned back to him in a fury. "Chaos always needs harmony, there must always be a balance or we go too far in one direction. And now his sweet smile and silly giggles are gone, his soft hair and mismatched eyes are out of sight. He's not in our arms, I'm not holding his hand, you're not ruffling his hair and tossing him in the air."

"Stop."

"I brought this all on myself, on both of us!"

Axen pulled her back in and let her cry the tears she didn't know she had left.

"I've never thought for one moment that you needed any form of balance," he finally said when her breathing returned to an almost steady rhythm.

Her face went blank as she took a deep breath to consider his words, then a weak smile curved from a frown that had felt permanent. "Well that's because it's you."

They held onto each other, capturing the stillness as if they were stuck in some awful dream, but the sound of approaching footsteps crackled against the tarnished ground.

"Dylah." Sentry stood a few steps away. "Axen, there is news on your son." She smiled and it filled them with hope. "They're ready to start making a plan."

They followed the strawberry shine of Sentry's hair back towards the Fellowrock castle. Axen gripped Dylah's hand tightly but only in an effort to stop her nervous shaking. He looked over at her, stunned to see amethyst streaking through obsidian irises.

She was ready for the war that would bring back her joy.

Chapter 23

More Reasons

"Her camp isn't too far away," Keilon said as he sat at the end of a long table surrounded by his family. "They weren't too hard to outsmart the first time, but I expect they'll be more prepared this time around."

"They've set up three large tents," Bahn added. "We believe that it's a ruse to confuse us about which tent they are holding Cav in."

Brig sat to the right of his father. "After some diligent watch we have narrowed down the possible locations of Cav to either the far left large tent or a smaller tent towards the center of camp. Delin was spotted entering both multiple times."

"So as I see it, we have two options here," Keilon said while making amaranth eye contact with his sister. "Either we attack with all weapons and glory, or we split into teams and enter with stealth."

"The second option." Dylah narrowed her eyes. "The

thought of seeing the shock on her face when she sees what's coming for her is all that is keeping me going."

"Let's leave first thing in the morning then," Axen said with a nod. "Make a camp not too far away, use the night to our advantage to take our son back."

"We can use the rest of today to assess our plans and back up plans and assign our groupings." Keilon scanned the crowd until he met amethyst eyes sitting in the back corner.

"Both of you have taken your titles well." Old Keilon smiled. "We'll have no trouble getting our Cav back."

"Our?" Dylah whipped her head to face him.

"Yes," he answered calmly. "He in no way belongs to her, he's ours and we'll get him back."

"That's a nice sentiment." Axen laid a hand on his wife's arm. "Perhaps a little confusing in the current situation."

The group broke away, each person tending to their respective duties, Navent and Sentry followed Axen to the Hightree castle.

"This castle is beautiful," Sentry noted as they approached the gate. "We could see it from so far away, it is probably the largest castle we've come across in all of our travels."

"Yeah it's pretty prominent." Axen flashed a distracted smile.

"Well, not the largest we've seen." Navent chuckled. "We've seen two that were much much larger."

"Really?" Axen raised an eyebrow. "Where?"

"Don't listen to him." Sentry elbowed her brother. "He's referring to where we lived each time we were cursed."

"Grand castles!" Navent continued. "Ornate ceilings miles above your head, black marble floors that stretched to the horizons, intricate windows that let in every ounce of light the sun had."

"And do you miss it, Navent?" Axen lightly laughed. "I may know someone who could return such wonders to you."

"Oh goodness, no!" Navent stopped in his tracks just before entering the castle.

"He had a traumatic run in with a cricket." Sentry muffled a laugh.

"I know it makes my wife and in-laws uncomfortable to think of how you all were living with no break from the curse," Axen said before clearing his throat. "I've seen my fair share of the curse's effect, I am perplexed how you all survived for so long, and I would like details."

"Really?" Navent caught up to him. "It's not too interesting."

"We don't know each other very well, but you should know that I was the one who broke your curse purely based on my own childhood curiosity. Really, I'd love to know." Axen flashed another half smile. "And I could use the distraction."

"We thought Dylah broke the curse." Sentry's eyes darted over to her brother. "It was you?"

Axen began to explain the intricate stipulations of the centuries old curse. How it was made to keep out the first Keilon, how Teyle thought no one would be able to love the chaotic soul, but that Axen began loving the owner of the soul when they were only children until they were torn apart and his memories were stolen. He then spun the tale of the deal he made with a now enemy in a secret tunnel, how only a few days later he was handed the cursed princess of Fellowrock. He went on to describe the friendship they developed, the kiss they shared, the realization that it was her the whole time, and how their love for each other finally broke the curse. It was during this tale that his first nearly genuine smiles could be seen.

"That's beautiful." Navent looked to the ground to compose himself as Axen grabbed handfuls of supplies.

"But then it came back!" Sentry added with an arched eyebrow. "So what happened?"

"Oh yeah, I bet that was terrifying for you." Axen sighed.

"We had just escaped our mother, luckily we were with

our father's allies and they accommodated us." Sentry tried not to smile. "Although, the castle had a cricket problem."

"Sentry!" Navent whispered fiercely.

Axen laughed, took a deep breath, and began to spill more of his past as he led them back through the castle. He explained the change in Dylah before a war, the ghost that was stuck in her mind, the power she built, the ancestors that were revived, and through trials and death, the curse was banished for good.

"She kept it," Axen finally said as they stood in the target fields beside the Hightree castle.

"What do you mean by that exactly?" Navent looked uneasy.

"You'll have to ask her for the specifics." Axen fidgeted with a dial hanging off his hip. "Do you two know how to shoot?"

"Yes, but Navent is the better shot." Sentry instinctively fidgeted with the handle of her rapier.

"Here's the thing," Axen began to say, "we are traveling with a small group, in that group there are only four archers, myself, Kremon, Kunor, and Dylah. But Dylah can only use weapons that she can wear, and through some trial and error we found she can not carry a bow."

"Could you, perhaps, clarify?" Navent smiled.

"You'll have to ask her for the specifics," Axen repeated. "So I'm letting you both try out the special tips I've invented before we take them out into the fight." He handed them each a bow and quiver. "Attach the canisters here, spin the dial, it changes the tip." He waited for them to situate themselves. "For this venture we'll be using mostly paralyzing tips, but feel free to try the ice, fire, and shock tips while we're here, because you never know what could happen."

"Oh!" Sentry smiled and smacked her brother's shoulder.

"You're the guy with all the arrows!" Navent matched his sister's excitement as he tied his hair back.

"You've heard of my arrows before?"

"Yes!" Sentry clapped her hands in front of her mouth. "We've been told so many stories of the men who thought they had died in battle only to wake up hours later with nothing more than a pin pricked scar."

"We should have put two and two together sooner!" Navent shook his head with wide eyes. "The tales of whole battalions falling asleep after the sight of a green cape."

"You've heard of the sleep bombs too?" Axen raised an eyebrow. "What kingdoms have you been frequenting?"

"Our father's army was an ally to many, we've traveled all over, it's hard to match the stories to the regions." Sentry finally composed herself.

The three stayed at the range for a few hours, practicing their aim and testing their quickness. All while Axen asked them countless questions about their cursed childhoods and their mother's rise to power.

When the sun was just beginning it's return to the horizon, the young siblings were led into the Fellowrock castle until they were sitting across from Dylah, who was staring into a mug filled to the top with cold coffee. She barely noticed their arrival.

"Tell her," Axen's voice finally made Dylah look up. "Tell her what you told me."

"Tell me what?" Dylah's voice was raspy.

"Our mother has done terrible things." Navent looked into Dylah's green eyes.

"We'd like to finally tell you about what led our father to steal us away from her." Sentry gulped.

"Go on." Pink streaked through Dylah's eyes. "Give me more reasons to kill her."

The siblings shared a look, until Navent took a deep breath and formed the words. "We were cursed for so long, not many of us believed that we actually used to be a proper size. Verinas treated us well, but there were certain jobs only we could do, demeaning jobs." He paused. "Our father followed his family's trade and became an engraver, a regal job, but still quite dangerous. And our mother, despite carrying the last name of Sorner, had the lowly job of desk maid."

"Desk maid?" Dylah almost growled.

"Yes, it's exactly as it sounds." Sentry sighed. "As children we sometimes helped her."

"Constantly tidying up the desk of some pompous noble." Navent rolled his eyes. "Sweeping away pencil shavings, erasing mismarkings, moving pens." He scoffed. "Have you any idea how heavy a pen is?"

"I do actually, stole a few when I was living with the curse." Dylah concealed the inkling of a smile as she flashed briefly amethyst eyes at Axen. "Continue."

"Well, our mother started talking to her assigned nobleman, listening to his worries, he found comfort in her, and word began to spread." Navent let out an aligning exhale. "She rose to the top, she wasn't even tidying a desk anymore, she was kept for comfort. The man who governed Verinas took her advice because she always took small steps to ease his worries, and like they all do, he gave her what she wanted so he could have more answers, more peace."

"And after the curse was broken?"

"There was a bit of a revolt." Sentry shrugged. "You have to understand, we felt unstoppable."

"It wasn't easy for them to get control back in Verinas." Navent looked down at the table. "So many took out a lifetime of aggression on their employers. Our people were treated like slaves, pets, belongings, and they finally had the means for revenge."

"Our mother was calculated in her rise to power." Sentry took over after noticing her brother become uneasy. "She continued to offer her comfort to the man in charge, she arranged for our people to be granted their rightful place in a kingdom they had been a part of for so long. He was sometimes reluctant to do so, but eventually everything was at peace. She wasn't even being an awful mother, but then she snapped."

"She murdered him." Navent finally looked up. "The man who had governed Verinas, she murdered him, publicly, and assumed his position of power."

"Our father didn't stick around long after that, a kingdom was calling for aid and he elected his army of our brethren soldiers to join the cause. And we never looked back." Sentry nodded to her brother.

"Until what," Axen added with an insisting tone.

"She and her followers began trying to spread peace to other kingdoms." Navent gulped. "My father knew that one day we would cross paths. It wasn't until the uprising she caused in Gomdea that they finally met again, and for the last time."

"Gomdea?" Dylah whispered, black and blue eyes locked on Axen.

"Yes," Axen replied. "And for now, I hope that information is just kindling to the fire you already have."

Chapter 24

Sunshine

The group joined together with the rising sun to ride towards revenge. They were no longer just siblings, or spouses, or even strangers and a disgraced ancestor, they were a battalion forged in blood and justice. Eleven horses, taking the roads untraveled to stay out of sight, inching further away from the damage and closer to the violence.

"Sentry," Kunor said as he forced himself to sit up a little straighter on his horse. "Would you like a travel companion?"

Sentry kept her eyes forward. "I have my brother."

Kunor glanced over to where Navent was riding next to Axen, firing many questions his way. "It looks like your brother is busy chatting up my brother."

"I thought your brother was the king?"

"My brother is the king." Kunor laughed nervously.

"I didn't mean Axen, I meant the king of Fellowrock, isn't that your brother?" Sentry was growing impatient.

"Oh no, you're mistaken." Kunor smiled widely. "Axen,

the king of Hightree, is in fact my brother, half brother to be more specific, but Keilon, the king of Fellowrock is my father."

"Oh."

"Yes, it seems as if he was a bit of a wild teenager." Kunor laughed loudly but paused to make sure his father had not heard. "So yes, I am the heir and I will be the king someday."

Sentry pointed a sweet smile to him. "I believe the monarchy is an aged practice that should die."

Kunor gulped. "Um yeah, me too."

Old Keilon progressed from the back of the group to the front until he was riding next to Dylah, who was silently staring off at nothing in particular.

"Has she said a word since leaving Fellowrock?" Old Keilon asked Keilon who was on the other side of Dylah.

"Some mumbles, no words." Keilon sighed. "Sometimes her eyes change, blue, gray, or black. Nothing else."

"Dylah?" Old Keilon reached over and grabbed her shoulder. She slowly turned her head, met his gaze, and returned to staring into the distance. "We need to stop." He pointed the words at the king. "Now."

"I don't think that's a good idea, and I don't know what makes you think I'm taking orders from you." Keilon rolled ignited eyes only to meet the matching eyes of his predecessor. "Wait, why?"

"She's slipping." Old Keilon's eyes faded to green as he glanced at Dylah. "We need to stop."

Keilon sighed with indecision until finally holding up a halting hand to stop the horses near a stream. The others dismounted their horses and stretched their legs. Bahn and his sons, along with Kremon decided to walk ahead for some scouting, Axen helped his still silent wife off of her horse, Kunor repeatedly offered to fill Sentry's canteen.

Axen led Dylah to the stream where she stood almost entranced by the sparkling water.

"Walk with me, youngblood." Old Keilon put a hand on

her shoulder and nodded to Axen. "Let's talk."

They followed the stream beneath spaced out trees and scattered bushes. Dylah never looked up from her boots.

"Dylah, we are now far away from your husband, your brothers, everybody." He held onto her shoulders hoping to capture her focus. "Whatever terrible thing you've been wanting to say, you can say it to me, because I can assure you I have thought the same terrible things."

"I hate what I am," she whispered.

"I know."

"Don't." She pushed herself away. "Don't pretend like we are any bit the same when you were the one teaching me to use what I am for malicious purposes." She shook her head. "I appreciate the help you are offering now but I will never forget the evil you brought to my kingdom and the hurt you caused my family."

"I know," he repeated. "Coming back that first time re-ignited the same feelings I had when my own soul first matured. You should know that I had been waiting for you, I had so many stoic plans but the moment I had a heartbeat again all I wanted to do was repeat the mistakes of my youth. I was a terrible ghost, but this time is different."

"I doubt it," she sneered.

A stillness rattled the silent connection they had, a feeling of disjointed sadness and regret made Dylah look to her one time nemesis as if he were some scared lost child.

"I had three children." He turned towards the rushing water. "I wasn't the best father, purely had them to carry on the Rilonck name after destroying most of it."

"You should have let it die."

"Don't talk like that." He sighed. "I'm just saying that I understand your pain, it's a terrible thing to see a piece of you hurt."

"I was unaware you were capable of feeling such a way." She swallowed the words when she saw his face fall as he looked at the ground.

"My daughter, she was terrified of me." He shook his head. "But she was the cutest kid, the best thing to ever come from me. I was so perplexed that I could have had a hand in making something so pure that I even accused her mother of sneakiness, but my suspicion soon went away because I swear sometimes I saw the smallest hints of purple in her eyes. She was the greatest kid, kind to everyone, she listened, even after seeing me use my eyes on the soldiers, and even her mother once, she still tried to keep a relationship going with me. But, at about eleven years old she got sick and didn't make it."

"I'm so sorry."

"As she was taking her last breaths all I could think about was the time I wasted succumbed to this soul I have and the pain and fear I caused her within her short life. I watched the purest part of me fade from this life while I was allowed to live well into old age, and to come back twice." He clenched a fist. "I never understood the demand for balance when life is already so unfair."

"When we came back from Gomdea we were all so battered, Cav saw us with bandages and crutches, he seemed to be holding back everything he wanted to ask, kids don't do that, but he was so shaken." Dylah finally looked up at her ancestor. "There was so much I couldn't explain to him that when I left for another battle I lied to him and told him I was after some lost arrow. But what did that save him from? Look what happened because of me."

"Keilon told me about that battle, you can't put that on yourself."

"I can, there is now new information." Her face fell into her hands as she muffled a frustrated growl. "Nevely started that war, a war we wouldn't have gone to fight if not for my actions in Arizmia when this chaotic connection of ours first came to light. When I kept hearing your voice in my head, when I had the drive to kill their tyrant and demand the creation of peaceful ties." Her hands fell into fists at her sides as she stared off at nothing. "Because we became their allies we went to Gomdea to help them, we lost so many men, we all have scars, and what did I leave that battle with?" She let out a misplaced laugh. "I left as the queen because the chaos that came forth from such a wicked twisted string of events finally rewarded me for the blood I gave it."

"Dylah, stop."

"And what's worse is that my mind should be flashing images of my son, his smile, his eyes, his laugh, the peaceful look on his face when he sleeps. Instead, the soul demands that I plot my next move." Her pink eyes tilted up to him. "Every moment I am thinking of another hundred ways to take down that dreadful woman, rescue my son, retrieve my brother, free her people from her clutches, it just won't stop."

"I am probably the only one who understands exactly how you feel." He met her powerful gaze with grieving eyes. "That was the one thing I leaned on Sorner for, he always seemed to quiet the constant voice. I'm sorry Nevely wasn't the calming presence she was meant to be for you."

"I let her look into my worries once, that's how I learned I did the impossible when I had Cav." Dylah looked back to the babbling water. "She thought she was fixing one worry, but instead caused so many more."

"It is an odd experience, looking into their eyes while they do that party trick." Old Keilon chuckled. "It's not like our eyes that are always different colors."

"Yeah, hers are just every shade of green."

"Except when they do the trick and they're as yellow as the sun." A half smile formed on his face. "I think that's what I found the most comforting."

"Yellow?"

"Yes." Old Keilon laughed. "Like laying in a field of flowers and looking up at the sun on the most temperate spring day."

"That's not the experience I had." Dylah grabbed the shirt fabric above his elbow and looked up at him in a panic.

"Her eyes went from bright green to dark green but looked into mine as a steady jade, no bit of sunshine with her."

"That can't be right."

As they were locked into a confused and calculating stare a rustle of shrubbery came from behind them as Keilon walked onto the scene.

"Hello?" he said. "You've been gone for a while, just making sure my sister is still alive."

Their heads tilted towards his voice and he was shocked to see their eyes full of storm clouds, which only made his swirl into the same color.

"Something isn't right, Keilon." Dylah took two steps away from her predecessor shaking her head. "Nevely isn't what she says she is."

"What do you mean?"

"When my brother used his soul on me his eyes turned yellow." Old Keilon was also shaking his head. "But Dylah says Nevely's don't turn yellow, she's not the soul of harmony."

"Well that sure does explain all of this," Keilon said with a sigh. "Wait, no, she has to be, she read Dylah's worries that's what got us into this!"

"Could she have guessed?" The first Keilon wrapped a hand along his jaw in contemplation. "Maybe she's just a dealer of cheap tricks."

"No, I was keeping so much of that pain to myself." Dylah slouched with half of her face covered by her hand.

"So she's just missing a color then?" Keilon gripped the bridge of his nose.

The chaotic souls stood in silence as they thought over the ironic unbalanced nature of their own supposed balance.

"Not missing a color!" Dylah finally looked up and laughed. "It's so obvious, why didn't we see this before?"

"Explain, what did we miss?" Keilon seemed almost annoyed. "How could we have caught on to this misalignment during her bout of going haywire and-" he paused when his eyes met his sister's. "She's missing a color because she's missing a piece."

"Just like when I didn't have the full soul and I couldn't maintain my power." Dylah smiled. "She doesn't have the full soul, that's why she's going too far in one direction."

Old Keilon grinned. "I knew my brother's soul couldn't cause such devastation."

"It does make sense that because she was only given her soul after I was born with a portion then she too would only be given a portion." Keilon nodded his head to agree with his logic.

"Balance." Dylah whispered. "So she must have the majority of the soul of harmony because she does have most of the power in her eyes."

"So who has the other portion?" Keilon asked as he and Dylah stared at their ancestor.

"Right, that's something I'll need your help with to figure out." Old Keilon seemed deeper in thought. "Chaos will always come first, then harmony immediately after. And it is always given to a Rilonck."

"Derck is barely a year younger than me, she must have been born sometime in between us." Keilon returned to pinching the bridge of his nose. "Could the other half be Delin? He seems to mesh with her pretty well."

"No," Old Keilon sighed. "Chaos must come first."

"But I'm the last Rilonck," Dylah answered as if she were asking a question. "There wasn't another one on our side until the nephews were born."

They seemed to reach the same conclusion as yet another rustle was heard through the nearby bushes.

"Are you three about ready to go?" Kunor asked with a calm smile. "Why do you all look so worried? Can I help?"

Chapter 25

Peace Be Damned

The banded trio of the same soul walked close together at a distance behind Kunor.

"We have to tell him," Dylah whispered.

"We can't tell him," Keilon argued. "He worries so much over big news."

Dylah smacked her brother. "Of course he does!"

"Everything okay back there?" Kunor turned around with a wide smile. "I don't like when you two fight, it throws everything off."

After he had turned around Dylah smacked Keilon again with an insistent look.

"Now that kid does remind me of my brother." Old Keilon smiled. "We should tell him."

"No!" Keilon whispered through clenched teeth.

"You just love keeping secrets from your kids, huh?" Dylah muffled a laugh.

"Did you just refer to yourself as my kid?" Keilon

laughed.

Dylah shrugged. "By default."

"Your mother always talks about how great of a parent you were for her." Old Keilon smiled.

"That's true!" Dylah added. "She said the same thing to me after this kind man threw me off of a balcony."

"It is a little bit funny now, right?" Old Keilon chuckled with a wink as Dylah rolled mostly amethyst eyes.

"We're not telling him," Keilon said in a hushed shout, ignoring their bleak jokes. "I lied to Dylah about a lot of things and she still turned out just fine, he can wait a little longer to figure out what he is."

"A lot of things?" Her eyes ignited under an arched eyebrow.

"It's all in the past," he said as his eyes matched hers. "So fix your eyes."

"Fix yours," she threw back with a sly smile.

"Really, is everything okay?" Kunor turned around again.

Old Keilon broke away from his prodigies and walked towards his brother's. "So tell me, Fellowrock prince, how do you feel about the color yellow?"

Keilon glanced over at his sister just before they rejoined the rest of the group. "You seem a little lighter."

"Oh no, I still feel as if there are a hundred swords piercing my heart." Dylah lightly laughed. "But to know that this awful thing isn't purely to justify the thing I am, but it's only an action from an actual mad woman, I feel a little better."

"Well, that's one way to look at it."

"Dylah?" Axen walked up and was confused by the genuine smile on his wife's face. "Are you okay?"

"Yes!" Her eyes lit up with pink. "I'm going to kill that half cooked batch of crazy and get our son back." She walked away to join Navent and Sentry.

"Are you going to explain?" Axen looked at Keilon.

"I would rather not."

"Alright then, let's keep moving."

They rode for two more hours before they saw the beginnings of Nevely's camp on the horizon, they stopped their horses in a group of trees to stay hidden until nightfall. The group rested, they ate, they planned. At the first signs of evening they began donning their black clothing.

Dylah stood by her horse pulling out her leather armor from bags strapped to its sides. She slid a dagger into a special pocket in each of her boots. Two more daggers were slid into sewn in sheaths on the sides of her thighs. Another pair were placed on her back along the angle of her hip bones, while two more fit along the contours of her ribs. The last of her nine daggers was hidden on her left arm.

"Can you be so heavily armed and still do your little trick, youngblood?" Old Keilon asked after watching her secure the last dagger. "Well, I guess we did still have our swords during that first day."

"You were gripping them quite strongly, right?" Dylah looked up at him and smirked. "We found a loophole in the curse, the things that you're wearing or holding on to very tightly shrink with you." She chuckled. "That's why when I came back from Hightree after the war I was returned to my towering height wearing a very elegant doll's dress."

"So daggers?" He raised an eyebrow.

"I could never find a sword that was comfortable enough to wield and still cause my preferred amount of damage and for some reason the bow doesn't shrink with me. The daggers were the easiest thing to make wearable, and honestly the most fun to use."

"And are you ready?"

"Do you even need to ask?" Her eyes streaked with power and obsidian.

"I'd like to accompany you on this mission." He was uncharacteristically quiet. "And I understand if that is worrisome for you."

"I trust you." She smiled. "Not that I fully forgive you

for killing me or anything, but the more I think of my son's young life, the more I understand that you have always been there for him."

"Yes, I've known him for a while now." He nervously ran a hand through his golden hair. "He really missed you." Old Keilon read the quizzical look on her face. "I visited him each time you were away." He smiled. "Meeting him wasn't on purpose, I felt a shift in the soul and decided to visit you. I thought something had happened to you, it was such an odd feeling that I couldn't ignore. But instead I saw a baby, as you know, I can rarely see the living I visit, but I saw him, and I saw you. You were asleep and holding him, but he woke up and just looked at me."

"Because we both died, that's how you could see him?"

He nodded. "It seemed you were doing well, but his presence bothered me and so I kept visiting."

"The night terrors when he was two." Dylah laughed to herself.

"I just want you to know that he is very important to me and I'd like to be there when you get him back." His pink and amethyst eyes met hers. "So I can protect both of you."

"I'm not sure I like this softer version of you, I think I preferred when you were knocking me to the ground over and over and telling me to rise." She smirked.

"Well you rose and now you have my allegiance."

"I already have an idea of who needs to be paired with who, and you're not going with me." She flashed a wide grin before walking away to meet the others.

Darkness fell, the fire was extinguished, the teams were assigned, glowing pink eyes shifted to one another as the plan was about to unfold.

"And you're okay with us being split up?" Dylah asked cautiously.

"I would love to be reunited as a family," Axen said as he counted the arrows in his quiver. "But you're right, we have a better chance of finding him if we're split up."

"We'll all be together soon." She smiled.

"I understand your groupings." Axen glanced over at his brother. "But why isn't Kunor coming with my archer group of Kremon and Navent?"

Dylah watched as the two Keilons conversed with her nephew. "He's in good company."

"You're hoping one of them tells him?"

"Shush! You're not supposed to know!"

"It does make sense, though, I can see it." Axen smiled. "How come Fareins never get the ancient trickery?"

"Because you marry into it." Dylah flashed a smile.

The group gathered around them, standing closest to the ones they'd be charging into the unknown with. Bahn and his sons, the Keilons and Kunor, Axen with Kremon and Navent, and Sentry with Dylah.

"You all know what our objective is." Dylah's magenta eyes scanned over the crowd of her brethren. "Tonight we are bringing home our joy, tonight we let the havoc win, peace be damned!"

"We all know which actions to take." Keilon took over. "You know your backup routes, our meeting point and our backup meeting place." He nodded. "Where we will be spaced out we will also be close together, if your group gets overwhelmed you know the signal to call for help."

"If possible, take Delin peacefully," Kremon added.

"And take Nevely violently." Dylah's eyes matched the night.

Words were shared, encouragements slapped on backs, siblings parted ways, the lovers met in an understanding embrace knowing soon their child would also be in their arms.

Dylah and Sentry watched as first Bahn and his sons faded into the night, then Axen's group, finally Keilon's.

"Are you ready to go get your mother?"

"I'm ready to avenge my father." Sentry spoke in a stoic voice that only stems from living through pain.

"Good," Dylah responded in the same tone. "Let's go."

Chapter 26

Wolves

The moon hung in the sky as the tiniest sliver of reflected light, as if it had poked itself through the stars just to sneak a peek at the scene unfolding below. An ominous howl drifted over the camp, the chorus of a wolf admiring the moon's slight presence, but a separate howl echoed on the other side of the camp. Many left their tents to investigate the sounds. More howls floated through the still night, there was no way to know which direction the wolves were approaching because their war songs were coming from all sides of the camp, until another cry joined the symphony, a scream.

A boy looking to be in his teens ran through the center of the camp, he was gripping his arm in pain. His quick strides were jagged and clumsy and he was constantly looking over his shoulder. Many of the campers tried to stop him but he was so stricken with fear that he just kept running, causing a panic through the camp as they looked for the blood thirsty beast that had lost its prey.

He retreated into the nearby woods, his scream stopped abruptly but was soon replaced by ferocious growls, rustling of foliage, and sounds of a scuffle and tearing until a finishing chorus of victory howls.

"Do you think they bought it?" Kane whispered to his father hiding behind a nearby tree.

"Definitely." The shine of Bahn's grin shone through the dark woods.

They noticed a pair of soldiers approaching, their drawn swords shaking in fear.

Brig cupped a hand over his mouth and began to repeat the same predatory growls he had made moments ago. The soldiers ran away. "Pathetic," he whispered with an eyeroll.

The father and sons waited until the panic seemed to calm, and when the campers felt they had escaped an attack, the trio of howls filled the air once again.

The soldiers of the enemy camp quickly channeled their adrenaline and began walking towards the woods to challenge a fate of jagged teeth and torn flesh. But then a new fate fell from the sky, a fate of fire. They watched in horror as flames soared above them and crashed to the ground forming a blazing wall around their camp. Howls rose again as the fire crackled, those in the camp started to scramble for fear of deciding which fate was worse.

After lining the camp with fire arrows, Axen, Kremon, and Navent progressed into the temporary village. They hid behind tents and when a soldier was seen by himself, a paralyzing arrow would be lodged into his neck before he was dragged into the shadows.

"You're a pretty good shot, Navent!" Axen whispered with a smirk as they slid a soldier against the sides of a tent.

"It helps to be working beside a legend." Navent flashed a smile.

They peeked behind a tent to watch the frantic display.

"There's only one way out for her." Kremon almost chuckled.

"Well then we better make sure she gets there with as few guards as possible," Axen said with rattling determination.

A nod was shared between the three before they split off in different directions as the chorus of howls rose once again, signaling the other trio of shadows to fall into the chaos that called to two of them.

"There surely is something special in the blood of Fellowrock kings." Old Keilon laughed after sending a charging soldier to the ground with a swipe of his elbow. He pointed pink eyes at his teammates. "Don't you two agree?"

"I'm not the king yet," Kunor mumbled as he shot an arrow into the leg of a passing soldier. "One day."

"Of course you're one to correct me, boy." Old Keilon smiled.

Keilon tossed another soldier to the side after a successful sleeperhold. "Now is not the time to discuss lineage."

"Actually now is the perfect time to discuss bloodlines!" Old Keilon raised an eyebrow. "You know, there's an easier way to handle them if they really are of Fellowrock blood." His grin widened. "Time for your first lesson!"

"I need no lessons," Keilon huffed after slamming his fist into a passing jaw.

"You're going to change your eyes to gray and you're going to do it right now," the ancestor growled as he dodged the swing of a sword, grabbed the soldier by the fabric on his chest and threw him an impressive distance. "Come on, your little sister mastered it in just one day."

"I just think of the color?" Keilon asked reluctantly.

"Yes!" Old Keilon's knee met a progressing soldier's stomach, he smiled at the familiar sound of cracking ribs. "But proudly, you're a damn chaotic soul, act like it!"

Keilon took a deep breath, he remembered how Dylah explained her power as seeing storm clouds pulsating with trapped lightning. He envisioned it for a moment, he could feel her waiting at the edge of camp along with the swirl of spent energy that surrounded their predecessor, and soon a twitch was felt in his eyes.

"Perfect!" Old Keilon chuckled as he grabbed a passing soldier. "Now command this brainwashed yuppy to do anything you'd like!" The soldier kicked his dangling legs, Old Keilon leaned into the man's ear. "Do you really think that will help you escape, sir?" He flashed a smile at Kunor who looked uneasy. "I've really missed this."

Keilon stepped to face the captive, when their eyes met, the man relaxed. "Tell us which tent holds your extra weapons." The soldier offered no words, he just held up a straight arm pointing to a tent not too far away. "Thank you."

"Not so fast, keep your hold," Old Keilon commanded before his scowl curved into a smile. "Don't forget to have some fun."

Keilon grinned feeling the power surge within him. "Would you like to help us set it on fire?"

"I would love to," the soldier responded in a monotone.

Old Keilon released the prisoner and they followed his stiff steps as he led them to the armory tent.

"I don't like this," Kunor whispered.

"Yeah, I bet you don't." Old Keilon chuckled and elbowed his own prodigy with an insisting look.

"Maybe it's just the Hightree half of me that makes me not enjoy war as much as the Riloncks do." Kunor shook his head.

"Trust me, kid." Old Keilon put his arm around Kunor's shoulders. "It is very much a Rilonck trait."

"Don't listen to him." Keilon glared at his ancestor. "Kingdoms and names don't determine your morals."

"I'd have to disagree, your majesty, King Keilon of Fellowrock." Old Keilon winked.

The man stopped in front of a tent, then was hit in the back of the head and thrown to the side. Kunor placed two fingers between his lips and whistled sharply three times. Moments later Axen and Navent appeared from the shadows.

"Where's Kremon?" Keilon asked.

"He's following a group of her soldiers that he thought was suspicious, but we've taken out most of the stragglers." Axen adjusted the dial on his canister. "Okay, let's light it up."

"You two look like you are having a grand time!" Navent flashed a smile before noticing Kunor. "You not so much."

"It's a damn frenzy out here." Kunor shook his head as he clicked his own canister.

Axen and Navent stood on either side of the armory tent piercing it with countless fire arrows. After they retreated into the shadows with the two Keilons, Kunor lined the perimeter of the tent with ice arrows to prevent anyone from trying to extinguish the flames.

"All that's left to do is keep an eye out for that witch." Keilon's pink eyes darted in the shadows as the group moved further into the frantic camp.

Old Keilon gripped Axen's shoulder. "I'll be at your side when we find him, all you need to do is take him and run, I'll take care of the rest."

"Unless Dylah gets to her first." Axen smirked and fired into a group of progressing soldiers.

Kremon ran by but took backwards steps when he recognized his family. "Your plan done?"

"Yes," Keilon nodded. "Just crowd control now."

"Great!" Kremon grinned. "I'm following Delin, he snuck off this way."

Before the others could follow him he slipped away, fearing how the two with the same name would handle his rogue brother, and how the distraught father would deal with the one in connection to his son's kidnapping. Kremon knew he needed to be the one to catch and diffuse Delin.

Kremon crept in the shadows, he rolled his steps to ease the crunch of his boots against the well disturbed soil. As soon as Delin slipped into a tent, Kremon followed. He wrapped the crook of his elbow against his younger brother's throat while simultaneously covering his mouth with his other hand.

"Don't say a word or I will put one of every arrow in you." Kremon squeezed his hold on Delin's throat to force his agreement, then released.

"So you're all here?" Delin whispered and coughed.

"And some new friends." Kremon stood with arms crossed blocking the door. "She will lose and you will have to answer for your betrayal."

"You don't know that she'll lose."

"I think we both know she will." Kremon narrowed his eyes. "Where is she keeping Cav?"

"I can't tell you that." Delin looked to the ground. "He's safe."

"If he's away from his parents, he's not safe." Kremon shook his head. "How are you okay with causing our sister so much pain?"

"I'm not." Delin gulped. "But it's what makes sense, just ask Nevely, she can explain it to you all."

"If I see your master I won't be asking questions, I'll be taking action."

"You don't understand!" Delin took a strong step towards his brother. "She knows peace, she settles your soul, she heals."

"She corrupted your mind! You burned our trees!"

"I had nothing to do with that!"

"You still let it happen and that's worse." Kremon took his own step forward glaring up at his brother. "But there is still a chance to mend what you helped shatter."

Delin was breathing heavily, his eyes darted from his brother to the door, to around the small tent, then to the floor. He took one deep breath to steady himself. "Nevely took Cav towards the surrounding trees." He sighed and met Kremon's relaxed stare. "But you'll never catch us."

In one quick motion a blade sliced from Kremon's right shoulder down to his elbow. He shouted in pain and tried to aim at his escaping brother but his arm was surging with pain and slowly becoming numb. He ran out into the camp gripping his heavily bleeding arm, jumping over fallen soldiers, and looking desperately for his failure.

With the camp surrounded by fire, a sudden fire also breaking out in the center of the camp, the spaced out constant howling of wolves, and their soldiers slowly dwindling there was nearly no option for an escape. Except for a clearing that led to a road, it looked like the camp's only safe haven, but little did they know that that is where she was waiting.

First a scared quartet of leftover soldiers entered the clearing, there was a zipping sound through the air, then only three soldiers stood looking at the man with a dagger in his neck.

"Gentlemen."

They turned around towards the call of a sweet voice, they gulped at the sight of their master's pink tinged hair. She stepped closer, but her features were younger, she was wearing all black pants and armor instead of pastel skirts, and her smile curved with drive not power. She slashed the air twice with her thin sword. The only standing soldier met her sly grin with wide eyes. He backed away only to feel the chill press of a blade against his neck.

"Where is the child?" the second assailant growled in his ear.

"He's with her," he trembled.

"And where is she?" Dylah pressed the blade against his throat with a gruff force.

"She's coming," he whispered.

Dylah and Sentry shared a nod before the man was sent into a deep sleep from the hilt of the dagger against his skull.

The ladies pulled the bodies to the side and returned to the shadows.

"You're proving to be a good distraction." Dylah winked a magenta eye at Sentry.

"When this is all over, would you mind helping me

change my hair?" Sentry lightly laughed.

"Here's the thing," Dylah whispered, remaining vigilant to her surroundings. "Sometimes we are given features we didn't ask for. And the moment you decide that you want to make that thing belong to you, and answer to you only, that's when you become your strongest." A single soldier walked into view. "Just watch."

Dylah jumped into the clearing and threw a punch at the soldier, she crossed her arms waiting for him to hit her back, she let her eyes wander to the girl waiting in the trees. Before the soldier's fist could make contact, Dylah seemed to disappear only to come back with an uppercut that crashed into the soldier's chin. He stepped back from the shock, threw another punch that hit only air, then a boot hit his chest. The soldier clenched his teeth and made another drive towards Dylah, she sighed with boredom. He seemed to run right through her but as he was trying to deduce her constant dodging, tight pressure wrapped around his neck and he fell asleep.

"Like that." Dylah flashed a smile as Sentry helped her drag the sleeping soldier away.

"How did you do that?"

"I used the thing that makes me the weakest and turned it into the thing that makes me the strongest." Her amaranth eyes seemed to brighten. "And I was only able to do it after accepting the thing I never asked for."

Sentry checked her surroundings. "Could you explain a little better?"

"I kept the curse." She grinned. "The terrible thing that made our people weak for centuries, that made us seem like we weren't a threat. It's now mine to wield and use to my own advantage."

"I can't imagine overcoming such an obstacle."

"I think you underestimate yourself." Dylah nodded towards the shouts that came from the camp. "You already did, and neither of us are done rising."

They waited in the trees, some soldiers were met with the stab of a rapier, others were hit with thrown daggers and disappearing punches. Families and innocents stared deep into commanding gray eyes and ran away as fast as they could.

Howls rang out, instead of a warning, the trio now sounded like a pack celebrating a successful hunt.

"They've done their jobs," Sentry whispered.

Dylah nodded as she noticed a large group walk into the clearing.

"Why so many and why now?!" Sentry began to breathe deeply.

"It's a distraction." Dylah's black eyes scanned her surroundings until she saw a pair of shadows stomping towards the trees at the edge of the clearing. The larger shadow pulled along a small shadow.

Dylah's heart raced. She glanced at the oncoming ranks, she knew everyone else was on their way but not close enough. Her window was closing and she had to think fast or lose the chance to retrieve her son.

"What do we do?" Sentry gripped her sword.

"Well you only have two jobs left to do, are you ready?" Dylah waited for a quick nod in response. "First, you're going to throw me, then you're going to slip into the shadows and collect everyone."

"Throw you?" Sentry's eyes went wide. "Like, actually throw you, you'll be tiny, and I"ll-"

"Throw me, yes!"

"I'm not sure you should be putting so much trust in me."

"Don't worry, it'll be fine!" Dylah quickly counted her daggers and made sure they were secured in their sheaths.

"I don't want to hurt you." Sentry gulped.

"You probably won't." Dylah shrugged. "Hurry!" Within a snap she stood among the grass and twigs.

Sentry offered a hand, watched as her now tiny advisor

pointed to the still moving shadows and braced herself.

Nevely had one hand gripping her long skirts and another pulling Cav who was taking slow heavy steps.

"Come on!" Nevely yanked his arm forward.

"No!" Cav shouted. "Where's Uncle Delin?"

Nevely huffed as she pushed them closer to a thick grouping of trees, she smiled knowing she was almost in the clear. A shadow soon flashed in her peripherals followed by Cav's hand slipping out of her clutches.

Upon her landing, Dylah wrapped an arm around Cav and used the other to brace his head. They rolled against the grass but Dylah quickly stood, easily holding her son with one arm as he held on to her so tightly in return.

"Mama," he muttered into her ear.

"We're going home, Cav." She kissed the top of his head.

"No!" Nevely stomped towards them, a firm scowl plastered over her lovely features. "Wolves, flames, senseless brawling, is that all your soul craves? You deem this as justified? Harmony would never condone such havoc!"

"Actually." Dylah began taking slow steps away. "The other half of your soul helped." She grinned. "But I imagine that he'll receive your own half before the sun rises."

"Other half?" Nevely whispered with a subtle tilt of her head.

Dylah used Nevely's shock as her chance to retrieve a dagger from the sheath on her thigh.

"Look at the stars, kiddo," she whispered in Cav's ear.

She shifted her weight to her back leg, ready to make an escape, then threw the blade at Nevely's stomach. The blood immediately began to stain through the pastel satin of Nevely's bodice, she clutched the wound while still progressing towards the mother and son.

Dylah's eyes pierced the night with pink lightning as she removed a dagger that was settled along her ribs and let it soar at just the right angle to slice her adversary's cheek.

"We're racing your dad to the horses." Dylah smiled at

Cav as she darted towards the designated meeting place. "So let's run!"

"We're going to win!" Cav giggled.

Dylah ran in a jagged pattern through the surrounding trees, stopping every so often to hide behind a trunk before changing her direction to make sure she wasn't being followed. Her heart pounded with relief, she felt the loving pull of her child nestled safely in her arms, and when they arrived in the dark clearing she finally stopped and knelt in front of him.

"Are you okay?" She pressed her hands against his face and kissed his forehead repeatedly. "I need you to tell me everything."

"She was so boring, mama!" Cav giggled. "Where's dad?"

"He's coming!" Dylah watched the shadows for the rest of the group. "We won the race!"

"That's not fair." Cav's eyes widened. "Uncle Kremon got hurt."

"What do you mean?"

"They're helping him."

"He'll be okay, and soon we'll be back home and you're never leaving my sight again, okay?" Dylah pulled him into her. "I love you so much, Cav, you are the best part of me."

There was a rustle drawing near and Dylah let out a sigh of relief knowing they had pulled it off. She had her son back, her family was whole.

A stinging sensation sunk into her back thigh.

She wrapped her arms around her son even tighter as a large shadow fell on them.

But her arms grew weaker with every passing moment.

"Mama," Cav whispered in her ear. "Look for the feather on the door."

Weakness overcame her, in a nightmare of events her arms went limp and fell away as she glanced into the calm yet sinister green eyes of her brother.

She tried to stand as her son was ripped from the hold he

had on her and held out of reach, but the injection made her legs numb.

"I'm sorry it has to be this way, Dylah." Delin clutched a squirming and screaming Cav. He reached into his pocket and sprayed a mist over his nephew's face. "He's safe with us and he'll live a happy life."

She screamed as Delin carried her sleeping child towards the darkness.

In one last bout of strength she grabbed her dagger from her shoulder sheath and threw it into the back of Delin's knee. He yelped in pain but faded into the shadows as she crashed against the ground into a darkness induced by tainted harmony.

Chapter 27

Pointing to the Trees

Dylah wasn't asleep, but she wasn't awake either. She couldn't feel her body, but she could feel each new crack form as her heart shattered into a million pieces. She couldn't see her surroundings, but she could hear her husband's frantic voice when he found her. She was trapped in the moment of her failure and it felt like there was no escape, until even her mind went dark.

It wasn't until hours later that her eyes could finally open on her command and let in the unwelcomed shine of a new morning. She sat up in a fog looking around an unfamiliar tent with the familiar muffled voices floating in from outside. Dylah stood and steadied herself when her injected leg shook bearing her weight. She stopped herself a step away from the flap of the tent, she tried to align the words that would apologize for her shortcomings as she feared the consequences of yet another failure. She contemplated slipping off and chasing after them herself, but she needed to see

Axen, to comfort him and hoped he could do the same for her.

Outside the tent she flickered her eyes to adjust to the bright light, she was in the center of the camp they had conquered in a fruitless mission. Voices bounced off the vacant canvas to her right and she took slow steps towards them.

The faces of her brothers, nephews, new allies, and husband turned to her. Axen immediately ran to her and wrapped his arms around her.

"You're awake," his words muffled into the crook of her neck.

Dylah's arms finally held on to him in return. "I am so sorry."

"Dylah, no." He squeezed her a little tighter.

"I had him," she began to sob.

"Take a breath." He held her out and tilted her chin up. "You did your best."

"It wasn't nearly enough."

"More than enough." Axen smiled and it felt displaced.

Dylah's mind was in a frenzy but her voice couldn't form the words to question the calmness of the situation that had gone so poorly. All she could do was follow Axen through the crowd of their family until they stood in front of a tent with a feather hanging from the door. Her eyes went wide as she remembered the words of her child, and just as she was floating in the awe of her own disbelief she heard his soft laugh.

She burst through the canvas opening to see her son giggling wildly as he playfully slapped at the hands of a man who had always visited his dreams.

"You're too slow!" Cav shouted through his laughs.

"Maybe you're too fast!" Old Keilon winked back at the child.

Dylah turned to see the insisting nod of her husband.

"Hey, old man," Axen said, catching Old Keilon's attention. "Let's give her a minute." He turned his head again looking at his bewildered wife. "I'll explain later."

Dylah didn't feel the steps she took towards her son, only reveled in the feel of him in her arms. She kissed his face and forehead repeatedly, ran her fingers through his fawn colored hair, and tapped at his shoulders just to make sure that he was actually in front of her.

"You were so sleepy, mama!" Cav giggled.

"You should have woken me up!" Dylah tickled him in response.

"I tried!"

"Cav," Dylah's amethyst eyes connected with his mismatched stare. "How did you know about the feather on the door?"

"I just knew!" He shrugged. "And our friend is here!"

Dylah took a breath wondering what other premonition he could be telling her. "What friend?"

"The one who calls you that funny name!" Cav pointed to his bright eye. "With eyes that are this color."

"His eyes are purple around you, kiddo?"

"No, mama, lavender."

"I am so sorry, you're right." She smiled feeling the weight of distance and failure fade away with his sweet face.

Axen entered the tent, and the family met in the embrace that they had been dreaming of since the trees were still smoldering. The embrace turned into a fit of laughter as their family normalcy paved through the trauma of the night. Cav's smile proved to be strong enough to lift the burdens they both still carried over losing him so easily.

It all felt complete but there were still questions to be answered.

Old Keilon and Kane entered the tent two hours later to keep a watch on Cav while Dylah was told of the events that happened after her injection and what led to the success.

She calmly walked up to the circle of her family, Kremon's arm was bandaged, Navent had a black eye, but despite the injuries they all seemed to have the same calm elated air about them.

Keilon wrapped an arm around her and led her to a log in the circle.

"I need you to stop falling asleep for undetermined amounts of time." He laughed and squeezed her shoulder. "But, I knew how worried you were while you were out. I tried to tell you how right everything went but I know you couldn't hear me."

"I could hear, though." Dylah shook her head. "I heard you find me, then nothing for so long."

"We'll get more answers about that later," Axen said as he glanced around the circle. "But for right now, we need to tell you what happened that brought our son back to us."

"I led them back to you just like you told me to," Sentry said with a sigh. "But we saw you lying there so still."

"I ran up to you." Axen held her hand. "You weren't responding, but your right arm was still extended, pointing to the trees."

"The boys and I followed the hint," Bahn began, "and not too far into the trees we found your dagger."

"After that the grass seemed to be more disturbed on one side." Brig nodded to his father. "Like someone dragging a leg."

"With the commotion going on around you, the ghostly man and I followed them into the trees." Navent grinned at her. "That's when we saw the slow moving shadow."

"I heard Navent's whistle," Axen said. "Keilon and I left you and Kremon under the watch of Kunor and Sentry."

Kremon nodded with unnatural silence.

"We quickly surrounded Delin." Keilon's gray eyes met hers. "He wasn't moving very fast."

"But he put up a helluva fight!" Navent clapped his hands together. "As soon as we had him surrounded, all madness broke out!" He pointed to his black eye. "I myself hit the wrong end of a rather pointy elbow!"

"It was a scramble," Axen said with a smile, "but I grabbed Cav and let them handle the rest."

"And the big injured guy was really mad about that!" Navent continued in an excited ramble. "But the king and that even bigger guy took over!" His eyes went wide. "I know it was quite dark and I only had one well working eye, but I'm pretty sure I saw that ghost throw the madman over his shoulder."

"I did!" Old Keilon's voice chuckled behind them.

"So where is he then?" Dylah held her breath waiting for an answer.

"Captured, and heavily restrained," Axen reassured. "We'll take you to him, he's not saying much yet."

Dylah nodded, stood, and removed the three daggers she still had in various locations on her person.

"What are you doing?" Keilon asked.

"I'm going to talk to our traitorous brother." She checked a boot and was delighted when an unexpected dagger was nestled within it. "I feel it would be best if I did not come in with sharp objects."

Navent elbowed his sister. "Is she implying that she's only dangerous in the presence of sharp things?"

Sentry muffled a laugh, and Kunor soon joined in with a light yet forced laugh.

"The chances of a sudden death are a lot lower if I'm unarmed." Dylah smirked as her eyes zeroed in on Navent with pink lightning. "But still pretty high." She nodded at her husband. "Take me to him."

"I will," Axen paused to shake his head. "But I'm not going in there."

"We'll go in with you." Keilon stood with a nod to the ancestor.

"Yes." Old Keilon grinned. "And the kid." He gestured at Kunor who was fixated on a lovely presence. "You know, for balance."

"Kunor," Sentry said loudly to break his trance.

"Yes?!" He smiled with all his teeth. "What do you need from me?"

"You're coming with us." Keilon crossed his arms. "Weren't you listening?"

Axen led the bearers of ancient souls through the camp towards the tent that held the person they never thought they'd have to hate.

"I think Kunor has a little crush," Dylah whispered loudly.

"She's so pretty." Kunor sighed.

"You're not going about it very well." Keilon elbowed him. "Are you sure you're mine? Our side is usually quite vexing."

"I had that guy on the hook since we were twelve!" Dylah laughed as Axen rolled his eyes.

"Maybe he gets his shyness from the other side." Keilon chuckled at his son's uneasiness.

"Not a chance," Axen said. "I did pretty well for being a heartbroken kid."

"That shyness is definitely a Rilonck trait," Old Keilon added with a knowing look. "I had a brother who acted the same way around a lovely suitor when they first met."

Axen's feet froze outside of a tent. "Here." He turned to his wife. "I'm sorry, but after seeing that crazed look in his eye when I grabbed Cav from him, I just can't bear to see him yet."

"I understand." Dylah smiled as her eyes went black. "I can handle him."

Chapter 28

Scum

Old Keilon entered the tent first, then Keilon and Kunor, and finally, Dylah. They stood with arms crossed staring at the hunched over figure with ties on his hands and feet. Delin was staring down at the dirt floor of the tent, he hadn't even noticed their entrance.

Dylah huffed, grabbed a fist full of dirty golden hair above the nape of his neck and reared his head back, forcing him to look at her.

"I have a few questions," she said with a smile and eyes like night.

"Answer mine first," he managed to say.

"And why do you think you deserve any answers?" Old Keilon barked from behind Dylah.

Dylah held up a halting finger to her predecessor. "Let's see what the questions are first."

"Where are the others in the camp? Most were innocent, what did you do to them?" Delin's voice wavered.

Keilon stepped forward with a smile. "Some of the captured soldiers were corralled so we could get information from them later." He blinked and opened his eyes to reveal a striking pink. "The others were told to go very far away."

Dylah looked from the ghost to her brother and back. "He can do that already?"

"Yeah!" Old Keilon slapped the king's shoulder. "Picked it up quick! I'm very proud!"

"Good job, big brother!"

"No!" Delin shouted, breaking the celebration of the chaotic souls. "I split it evenly but I kept the power in Dylah's eyes."

"Here's the thing," Old Keilon chuckled. "Chaos and harmony are plagues, given a host and the right conditions, they will spread like wildfire." He took a step closer and leaned over the prisoner. "He was already a host, you just gave him the right conditions." He grinned. "And that's why I'm here, so thanks for that."

"And where is Nevely?" Delin whimpered and his eyes went wide when he saw the calm smile on Dylah's face. "What did you do to her?"

"Well, the last I saw, she was indeed alive." Her smile fell. "But I'm guessing the dagger I threw at her stomach isn't helping her much."

Delin's head fell as he began to cry.

Kunor stepped forward when the other three were at a loss for words.

"Why does she mean so much to you?" he asked. "She kidnapped a child and set your kingdom on fire. What makes you think that you owe her so much of yourself?"

"She settles me." Delin sighed. "She takes the worries I have, she lets me breathe."

"Did we as your family not do that?" Kunor knelt in front of Delin and placed a hand on his shoulder. "If we failed you before let us make it right, but don't seek out any lovely stranger to fill whatever gap we've left. Tell us, let us fix it."

Delin raised his head and looked into Kunor's eyes. "You seem familiar."

"I should," Kunor said slowly, "I'm your nephew."

"That's not what I meant, it's similar to-"

"Now answer our questions!" Keilon interrupted.

"But, Keilon, your son!" Delin shook his head. "It's almost uncanny how-"

"How much like his father he is?" Dylah quickly added. "We know!"

"Delin," Old Keilon said with a nod. "We know but we'll handle it later, you have some answering to do."

"And what gives you the right to make commands?" Delin clenched his teeth as he pointed a glare at the ghost. "You killed my sister!"

"She looks alive to me." Old Keilon shrugged. "I honestly don't see the issue here."

"What did you do to Dylah to steal Cav away?" Keilon asked. "Why did you leave her in the grass as you ran off with her child?"

"Did you inject me with poison?" She glared.

"No," Delin said with a sigh. "It was a serum. Some in the camp were from a different kingdom, they introduced me to their weapons and explained that they use a serum that makes the body completely numb and in a state of limbo when at its most potent. I diluted it and that's what I used on Dylah."

"Despicable." Old Keilon rolled his eyes.

"You're one to talk!" Delin pulled against his bonds trying to progress towards the ancestor. "You're the worst of them all, the reddest stain on our history," he paused and let a sly grin form, "the scum at the bottom of the pond." His eyebrow raised. "But of course, you know all about that. Don't you?"

The first Keilon's eyes went wide and mixed with storms of azure, but in a well practiced reaction, he changed them to pink electricity.

Dylah noticed the hidden pain of a man she had slowly come to respect. She raised a flat hand and slapped Delin across the face.

"You're the one on trial here!" she sneered.

"This serum, you said it leaves the victim in a state of limbo and that they brought it from their previous kingdom?" Keilon asked calmly. "Dylah, why don't you explain to him where some of his new friends used to call home."

Dylah smiled, she pushed back the loose strands of dewy blonde hair on Delin's forehead and slowly traced a scar. "Gomdea."

"No." Delin shook his head.

"But, good news for you, little brother." Keilon smiled below burning irises. "Your sentence will now be finding an antidote for that serum, and saving Arkon."

Dylah let the Keilons and Kunor leave the tent, but she remained in front of her brother.

"I should kill you." She let her hand glide over the empty sheath on her thigh. "You nearly broke me for the sake of a stranger, but I have to remember a time when you were the one I went to with every nightmare and broken bone. I hope you come back again, brother."

"I just don't think I can choose the side of chaos, Dylah."

"What a shame." She shook her head. "We'll collect you before our departure."

Kunor followed silently as the past king and the current king joked about things he didn't know could be funny, such as weapons and rebuttals, but he was waiting for his moment.

Kunor watched as his father joined Axen and Cav, he also kept an eye on the person with the same name.

Old Keilon made his way to the edge of the camp, after a three hundred year old memory was thrust into his face he needed the air. His mind flashed to crystal waters and hands holding his shoulders down as he violently fought for a single breath. He heard the muffled echoing words of those he had trusted as he looked up through the distorted reflected sun rays. His eyes twitched as the memories warped to crimson and the voices turned to screams.

"Hey."

The friendly voice shook him out of his nightmare. He turned to see his prodigy's son, Kunor.

"I'm sorry, I just don't really know what to call you." Kunor shrugged. "I knew my father by the same name and as the king for so long, it's odd to think there's another one with his name."

"You don't have to call me anything." Old Keilon forced a smile.

"Oh, um, okay." Kunor laughed nervously. "I just need to ask you something really quick."

"Is it about a legend? Perhaps about your father or aunt?" A genuine half smile curled. "Or would you like some advice on how to get the girl?"

"No, none of that." Kunor tapped an anxious finger against the side of his leg. "I was wondering if you could tell me what my father and Dylah aren't telling me."

Chapter 29

Spark

"I'm what?!" Kunor shouted just before Old Keilon muffled his mouth and effortlessly pulled him even further from the camp.

"You're not supposed to know yet," he grumbled as he pushed the prince into the nearby trees.

"Harmony?!" Kunor tried to catch his breath as if he had just sprinted up the steepest mountain. "My soul?!"

"Yes." Old Keilon grabbed his shoulders to steady his panic. "You are meant to be their balance, do you understand?"

"I have to tell them that I know!"

"I know you really think that, because of course you do, but you can't." The first Keilon smiled. "Just keep it to yourself, with that other witch nearing death I imagine you'll get the full soul soon!" He turned to walk back to the camp. "And I'm the only one who knows you know and they'll probably kill me anytime now, so don't worry so much."

"Soon." Kunor lingered on the word. "What do you consider to be soon?"

"It's not in my nature to specify."

"They're going to hate me." Kunor started to walk in a circle around a tree.

Old Keilon sighed and turned back. "What makes you jump to that conclusion?"

Kunor gestured to the camp. "Remember just last night when you were throwing soldiers all about?"

"Yes, quite the party." He grinned. "Are you worried that we only attacked because we hate harmony?"

"No, I understand why this action had to be taken, it makes sense. I wanted my nephew back." Kunor shook his head. "But Dylah and Nevely never even tried to see eye to eye, and well, you and your brother."

"Nevely was a mad woman, and as for Sorner, that was entirely my fault, you don't need to worry." He watched as Kunor took panicked breaths trying to untie the knots of his mind. "Balance is possible, I know that because I had it and I cast it aside." He clapped a hand to his shoulder. "And hey, it might take awhile for it to rise in you. Look at your father, damn near elderly and finally full of lightning."

"I don't want to be full of lightning." Kunor gulped.

"You won't be." Old Keilon pushed Kunor towards the camp. "Your spark is different than ours. Where sometimes we strike with abandon, you are like the sunlight, constantly burning bright. Do you need any better metaphors for chaos and peace?"

Dylah had a tight grip on her son's hand as they ran past rows of empty tents muffling their giggles. She stopped against a canvas wall and peeked around the corner. She raised a single finger to her lips as her eyes sparkled like amethyst.

"Princess?" Axen called out with a laugh in his voice as he walked slowly through the empty camp, checking around each corner. "Cav?"

He took another step, then the familiar giggle escaped to his left.

"Almost," Dylah whispered crouching next to Cav, she handed him a small sachet. "Get ready to run, kiddo."

Axen jumped into view where he knew his wife and son would be hiding. Although he was expecting it, he was still surprised by the cloud of dust blocking his vision.

Dylah let Cav pull her along as they ran away.

"We did it!" he shouted.

"So you like escape training?" Dylah laughed. "What do you say?"

Axen was brushing the dust off of his arms when a familiar phrase said in his son's voice exclaimed from not too far away.

"I will always try to escape!" Cav followed it with a giggle.

Dylah waited for Axen to catch up to them, together they walked back to join their family and make a plan to return to their kingdoms.

"Escape training, huh?" Keilon asked almost immediately. "You sure are starting that a little too soon."

"Just want my kid to be able to get away from the situations he shouldn't be in." Dylah smiled as Axen took Cav to where Navent was sitting. "You had me start my own training very soon after Nanny's pillow incident. You should understand, this is as much for his safety as it is for my sanity."

"I will warn you about escape training." Keilon grinned. "It tends to make kids a little wild."

"That's fine!" Dylah laughed. "Are we about ready to leave?"

"Yes." He nodded. "Bahn and the boys are still scoping out the tents for anything useful, Kremon is off sulking somewhere, and I don't know where the old man and my son went."

"Wait, together?!"

Keilon laughed loudly. "Of course not, how absurd!"

Moments later two more people joined the group, mumbling to each other until the moment they spotted eyes on them.

"And that is how you make a man forget his name for three days!" The first Keilon elbowed Kunor, suggesting that he fake a laugh with him.

"Genius!" Kunor laughed slowly.

Keilon was unamused and decided to check on Bahn's progress.

"What are you two doing together?" Dylah soon stood in front of them with arms crossed.

"I was walking the perimeter when I noticed he was walking too," Kunor stammered, "and uh, we decided to walk back together."

"Is that so?" Dylah pointed fiery eyes at her predecessor. "Talk about anything interesting, old man?"

"No!" Kunor laughed.

"Old man," Dylah repeated.

"Simply discussed the weather and shared a few jokes." Old Keilon shrugged. "That's all."

"He told me." Kunor immediately covered his mouth with his hands. "He told me absolutely everything."

"You what?!" Dylah quickly punched the ghost in the stomach. "Kunor, go distract your father while I handle this." She pointed a finger up to him. "And don't tell him a thing."

After Kunor had taken three large steps to get away from the scene, Dylah pointed black and pink eyes at her predecessor.

"Okay okay," Old Keilon coughed with a smirk. "Can we just note that of course he couldn't keep the secret?"

"Keilon is going to kill you!" Dylah shook her head.

"I thought that was the plan already?"

A green cape quickly approached.

"Hey, so my brother just informed me in passing that his soul is full of harmony and he's freaking out." Axen furrowed his brow. "So, chaotic people, who told him?"

"Look, we talked." Old Keilon held up his hands. "He could already sense there was something off about him and that we were keeping a secret."

"Keilon is going to kill you," Axen grumbled.

"Yes, that has been established." The ghost smirked.

A few moments later after some subdued bickering, the reigning Keilon stomped towards his predecessor and promptly landed a fist against his cheekbone.

"So he told you too, huh?" Old Keilon shook the pain off.

"We're leaving within the hour," Keilon said to Dylah and Axen, ignoring the ancestor. They took the hint and walked to get their things together.

"He needed to know," the first Keilon said.

"I do not need you to tell me how I should be running my kingdom, and especially how I should be discussing things with my adult son." Keilon rolled ignited eyes. "You will be escorting Delin back to Fellowrock, and then I'm executing my end of our deal."

"Understood."

Chapter 30

Often Finicky

It was decided that they would return in two groups. The reunited family, along with Kremon, Navent, Sentry, and Kunor, left first. Then about an hour later, Keilon, Bahn and his sons, and Delin under the careful watch of the first Keilon, began their journey back.

Not only was this a strategy to keep a watch on any lingering threat, it also kept those that had become weary of each other separate.

"Scum on the bottom of the pond," Delin pointed the loud whisper at the living ancestor.

The first Keilon shook the water out of his ears from centuries before but every so often, he'd hear the words again and begin to picture a life of torment and failed rescue attempts.

"Are you wondering how I know that bit of history?" Delin managed to say when he noticed their pair of horses had fallen slightly behind.

"It will all return to history soon."

"Sorner kept a written record of your life, even after exile he compiled the updates he was given. The letters that escaped your ever roaming eye." Delin smiled.

"I bet those are interesting to read."

"I wonder just how many bones are at the bottom of that pond my sister used to run around as a child."

The former king's eyes turned to black thinking of the sound of thrashing water. He turned to Delin. "I lost count."

"What will you do when the people you have somehow swayed discover just how much blood you spilled?" Delin's laugh was low. "How you managed to clear so much of our kingdom's records is quite impressive. And especially considering the most heinous events, you're a monster."

"Like I said," he began with a sigh, "I'll be returned to history soon enough."

In the caravan riding just an hour ahead, Cav had fallen asleep in his mother's arms as she gripped the reins of their horse.

"Is he out?" Axen said softly, riding next to her.

Dylah wiggled a shoulder and smiled when her son continued to dream. "Yeah, remember we'd have to take him on rides when he was a baby to get him to fall asleep?"

Axen smiled back, thinking of the innocence he was trying to save. "When we get home, I think you should do it."

"Oh," Dylah said through a sigh. "Are you sure?"

"Yes." Axen nodded. "I want that woman erased from his head."

"Me too."

When Axen had first suggested they use Dylah's power on their son to help him recover from the kidnapping and frenzy of the rescue, she didn't think he'd want to follow through with it. They decided to consider it and decide by the time they arrived home, and it was apparent that the decision had been reached. Thinking of connecting her gray eyes to her son's sweet gaze rumbled a rawness within her that she hadn't felt since her pink eyes first emerged.

She understood where Axen was coming from. The fear that Cav might bear felt weighted on their shoulders and she didn't doubt that if her husband had the ability, she would be pushing him to use it as well. On the other hand, she wanted the council of souls like hers, one that had just felt the power arise and the other who had used the power too much. Instead, she turned to the opposite side of the same scale.

During their last stop, Dylah passed Cav over to Axen and when everyone was distracted she pulled Kunor by the arm.

"Everything okay?" he asked slowly.

Dylah stood in the light of the sunset gazing up at him.

"Am I in trouble?" he asked quickly.

"No." She shook her head. "I think I need one of the Keilons instead, sorry."

"Wait, no," he laughed. "Just tell me."

Dylah took a deep breath. "Is it wrong to use my eyes on Cav?"

"Yes."

"I know, I just have to explain that to Axen."

"Oh this was Axen's idea?" Kunor looked to the sky in thought. "Then it's probably okay."

"Hey!"

"I don't mean to offend." Kunor tried not to laugh. "I'm just saying that if the suggestion came from the most level headed person I know then you know he has thought of every terrible thing and trusts that it won't happen."

"Yeah, that makes sense." She pointed green eyes up to him. "Actually this did feel pretty great!"

"I'm not sure I follow."

"Balance." Dylah smiled and returned to the horses.

The night was still young when the second group made it to the Fellowrock castle. They immediately led Delin to the cells in the basement. When they entered the foyer they were surprised to see Dylah sitting on one of the lower steps.

"What happened?" Keilon took quick steps to her.

She yawned. "Nothing, I just need some help with something." She fought another yawn. "What took you so long?"

Keilon rolled slightly fiery eyes. "Brig and Kane got into a bit of a heated discussion, and Bahn, being the nurturing parent he is, made us stop so they could fight it out." He huffed. "It was a very even fight and it took a bit longer than we thought it would."

Dylah glanced over to where their ancestor was lingering by the doors. "And did he prove to be helpful?"

"Barely said a thing." Keilon shrugged.

"Well I need both of you so grab him and come on."

Dylah paced the hall outside of her old bedroom until she saw the two with the same name approaching. Her heart was racing with nerves and she feared what was coming next.

She turned to them to begin explaining the situation at hand but before a word could be uttered she was interrupted by a ghost.

"Stop forcing your eyes to be green." Old Keilon crossed his arms.

"Don't talk to her like that!" Keilon growled at him. "She's not doing that!"

Dylah sighed and let the blue thunderstorm show through her eyes. She explained to them that she was about to use her eyes to help Cav move past the days they didn't want him to remember. They reassured her that it was a warranted act, that it didn't make her a bad mother, and they promised to be there too.

They entered to see Axen on the bed, with a sleepy-eyed Cav in his lap flipping through the pages of a book.

"I almost couldn't keep him awake," Axen whispered. "What took so long?"

"Fist fight," Keilon whispered back.

"Riloncks." Axen rolled his eyes. "Are you sure you're ready to do this?"

"Yes." Dylah nodded before crouching in front of her husband and taking her child's hands in hers.

Axen kept a firm yet gentle grip on Cav's shoulders and tried not to look when Dylah's eyes filled with the color of mindless melancholy.

"Cav," Dylah said slowly.

"Yeah, mama?"

"The last thing you remember was mama and dad tucking you into this bed after the fire, okay?"

Cav blinked at her. "No, I remember that lady with the pink hair and Uncle Delin taking me on a trip, and I remember you in the woods, mama you flew!"

Dylah raised an eyebrow. She looked up at Axen then both of them looked to their added support.

She took a deep breath and tried again. "Cav, the last thing you remember is your dad and I tucking you into this bed after the fire, okay?" Her eyes went wider. "Tell me you agree."

"But we were just on a trip!" Cav giggled.

Old Keilon turned to the king. "Your turn."

"What?" Keilon shook his head. "If it didn't work when she did it, why should I try?"

"There's a chance that it didn't work for her because she had apprehensions about using it." Old Keilon gestured to the king. "So you should try."

"And you think that I don't have apprehensions?"

"Yours aren't the same as a mother's," the first Keilon replied calmly.

"Please," Dylah whispered.

Keilon took Cav and paced the width of the room to prepare himself. "Hey, Cav," he finally said to get his nephew's sleepy attention.

"Uncle Keilon, your eyes are different."

"Yeah, remember when you asked me if they would

change?" Keilon smiled. "Well they finally did."

"I knew they would." Cav smiled with a yawn.

"Okay look at me, kiddo." Keilon closed his eyes to imagine the clouds he was conjuring. He opened them and held his young nephew's gaze. "The last thing you remember is your parents tucking you in after the fire, okay?"

Cav tilted his head. "No, I remember going with Uncle Delin and that other lady on a trip, and the wolves, and mama flew!"

Keilon handed Cav back to Axen and the three chaotic souls returned to the hallway to address their shortcomings.

"Are you sure you were doing it right?" Dylah groaned.

"Yes," Keilon fired back.

"Does it just not work because he's my kid?" She rubbed her temples.

"No, I used it on my kids all the time." The ghost smiled. "Sometimes I told them they didn't have voices." His smile grew. "Sweet silence."

"You're the worst," the other two muttered in unison.

"What did he mean by knowing that your eyes would change?" Old Keilon asked.

"Oh." The king shrugged. "It was just something he mentioned not too long ago."

"Why do you ask?" Dylah turned to the ancestor.

"Is that the only time he has said something like that?" Old Keilon seemed to lock onto her. "Or have there been other predictions? There have been, huh? How many?"

"A few," Dylah whispered through her shock. "He knew that Keilon was angry one day, he told me to help Aloria first though I did not understand it at the time, and when Delin was ripping him away from me he told me to look for the feather on the door." She sighed. "What does that mean?"

Old Keilon didn't answer, he just opened the door and politely asked for the child. After a nod of approval from Dylah, Axen allowed the ghost to hold their son.

"Cav, do you know you're named after someone who

lived a really long time ago?" Old Keilon asked.

"No, my name means joy," he yawned and his eyes blinked longer than normal.

"That's a fair observation." He tapped under Cav's left eye. "One more question and then we'll let you go to sleep."

"Aren't I dreaming?"

"No, I'm actually here for now."

"Right." Cav's exhausted eyes widened slightly at the realization.

"Cav, can you tell me about something that's going to happen soon?"

"Uncle Kremon is going to get stitches, he's not going to like it, they'll give him medicine that will make him silly." A sleepy grin slowly formed.

"I bet that's going to be funny!" The first Keilon laughed before handing the child back to his mother and gesturing for the kings to follow him to the hallway.

"Are you going to explain?" Axen asked.

"I would like to wait for youngblood."

"Are you ever going to not call her that?" Keilon crossed his arms.

"Actually." The ghost grinned. "You're a youngblood too, youngblood."

Dylah appeared as if from thin air. "I thought I was youngblood."

"You are," Keilon said as he pointed a glare at the still grinning former king. "I am not."

"Now can you explain?" Axen asked with subtle aggression.

"Yeah, your power will not work on that kid." Old Keilon's smile fell. "But you shouldn't be surprised about that gift he has."

"What are you talking about?" Dylah asked.

"Really?" The first Keilon raised an eyebrow. "You all can find a way to cure a curse but don't understand the workings of family traits?"

"Of course!" Axen shook his head with a smile. "Junia!"

"If she could pass the gift on, why didn't any of her six children receive it?" Keilon added.

"Your mother's bloodline is strong but often finicky," Old Keilon replied. "I saw the gift skip generations within a family back in my day."

"And that's why the power doesn't affect him?" Axen began to think out loud. "Are the two connected somehow?"

"What do you mean back in your day?" Keilon narrowed smoldering eyes.

"The power didn't always work on that particular bloodline even though they are Fellowrockian, even those without foresight." Old Keilon blinked the tinges of gray and blue from his eyes. "I'm sure it's the same for Cav. For some reason they can fight off our mental takeovers."

"And how would you know that?" Keilon asked.

"It doesn't matter," Dylah quickly added.

"Let's consider this matter solved then." Keilon nodded. "We'll make sure Cav heals well from his experiences. He'll be okay." He sighed. "Old man, I'll be showing you to your room and locking you in it."

"Fair enough." He shrugged back.

"Dylah, we'll have a meeting in the morning." Keilon pointed electric eyes at her. "To discuss certain matters."

"Understood," she paused to think over what that meant. "I'll lock him up."

"What?" Keilon took a step towards her.

"I will remind you, big brother, that I have killed this man once before."

Keilon wanted to forbid it, but a second thought had a deepness to it.

"It's fine." Axen nodded at both of the Keilons. "She'll make sure he's really dead this time, right?"

"And I'll hold one hand behind my back so she definitely has the advantage." Old Keilon grinned. "But the left hand, because I don't want to make it too easy for her."

"Yes!" Dylah smiled. "And I'll kill him on the ground level so there will be no throwing."

"Still don't like jokes about your death, little sister."

Axen slipped back into the room with Cav, Keilon went to his office to check over various matters, and Dylah slowly walked the remaining Keilon to a door at the end of the hall.

"I've been in this room before too," he muttered to himself.

"I'd imagine you've been in every room of this castle." Dylah laughed.

"I meant as a ghost."

"That makes sense, this was Keilon's room when we were growing up." She pointed a smirk towards him. "One of your haunting victims."

A smile lightened his face as he was lost in thought. "It does make sense." He chuckled. "There was one night I was trying to visit him, for some reason I ended up in another room but I could feel the soul there so I stayed. I heard the screams, I tried to explain myself, but then I felt two parts of the soul."

"Why do you get so much joy from haunting small children?"

"I wasn't trying to visit you at all, the idea of the soul being split was absolutely ridiculous to me until I felt it when the two of you were together."

"I actually do remember that night," Dylah fiddled with the key. "Our parents had just died, I had a nightmare, I don't remember it but I'm assuming it was my future murderer." She smirked. "And Keilon stayed with me." Her smile fell. "There is one part of the dream I remember, because it never made sense to me and I used to think it was quite funny." Her irises streaked with pink. "I heard you say 'two?' but I was only six, how could I have figured that out so long ago."

"I'm glad you both grew up not knowing what you were." His eyes matched hers. "It's better that way."

"I have a few questions before I lock you up." She took a

step towards the door. "Will I get to do that? Pop into dreams and what not?"

"Yes," he said with pink eyes and a nod. "It'll be your job to find and guide the next vessel for the soul. I heard Dycavlon, you and Keilon heard me, the next one will hear you both."

"Interesting."

"Next question so I can get on with my last night of life." He crashed on the bed and stared up at the ceiling.

"Right." She crossed her arms. "Why are you such a hypocrite?"

"Excuse me, youngblood?" He sat up with irises ablaze.

"You tell me not to hide the colors in my eyes yet I caught you doing the exact same thing." She pointed fire back at him. "When talking about my mother's bloodline I saw the change you decided to hide. And even back in the tent with Delin. Why did you do that?"

"It is not necessary for you to know the reactions I have to the things in my past that are irrelevant to you now."

"I don't know about that." Dylah was about to leave.

"It all dies again with me tomorrow."

"And you're okay with that?"

"Yes," he said as he fell back on the bed. "I've lived two times too many." He waited for her to close the door before he muttered, "Perhaps three times too many."

Chapter 31

Brief Chokehold

Although most slept well into the morning recovering from the frenzy of days that had preceded, it was apparent that three were too lost in thought to stay asleep past the sunrise.

Keilon was first in the kitchen, but Dylah quickly entered, demanding he add another scoop of coffee to what he had already measured.

"See, this is too strong," Keilon mumbled after one sip.

"Could be stronger." Dylah sat at the table. "Have you made a decision?"

Keilon thought for a few moments as he sat across from her. "It was never a decision."

"I think we should still discuss it."

"And why would we need to discuss it? I'm not budging on this, Dylah."

Another person entered the kitchen, making the brother and sister halt their conversation.

"You're talking about me, aren't you?" Old Keilon laughed as he filled a mug. He took a sip. "Could be stronger."

"Are you drinking coffee?" Dylah's eyes streaked with black. "Of all the times you told me it clouded my mind and affected my judgment and you stand here in front of me drinking it?!"

"I trained you the way I was trained." He shrugged. "That's all."

The black in Dylah's eyes quickly changed to a fog.

"I didn't unlock your door yet, old man." Keilon raised an eyebrow.

"Right," he laughed. "I used the window. Don't you know how easy it is to escape out of those rooms?"

Dylah's eyes grew cloudier. "Yes."

"No," Keilon growled, not as an answer to the question of a ghost but to point a command at his sister.

"Excuse us," Dylah said as she pushed in her chair. "We're going to have a discussion."

Keilon stood with a blaze in his eyes. "It will be a short one."

Their walk to the fifth story was silent. Each of them rehearsing the lines they would say to support their claim, each of them also feeling the opposing anger of the other and choosing to ignore it.

The office doors latched followed by a rapid firing of statements, slight threats, and curse words coupled with fists hitting the desk for added emphasis.

"Absolutely not, Dylah!"

"Think about it!"

"No!"

More sharp words were tossed around the room in a practiced dance that originated over two decades before. Scorching eyes locked on each other, then even the darkest of nights were seen in each iris.

"You think I'm willing to risk that?"

"Maybe!"

His finger pointed down at her while hers pointed up at him. At one point there was a brief chokehold on the king, which proved to be the turning point in the conversation that they needed.

"So, you're sure?" Dylah asked, catching her breath. "That's what we're doing?"

"Yes." Keilon nodded. "It will be better this way."

Dylah left Keilon's office and headed into the forest as flurries began to stick to the remaining leaves. She caught sight of Bahn and rushed over to him.

"Hey, have you seen the old man?"

"Uh, yeah," Bahn said but he matched her slight panic. "Have you seen Kremon? The medicine they gave him during his stitches made him a little silly, he might be in a tree."

"That's peculiar," Dylah said, slowly thinking of Cav's prediction the night before. "But the old guy?"

"He went off that way not too long ago." Bahn pointed well past the castle.

Dylah raised an eyebrow looking into the thickest part of the Fellowrock forest, but she trudged on until she saw his figure staring at a small space of land where no trees grew. As she stepped closer she felt a shift in the air, a heaviness she couldn't quite explain.

"What is this place?" Her question made the strong ghost flinch. "Did I just scare you?"

"I'm just assuming it's my hour of reckoning."

"It's not."

"What?" Old Keilon said almost angrily. "But we're back, we accomplished what we set out to do, you have no use for me. When will Keilon be killing me?"

Dylah took a slow step closer. "Why don't you tell me why you came to this particular place and I'll explain our decision."

There was a brief silent exchange of shifting eyebrows and many shades of irises before the past king finally conceded and began digging up the past.

"When I was a kid," he paused when saw her odd expression. "Yes, I know, that was many lifetimes ago, but I still remember this place." He slightly smiled. "My best friend was my cousin, her name was Enfy, she lived right here. You see, I was born knowing exactly what I was, and for that reason I was treated like an entity. They put me through countless dangerous tests, but Enfy was the one who kept me level. She made sure that I knew that even though I was special, I was still human. She'd bring me here to escape the weight of it all."

"I'm glad you had her," Dylah said slowly, "but I'm sorry, what happened? Because you weren't too level headed in your youth."

"They killed her."

"Why?"

The first Keilon took a deep breath as a pain that began centuries before bubbled up to the surface once more. "They weren't sure what power the pink eyes held and they did everything they could think of to force it out of me. But when mine finally changed they were so happy to figure it out, they didn't care how many times I nearly died for the sake of their curiosity. Enfy was there to tell me to use it for good, to not overuse it, she helped me visualize peaceful things, she made sure Sorner and I worked together." He swallowed. "When Tovin attacked me in the woods, Enfy was the one who made sure I healed quickly, she whispered to me as I was sleeping that I would conquer my pain and restore peace. I wouldn't have lived much longer if not for her."

"She sounds like a great woman."

"She was." His eyes were quickly engulfed with a deep blue ocean. "But she had challenged the forest elders one too many times, and they decided they could do without her." He gazed around the empty patch of forest. "The most important thing to know about Enfinella Rilonck is that she built her hut herself and would spend days weaving her own thatching. She lived a simple life, renounced her Rilonck lineage, and lived in gratitude to nature. Where the elders were blinded by the power Sorner and I held, she stayed true to the ancient practices. One day I came to visit her, I was trying to plan my next move against Tovin and I needed her blunt honesty. But I saw the flames from far away. I ran as fast as I could, I pulled her out of the burning house but she had also been stabbed in the chest." He shook his head as his eyes glossed over staring at the memory in front of him. "I was too late."

"What did you do after that?"

"I used my eyes to command my father to put the forest elders to death." His voice went dark. "I drowned them just like they had tried to do to me in the name of conditioning chaos."

"And a monster was born."

"Yes." He finally looked at her. "So, what's the verdict, youngblood?"

"Well, Keilon really wanted to kill you but then he suggested we keep you around for the purposes of war, because you are rather effective in that area of expertise." She laughed. "But even he decided that wouldn't be a fair setup for your second life."

"This is my third life."

"Yes, I know." She rolled her eyes. "I remember the last life particularly well!" Amethyst eyes pointed up at him. "But you don't seem like you're that person this time around so maybe it doesn't count, and I honestly could not bear to explain to my son why his new favorite person is suddenly only in his dreams again." She pushed against his shoulder, beckoning him to follow her back to the castle. "So sorry to tell you, you'll be sticking around this time." She lightly laughed. "You may have lived two lives too many, but we'll just say those were your first two lives." She paused thinking of the words she wasn't meant to hear after locking the door. "And certainly not three times too many."

He walked with her through the forest silently thinking

over the possibilities of his new life. His feet stuck to the ground and he grabbed her arm. "Dylah."

She turned to him with a confused expression, but before she could say anything his arms wrapped around her.

"Thank you," he whispered.

"This is weird." She laughed but hugged him back. "You're welcome."

He dropped his arms and looked at her with clouded eyes swirling with pink lightning. "But if I get any step closer to the person I was before-"

"I'll kill you, then Keilon will kill you, I think Axen would like to kill you too." She grinned. "We got it covered." She punched his shoulder. "Come on, youngin."

"Excuse me?" he said with a chuckle. "I am upwards of 330 years old, youngblood."

Dylah stopped and quickly scanned him. "You look like you're about twenty-six."

"I am not!"

"Did you just sass me, boy?" Flames pointed up at him above a slight smirk. She continued on through the forest as he followed. "I am older than you by a few years."

"I had grandchildren!"

"Oh you poor boy, I think you've gone mad." She laughed. "You see, maybe you really are the first Keilon, but there are very few records remaining of that legend, so as far as I can see, you are just a boy who is arguing with the Second in Command to the Fellowrock armies and the queen of Hightree." She lowered her voice. "Choose your next words very wisely."

"What am I supposed to do?"

"Easy." She turned to him with a wide grin. "I need a nanny."

"You want me to protect Cav?"

"Yes." Dylah continued to walk. "And be his friend, care for him when we can't, teach him things you wished you'd known, ya know, nanny stuff." She concealed her wide grin.

"I should warn you that he does occasionally have night terrors, though I do think they have stopped."

"Dylah, I killed you."

"I killed you too, little one, come on."

Old Keilon stood bewildered as her navy cape inched further away. "I don't think I've ever been called 'little one' in any of my lifetimes."

"I suggest you get used to it, little one."

"You do realize that your line of sight is very much below my shoulders, right?" He chuckled.

"Sometimes even lower." She quickly disappeared and reappeared in an instant.

He followed her silently. He thought over the second chance at living a life untainted by hurt, betrayal, and heartbreak. The thought of helping to raise a child he already adored kept his eyes a seemingly permanent lavender. The anticipation of what was to come was slowly erasing the burden of what had been.

"I really don't know why I always come back at this age," he finally said.

"I think there's a definite reason why you keep coming back young and strong." She stopped once more. "Because this is the point where it started to go wrong, at this point in your first life maybe you had done a few terrible things but you hadn't yet descended into tyrannical chaos. I don't know what bookmark in your life sealed you in your youth, but I'll be preventing such evils this time around."

It was in that moment that the first Keilon realized he was in fact, only twenty-five, the age he was when he forced his brother into exile.

Chapter 32

Crimson Dripping

Axen led a group of ten guards to his sleeping brother's chambers, walking in the center was his heavily restrained brother-in-law, Delin. Axen commanded the soldiers to wait in the hall as he entered the dark room.

He sighed looking at his brother's still frame on the bed. With all the commotion he hadn't visited Arkon in over a week. Axen opened the drapes, he spoke as if Arkon could hear him, he filled him in on the happenings around the kingdom and the adventure they had to take for the sake of Cav. It never got easier for Axen to talk without a reply.

After taking a few moments to soak in the stillness that called for no regal responsibilities, Axen called Delin in. He still couldn't look at the man who had seemed so feral in the forest. What hurt even more was the realization that a once solid friend had turned into an enemy so quickly.

"Knowing what you know now, can you reverse the damage?" Axen asked as Delin inspected the black circle that still remained on Arkon's neck. "Can you confirm it is the same serum you used on your sister in an attempt to steal your nephew?"

"I'll see what I can do," Delin replied dryly. "Can you take these off?" He lifted his bound hands.

"Not a chance."

Delin managed to roll Arkon onto his side, he inspected the wound that hadn't changed since the night it appeared. "It's the same."

"And you're sure?" Axen asked slowly, hiding the reaction he didn't think Delin deserved. "Because Dylah immediately lost consciousness but Arkon was awake for hours after it happened."

"The serum often varies depending on who made it, but the end results are always the same."

"And you think you can find an antidote?"

"Yes." Delin nodded. "If permitted and my jail cell is stocked with the needed equipment I can begin making a few tests." He took in a shaky deep breath and shook his head. "Again, only if that is allowed within my confinement."

"You talk like your captivity is unjust." Axen rolled his eyes.

"I just find it odd that I am constantly bound yet needed," he scoffed back, "but the man who should be bound is seen as only needed."

"You'll have to consult Dylah about that."

"You're okay with the man who killed your wife being the caretaker of your son?" Delin laughed. "If only you knew his history."

"I am aware that his history is pretty unsavory." Axen busied himself changing the low candles on Arkon's nightstand. "But my wife seems to trust him, my son adores him, he's not a bad conversationalist, and well, we once thought the world of you and you still betrayed us." He stopped and turned to Delin. "So maybe the past doesn't matter."

"I assure you that Cav never saw any malicious act."

"He saw you inject his mother. He was wide awake when you ripped him from her arms." Axen didn't give him the chance to defend his actions. "And we can't even erase that pain."

"Dylah's power doesn't work on him?" Delin asked. "Nevely's didn't either."

"You allowed that lunatic to try her power on my son?!"

"You allow a murderous tyrant around your son?!" Delin fired back.

"If Old Keilon has any ill intentions I assure you that Cav will warn us prior," Axen said with a smug smirk. "As you probably know my son sees the future."

"He told me there would be wolves." Delin shook his head. "He was howling that entire morning."

"And you still believe he wasn't meant to be ours?" Axen laughed if only to contain his anger. "Even with his eyes and your mother's gift you're still convinced that my son was the result of some tainted cosmic lottery."

"I've never had a problem with Cav's existence, it's the ripple in the laws of an ancient soul." Delin's demeanor darkened. "Can you really see my sister taking in her murderer like some lost puppy and believe that she is a fit parent?"

"I don't think you understand the deep rooted aspects of that ancient soul, of course she's giving him another chance, he's a part of her too." His usual smirk returned. "And I see that as being quite motherly."

"After everything our kingdoms have been through together, I can't believe what you've turned into." Delin shook his head. "I should've never met you in that tunnel."

"Actually, Delin," Axen said, meeting his dark gaze with a wide grin. "You never should have sent me away so many times when I came back looking for my friend. You should have just let us live our lives and make our own decisions. You never should have meddled. You cost me a decade away from my best friend and the love of my life." He watched as his brother-in-law tried to form the words but grew tired of waiting for any weak response he would spew. "Your treachery doesn't seem so spontaneous anymore, not after thinking of the way you've butted yourself into everyone's lives. Even meddling with that ancient soul you believe to be so precious, you split it like firewood and thought nothing of it until you were so easily swayed. You're only slipping now because you've actually gotten a consequence."

"Axen-"

"No need to be so friendly." Axen opened the doors and had the guards surround Delin. "You will address me by my title or not at all." He smiled as the guards pushed him out. "I would actually prefer not at all, not even through a message on a ribbon."

The guards were leading Delin through the halls of the Hightree castle, descending lower and lower to lock him up in the basement cells. Even though the castle was an architectural wonder with its vast workings of hallways and endless stairways, two people still managed to cross paths.

Delin looked past the surrounding guards and locked on him with a malicious grin as they drew closer.

The first Keilon willed his eyes to remain a steady green.

"Scum!" Delin barked.

"Silence!" a guard demanded.

"I'm not the one in chains, my friend." Old Keilon forced a laugh.

"You should be," Delin growled as they passed each other. "Weighed down with chains sinking to the bottom of the pond where you've always belonged."

The ghost tried to shake the words off, he had been focused on his new life for a few days now and was finally feeling like the terrors of his past were all just a bad dream. But as he walked towards the innocence of a child, he heard the low murmurs from the prisoner.

"Drowned, beaten, poisoned, exiled, betrayed." Delin laughed lowly. "And you were their king, the silver stag with crimson dripping from his antlers."

Chapter 33

Different

It was a calm morning for the small royal family in their suite of rooms. Dylah was drinking coffee as Cav sat across from her drawing page after page in a sketchbook his new caretaker had given him in an effort to channel and chart his visions. In the weeks since starting his third life, the first Keilon had been trying different tactics to help Cav feel confident in his power, and drawing seemed to grasp both joy and progress for the child.

"It'll snow tomorrow," Cav said as his pencil swirled depicting the clouds he knew were coming. "Uncle Keilon hates the snow."

"Again?" Dylah laughed. "We've gotten so much already."

"Can we throw snowballs at Uncle K?"

"Absolutely," she leaned closer with a sly grin. "It'll be an ambush."

She smiled at the thought of a game with her son who

found so much bliss in the clean snow, but since the events of a past battle, she'd always picture the snow tarnished by red and black.

"War eyes!" Cav giggled.

Dylah shook her head and forced her eyes to a happy lavender. "That just means that mama needs more coffee."

"And how many times have you gotten more coffee already?" Axen laughed as he walked into the room, fastening his green cape to his shoulders. He leaned over his son and looked at the page he was drawing. "A hand?"

Cav sighed. "I don't know how to draw it." He put his hand on the table and rapidly tapped his finger.

"Yeah I bet that's difficult to draw." Axen looked to his wife who was wearing a similar confused expression.

"Cav, why don't you go find your cape and wear it navy side out?" Dylah smiled. "To the trees!"

"Unmatched, unbroken!" he giggled back.

"Ah yes, the future king of Hightree." Axen laughed. "Were you planning on taking Keilon?"

"Be more specific."

"The twice resurrected legend of a man known for being a strong warrior that we have somehow managed to hire as our four year old son's nanny."

"Why didn't you just say that?" She grinned. "But yeah, why? Do you need him?"

"We're getting the first test from Delin today," he said flatly. "I already have our Keilon ready to use his eyes to make Delin truthfully say if he meddled with it at all. But I need the other Keilon to restrain him while he does that."

"That's a helluva plan, your majesty."

"Every precaution is necessary." His eyes met hers. "And I don't want you seeing that."

"Ah yes, I am quite dainty and easily frightened." She laughed.

"He's not the same anymore and it's difficult to see. You two grew up just a door apart, I want you to keep those memories."

"Fair enough."

The suite doors opened as the past and current kings walked in.

"I hate the snow." Keilon scowled. "Are we about ready?"

"Yeah, hope you guys have fun with that." Dylah took the last gulp of her coffee.

"Aren't you coming?" Keilon asked. "I'm holding him back, you're using your eyes."

"When I said Keilon would be holding back Delin, you agreed." Axen tried not to smirk.

"And he was referring to me." Old Keilon laughed. "Obviously."

"I thought you were talking about me, because then you said we'd use the eyes." Keilon shook his head. "I suppose that does add up, then what is Dylah doing?"

Dylah filled a thermos with the remaining coffee. "I am taking the boy to the trees for some added escape training."

"To the trees!" Cav ran into the room.

"We really should be specifying better." Keilon crossed his arms. "If he's sticking around this will get rather confusing."

"I said Keilon would be holding him back." Axen laughed. "Why would I talk about you like that if I was talking to you directly? Have you ever spoken to me and said 'Axen will be firing the arrows?'"

"Axen can stop talking now." Keilon grinned with a flash of embers.

"How much did you draw today?" The first Keilon asked as he made his way to the sketchbook on the table.

Cav opened the book and flipped through the pages. He explained each scribble with a wide smile, he reenacted the fast tapping finger, but when he flipped to the next page, the ghost's eyes streaked with pink.

"Care to explain this one, Cav?" he asked slowly.

"Yeah!" Cav giggled back. "The sun is going to be empty!

That's so weird!"

Old Keilon smiled. "That's called an eclipse and it's a sign of something big happening." His electric irises caught the two pairs of cloudy eyes staring back at him. "It's a sign of harmony."

"Okay, kiddo!" Dylah rushed over and slipped a thick knit cap over his head, letting her hands linger over her son's ears just long enough for her to whisper up to her predecessor, "Kunor?"

He nodded. "We come with lightning, he comes with sunlight."

Across the kingdom Kunor was lingering in the foyer of the castle, he couldn't help but pace and he tapped his fingers against his legs.

"Are you okay?" Sentry giggled.

"Uh yeah!" Kunor smiled after waiting so long for her to come down the staircase.

"I was wondering if you could finally give me that tour you offered when we first arrived?"

"It's very cold, are you sure?" He wanted to smack himself for nearly rejecting her offer.

"I guess we could wait."

"No!" Kunor said too eagerly. "It's a small kingdom, we won't be outside for too long."

He quickly grabbed the navy fur lined cloak he had waiting nearby and offered the other black one he had brought for her.

"This seems a bit small for you, why do you have this?" she giggled.

"Dylah keeps a few extras here, she won't miss it." His eyes went wide. "Well, at least I hope she won't."

"You worry differently than my mother does."

"Is that a good thing?" Kunor asked as he opened the castle door for her.

"I'll let you know."

Kunor showed her each training ground, he pointed to a clearing of purple light and adamantly told her that no one was allowed there without Dylah's permission. He walked her through the rundown neighborhood where he had grown up with a foster father that he would always adore. She said very little in return, just slowly nodded along to what he was saying.

"So you didn't know you were a prince until you were seventeen?" Sentry finally asked.

"Yeah, it's a long story, I only found out because I punched Dylah." He shrugged.

Sentry broke out into hysterical laughter. "You absolutely cannot leave it there, I need the whole story!"

"Aren't you getting cold?" he laughed back.

Her sigh released a cloud into the brisk air. "Yes, anywhere you can show me inside?"

Kunor looked to the ground in a string of thoughts with the common goal of staying at her side for as long as possible. "Yeah, actually!"

In a bout of excitement he grabbed her hand and pulled her in the direction of the castle courtyard, before realizing his quick advancement and releasing her fingers.

Sentry turned to study a nearby house in an effort to hide her wide smile from him.

Kunor led her to a door, then down a staircase that grew mustier with every step. Throughout the trek he told the story of his wild commander teaching him how to throw a punch, and how he had unintentionally shrank her due to a curse that protected his mother's bloodline.

"And that's how I found out Axen was my older brother." They descended even lower and the hall of steps narrowed. "After some digging he discovered that Keilon was actually my father through some rambunctious teenage love story. Well, actually he was the only teenager in the relationship." He paused. "My mother was a bit older than him, and we really don't talk about how terrible that was."

"Your mother sounds just about as great as mine."

They were now nearly shoulder to shoulder with no clear destination, and just when she was about to utter her first complaint she saw the long strip of torches in a tunnel that looked endless.

Kunor stepped further into the tunnel. "And when Dylah was planning a dangerous ruse on the ghost they snuck me down here to hide me in Hightree."

"This leads to Hightree?"

"Yeah! This is where they tested the cure, follow me!"

Finally they could hear the rushing water overhead, and soon came upon the prominent white line.

"So now you've seen all of Fellow-"

Sentry pushed him against the stony walls of the tunnel and planted her lips against his. "You're different," she said with a smile.

"In a good way?"

"Your bright eyes actually look happy, so yes, in a good way."

"My bright eyes?" Kunor laughed nervously.

Sentry pulled out her rapier and Kunor flinched when she held it up to his face.

"See, bright green, you must be happy."

Dylah pulled Cav through the forest, the sun reflecting off of the fresh snow was thrusting the thought of an impending eclipse to the front of her mind. It was exciting to think of Kunor taking over the full power of the soul, but there were also worries after seeing what that power could demand. Dylah squeezed Cav's hand tighter and trudged on.

They played hide and seek in the forest, she let him land punches against the palms of her hands, they found the perfect spot for their snowball attack the next day, and ended their chilly adventure by throwing rocks at the frozen pond. They challenged who could slide the rocks the furthest or who could knock the other's rock out of place. When they just couldn't stand the cold any longer they decided to head for the castle.

As they entered the courtyard Cav paused to study the facade of the castle.

"Can you guess where your Uncle Keilon's office is?"

Cav pointed to the fifth story. "The three windows."

"Right, and those don't open just for future reference." Dylah laughed.

"Why is there a deer on the banners?" Cav asked, studying the navy banners that hung on either side of the door.

"It's a symbol of Fellowrock," Dylah answered. "Your grandma made those banners before your Uncle Keilon was born," she shrugged. "I don't know why it's a stag, I think she just thought it looked tough."

"I like the antlers," he said looking up at his mother.

"Me too, kiddo." She smiled back, but the approaching laughter piqued her interest.

"Aunt Dylah," Kunor stammered as his eyes went nearly white from the shock.

"Your eyes are different," Cav loudly pointed out.

"Did he try the trick yet?" Dylah aimed the question at Sentry.

"No, he's still a little bit shaken up." She elbowed him, prompting him to turn with a grand smile and lime green eyes.

"Well it seems there is one emotion in common with sparking both chaos and harmony," Dylah said with a grand smile as amethyst eyes darted from Sentry to Kunor and back with a wink.

"Are you all having a meeting?" Keilon asked as he and the ancestor approached.

"No, just enjoying the lovely day." Kunor smiled.

"Now you decide to lie?" Old Keilon laughed. "You know we can see your eyes trying to pick a color, right?"

"Can he do the thing yet?" Keilon asked, leaning closer to his son with narrow eyes as Kunor tried to slowly take a step away.

"No, I already asked." Dylah turned to the ghost. "I thought you said the eclipse would mark his eyes changing?"

"I said no such thing." He rolled his eyes. "The eclipse marks the maturing just like the thunderstorm marked both of yours."

"Eclipse?" Kunor nearly whispered. "When?"

"When did you see the empty sun, Cav?" Old Keilon put a flat hand on the boy's head.

The boy shrugged. "There was no snow on the ground," Cav replied with his head tilted back to look up at him.

"Good. I hate snow," Keilon muttered.

"But you were born in a blizzard." Dylah concealed a laugh.

"Uncle Keilon, why is there a deer on the banners?" Cav turned his head to the king.

"Yeah, I've always wondered that too," Kunor added, happy that the subject had changed.

"It's not a deer," Old Keilon answered, studying the shine of the embroidery. "It's a silver stag."

Dylah noticed the familiar look of regret on his face. "Why don't you take the kid inside to get warmed up?"

The first Keilon wanted to say anything in return that would back pedal from the reaction of his answer, but he watched as she blinked briefly blue eyes to him followed by a nod to the doors as if to silently say she understood.

"How odd it is to watch you be so protective of a legendary warrior." Keilon laughed when the others had retreated into the warmth of the castle.

"Don't you feel the heaviness that surrounds him?"

"I do." He sighed. "When are we getting to the bottom of that?"

"We aren't." Dylah pointed fiery pink eyes up at him.

"Very odd." Keilon raised a brow over cloudy eyes.

"Any news on Arkon?" Dylah asked to change the subject.

"Yeah, actually." Keilon smiled. "He started tapping his finger!"

Chapter 34

Except Rocks

Dylah's back was flat against the bark of a tree, she took slow breaths pointed downward to hide the clouds that were rising with each exhale. A twig snapped, she was given her first signal. Her heart stopped, her narrow gaze found hazel eyes across the snowy forest.

Axen's eyes locked with the vibrant color of power only amplified by their bleak surroundings. He watched as she stood completely still, her hand tightly at her side ready for the attack. She flashed her eyes blue then green, the signal telling him to get ready.

Dylah waited until the crunching of steps grew almost too close for comfort, then she nodded and all hell broke loose.

Thunderous shouting rose as projectiles were thrown in a panicked haste. A mad scramble to see through the bombardment to determine who was the victor.

But victory came swiftly as their target fell to the trampled snowy ground in exhausted defeat.

"Are you kidding me?!" Kremon shouted with a laugh. "I just got my arm out of a sling and you pelt me with snowballs?"

Cav giggled. "I thought you were Uncle K."

"But I technically am Uncle K." Kremon tilted his head in the snow.

"He means the old guy," Dylah added.

"We gotta work on your observation skills, buddy." Axen laughed as he helped Kremon to his feet.

"No need." Dylah calmly tossed a tightly packed snowball in the air and caught it. "Everyone is a target when it comes to a snow battle."

Kremon's eyes lit up. "We haven't had a snow battle in ages!" It was the happiest he had seemed in the weeks since the altercation at Nevely's camp. "Let's make it a big thing like old times, I'll go grab my kids!" He shifted a questioning eye on Dylah. "All the same rules?" he whispered.

"No." Dylah rolled her eyes. "The king told me I can't put rocks in the middle, apparently that wouldn't be fair."

"Also dangerous," Axen added with a sigh. "Very dangerous, how do any of you still have eyes?"

"Meet in the foyer in an hour?" Kremon grinned. "I'm comin' for you, kid."

"My mama is going to punch you in the face."

"Oh." Kremon's smile fell. "Is that something that you saw?"

"No." Cav grinned.

Within the hour a crowd had gathered in the Fellowrock castle foyer. Kremon brought his twin sons, Taron and Terner, Bahn stood with his wife, Chany, along with their teenage sons. Also joining were Keilon and Kunor, Sentry and Navent, Axen, Dylah, Cav, and the first Keilon. They were all dressed in warm layers, warm beverages were passed around, as was a flask filled with a different type of warming liquid.

"Okay!" Dylah finally said to get their attention. "Same rules as always, well, except no rocks." Her eyes shifted to Axen and the Riloncks all visibly slouched with groans and murmurs.

"Dangerous!" Axen defended himself.

"Anyway!" Dylah began again. "We get out to that part of the forest, we scatter, it's a free for all, anything goes-"

"Except rocks," Bahn growled.

"Almost anything goes." Dylah laughed. "Everyone okay with battling in the snow again?" Her eyes went black and blue hoping the veterans of the same war understood what she was referring to while saving the innocence of their small children. "If needed, Chany has the thermoses of coffee and tea, or the kings each have flasks of a stronger brew."

"I will gladly trade a thermos for a flask." Chany grinned.

With very little warning they raced off hoping to be the first to claim a treasured hiding place. Dylah crouched next to Cav behind a particularly wide trunk as Axen stood close by. Brig and Kane had chosen to hide in the branches. Kunor and Sentry were not yet spotted while neither of the Keilons managed to hide their broad frames from view. It was all too still, then small shouts rang out causing everyone to scoop handfuls of the surrounding snow in their hands.

Dylah tilted her head to catch a glimpse of what was coming. The twins ran, just barely four year olds but their eyes were crazed as they progressed through the forest. Their arms swinging like windmills hurling the snowballs their following father supplied for them as he laughed hysterically.

Dylah's wide eyes met Axen's similar surprised expression.

"What do we do, mama?" Cav whispered. "They're getting closer."

Dylah's soul switched to commander. "Your father is going to stay here throwing snowballs at their weapon supply, while you and I gather at least one reinforcement to flank them."

After a collective nod, they split. Along the way of dodging between the trees, they ran into Keilon.

"Are you trying to take out these insane kids?" he asked with signs of distress and a swig from his flask.

"We're flanking!" Cav smiled.

"Great plan, Third in Command!" The king beamed.

"How about you stay with the kid," Dylah suggested, "and I'll sneak across and at your signal we knock 'em out."

Dylah jumped into the branches overhead hoping to sneak over the twins' path of destruction. She came across two other sets of green eyes shocked to see her in the trees.

"I am requesting an alliance," Dylah said with a grin. "Agree or perish."

Brig and Kane quickly nodded and followed her to the other side.

Below, the steady stream of twin fired snowballs had become intermittent as Kremon fended off relentless snowballs to the face.

Axen had gained the support of Navent who agreed to help with the front attack, allowing Dylah more time to form the other offenses.

At the sound of three sharp whistles a barrage of snowballs fell on the assailants, and soon everyone jumped through the trees in a free for all that was unlike any frenzy the non-Riloncks had ever seen.

Cav was on Old Keilon's shoulders, making him untouchable. Bahn and Chany stood back to back, seamlessly handing each other new well formed snowballs in a dance that seemed too well practiced. Kunor and Sentry had still not joined. Navent and Axen stayed in their strategic spots, Axen had quickly fashioned a strip of leather to the string of his bow, making him able to hurl snowballs from a great distance. And when Dylah felt an icy sphere crash against her head, she assumed it was Kremon and punched him in the face.

The snowballs flew from every direction and with such consistency that it was almost maddening trying to decipher which trajectory belonged to each person.

The fight continued with some running off to refill their supply. Chany began pulling the children out to offer them a thermos of warming cinnamon tea with hints of sweet vanilla. The adults took turns seeking out the kings for the contents of their flasks that warmed like fire and tasted like steady motivation. Between the whiskey and the constant laughter, the soldiers were kept in the present moment of fun, instead of being reminded of a past attack.

"Having fun?" Dylah laughed as she caught sight of Old Keilon stacking snowballs behind a nearby tree. She scanned the crowd to see that Cav had been passed to her oldest brother.

"This is madness!" he chuckled in reply. "How long has this been a tradition?"

"I think Keilon started organizing these soon after our parents died." She smiled. "It was either as a distraction for us or for him to subtly beat up his annoying siblings." She shrugged.

"How long does it last?"

"Usually until Bahn and Kremon get in a fist fight." She pointed to the crowd just in time for them to watch as Kremon lifted Terner to allow him to smash a snowball in Bahn's face. "So anytime now."

"And what happens after?"

"We can slide rocks across the pond." Dylah flashed a smile. "Cav likes that, but so did I when I was a kid."

"Not a fan of the water."

"Oh because of the old saying?" she asked just before taking aim at Brig.

"What old saying?"

"You know, well, maybe it wasn't around back then." She met his steady green eyes. "Don't go to the water, legend says you won't come back."

In a single blink Old Keilon's eyes went cloudy and blue.

"Oh, there's the fist fight." Dylah laughed before joining the group as they reached an armistice.

The first Keilon leaned against a tree to support the realization that the horror of his reign had somehow turned into a passing phrase.

Chapter 35

Laziest Day

Dylah and her oldest brother were waiting in the hall outside of Arkon's chambers.

"Last treatment gave us no results, still only tapping fingers." Keilon sighed. "Maybe we gave the doses too close together, it's only been a week since that first movement."

"I didn't want to tell Axen, I'd hate for him to get his hopes up," Dylah paused, "but Cav's prediction this morning included a nodding head."

"Has he given any updates on the eclipse?"

"Never mentioned it again."

"Well, at least you're probably feeling comforted that Nevely is dead." Keilon nudged her with his elbow. "One less thing to worry about."

"We don't know that for sure." Her voice was full of gravel. "You and I both have the changing eyes, so Kunor getting his doesn't mean she's dead."

"And that's why you have the ghost guarding your son?"

"One of the reasons, yes." She nodded. "Can we meet at the sparring field after this?"

"Always happy for the chance to throw a punch at you."

"Then why do you rarely land them?" she snickered back.

The door creaked open.

"Okay, you two can come in," Axen nearly whispered.

The room looked as cheery as it could. Orange drapes opened to let in the bright winter sunlight, flowers in ornate vases staggered throughout the available surfaces, the clean scent of fresh candles filled each of their slow and steady breaths as they approached the bed.

"You damn Farein," Keilon managed to say with cloudy eyes.

Dylah watched in amazement as Arkon's right pointer finger began tapping.

"He just called me a wretched Rilonck." Keilon laughed watching the finger tap faster as if to agree.

"Will you roll him so I can administer the next treatment?" Axen pointed the question at Keilon.

With Arkon on his side Axen poured the gel Delin had made on a swab and pushed away a few long hairs blocking the wound that was now only a dark shade of gray.

"Remind me to ask for the name of the nurse in charge of cutting his hair." Axen sighed. "Unacceptable."

"Being a king really does shorten your nerves," Keilon added, hoping to ease Axen's worries.

"Yeah," Dylah chimed in. "Keilon once fired a maid because she showed up in a wrinkly dress to clean his room first thing in the morning."

"That sounds odd." Axen half laughed as he readied the needle. "Care to explain, your majesty?"

Keilon sighed, and if he were not helping to keep Arkon on his side he would have pinched the bridge of his nose too. "Dylah, she wasn't a maid."

Dylah laughed. "Well if she wasn't a maid then-" She

read his arched eyebrow. "Girlfriend, got it."

"I'm glad it took you so long to realize that." He chuckled. "The repercussions of that interaction sent me into an existential crisis."

"Well I remember that part."

Axen was grateful for the distraction as he injected the center of his brother's ominous wound. He was stuck in a whirlwind of excitement, relief, and not wanting to get his hopes up over a few wiggling fingers. They lowered Arkon back against the bed and stood in a moment of silence that rang loud with questions and worries.

"Now we wait," Axen said, breaking the quiet.

Cav was skipping through the castle gardens as the first Keilon slowly followed, his eyes reflecting the true joy he was experiencing in the presence of the child, but his fake grin hiding the thoughts in his head.

A week had passed since he learned that the phrase that originated three hundred years prior somehow survived the ages but lost the intended meaning it once bore. Old Keilon often woke in the middle of the night gasping for air as the water in his dreams filled his lungs and drowned his mind. He knew that his newfound friend was starting to sense his wavering mood, he saw her worry in every quick glance, but he just couldn't bring himself to finally put his first life and death into words.

"These ones are lilacs! But they aren't blooming yet!" Cav shouted. "Mama has a whole field of them!"

"Does she?" The first Keilon's smile curved with a genuine tinge of happiness.

"We should go to Fellowrock!" Cav jumped on the edge of one of the raised planters and tiptoed along the edge. "We haven't shown you all of Fellowrock yet!"

"I bet it's a very beautiful place, Cav." He laughed, not wanting to break the child's illusion.

"You have to ask mama to show you the field though, or

she'll be mad and show you her war eyes."

"Sounds scary!" He changed his eyes to black. "Do they look like this?"

"Hers are scarier!" he said with a giggle. "You can ask her to take you there after she shows you the pond." Cav jumped off the planter and ran to the next row.

"What?" He tried to remain calm as he took brisk steps after him. "The pond?"

"Yeah!" Cav flashed a smile. "You'll like it! We can catch toads some time!"

"Your mama and I are going to go to the pond?"

"She's going to be sad," Cav shrugged, "probably because she hates toads."

The ghost swallowed the words and shuddered when they tasted like murky water.

"Any other fun places I should know about?" Old Keilon asked when he knew he no longer had to force the color of his eyes.

"There's a tunnel!"

"Really?" He turned and muttered into his shoulder, "How long has that been there?"

An hour had passed since Arkon's injection. Axen was called to address a matter he didn't find very important, but while he was gone, the oldest and youngest Rilonck siblings sat in a slow going conversation hoping the words would spark Arkon's consciousness.

"Any particular reason you're wanting to fight me?" The reigning Keilon laughed. "Is there something I should know? A certain grievance against me that I haven't caught on to yet?"

"No." Dylah rolled her eyes. "There's just something I've been wanting to try."

"Have I not already trained you in everything?"

"I want to be dual wielding."

"Dual wielding?" Keilon raised an eyebrow. "Is carrying

nine daggers not good enough?"

"I like throwing the daggers and having one handy at all times." In an instant she held a dagger in both fists. "But I want to fight with one in each hand."

"Okay, I don't have a whole lot of pointers in that matter, but we can try it."

Axen opened the door followed by an immediate head tilt. "Daggers?"

Dylah quickly returned her weapons to their sheaths. "Don't worry about it."

"Of course, princess." Axen smirked. "Any change?"

"Nothing yet," Keilon said with a supportive nod. "Key word being 'yet!'"

Axen stood at the edge of the bed. "Aloria got her stitches out today," he said to his brother and watched as the fingers tapped slowly. "She's getting her energy back." The fingers tapped faster. "Avalia is at the point in her pregnancy where she runs out of the room every twenty minutes, it's still as funny as it was the first three times." Axen stared at the fingers tapping out the cadence of a laugh he hadn't heard in half a year.

"You have about thirty more siblings to update him on." Keilon grinned. "Want me to pull up a chair?"

"The point is to make him want to answer, not bore him further into his sleep." Axen laughed. "And I can't tell him what I know about Kunor because, well, you're here."

"I'll have you know that I am mildly aware of my son's friendship situation." Keilon rolled his eyes.

"Maybe today just isn't the day." Dylah stared at the former king's still face.

"Yeah, maybe." Axen slumped slightly. "We'll give it another hour then I'll post the rotation of nurses."

"Let's move our training to tomorrow morning." Keilon flashed electric eyes at his sister. "Because we're staying here as long as it takes."

"That's right!" Dylah grabbed Axen's hand.

Sunlight dulled as moonlight brightened. The room remained still, except for the fingers still tapping in response. Dylah stepped out to check on Cav and the other young man she had decided was in her care too. Keilon held a brief whispered meeting in the hallway to assign certain duties to his brothers and son. Axen supervised a haircut.

The candles were nearing their last inches of wax as Dylah's loud yawn shook the kings awake.

"Let's get some rest," Axen answered with his own yawn while stretching his arms.

"Are you sure?" Keilon asked.

"Yeah, it's okay, we'll try again in a few days." Axen nodded.

"Let's not tell the others that we all basically just took the laziest day off." Dylah muffled a laugh.

"I think we deserved it." Keilon chuckled. "And, hey, I bet Arkon enjoyed the company!" He stood and laid a hand on his friend's still shoulder. "Isn't that right, you damn Farein?"

Keilon's eyes fell to the fingers he'd hoped would tap back a voiceless response, but instead, with eyes still closed, Arkon nodded.

Chapter 36

The Silver Stag

Cav was spending his morning scribbling the images he had seen in his dreams. Axen stared out the window at the thawing kingdoms below, he yawned into his coffee mug and glanced over to be sure his son was still occupied.

The night had provided him a victory in the form of head nods from Arkon. Where he had let Dylah and Keilon go, he stayed until the sun was peeking over the horizon promising the joy of another day. Axen asked Arkon countless questions and every subtle up and down or side to side shake of his head seemed like the most impressive physical feat.

He returned to their suite and soaked up two hours of sleep before his mind told him to make a plan. Within Dylah's first cup of coffee and before Cav had woken up, Axen had charted his prediction of response progression in Arkon. First the tapping of fingers, now the nodding of his head, and soon opened eyes or even spoken words were possibilities.

"What's the news, buddy?" Axen asked walking to refill his coffee, thankful that Dylah wasn't there to point out the first signs of an acquired addiction.

"The snow will melt today," Cav mumbled as he continued scribbling. "Who hasn't seen you in a while?"

"What do you mean?" Axen sat across from him. "Is that something you saw?"

"Kind of." Cav shrugged. "I heard 'I haven't seen you in so long' then I saw your face go like this." He mimicked his father's usual surprised wide eyes.

"I don't look like that." Axen smirked. "Both of my eyes are brown."

Axen's mind began narrowing down a list of names of people he hadn't seen in a while. They ranged from far off dignitaries and former possible suitors from what felt like a lifetime ago. Soon, it clicked. His brother's voice. The thought woke him up more than his third cup of coffee had.

The door to the suite opened.

"Sorry to barge in." Old Keilon slowly closed the door.

"I knew you were coming." Cav grinned without looking up from his paper.

"Thanks for the warning, kid!" Axen laughed. "But really, I thought Dylah told you to take the day off since you ended up hanging out with Cav all day yesterday?"

"She did," he answered slowly. "I was actually hoping to talk to her, is she here?"

"Mama took her daggers to Fellowrock." Cav looked up. "A lot of daggers."

"Keilon is going to help her with a new skill she's been meaning to try," Axen added for clarity. "They're at the sparring fields behind the Fellowrock castle."

"Thanks." He turned back towards the door but after a breath he looked back at Axen. "Ya know, you really do remind me of him."

"I'm sorry, who?" Axen smirked.

"Brennit." Old Keilon smiled. "It's not just the cape and

general Farein features." He paused and studied the way Axen leaned towards his son. "You both just really strived for peace, I hope you recognize how great that is."

Axen shifted his eyes to make sure his son wasn't paying attention. "Third life making you a little soft, huh?"

He turned back to the door with a chuckle. "It really is."

Dylah already had one wooden dagger slapped from her left hand, and in one fluid motion she jumped, aiming her remaining dagger at Keilon's shoulder. He hit his forearm against hers throwing off her trajectory and loosening her grip enough to disarm her.

"Why is this so hard?" Dylah asked, catching her breath.

"Why are you so set on doing it?" Keilon handed her the training daggers she had dropped. "Want to keep trying?"

"Absolutely." Her pink eyes triggered his to reflect the power that fueled them both.

Dylah positioned herself on the edge of the circle, Keilon across from her. She gripped the wooden daggers as Keilon held the familiar wooden training sword he typically used. With the smallest nod that she had known to be the signal for decades, she charged forward. Dodging each swing he threw, jumping back and hearing the smack as she let her shorter fake blades crash against his single mimicked sword.

He threw an elbow, she ducked to miss it and looked up in time to see the dull wooden blade nearing her face, like a reflex she held up her crossed daggers to shield herself. The realization of a successful block made her lightning shine brighter and a wicked smile form on her face. She threw a knee into his side, kicked him back a few steps and began dodging his swipes while hitting his blade with more speed and accuracy than before.

Just like in any of their other successful fights, they soon had a rhythm of constant unwavering hits, but an end was approaching. Dylah once again shielded herself with daggers crossed, but funneled her strength into her right arm to keep the block as her left wooden dagger smacked at his knuckles. The shock gave her an opportunity to disarm him and finally hold the rounded point up to his neck.

"I think you're getting the hang of it, little sister."

"It would be more fun if I could use real ones." She rolled her eyes.

Keilon inspected the knuckles he knew would bruise. "I'd rather keep my fingers."

"Yeah," a voice emerged from the surrounding trees. "That wasn't bad, youngblood."

"Any pointers on dual wielding, old man?" She held the daggers by their faux blades prompting him to take the handles.

"Daggers, a few." He shrugged. "But I started dual wielding swords at just seventeen, and that's an entirely different method."

"Well, that's a coincidence." The reigning Keilon elbowed his sister.

"It's not." The first Keilon purposely ignited his pink irises. "Which elbow do you typically throw? Left?"

"Yes," Dylah replied with a raised eyebrow, pondering the similarities.

"So, until you've mastered the mid-fight flip," he said as he briefly flipped his left dagger in the air and effortlessly caught it with the blade pointing down. "Hold your left dagger pointing down so you don't accidentally fatally stab yourself while throwing an elbow strike."

"That's fantastic," Dylah whispered with glowing eyes.

"Yeah?" He chuckled as he calmly tossed both fake daggers, alternating which direction their points were facing. "And it's a great distraction." With his right dagger pointing up and his left pointing down he turned to the king. Old Keilon held the left dagger pointing at his prodigy's shocked face and his right dagger pressing into his stomach. "See if these were real, you'd be very dead."

"If I wasn't such a fair and patient king, you'd be very

dead," Keilon growled back.

Old Keilon flashed a smile and lowered the fake weapons.

"I think that's all I needed for today," Dylah said as her face held a steady smirk.

Keilon returned to the castle, Dylah organized the wooden weapons and sheathed the real daggers she had brought with high hopes.

"Are you off wandering the woods for the day, youngin?" she laughed.

"Actually," his voice slightly rattled. "I would like to show you something."

Dylah followed silently as he led her through the familiar woods, she kept her wits about her, confused by the situation at hand.

"Before we go any further," he paused to take a breath. "I would just like you to know that this part of our history has been cleared to the best of my ability."

"So what you're saying is that you're not the star of the fairytale I was told as a child?" Dylah smiled in the shadows of the trees. "I can handle it. Can you?"

His mind replayed the moment Cav had told him that Dylah would be standing by the pond with blue eyes. "Maybe."

Dylah walked past him and looked at the calm ripples. "Does this have something to do with you not being a fan of the water?"

"It has everything to do with that."

They stood on the edge staring at the water to avoid the other's nervous gaze, and with a deep breath, the first Keilon finally began to depict the horrors of his first life.

"They held me under," he started. "They thought that making me approach death would trigger the soul to rise for the sole purpose of saving me. Most of the time they did it in the winter, one time they even chiselled out a hole in the ice, and plugged it once I went under."

"Bastards," Dylah growled.

"I am just getting started, youngblood." He elbowed her and was thankful for a break at the beginning of his tale. "Other times they bound my hands to a fallen branch then lit it on fire, hoping that the impending burns would also ignite the soul." He paused. "When I was about eighteen they began renting me out to any passing army. I fought in wars for kingdoms I didn't even know the name of. I had been trained extensively, because again, they believed the strain of war would awaken my power." He finally looked at her. "I was quite skilled at dual wielding swords, I kept them sheathed in an X on my back. Because I was seen as so very special these swords were also special, their hilts were silver, and they stuck out from each shoulder. Thus, I got the nickname of the silver stag."

"Because the hilts looked like antlers." She smiled.

"Exactly." He returned to staring back at the water. "I finally got the power one day after Tovin told me he would not be accepting my proposal to Teyle. I remember she walked me to the treeline, I was so angry, and when I turned to look back at the castle, my eyes finally turned pink."

"Mine turned pink out of vengeance too."

"You know most of what follows, Teyle was sent away for awhile, she came back and we tried to run away, we were attacked in the woods, I nearly died. Then they killed Enfy, and you were right, that's what sparked my rampage." He sighed. "First I commanded my father to round up the five high elders. I looked at each one of them and told them to sink to the bottom of the pond they had held me under so many times. I felt nothing watching them drown. Then the war with Hightree was in full swing, I saw my opportunity, I killed my father." His voice lowered. "With a practiced flip of a dagger."

"Was there a reason?"

"Not a good one." Old Keilon looked to the dirt. "My oldest brother, Hekar, quickly became king. We actually got along pretty well but he was set on drafting peace agreements despite my commands. So in another battle, he fell too at my hand." He sighed. "The battles had slowed, so I poisoned my other older brother, Endast, making myself the king. The war continued, we lost, we were cursed. My mother succumbed to her own disappointment. Time passed and we were doing okay, then I exiled Sorner." His breath caught in his throat as he heard his brother's last words to him echo in the corners of his mind. "That was the most horrible thing I've ever done."

"That's where it went wrong, huh?" She stared at the ground too.

"Without his balance I became unstoppable." He shook his head. "I had the rest of the elders drowned, and that's how the religion Enfy had lived her life devoted to died. I took great satisfaction in that manner of death. Throughout my reign I had other tactics of execution and punishment. Fire, daggers, needles, the screams that echoed in this forest because of me became endless." He shuddered. "And that's when the second half of my nickname really bore meaning, the silver stag with crimson dripping from his antlers." The former king watched the ripples spread over the pond after a single fallen leaf. "But most of the time, I called them to the water for their death. Any small grievance, any signs of an uprising, anything, I called them here. A code began to circulate the kingdom."

"Don't go to the water," Dylah whispered, "legend says you won't come back."

"That's the one."

"I had no idea."

"Good, I made sure this part of our history died. I wanted the next one to be born not knowing what they were or how much they were capable of. You needed to grow into the power on your own, you needed to fail and feel terrible about it, you needed to see the good in it."

"I do."

"Because they thought they were preparing me to be a weapon, and now their bones are at the bottom of this pond." He closed his eyes tightly. "My bones are at the bottom of this pond."

"What?" Her quiet voice shook.

The first Keilon found the courage to look at her and saw the tears flooding her deep blue eyes.

"I lived a long life, almost made it to eighty." He let his eyes match hers in color and depth. "But towards the end I fell very ill. I could barely move and I was ready to die. It had become apparent many times in my wretched life that chaos never truly wants the evil of violence, but that's all I ever gave it." He blinked rapidly and turned back to the water. "My son was ready to become king so they didn't bother waiting, and I don't blame them. They chanted as they lowered me in the water. I remember seeing the sunlight swirl through the ripples, I remember sinking lower and lower, it felt just like home." He let out a sigh. "Then I woke up in a forest where time stood still, I was this age again, and I was told to wait." He slowly took a deep breath. "For you."

Dylah's face fell into her hands as she began to sob.

"Then I came back that first time, I saw you so new to the power, so unaware of what you could do. I was set on making you stronger so you could always keep your head above the water. But something clicked, the vengeance returned and instead of lifting you up I wanted to push you under and give myself another chance with all the same old tricks." He looked at her again, still lost in an overwhelming sadness. "It was a miracle that I was brought back for the third time, and I immediately saw Keilon with his brand new power treading water, and you, you have two feet on dry land at all times. You both are thriving and commanding with a natural grace that I had but couldn't wield on my own. That's why this time around all I can think about is the water in this pond weighing me down and sinking my bones further into the scum where they belong."

Her face finally tilted to look at him, tears still streaking her face, her eyes resembling the depths he was just describing. But she didn't say a word.

"I understand if you want me to leave and never see your child again." He shook his head. "I knew I couldn't spend another moment with him until you knew the truth."

Old Keilon was ready for any terrible thing she would say. His eyes glanced at her hand, and he knew that if she were to point a dagger at him he would do nothing to prevent the impending death she could give him once more. He was expecting to see fear and sadness in her eyes, instead Dylah grabbed his elbow and pulled him back to the forest.

"What are you doing?" he asked, fearing they'd soon be met by a council of those ready to put him to death.

She stopped abruptly, put her hands on his shoulders and began shaking him. "Your bones are here!"

"Dylah-"

She smacked his face. "You're alive again, don't you dare think for one more moment that you're the same skeleton at the bottom of that pond!" Her grip returned to his elbow as she continued to pull him through the trees. "Come on, you never need to see this place again."

He planted his feet into the dirt, the sudden stop made Dylah nearly lose her balance.

"I don't want to live this life in complete ignorance of the terror I caused, I tried, but it's all so haunting."

"But we never knew that history!" She glared at him, but her face softened when a question came to her. "How did you erase that history?"

"Eyes."

"Of course." She nodded. "Well you have a new job, old man."

"I understand."

"No, no, no." She laughed. "You're still my son's favorite person."

"Really? So what's the new job?"

"You're going to write down all of those terrible events, be the voice for the people you wronged." Dylah watched the blue deepen in his eyes. "And I will have it sealed for Cav to open when he's the king." She smiled. "So after we're both dead. You can add a note at the front explaining the situation and how he knew you as a different person. He'll understand."

"I can live with that." He grinned back.

They walked back towards the border of Hightree, Dylah explained she knew rooms where his writing would be kept private, she even offered to use the curse that he caused to put them in a place only she could find.

Once they took a single step through the ashen treeline they stopped, eyes pinned on the sun.

The eclipse had begun.

Chapter 37

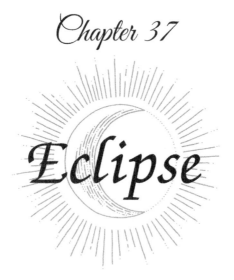

Eclipse

Axen yawned through a morning of kingly duties with his son at his side, before leaving him with Avalia to attend to their older brother. He couldn't shake the prediction of someone telling him that they hadn't seen him for awhile, and after Cav had successfully predicted the finger taps and head nods, he knew he must've meant Arkon too.

Keilon joined him too after his morning of fending off the newest dual wielder in the Rilonck bloodline.

"He found Dylah, right?" Axen asked. "He seemed a little worried."

"Yeah, I caught on to that too." Keilon smiled. "She'll get to the bottom of it."

"Remember the first thing you said to Arkon?" Axen smirked.

"My name is King Keilon Rilonck," he forced the proud voice he had used to intimidate them years ago when he declared the long awaited war. "Named after the first great Keilon Rilonck."

Arkon's fingers tapped and his head shook side to side in disagreement.

"And are you still holding on to that statement?" Axen held back a laugh.

"My name is King Keilon Rilonck, named after the first Keilon Rilonck, only much more level headed and planning to live just one life."

"Now that would have been a great introduction." Axen nodded along with Arkon.

"Actually, will I come back like the old guy?" Keilon seemed to slump in thought. "Or does that job only go to Dylah?"

"You're asking the wrong person." Axen shrugged. "Do you think Sorner came back when Nevely's power first rose?"

"Something tells me that resurrection isn't seen as harmonious to the rules of life." His eyes grayed as he mulled over the possibilities. "Does that sound right? Apparently I'm full of chaos and wouldn't understand."

"You're still asking the wrong person." Axen laughed.

"So you think he'll start talking soon?" Keilon straightened his posture and changed the subject. "How long do you think I have to prepare myself for one of his long winded meetings?"

"Hard to tell, Cav can rarely specify when these events will happen."

"Well let's just ask the guy!" Keilon propped his legs on the bed and nudged Arkon with his boot. "You going to talk to us?"

Axen tried not to smile when Arkon nodded.

"Now would be great!" Keilon added with a laugh.

Arkon shook his head.

"You don't have to be so stubborn," Keilon huffed.

A shadow seemed to fall over the room. Axen stood and went to the window.

"It's happening," he whispered before turning back to

Keilon. "You need to go find Kunor."

Keilon was on his feet and out the door before Axen could add another word.

Axen's eyes darted from his sleeping brother to the door leading to their younger brother. He wrestled with who needed his attention more, then headed to catch up with Keilon in the hall.

Dylah and Old Keilon checked the Fellowrock castle, but came up empty. Sentry joined them too, she told them that she was very young when the eclipse came at the emergence of her mother's power and that it made Nevely frightened and disorientated. Old Keilon added that when the eclipse came for Sorner it made him incoherent and unlike himself. The three of them ran through the trees, then Sentry thought of another place.

"Are you sure this stairway was made by Riloncks?" the first Keilon said, ducking his head and sliding against the wall as they descended lower.

"Made to deter the weak," Dylah responded with a smile.

Seeing the torchlit tunnel made them pause to take a breath.

Sentry didn't wait for them and kept stomping forward, looking for her newfound love.

"How long has this been here?" the ghost whispered, his head on a swivel.

"Delin once told me they built it less than two hundred years ago, so not made in your time." She too kept walking forward. "They employed allies to build the other side."

They walked further until Dylah stopped and held up a halting hand.

"What's wrong?" he asked with wide eyes.

She pointed to the ceiling. "We're about to be under a river, you'll be able to hear the water, just wanted to warn you."

At the end of the tunnel they finally caught up to Sentry

who was tapping her foot.

"I don't know how to open it!" she nearly shouted.

"Just take a step, it'll open." Dylah tried not to laugh at Sentry's quick transition from rage to amazement.

Emerging from the tunnel prompted confusion, as mid day was barely brighter than the night. All three stared at the blocked out sun as the dark circle slowly began to uncover it.

Sentry went towards the target fields.

Dylah said she would check each of the three decks.

Old Keilon elected himself to weave through the endless hallways.

They split in separate directions with a nod.

Axen was unable to catch up to the reigning Keilon, but he figured that if it was his son he'd be sprinting to his side too. He went up and down many stairwells, through hallways only used by maids and nannies. If Kunor was anywhere, he wasn't in the Hightree castle.

Axen paused to take a breath and catch a glimpse at the eclipse. The sun was quickly returning to it's full circumference and he hoped that someone had found his little brother who was now in complete possession of an ancient soul.

He walked a little slower as he made his way down the main stairway, deciding to collect Cav from Avalia and head to Fellowrock. But, as he turned a corner he was slammed into the wall, a strong forearm against his chest, soon staring up into bright green eyes.

"I haven't seen you in so long!"

"Do we know each other?" Axen asked the strange man.

"Has it been too long?" The man released his grip. "Do you not remember me, Brennit?"

"Brennit?" Axen shook his head. "My name is Axen, I'm the king of Hightree." He took a step away from the man's stare. "Who are you?"

The man shook his head in disbelief. "Axen?"

"No," Old Keilon said from down the hall, he was quickly

at Axen's side.

"It's not so nice to see you again, Keilon." The man's voice darkened.

"Who is this?" Axen asked, growing agitated but noticing the blank cloudy gaze of the ghost.

"Sorner."

Chapter 38

Bunnies

"Keilon, please." Sorner rolled dark green eyes. "You don't have to force that blank color for my sake. Let me see a wild one!"

"I'm not." Old Keilon shook his head. "I'm entirely shocked and they won't pick a color."

"Why are you so young? Why am I so young?" Sorner took a step closer to his brother. "This is the Hightree castle, how are we here? And tall, so tall. I simply forgot the feeling of being tall! It's somewhat frightening to be so tall."

"Do you want to tell him?" Axen asked with wide eyes pinned on the first Keilon.

"And you've changed your name?" Sorner again stood too close to Axen. "Brennit is a lovely name, why change it to Axen?" The syllables of the unfamiliar name seemed to combat in his mouth.

"Are you not here for Kunor?" Axen took a step back.

"Who?"

"Your prodigy." Old Keilon methodically propped a

straight arm against the wall to make a barrier between his brother and Axen. "The new soul of harmony, the eclipse came, he has the full power. Are you not here to teach him?"

"Did you already come back for your other prodigy, Nevely?" Axen added.

"Who?!" Sorner repeated.

"Something is off here," Axen whispered.

"Sorner, it's been three hundred years since the curse was placed." The first Keilon held up empty hands hoping to break the news gently.

"Come on, you've told better jokes than that!" Sorner crossed his arms. "You expect me to believe that three hundred years have magically passed? What did you do, brother? Execute death so you could live forever?"

"No, Sorner, I've already died twice now." He grinned. "I came back once to teach my prodigy, Dylah, and I've come back again to teach the other half of the new soul, Keilon."

"And now you think I've come back to do the very same?" Sorner chuckled nervously in the gaps of quick deep breaths. "Being a living ghost is preposterous! You think I would allow such a twisted turn around the most basic rule of life?"

"I was just discussing this this morning," Axen whispered to the ghost he was most familiar with.

"More importantly, you think I wanted to see you again? You dislodged nearly every morsel of joy I had in my life and had me sent away in a basket," Sorner scoffed. "Not you, Brennit, I of course missed you terribly."

"I appreciate the sentiment," Axen started, "But I am Axen, not Brennit. I am very sorry."

Sorner calmly tilted his head. His golden curly hair was tightly pulled back into a neat bun that rested on the curve of his skull. His eyes warped between shades of green as he switched from confusion to panic within each blink.

"Sorner." Old Keilon held his brother's shoulders tightly. "I know this is a lot to take in, but there is a young man somewhere in these two kingdoms who has just felt a fire light in his soul, he is scared and he will need your guidance."

Sorner kept his constantly changing eyes on Axen. "You trust my terrible brother?"

"I do." Axen nodded. "He helped save my son."

"That's odd." Sorner turned to his brother again. "The thought of you with children is a little incomprehensible for me. Actually, quite laughable. Though, I never got to see you as a father, did that change you at all?"

"Not at all, I was a horrible father."

"So my instincts were correct." Sorner took a deep breath. "Fine, take me to this supposed prodigy."

Two sets of steps were heard approaching down the hall. The first Keilon stood to hide his brother from any passerbys, as Axen peeked around the corner.

"Oh good," Dylah said with a relieved smile. "Sentry is with Kunor in the gardens."

"He is in a bit of shock," the reigning Keilon crossed his arms. "And decided he didn't like our, how did he put it again?"

"'Bag of pine needles and mud souls.'" Dylah smiled widely. "We thought maybe he'd talk to you." She glanced around the corner.

"Are you kidding me?!" Sorner raised an eyebrow. "This one's got the eyes too!"

"Who are you?!" Keilon took a step closer.

"You too?!" Sorner smacked his brother's shoulder. "You really weren't lying, that is a lovely surprise."

Dylah read the strange man's features. Took note of his familiarity with the man who was seen as a ghost to so many, and his changing eyes.

"Well that makes sense," Dylah said. "Of course you'd come back too!"

Sorner took a step to study his brother's prodigy. "And this one is a Rilonck?" He raised an eyebrow to his brother.

"Yes," the first Keilon responded slowly.

Sorner glanced back at Dylah, then whispered, "Are you sure?" He glanced at her again. "She's quite small for our bloodline."

"I'm sure." He flashed electric pink eyes at Dylah.

She took the hint and made her eyes transition through every color as she immediately drew two daggers, spun them, and returned them to their sheaths. "I'm a Rilonck."

"Married to a Farein, though," Axen added with a laugh.

"Hm." Sorner thought through the new developments in a list of many. "The panicked boy first, then I have an insane amount of questions. To the gardens then?"

Axen led them through the castle gardens, fending off the constant stares of the newest tall blonde man.

"You say it's been three hundred years?" Sorner pointed the question back to his brother. "And this isn't Brennit?"

"I'm still just Axen."

"Never refer to yourself as 'just' anything!" Sorner forced himself to look ahead, slowly coming to terms that the man next to him was not his former lover. "You are so much more than 'just' you!"

"Has he always been so uplifting?" Dylah elbowed her predecessor.

"His training was vastly different than mine," the first Keilon whispered back. "Kittens were involved quite often."

"Perfect!" Sorner clapped his hands together before scurrying down a row of flowers.

The group watched with confusion as the newest ghost tiptoed gracefully, then lunged out of sight only to return calmly petting a rabbit.

"He's down this way," Keilon said, breaking up the odd moment.

Kunor was sitting on the ground, his back against a tall planter, he was slowly spinning a daffodil in his hands, staring at it with blank pale green eyes.

Sentry stopped the group a few steps away.

"He seems to be calming down, but still not saying

much, just making overly happy descriptions about his surroundings." She turned back to him and half smiled.

"Sentry!" Kunor called out. "This daffodil is the color of the most graceful butterfly floating on a calm breeze in mid morning! Don't you think?"

"Yes!" Sentry answered quickly before turning back to the group and letting her smile fall. "See, sappy stuff like that."

"Your hair is beautiful!" Sorner stepped forward and loosely held one of her tight curls while still cradling the rabbit in his other arm. "My children's hair was a similar color." He smiled. "Like copper gently kissed by berry wine and oh so curly! Absolutely lovely!"

"Yours is curly too." She tilted her head.

"No, no." Sorner pointed to his head. "Mine is actually in a bun."

"Do I know you?" Sentry furrowed her brow.

Old Keilon stepped forward with a hand on his brother's shoulder. "Just talk to the boy."

"Always the hasty one, Keilon." Sorner huffed, then patted the rabbit's head. "Never one to stop and take in the subtle brush strokes of life's great painting."

Sorner sat with his back against the planter next to Kunor.

Kunor turned his head to face the strange man. "You give off the air of blooming flowers after a clean brief rain, and the sun has broken through the clouds making the raindrops smile."

"That was beautiful." Sorner grinned. "And also absolutely correct."

"Souls of harmony," the first Keilon muttered through a sigh, as his prodigies covered their smirks.

"Here, hold this precious creature." Sorner placed the rabbit in Kunor's arms. "He is the personification of what we are."

"Bunnies?" Kunor said slowly as his fingers felt the soft

fur.

"We are harmony, peace, order, alignment." Sorner placed his hand on the rabbit's head and began to gently rub its ears. "Just like this creature we roam these lands quietly, we approach with softness and clarity. We flourish in the spring, we become a loving part of our surroundings."

"Oh." Kunor nodded.

"Look at me, watch my eyes."

Kunor tilted his head. "They're like mine."

"Actually, yours are like mine."

"Who are you?"

"Sorner Rilonck, soul of harmony, you're my prodigy, youngblood."

"Did he just?" Axen whispered to Dylah.

"I'll explain later," Old Keilon whispered back.

"Look at my eyes, see the yellow?" Sorner asked Kunor.

"Yes, how do I do that?"

"Think of a dark cloudy day and picture the sun growing so large it dissipates the darkness and the clouds." Sorner smiled. "Be the sun."

Kunor closed his eyes and took a deep breath. When he opened them they shone like sparkling sunlight. "Now what?"

Sorner turned to the waiting crowd. "Any volunteers?"

Keilon took quick steps and joined the opposition of his own soul. He sat on the other side of his son. "Let me have it."

Kunor calmly placed the rabbit on Keilon's lap.

"No," Sorner laughed. "He meant use your power."

"Why didn't he just say that then?" Kunor raised a brow.

"Souls of chaos." Sorner grinned showing all his teeth. "They tend to not be very clear."

Kunor turned to his father. "This feels weird."

"That's perfectly fine." Sorner put a hand on his shoulder. "Lock on to his gaze and hold it."

Yellow irises met clouds, but soon the clouds parted to show the green underneath.

"Why would you worry about that?" Kunor smiled. "How were you to know you had a child so close by? I hold no resentment towards you." His smile fell as his hold remained constant. "You carry so much concern for all of us, of course you do, you've kept the same worries for so long now. She's okay, he'll come around, he's safe, they're happy, we're all doing fine. And you, why would you ever think so lowly of your great accomplishments?" Kunor closed his eyes and turned away. "That felt invasive."

"You'll get used to it." Sorner stood and rejoined the group.

"You're Sorner?" Sentry whispered in disbelief. "I come from your line."

Sorner looked at her again. "Yeah, that adds up."

Keilon helped Kunor to his feet, Kunor released the rabbit into a nearby planter and took a few deep breaths.

"I'd like to go to the trees," Kunor said proudly.

"Yes! The trees!" Sorner smiled. "Let's do that!" He turned to his brother. "Assuming it's all still standing."

"It is!" Dylah interjected in his defense.

"How odd it is to see my brother's likeness in someone so very much his opposite." He raised an eyebrow and took a step closer to her. "But you're different, more drive, less anger. Very much a Keilon but also more of a-" Sorner tapped at his brother's shoulder. "You know who she actually reminds me of?"

"I know." The first Keilon smiled.

"Although, again, and I cannot stress this enough, much much smaller than she was." Sorner smirked.

"Yeah, I get it." Dylah rolled her eyes.

Sorner leaned close to her face. "Black streaks from just a small observation?"

Dylah commanded her eyes to full obsidian. "Is personal space not considered harmonious?"

"Not to him." Old Keilon chuckled.

Sentry looped her arm with Kunor's as the group followed, deciding to head back to Fellowrock to let the newly emerged soul soak up its homeland. The first Keilon did a double take, and realized his brother had slipped away. Dylah quickly noticed too and nodded to the back edge of the gardens with a smile as they parted ways.

Beyond the gardens laid the royal cemetery. Sorner was tiptoeing around the headstones, reading each one with worrisome anticipation, until he found the name he dreaded to see carved in stone.

"He was a good king." The ghosts stood side by side reading the dates. "Passed shortly after you did."

"You kept contact too?" Sorner whispered, dark eyes pinned on the well worn stone.

"Not as much as you did, a few letters here and there." He shrugged. "A handful of meetings, I may have broken his nose once."

"We wrote, he visited Verinas a few times too." Sorner sighed. "Though, those interactions were quite different and overall lacking in a certain intimacy we were fond of."

"But you were safe, right?" Old Keilon whispered. "You had a long life, you had more children. Were you safe, Sorner?"

"The trip there was definitely traumatic." Sorner shook his head. "But to answer your question, yes, we lived well under our condition."

"Good," he swallowed. "I'm glad you're back, Sorner."

"Why?" Sorner laughed loudly. "So you can have a second chance? Big plans to destroy my life differently?"

"No, just a second chance to keep you around."

"Brennit made it very clear to me that yes, I could blame you for the terror you caused us." He sighed. "But also that it was you who made sure we would be taken care of, that you begged him to save us, you gave him every detail of the exile. You gave us our sentence and our salvation hand in hand and I always knew that, Keilon."

"I tried to tell you." He elbowed his brother. "But you

wouldn't believe me."

"I was a little panicked that day, you'll have to forgive my inability to read through your trickery."

"Now what?" Old Keilon nearly whispered. "What do we do now?"

"Hm." Sorner narrowed his eyes. "Neither of us have the power anymore, just like when we were kids."

"Yes, it's a bit of a relief."

Sorner wrapped an arm around his brother's shoulders and turned them to leave the burial grounds. "What would our lovely protective cousin Enfy say to us in a time like this?"

The first Keilon wrapped his arm around Sorner in return, and with the other hand pointed to the calm shade of blue over their heads.

"Keep your eyes to the sky, youngbloods!"

Chapter 39

Absence of Harmony

Despite their hurtful goodbyes so many years ago, chaos gripped onto harmony as they neared their homeland.

"I have worries," Sorner said.

"So nothing's changed?" His brother smirked back.

"I know we're tall right now, but I have very vivid memories of not being so tall." Sorner raised an eyebrow. "How can I be sure that the next time I step over this border I won't return to the likeness of a plaything?"

The first Keilon pondered the thought for a moment. He knew his brother's staunch need for visual reason. "Wait here."

Moments later Sorner watched as his brother returned with his small prodigy.

"The curse is gone." He locked pink eyes on his brother. "Dylah will demonstrate."

"We're all waiting for you back at the castle," Dylah groaned, "but sure. Watch closely."

Sorner held his breath as Dylah took a step away from the protection of the trees, then disappeared.

"You liar!" Sorner fell to his knees hoping to find her. "Why must you put so many in danger?"

Dylah quickly reappeared. "The curse really is gone, Sorner."

He stood and brushed off his knees with an annoyed glare pinned on Dylah. "I don't think I like you."

"Dylah kept the curse." Old Keilon watched as his brother's eyes brightened.

"You what?" Sorner grinned in amazement.

"Still don't like me?"

Dylah smiled as the two brothers followed her, acting as two brothers in their mid twenties would. Laughs, elbows thrown, a brief argument here and there all throughout the short walk to the castle.

Sorner planted his feet in the courtyard. "I never thought I'd be here again."

"Me neither." His brother sighed.

"I see you're at least remembered." He elbowed him with a nod to the banners. "When will you be bringing back the antlers, silver stag?"

"Never," he whispered.

Sorner stepped into the Fellowrock foyer as his eyes darted around the interior. "How has none of this changed?"

"We're lazy," Kremon laughed. "No motivation to change a damn thing."

"Except centuries old curses," the reigning Keilon added. "And injustices."

"Actually." Sorner squinted his eyes at the kitchen doorway. "When did the kitchen change? Keilon?"

Sorner went to turn to his older brother, to ask him many questions to help him clarify the swirl of worries in his head, and offer him any reasoning. He wanted to point out that the Riloncks in front of him so greatly took after his brother. Instead when he turned to his brother with the bloodstained history he saw him laughing with a young child.

"Who's the new guy?" Cav asked with a glance over to the stranger. "I saw that he wasn't very happy to see you."

"That's my little brother." Old Keilon put a hand on Cav's back and guided him towards Sorner.

Sorner immediately raised an eyebrow. "Child, I would like to hold you."

"Why?" Cav and the first Keilon asked almost in unison.

"He is a child, therefore much shorter than I am." Sorner pinned his gaze on Cav. "I would like a closer look."

With a sigh, Cav was handed over to Sorner. "His name is Cav."

"His eyes." Sorner looked in amazement. "How is that even possible?"

"This kid has found his way around many truths of life." Old Keilon smiled and ruffled Cav's hair.

"It does seem that way." Sorner shook his head and looked at his brother. "You've been living this other life long enough to produce more children?" He looked back at Cav. "And named him after your predecessor? My youngest daughter was named after Allinay."

"No, you're mistaken." He laughed.

"Hey, kiddo!" Dylah took Cav from Sorner.

"Your child?" Sorner asked.

Dylah froze, her eyes were immediately rivers of storm clouds as she gripped her son tightly, remembering how his existence spiraled the other soul of harmony.

"Yes," the first Keilon answered for her. "Axen is his father."

"You do understand the condition your soul inflicts when given to a woman, right? It was outlined so clearly in writings that were considered ancient even in my time. It is a basic law." Sorner met her eyes with a dark gaze. He took a step closer to her, her eyes widened and she took a step back. "Sometimes in the absence of harmony it is chaos that must step in." His eyes brightened and he smiled. He wrapped an arm around her and lightly kissed the top of her head. "And sometimes chaos produces such beautiful miracles."

"I don't think I like you much either." Dylah laughed. "But thank you, I know."

Old Keilon whispered to Sorner.

"Oh!" Sorner shook his head with a chuckle. "Had I known the prior circumstances and events caused by others claiming to be harmonious I would have worded that much differently." He shrugged and walked towards the others.

Dylah let Cav run off to play with his cousins, her gaze quickly pinned on the sight of Sorner and Kunor talking. "I don't think Nevely had a shred of what he is."

"After Sorner got his power, that very first morning after the eclipse, I woke up to the yellow eyes staring at me," the first Keilon said. "He wanted me to start each day free from whatever worry I had from the day before."

"No personal space."

"None." He laughed. "But it was nice growing up with someone who understood such an incomprehensible part of me."

"I know." Dylah nodded over to where her brothers were standing together. "They've always been my lifeline."

"I often wonder what would have happened if Sorner and I just had each other, what we would have been without the influence of our kingdom and family." It seemed like he was thinking out loud.

"I think you need a drink." She began walking towards the congregating family. "It's been a very enlightening day."

The Riloncks of varying descendancy, and those that married into the family mingled together in celebration of what had been and what was to come. Kunor practiced his new talent on whoever volunteered, he was rewarded with an extra drink when he became the first to make Bahn cry. Navent and Sentry were in awe of Sorner, and he bathed in every ounce of their attention. The castle was bustling with excitement from every corner.

The doors opened, and Sorner was shocked to see yet another familiar face.

"Teyle." He immediately stood in front of her with his arms crossed. "I do not like you."

"Hello again, Sorner." She smiled. "You haven't changed."

"I surely hope you are not here to vex my brother into havoc and bloodshed." Sorner pinned dark eyes on her. "I apologize, that wasn't your fault in the slightest. On an unrelated note, I miss your brother severely."

"He missed you too, all the way up until he passed." Her smile turned solemn. "I'm sorry he is among those unable to be brought back. Though, it is rather odd how many of us were able to come back."

The reigning Keilon slipped past Sorner and looped his arm in Teyle's. "I guess I don't have to explain to you how odd that one is," he whispered in her ear as he led her away.

Sorner stomped over to his brother. "Doesn't it bother you that your long lost love is also living but with the man who bears your same name?"

"Not really." Old Keilon shrugged as he took a drink. "Teen love, that's all."

"Really?" Sorner raised an eyebrow. "We fought a war and were cursed for what you are now deeming as 'teen love?!'"

"There was another."

"Right, I do remember getting word that you had married, then married again."

"The first wife's sister." He winked.

"So which sister did you love more than Teyle?"

"Neither." He laughed. "There was another."

"Interesting." Sorner took a drink. "I had many. The most harmonious aspect of love is how freely and abundantly it can be given."

The party continued on into the night. Sentry and

Navent retired for the evening along with Kunor shortly after, while some children fell asleep on any given surface. Drinks were continuously poured, all eyes were pinned on Sorner as he told the tale of slowly being drowned as his brother ran through thorny vines, trap doors, wolves, and fire to get to him.

"Don't forget the brick wall at the end." The first Keilon rolled his eyes.

"How would I know about what was at the end?" Sorner laughed. "By that point I was underwater! If you wanted me to tell the story correctly perhaps you should have run faster."

"Perhaps I should have walked."

Others shared with their ancestors tales of the war they fought to avenge the curse.

"So he didn't know it was me at first," Dylah started with a smile pointed at her husband. "When he came to help me up I used a fake voice."

"Not that I believed it was actually her when she finally did reveal herself." Axen smirked.

"I shot my own countryman in that battle." Kremon laughed lightly and raised his drink.

"You did what?!" Keilon's eyes went wide and orange.

"Not fatally, just to get him out of Dylah's way."

Eventually the jubilee began to wear down. The ancient Rilonck brothers wandered around the foyer of the castle, absorbing the quiet they rarely had in their youth.

Keilon stood at his predecessor's side. "I'd like to talk to you."

"You'd like to?!" Old Keilon smiled.

"My son looked into my eyes and said that it is imperative that I tell you that I no longer wish to kill you."

"No kidding?" He laughed, then his face fell. "Wait. What did Dylah tell you?"

"She didn't have to tell me anything." Keilon looked at him with stormy eyes. "The soul just feels lighter somehow."

"Yeah." Dylah appeared as if from nowhere. "It does."

"New Riloncks," Sorner stood by his brother. "I am now in need of lodging, and seeing as how I in no way asked to be given life again, I believe you are the ones who must provide such accommodations."

"Dylah already thought this through." Keilon elbowed his sister.

"Follow us." She flashed a smile as she walked towards the door where Axen was standing, clutching their sleeping son.

The brothers followed the small royal family silently, one in a state of confusion, the other in awe of his nostalgic surroundings.

"The forest at night was always so peaceful," Sorner whispered. "Like the sound of the crickets made the world pause."

"Always the poet." Old Keilon rolled his eyes. "The thorn in my side."

"And yet you still don't pluck me out."

"We're here," Dylah interrupted as she nodded to the porch steps.

"This is your house." The first Keilon raised an eyebrow.

"No, Dylah is the queen of Hightree," Axen whispered. "She lives in the castle."

Axen waited with Cav in the kitchen as Dylah led the ancestors up the staircase and pushed them into rooms right next to each other.

"You're staying here," she demanded. "You're going to get back what you had so long ago." Her eyes glittered with pink. "Together you're going to document the history that was destroyed. Understood?"

"Perhaps, I like you." Sorner smiled. "You're a little miniature Enfinella."

"Did you even need to say little if you were already going to say miniature?" She scowled. "But, thank you, from what I've heard about her, I would've loved to have known such a woman."

The brothers were given a brief tour, Sorner was pulled away from a lightswitch that he found rather fascinating and was given an explanation on the intricacies and dangers of electricity. Dylah explained that the master bedroom, Axen's workspace, and Cav's old room were completely off limits but that the house was theirs to be a family again.

She promised to visit them in the morning to drop off Cav before she went to command various trainings. After handing them each too many blankets and receiving words of gratitude from the holder of her same eyes, Dylah finally rejoined her husband as they walked towards their towering home.

"You know I support your decisions, princess," Axen started to say. "When you first suggested giving him another chance, I understood that I may never understand where you were coming from." He sighed. "So clear some things up for me, why try so hard for him?"

"I'm not sure I can explain it."

"Will you at least try to?" He half laughed. "Put it as vaguely as you need to, I'd just like some perspective."

Dylah thought for a while. She mulled over the bloody history given to her by the pond, she envisioned the bones beneath the water, and the lifted regrets that seemed to conjure an atmospheric phenomenon.

"Because," she began with a sigh, "he's what I would have become if I didn't have you."

Chapter 40

Same Reason

"I swear I will shove another dagger through your heart!" Dylah pointed a strong finger up to her predecessor.

"I feel as if that is a tad bit dramatic in this situation." Sorner chuckled watching the altercation.

"Dylah, really, I was just about to-" the first Keilon started.

"I don't need any excuses! Look at this kitchen!" she shouted. "Filthy!"

"Keilon has never been one for neatness." Sorner grinned. "I often woke in the middle of the night to tidy his side of our room just so I could get some decent sleep."

"So why didn't you clean the kitchen?" His brother shot a burning glare at him. "How could you even sleep with it in this state?"

"I had a very cozy blanket, thank you very much."

Dylah rolled her eyes. "Please tell me you at least wrote enough pages last night to make up for your falling behind this past week."

The brothers shared a glance, Sorner let a lone laugh slip out.

"Seriously?" Dylah began to count the empty mugs on the counter and in the sink.

"You must understand." Old Keilon muffled a laugh and elbowed his brother to quiet down. "We are digging up some long dead memories, and many of them remind us of others."

"And most of them are vastly hysterical," Sorner added. "Well, up until a certain point."

"I'll be the judge of that." Dylah slid out a chair at the table. "Sit."

The brothers glanced at each other again as if to silently argue who would approach first.

Old Keilon sat across from her, then Sorner next to him.

"Keilon stabbed the ice once," Sorner started. "Which was a rather impressive feat even for someone of his strength. They trapped him beneath the ice and he had just barely escaped death."

"It was actually twice," he corrected. "Once on each end of the pond."

Sorner continued, "The whole ordeal was pretty horrific for him, but some of the elders and our brother, Hekar, fell in after the cracks spread."

"That doesn't sound too funny." She raised an eyebrow.

"I ran away after that, I went to Hightree to see Teyle with plans to escape far away." He was tapping his hands nervously.

"But he didn't do that!" Sorner laughed. "Instead, he decided to hide out in that castle for a few days trapped in a room with his lady."

"I see." Dylah's eyebrow seemed to be in a permanent arch.

"Then one day our father and brother came looking for me again." Old Keilon fought a smile. "But the room had an attic, so I hid. When Hekar tried to move the opening, I was on the other side keeping it in place."

"And then what happened?"

"Oh, uh, I let my grip go because they made it sound like they left the room." He shrugged. "Then they sent me to wars for a year."

"Don't you mean war?" she asked. "Singular."

"No." He sighed. "I mean wars."

"See, hilarious!" Sorner pointed an insisting smile at her. "Don't you agree?"

"Yes, hysterical." Dylah shook her head with a slight smile. "Well, get it together boys! I need more effort."

"If you're done, are you almost ready to go?" Old Keilon smirked. "I'm sure you're ready to throw a few punches at me anyway."

"Absolutely." She waited until he had left the kitchen, then she leaned closer to Sorner and whispered, "Have the dreams stopped yet?"

"Yes," he paused, "but only because he rarely sleeps."

"Do you think it's because we're stirring up those memories again?"

"Oh, sweet little Dylah." Sorner smiled. "We haven't even touched the terrible things yet."

Dyah steadied herself with a breath, she had gotten used to Sorner's dramatic way of speaking. "But soon, right?"

"Yes, soon." He slouched. "I hope he's preparing himself for the discussions."

"I'll see what I can do." Dylah nodded and quickly caught up with the first Keilon outside.

In the three months since Sorner had appeared there had been a shift in the air. What once held a heaviness now seemed lighter, where there used to be constant questions, slow answers began to close the gap. As more and more history was uncovered it made the present feel steadier, like chaos had truly been balanced.

Across the treeline high in the monumental castle, Axen

opened his brother's bedroom door and let Cav race in to greet him.

"Well, ask him." Axen laughed watching Cav tiptoe towards the bed.

"Uncle Arkon," Cav started, "are you taller than my dad? I don't remember."

"Mhmm," Arkon murmured.

"Told you." Axen ruffled Cav's hair.

"When will he talk again?"

"I was hoping you would be able to tell me that, buddy."

Arkon had made great strides in the past few months. He was now able to move his hands freely, he nodded and every so often opened his eyes. Most recently he started answering in groans and other almost word-like responses. Axen was hopeful that a recovery was approaching but the last two treatments had resulted in very little advancement and he was beginning to worry. Lately, he had been bringing Cav to visit hoping it would prompt some sort of vision.

A soft knock landed on the door before Kunor and Keilon walked in.

"Damn Farein." Keilon shook Arkon's shoulder.

"Mhmm."

"Well, he's getting closer to it." Keilon shrugged. "What's the news, kiddo?" he asked Cav.

"The funny one is going to meet us in a bit."

"He means Sorner," Axen added when he noticed the confused look on his brother and brother-in-law's faces. "What about your mama and Uncle K?"

"No, just the funny one." Cav laughed.

"Well, that's great." Kunor sighed with relief. "Holding Delin's gaze is still a little hard for me to do."

"When are you heading down to the uh," Keilon paused to check how well Cav was listening, "the rooms."

"Once we're done here." Axen nodded.

"Uncle Keilon," Cav said, staring up at him. "When I stay with you for a few days can we catch more toads? And do you think Uncle K will come this time?"

"When you stay with me for a few days?"

"Yeah!" Cav giggled. "When mama and dad go on their trip."

"That sounds fun!" Kunor smiled. "Where are you going, Axen?"

"I have no idea." Axen seemed unphased by the small detail of a future he would find out about later.

After keeping Arkon company for about an hour and dropping Cav off with Avalia and her protruding stomach, Axen, Keilon, and Kunor descended down into the prison beneath the castle. They walked along the long row of empty cells until they saw Kremon standing outside the bars with arms crossed.

"He's not feelin' it today." He shrugged. "Didn't laugh at any of my best jokes."

"Is Sorner here yet?" Kunor asked.

"Uh yeah." Kremon chuckled. "He saw a mouse and followed it down that way."

"Delin," Keilon said as he unlocked the cell. "How are we doing today?"

Delin answered with a low groan.

"Alright!" Sorner laughed as he appeared at the end of the long row. "I've caught the friend." He held a gray mouse to his chest. "He took a nibble out of my finger but I do believe we understand each other now."

"Can we get started?" Keilon mumbled as he opened the cell door.

They soon surrounded Delin who was sitting on his bed in a deflated position.

"Arkon is mumbling quite a bit," Axen said with a forced cheer in his voice, "but no other changes."

Delin didn't respond.

"Do you have any idea why the latest treatments aren't providing any new results?" Keilon asked with arms crossed.

"No no no." Sorner sat himself next to Delin on the bed. "You don't just bombard the fella with your demands, you check in on his soul first." He put a hand on Delin's back and lightly rubbed. Then, he raised a finger and called Kunor over. "Catch his gaze."

"No," Delin finally muttered.

"Come on." Kunor sat beside Delin after Sorner moved over. "You like it, remember?" He laughed. "Reminds you of the crazy lady."

"We don't refer to women as crazy," Sorner whispered. "Or hysterical. They can be evil without a label that hints at their gender."

"Oh." Kunor nodded. "Come on, just look at me, it'll be over before you know it."

Delin took a deep breath followed by an exhale that rattled with bottled up anger. He finally sat up and looked at his nephew.

"Okay, youngblood, give him the sunlight." Sorner glanced at Delin again. "You may need to give him every bit of it."

Kunor let the warmth flood his eyes and as he locked onto Delin's gaze he was overcome with worries so strong it felt like the most powerful gust of wind slapping his face. He saw glimpses of the calculations that filled Delin's every thought, he saw the unfamiliar image of Arkon full of life, and flashes of each and every family member he knew, including those he knew had gone before him. The image that lasted the longest spoke the loudest.

"You're losing him," Sorner whispered.

Kunor shook off his hold and put his hands on Delin's shoulders. "After all this time?" He smiled. "I understand, but if you could just put it into words maybe you wouldn't be locked up anymore."

"I don't know what you're talking about," Delin huffed as he returned to his folded over state.

"Delin, please," Axen said with a sigh. "We could really

use your brain right now, I'm at a loss." He shook his head. "I've tried but the formulas just don't add up to anything, I don't understand what we're missing."

"We are so close to having our brother and friend back," Kunor added. "We can try again but you need to look at me. We can expand on that worry."

"Leave." Delin's demand muffled into the hands that were covering his face.

Keilon nodded his head towards the exit, silently telling them all to leave. He let them slip out before he shut the barred door and shook the keys, making it sound like it had been locked. And when Delin looked up, thinking he was once again alone, Keilon only smirked back.

"So smart but still so easy to trick." His grin widened. "Remember when you were nine and messed up that spell and I ran down the hallway through-"

"What are you doing here, Keilon?" Delin sighed.

"You know what the problem is with the treatments, don't you?" Keilon crossed his arms. "Why won't you tell us?"

"Why don't you just use your eyes and make me tell you?"

"Because I still hold some trust with you and I don't think that would be necessary." He shrugged. "Come on, I thought you were coming back to us, just tell me."

"I see the ghost hasn't killed Dylah yet." He rolled his eyes. "How you allow such a tarnished stain on our history to roam about freely is enough of a reason for me to never tell you a damn thing."

"He has his conditions, along with Sorner." Keilon tried to remain calm. "Dylah has assured me that she has it under control and I trust her."

"Will I be granted permission to attend her funeral?" He locked eyes on his brother. "Perhaps even yours?"

"Stop," Keilon demanded as his eyes ignited with fire and power. "I'm not here to discuss your opinion on matters that don't concern you. I'm here to get the answers out of you that we desperately need because an innocent and honorable man is still confined to a bed."

"I don't have the answers."

"I know you do. You always have the answers." Keilon took slow steps and sat on the bed next to his brother. "Why won't you tell us?"

"I don't want to." He gulped.

"I just don't understand, Delin." Keilon sighed. "This isn't the kid who I watched grow up. The one who stayed inside reading, the one who let his kid sister sleep in his bed when she was too scared to come find me, the over protective big brother who berated me when I broke Dylah's ribs. The same over protective brother who wouldn't dare tell me the reason behind her broken eyes because you didn't want to tell her secret. And yes, the same one who committed treason behind my back for the most noble reasons. You were worried so many times about her young life, and even after she was married and a mother, you cared enough to meddle into the fabric of our souls. But you weren't just worried for her those times, you were lost and searching." Keilon shook his head. "Yes, we talk a lot about how I had to raise Dylah after our parents passed. But you know what, Delin? I raised you too, and I raised you better than this."

"It's the same reason," Delin whispered.

"What?"

"It's Dylah." He finally brought himself to look at Keilon. "I know what is needed for the final treatments, and the only one able to get it would be Dylah."

"And you don't want to put her in danger?"

"Yes." His face fell into his hands. "I haven't seen her since that camp. When she interrogated me, I didn't even recognize her through that anger."

"And you're surprised by that?" Keilon laughed. "You helped kidnap her son, you drugged her, you did everything against her. She grew up trusting you and you shattered that, so don't blame her for not wanting to pop by for a visit."

"I know what I did," Delin spoke quietly. "She's still my sister, I am feeling the weight of my actions, and at the center of all of my guilt is her."

"Well, helping fix Arkon may be the first step towards her forgiveness." Keilon put an arm around his youngest brother. "If anything, she'll have to visit so you can explain it all to her."

Keilon coaxed more information out of Delin, and when the situation became clear, he told Axen that Dylah needed to pay her brother a visit.

"No." Dylah tightly clenched a dagger in each hand.

"Perhaps, we should move away from this particular training field." Axen smirked. "Or at least put down the daggers."

She reluctantly sheathed her daggers on each thigh. "I'm not talking to him."

"He will only tell us what is needed for the final treatment if you're there to hear it." Axen sighed. "I don't like the condition either but we have to think about the bigger goal here."

"I completely despise the idea of looking at him again."

"I know, it hasn't been the same since his crimes." He grabbed her hand. "But I'll be there, Keilon hasn't left him all day, Kunor and Sorner will be there in case he gets too unhinged he can be given a breather."

"Fine." She looked away to hide the multitude of colors in her eyes. "Now?"

"The sooner the better."

"Understood." She turned back to the training field where the first Keilon was laughing against his adversary. "Sorry, Navent, you're going to have to fight him for a little while longer."

"I beg your pardon!" Navent yelled back through exhausted breaths. "I was barely winning with you helping me!"

"Definitely from Sorner's line," Old Keilon snickered.

Dylah pointed at her predecessor. "Don't kill him." She pointed at Navent. "Don't let him kill you."

She followed Axen through the woods as they listened to the sounds of arguments and light begging grow fainter.

"I see Navent hasn't gotten any better," Axen laughed. "Maybe he should stick with the bow."

"Hey, he said he wanted to learn more about fighting with a dagger and who am I to say no to someone who wants to acquire another deadly skill?" She smiled back.

Axen rejoined those waiting in the prison cell, he had an annoyed smirk on his face and avoided looking at Keilon.

"Where's Dylah?" Keilon asked as orange streaked through his eyes.

"Well, she agreed to come, but, um." Axen tilted his head towards the direction of the stairwell. "Kind of vanished once we got to the prison doors."

"Are you kidding?" Keilon gripped the bridge of his nose.

"Relax," Dylah's voice came from down the hall until she stood outside the cell door. "I just needed a minute."

Keilon wanted to call her out on her flightiness but he could sense her nervousness and anger grow with every step she took closer to their estranged brother.

"I'm here, Delin." She crossed her arms in the far corner of the cell. "Tell us what you need."

"If I may add just a smattering of advice," Sorner whispered in her direction. "Aggression is not the way to approach this situation."

"It's fine." Delin seemed to look through the crowd and lock on to her stormy and black eyes. "Dylah, there's a vine that grows only on the trees of the valley pass, the root of that vine contains the healing elements I need to save Arkon."

"That's it?" Dylah laughed. "After everything you need me to run an errand for you?"

"Dylah," Keilon whispered. "Just wait."

"No!" She stomped to where he was sitting on the bed and stood in front of him taking ragged shallow breaths. "Do you have any idea what you've done to my family?"

Delin's eyes fell to his feet. "I'm sorry."

"Look at me!" She shoved against his shoulder. The second he met her blue gaze, his eyes filled with tears. "Does this help you understand a mere fraction of the heartbreak you made me live through?" Dylah held the color of her eyes as she forced the sadness on him. "Do you feel how helpless I felt when my son was ripped away from me? The time that passed without him that felt like dying over and over again? The pain of seeing our home on fire? Can you begin to understand now?" She took a shaky deep breath. "I trusted you and all you gave me was suffering."

Axen grabbed her wrist and tried to pull her away but she refused to move. The others exchanged glances not knowing what to do.

"I feared this might happen." Sorner smiled. "It's always the smallest ones with the biggest rage." He elbowed Kunor. "You'll need to step in."

"She'll kill me," Kunor whispered.

"Her daggers are at the top of the stairs," Axen quickly added.

"That doesn't mean anything!" Kunor answered.

"I intervened with Keilon's rage countless times and I bear no scars." Sorner pushed him closer to Dylah.

Kunor felt an oddness within himself as he inched closer to Dylah, like the chaos building within her was somehow charging his own peace. He grabbed her shoulders and turned her to face him in one quick motion that she couldn't fight off. The sunlight of his irises mesmerized her instantly.

Kunor didn't hold her worries for very long, he only wanted her to take a breath.

"She's going to do it." Kunor smiled at Delin. "And none of the injuries she wishes to inflict on you are inherently fatal, so you should take some comfort in that."

"So, are you going to draw a map?" she asked with eyes she was forcing to remain green. "Perhaps a diagram so I can bring back the right thing?"

"Yes," Delin's voice seemed lighter and the beginnings of a smile settled into the corners of his mouth. "I'll have them drawn up in no time, but you cannot go alone."

"Oh?" She arched an eyebrow. "Are you fearing for my safety now?"

"Someone needs to immediately prepare the root so it can be used properly," Delin answered slowly. "And the only one I know who would understand the process," his head turned, "is Axen."

Without a word the king and queen of Hightree nodded to each other after only a few seconds of consideration, they tapped their fists twice as the other spectators waited for their answer.

"We'll go." Dylah turned to leave the cell. "For Arkon."

Chapter 41

Every Bit of Daylight

"So, kiddo," Dylah said as she gripped Cav's hand while they walked through the treeline. "Any fun plans with your Uncle Keilon while we're gone?"

"I asked him if we could take Uncle K to the pond to catch toads," Cav replied. "I think he's thinking about it."

"Hm, no, Uncle K is afraid of toads too, don't ask him to go to the pond." She smiled to hide the underlying reasons. "But maybe I'll try to help you catch some when we get back, okay?"

"Really?!"

"Yes, maybe my screams of terror will scare them in your direction." Dylah laughed. "So think about your tactics over the next few days and we'll execute the attack when I get back."

"It won't be a few days," Cav said calmly. "You and dad will be back really late tomorrow night."

"Are you able to narrow down the days now?" She

squeezed his hand. "Your grandma would be so proud."

"No." Cav giggled. "I saw Uncle Kremon say 'you weren't even gone for a day' to dad."

"Oh, well, that does help I suppose."

As Dylah was making her old bedroom comfortable for her son she rattled off lists upon lists of guidelines for her brother.

"You do realize that I have met the kid before, right?" Keilon rolled his eyes. "He'll be fine."

"We haven't been apart since, well, the fire," she muttered.

"He'll be fine, I promise." He grinned. "Maybe I'll just pump him full of coffee and chocolate and we'll just stay up the whole night. No one can sneak up on us if we never sleep!"

"He has to sleep." Dylah pointed fire at his amethyst. "Or else he doesn't understand the visions and he gets really frustrated." She dug into a bag and pulled out a small sketchbook. "So make sure he has this first thing in the morning."

"And when does the old guy come to collect him?"

"He won't while I'm gone." She laughed. "I'm giving him a pretty hefty assignment he doesn't know about yet so he will be quite occupied."

"And would you like me to check in on your other son while you're away?"

"Yeah just pop by if you could." Her eyes widened when she finally understood his joke. "You're not funny."

"You're leaving first thing in the morning?" He decided to change the subject.

"Yeah, unless Axen comes back with the maps and guidelines and decides we need to leave earlier." She looked into the now empty bag and double checked that she had brought everything necessary and unnecessary. "Cav says we'll be back by tomorrow night."

"Oh, any idea why it'll be such a short trip?"

The door opened and a green cape stepped in. "We need to leave probably within the next couple of hours." Axen sighed as he looked over the diagrams. "He says that we will need every bit of daylight to locate this thing."

"Doubt it." She rolled her eyes. "But I just have two more things to do then we can head out on this grand adventure."

First she checked in on Cav who was playing with Kane and Chany, they'd tell him goodbye right before leaving. Then she headed towards the house on the treeline.

Dylah decided to enter from the deck doors, the sky became cloudy as a light early spring rain fell. With her house in view and the soft raindrops hitting her hood, she was thrown into a past she had often pushed away.

"Hey there, youngblood."

"It's not very smart to stand in the rain," she walked past him into the house. "You'll catch a cold and that is not how The First Keilon dies."

"I'd take a boring death this time around." He chuckled as he followed her inside. "Drowned and stabbed were a little too dramatic."

"Next time I'll go out in a blaze of glory," she added. "Being thrown from a balcony was a little boring."

"You two," Sorner said through a sigh as he was strewn about one of the couches. "Why is death so appealing to the chaotic soul?"

"Because," Old Keilon said proudly, "at one point something has to be strong enough to conquer the storm, and it is vastly entertaining waiting to see what that will be."

"Dylah, the king tells me you're leaving soon." Sorner sat up. "Or have you changed your mind?"

"No, we're leaving just as soon as we're packed up." She noticed the confusion on her predecessor's face. "I just wanted to stop by first."

"She doesn't need you to go." Sorner fell back to the cushions. "Don't even think about offering."

"I wasn't going to." The first Keilon rolled his eyes.

"Yes you were." Dylah laughed. "Cav is all set up with my brother, he'll be fine." She took a pausing breath. "I need you to get the hard stuff on paper while I'm gone."

"Oh!" Sorner popped up again. "She means all the murdering!"

"Yes, that." She smirked and continued walking to the kitchen.

The older ghost pointed a glare at his nonchalant brother before walking into the kitchen to see Dylah standing on the countertops rummaging through the highest shelf.

"I know this looks odd." Her voice bounced around the interior of the cabinet as she shuffled the contents around. "But I hid some extra strong coffee up here after Axen threatened to throw it away." She laughed loudly. "He thought it made me too um, how'd he put it, annoyingly snarky."

"I don't blame him." Old Keilon laughed. "You're usually one or the other, I can't imagine the two together."

"Big talk coming from someone living in my house." She jumped down from the counter clutching her prized bag. "You're going to be okay, right?"

"I think I'll manage."

Dylah looked at him for a moment, and after noticing the strain of exhaustion, jumped back on the counter. She pulled out a jar of powder, jumped down and handed it to him. "When Cav was having nightmares we started giving him some of this in a glass of milk right before bed."

"And why do I need this?"

"Just in case." She shrugged. "You'll probably want about three spoonfuls, it doesn't taste terrible mixed with wine."

He was about to answer when the front door opened and Axen stepped into the kitchen. He quickly noticed the bag that Dylah tried to hurriedly hide.

"No." His eyes were wide and he shook his head. "It is only you and I on this trip, and I just might leave you there if you're all hopped up on those evil coffee beans."

"Now coffee beans are evil?!" Sorner shouted from one room over.

"Fine," she said as she set the bag on the counter. "I'll leave them here."

"Sure." Axen shook his head. "I'm getting some of the supplies he listed, so if you're going to sneak a cup or two before we head out, you don't have much time."

"You're perfect." She grinned as he disappeared down the hallway wearing a smirk.

"Is two cups going to be enough to keep you up through the night on your adventure?" the first Keilon asked.

"No." Her voice fell to a whisper. "But the six more that I'm putting in the thermos will."

"I'll tell him."

"I'll kill you."

"Do not kill each other!" Sorner interjected again. "I beg you, stop discussing death!"

"I'm hiding this again." She pointed pink eyes at him. "I know exactly how much is here and I will know if you try to switch it."

"Why would I-"

"I know you're not sleeping, that's why I gave you the powder. Hands off the coffee." She turned away from him as she poured the bulk of the fresh coffee into a thermos. "You only need to dig up that dirty past one last time before I hide it away for decades. Okay? I'm not going to question any of it."

"Three spoonfuls?"

"Yes." She smiled. "But stir well, sometimes it clumps and looks a little odd."

Axen emerged with a bag slung on his shoulder. "Did you have enough time to sneak the proper amount of coffee?"

"Not yet." Dylah slowly sipped from a mug. "Maybe you should go check on Sorner."

"Of course, princess." He laughed as he left the kitchen once again.

Dylah took two large drinks before she broke the silence in the kitchen. "I know it's hard digging up the silver stag, but maybe this time around you'll understand the dripping crimson."

After the ghosts were handed their set of final instructions, Axen and Dylah returned to the Fellowrock castle. They took turns holding Cav tightly and promising to be back as soon as they could. Dylah went over all of her overly specific directions with Keilon one more time. Then after a final hug and the common whispered words, the king and queen rode off with the falling sunlight.

"So, enemy prince," Dylah said with a laugh. "Did you think all of our adventures were over?"

"Not at all, I expect we have many many more to come."

"When we cure Arkon and go back to just having a lowly royal title, we'll take the kid all over."

"Who says I'll surrender my title of king so easily?" Axen smirked. "Maybe I enjoy the mountains of paperwork and buckets of stress."

"Should we turn back then?" She pointed amethyst eyes at him. "I'd sacrifice an adventure for you to stay the king."

"Absolutely not, princess."

Chapter 42

Complicated Roots

They traveled on horseback straight ahead until the sun began to illuminate the vast horizon. After staying up through the night they were growing tired before their true adventure even began, but in a flurry of pressure and spousal insulting, Axen conceded to drink the extra strong coffee in Dylah's thermos.

"We've traveled too much in the past year. Gomdea and back was enough for me, then to scope out that witch's camp twice, too much." Dylah handed the coffee over to Axen. "I miss the times when we couldn't go anywhere."

"You better take that back right now before another ancestor comes out of nowhere and curses you again." He laughed.

"Permanently cursed." She winked. "I fear nothing."

"Well, I hate to tell you," he said as he handed the thermos back over to her. "But you're just about out of coffee."

"That's not scary." She slipped the thermos back into a

bag on the side of her horse. "It's depressing."

Axen unfolded the map as soon as the rising sun allowed enough light to study the fine lines. His eyes darted from the parchment to the horizon and each side several times. "We should be coming up on the valley." He pointed ahead. "Then the hollow will be a pretty obvious turn."

"What makes it so obvious?"

"Delin said it would look a little spooky." Axen shrugged.

"We've seen our share of spooky things, I'm not sure we'll catch it." She grinned.

"The instructions do specify that it'll be on our left, so I guess that will narrow it down."

"Did he ever clear up why I had to be the one to get this thing?" Dylah asked slowly. "I understand that you two have always done the crazy experiments together so he would only trust you to prepare the root, but why do I have to get it?"

"He wouldn't tell me either." Axen sighed. "All he said was that it had to be you, and it would be obvious when we got there."

"His confidence in what he thinks is obvious sure is high."

The valley soon enveloped them, a wide open space filled with staggered trees whose branches stretched casting speckly shadows on the road. On their left was the base of the mountain that led in the direction of Gomdea and the sand countries. On the right, the mountain they could always see from the lilac field, the route that led to Arizmia. The same mountain whose summit became the place where Dylah's eyes first sparked.

"What if we never went to Arizmia?" she nearly whispered. "Do you think I'd ever get the power? Would there still have been a cataclysmic need for chaos?"

"Yes." He nodded, still looking ahead. "You were always meant to be who you are one way or another." He turned to her with a smirk. "It just so happens that a vengeful ex-fiance was enough to make it happen."

"I'm glad it was something I wasn't expecting." She looked up at the branches above their heads. "I always kind of had an idea that maybe my eyes weren't just a fluke like everyone said they were, but I'm thankful that it wasn't something we were all waiting for. It's better that it was a shock."

"Instead of how it was for the old guy?" He looked at her with a raised eyebrow and slight worry. "I thought you said you wouldn't be reading those pages anymore?"

"I had to." Dylah shook her head. "I didn't want to, but I needed to know. They were so awful to him." She gulped. "Some of those stories are bringing meaning to dreams I never understood as a kid. All those times I swore I was a king just because my soul was."

"What do you think they'll be talking through while you're gone?"

"Some of the early murders."

"I see, 'early,' nice of you to specify." He laughed.

She was silent for a moment as she stared at the horse's mane. "Is it okay with you that it's me?"

"What?" He halted his horse and she did the same. "Are you asking if it's okay that you're the soul? As if it could have belonged to anyone else, as if it didn't fit the very definition of who you are?" He grinned. "I don't even think your prodigy will measure up to the way you hold it."

"No, are you happy with the life you live because you chose me?"

"Well, that's a helluva question!" He dismounted his horse and pulled her into his arms.

"I just fully recognize that you are the one who balances me and I'm just worried that I don't do the same for you." Her eyes clouded over as she sank into him. "It's not fair that you quiet the chaos for me and I only bring it to you."

"But I like you wild." Axen rested his chin on her waves. "I think we've established this many times now."

"It's not just a matter of being wild, it's everything else

you've been put through since the first time you saw my eyes." Her voice muffled against him.

"Do you mean the peaceful ties that were forged between our kingdoms? Or maybe the winter wedding that I demanded? The tyrants that were rid from this world? Or are you talking about the perfect child that fought through the laws of destiny to be ours?" He lightly laughed. "Yes, I'm suffering." He kissed the top of her head. "It was always supposed to be us, princess."

Dylah pulled his face to meet hers with a kiss that said everything she couldn't.

"Have I ever told you how pretty your eyes are?" she finally asked.

He flashed a smile as he turned back towards his horse. "Thanks, I got them from my great great great great great great grandfather."

"Oh, so that's what makes you so special, huh?"

"Obviously."

"Hm, the soul of," she thought for a moment, "absolute perfection."

They rode for another hour until Axen pointed to a dark gap in the approaching trees. "Does that look spooky to you?"

"Perhaps a little bit." Her eyes that had been cloudy returned to a happy amethyst rimmed in pink at the first sign of a new thrill.

They tied their horses to a tree at the top of what they could now see was a dip in the earth to an open trail. Though the trees remained level with the surrounding woods it looked like the land had been carved out. Each step lower exposed more of the roots on the walls of dust and dirt. Soon the bases of the trees were high above their heads as they walked, studying the system of complicated roots that acted as a naturally occurring brick and mortar, forming what felt like a hallway in the middle of nowhere.

Dylah reached and felt the vulnerable yet strong middle of a gnarly root. "This is amazing," she whispered. "Have you ever seen anything like this?"

"No," he whispered back. "I wonder why he didn't explain this better." Axen looked around inspecting the aspects of nature that usually remained hidden deep beneath the grass. "Actually, this would be rather hard to explain."

They continued on, taking slow steps with hands tightly clasped and eyes that seemed enchanted to never blink in the presence of the unique environment.

"There." Axen pointed to an exposed tree root with a vine crawling up it. He studied it closely and followed the tangled green string to the base of the root wall. "And now I understand why you needed to come."

"Why?" Dylah stood beside him and looked down at where his gaze was pinned. "Oh. I hate him."

In the gap between where the wall met the road there was a crevice that the vines seemed to be rooted in. It would be a place too small for the skilled use of a hand, but a place ideal for someone who could change their size drastically at the snap of a finger.

"You don't have to go down there." Axen held her shoulders as he watched her contemplate the task at hand.

"I'm just wondering how they were able to get to this precious root without my ability." She lightly laughed before pulling out the diagram that Delin had drawn for her.

"He said they had a special tool that he didn't know how to recreate." He sighed in the middle of his own processing. "Really, we can just turn back."

Dylah suddenly remembered Cav's vision of them getting back earlier than planned, but giving up wasn't something they'd ever do. "In and out, no problem." She grinned. "For Arkon."

Axen sat on the ground and began to prepare the vials of colorful liquids needed to immediately extract the healing components. He double checked the instructions and lined everything up in the order it would be needed.

"Are you ready yet?" Dylah laughed.

"I only want you to have to do this once."

"I'm not dainty."

"You're about to be!"

"In and out." She smiled below sparkling eyes of joy and power. "And I'll do it as many times as necessary. The danger of it and any fear you might have doesn't eliminate the need."

"Well if you put it like that." He let out a defeated exhale through a genuine smile. "Go ahead, you nightmare."

Dylah crouched and looked down into the small opening, then placed her hand in to judge the space.

"It's not as deep as it looks and from what I can tell, no bugs."

Axen's eyes went wide. "I didn't even think about bugs."

Dylah looked over the instructions one last time, she needed to disconnect a tendril from the very end of a root without dislodging the root altogether then quickly get it back up to Axen. She traced the trail of the vine and zoned in on where it seemed to finally sink into the earth.

"Ready?" She waited for his nod after one last check of his supplies, then she enacted her curse and jumped down into the crevice.

Dylah slid her hands along the end of the vine until it dug into the ground. She loosened the packed dirt with her fingers and felt where the root seemed to split off into smaller tentacle-like extensions. She pulled until one popped from beneath the dirt. The sight of it was almost startling, although it had been in the rich soil it was stunningly milky white.

With extreme caution, Dylah drew a dagger from the sheath on her hip and began to slice, careful not to score the mother root. When the tendril was successfully disconnected she held it severed side up so as to not drip any of the honey like substance within it.

"Got it!" she yelled up into the opening. "Take it!"

Axen carefully took it from her hands and put it into the first vial of a blue liquid. "Are you going to come out?"

"I'm waiting just in case that one doesn't work."

"Of course, princess." He watched the blue liquid turned to green as the tendril slightly shriveled up. Then with a pair of small tongs he transferred it to the vial of red liquid. This prompted a more physical change, the thick substance separated from the root and floated to the top. Axen scooped out the ball of clear gel and moved it to the last vial of pale yellow oil. The gel and oil bubbled together then calmed into a salve.

"Can you get one more, just to be safe?" he asked, looking at the strange substance that had been created. "It's also just a very interesting process."

"You're having a fun time experimenting again, huh?" Dylah said up through the opening as she felt around in the loosened dirt for one more tendril, finding it easier this time. "This one is a little bigger, does that mean anything to you?" She didn't let him answer, she just cut in the same manner as the first time and let him take it.

Dylah pulled herself out of the small dip in the earth and returned to her usual size as Axen was on the last step of the process.

"I think this is good." Axen nodded, watching the odd bubbling of the gel and the oil. "And if not, this was a nice little trip."

"Yeah, we deserved a relaxing high stakes getaway." She grinned.

"Our next escape will require no miniature mining, I promise."

"How boring."

Axen secured both serums into separate well sealed jars, he then wrapped them in a plush fabric and made sure they were safe in the bag. After double checking that every chemical was inactive and each piece of equipment was safely packed away, they headed back up the sunken trail to their horses. Again they marveled at the systems of roots tangled into the dirt wall, they interlaced their fingers as they made plans to bring Cav back to such a fantastically interesting place.

They prepared for the journey back, securing the equipment and now unneeded directions into packs on their horses. Axen unfolded the map looking for a possibly faster route home.

"I'm going to explore a little bit down this way," Dylah said with her eyes pointed to the unknown.

"I see the thermos is also unpacked." Axen raised an eyebrow. "What a coincidence."

"It's going to be a long trip back and I just want to stretch my legs and um, re-energize myself." Her amethyst eyes sparkled in the early evening shadows. "And when I get back maybe we sneak off the road for a quick minute." She winked.

"Hurry back."

Dylah ventured off the road and through the surrounding trees taking in the similarities and differences of the forest her soul was rooted in. The slowly setting sun ignited a loving warm glow through the fresh spring leaves and Dylah couldn't help but take slow deep breaths between sips of her now cold coffee. She reflected on their successful mission and what that could mean for her family going forward.

Images flashed in her mind of returning to the house Axen had built and to a future burden being taken off of Cav's shoulder when he would no longer be the heir to Hightree. She breathed a sigh of relief when she pictured herself as just the princess and commander again. A bush of dark blue flowers caught her eye at the base of a tree and she decided to get a closer look before heading back.

Dylah snipped a few stems off of the bush with her dagger and smiled at how regal of a queen she was. She jumped when the sound of various murmurs could be heard approaching. On soft feet she drew nearer to the open road and tilted her head at the far off approaching convoy.

She stayed in the shadows and tiptoed even closer. This road wasn't too familiar to her and she couldn't narrow down which surrounding kingdom could be using it.

As the last rays of sunlight shot through the valley, a strawberry shine reflected off of the leader at the head of the convoy.

Without a thought, Dylah's feet and heart raced back in the direction of Axen. They needed to get to their kingdoms as quickly as possible to prepare for a full fledged battle.

"You look like you've seen a ghost." Axen laughed as she ran towards him. He noticed her black and gray eyes. "Dylah?"

Dylah crashed into him. Her fingers dug into his shoulders as she rested her head against his chest trying to catch her breath.

"It's Nevely."

Chapter 43

Rather Redundant

The reigning Keilon woke earlier than usual to tend to the many needs his young nephew might have. He walked slowly to avoid each creaking floorboard he had memorized many years before when another young child took up residence in the same room. His fingers wrapped around the knob as he gently cracked the door open.

"You're awake already?" Keilon laughed seeing his nephew sitting up in bed scribbling in his book.

"You're awake too." Cav shrugged.

"Drawing anything I should know about?" Keilon watched as Cav sketched an image of a pen and paper.

"Nothing really, but sometimes I don't understand." He sat his pencil down and finally looked at his uncle.

"Anything I could clear up?"

"Who is Hekar?"

Keilon let out a breath as he searched his mind for the unfamiliar name. "I don't know, who said that name in your vision?"

"The funny one."

"Oh." He felt relieved for a reason he didn't understand. "Sorner knows a lot of history so Hekar probably lived a really long time ago."

"Do you know a lot of history too?"

"Not really, there's a certain point where Fellowrock's history gets a little fuzzy." Keilon clapped his hands together to point away from the subject. "Well we should get ready to go so I can take you to check on your kingdom."

"What?" Cav giggled.

"You heard me!" Keilon crossed his arms. "Your parents are away which makes you the ruler of Hightree in their absence." He smirked. "Did you see that one coming?"

"No!" Cav laughed louder.

"After you, your highness."

Old Keilon shuffled down the steps of the borrowed house he shared with his brother. He stopped at the middle step to yawn, contemplated returning to bed, but reluctantly continued on into the kitchen hoping to somehow sneak the extra strong coffee Dylah had hidden. He knew she would be mad, but his exhausted state was purely her doing after she gave him the powder.

"I see sleep has finally welcomed you once again." Sorner grinned from the kitchen table. "The boy stopped by about an hour ago with your prodigy, he was confused about your lack of presence so I told him you were off fighting some terrible creature." He winked. "You might want to construct an exciting story for him." He paused for a moment and looked down at the blank pages in front of him. "We can start whenever you're ready."

"Let me wake up a little and we can dive right into it."

"Take your time, we are going to open up some rather deep wounds today." Sorner nervously tapped his fingers.

"Enfy?"

"Yes."

"Our father?"

"Also yes."

Old Keilon took a deep breath. "Hekar?"

"Yes, and that's where we'll stop for the day."

"Alright, then we better get started." He turned towards the counters and began to measure the usual coffee grounds, but decided to add two extra scoops to prepare for the hurt that would surely be coming.

They sat at the table in silence. Sorner's pen was ready to write the first word, but it wasn't coming to them. Enfy had long been their protector when the world only wanted to use them, she saw their humanity and recognized that their gifts were often burdens. She was the voice that rang in their heads and diving into the death of someone who had such a hand in the events that followed was something they weren't sure they could bring up while also honoring her memory.

"Skip it?" Old Keilon asked.

"I think Dylah will understand." Sorner smiled. "We can always circle back to it, perhaps some night when we are nice and drunk."

"That is exactly the state of mind Enfy would love to be remembered in." He slightly grinned. "Enfy Nothing, Lady of Nowhere."

"Then let's just start with our father's death." Sorner quickly wrote 'Nevik' at the top of the page. "We've already outlined much of your grievances against him, so no need to go into why you harbored such hostility. Just explain how you pulled that off in the middle of a battle."

The first Keilon took a long drink, he remembered the weight of dual swords on his back and the enticing scramble of war. In an instant he was back on the streets of Hightree feeling his heart pumping as he saw his father in a moment of vulnerability and took his opportunity. He began to outline to Sorner the ruse he played up until their father's last breath. How he played the role of a savior until with a flip of his dagger the once great king was left without a voice at the hands of his son who he made into a weapon.

"His death wasn't just through hatred, it was revenge." The former silver stag nodded to his brother.

"I remember the circumstances," Sorner said as he finished writing a line. "I outlined the reasons, they'll understand." He was quiet for a moment as he added a few extra lines. "I am in no way making you the hero, because this is still murder, but there is so much more to be understood about your decisions." He flipped to a clean page and wrote 'Hekar' at the top. "And now let's talk about the death that was my fault."

"You can't still think that!" Old Keilon groaned. "It was all an accident but if I didn't kill him in that battle I would have just killed him at the next opportunity." His eyes were locked on green to hide the oceans underneath. "I think you understand."

"History becomes toxic when it is only one-sided. Just let me tell my side of it." Sorner sighed as he again began to scribble. "I wasn't supposed to be there."

"But you were there because I told you to be."

"We're not arguing about this again, it feels rather redundant." Sorner didn't look up from his writing. "Yes, though he was our close brother, Hekar was probably doomed to fall in some way by your hand. But this is the way it happened and there was a purpose." His dark eyes darted up. "I know you hate to admit it, but his blood coats my hands too."

"I thought he was going to kill you, Sorner." He crossed his arms and sunk into himself. "I saw the rage in his eyes as he lifted his hand to strike you, and at that moment he was no longer my brother. His death wasn't entirely my decision, but saving you was my choice."

"Again." Sorner glanced up. "Rather redundant."

The brothers continued discussing the past until late afternoon. Sorner could tell that the topics were wearing down on the man he had always known as relentlessly strong. He gave an excuse for them to take a break so he would have time to gather the supplies to execute his next plan.

After an hour of staring up at the ceiling in contemplative thought, the first Keilon was shaken back to the present by his brother's usual grand entrance.

"Attention! Stop your sulking, for it is time!" Sorner shouted with a certain jovial timbre.

"Time for what?"

"No questions! To the table!"

Old Keilon shuffled after his skittering brother, ready to dull the high energy that seemed to make the house vibrate. But when he entered the kitchen and saw the pair of wooden cups, four dice, and a thin branch, a smile spread on his face.

"I can't believe you remembered this game." Old Keilon slowly laughed in amazement. "What was the silly name we called it?"

"Cropple Top."

"How long has it been since we've played this?"

Sorner laughed. "Brother, we've both been dead for upwards of three hundred years." His smile slightly fell. "But considering what ages we seem to be now, I'd say we last played this yesterday."

"Right." His eyes streaked with water and clouds. "This hasn't been played since that last real time we-"

"This was actually played quite a bit after that night." Sorner cut him off to divert from the saddening facts. "My two sons and I were avid players in their teen years."

"Really?" He sat down and placed a die in his wooden cup. "Did you always beat them like you used to beat me?"

"Oh no, Rone was far faster than me at rolling his die so he often won." Sorner smiled. "But he only rolled with such vigor because everytime Kei won he'd slap the stick so hard it nearly snapped."

"Kei?"

"You seem surprised." Sorner sat and rattled his own die in his cup. "I thought you knew I named my second son after you?"

"I did, I guess I just thought it wasn't true."

"Well, not entirely after you, Jelina wouldn't allow it and I was still quite angry with you at the time, understandably." He smiled. "They only named you Keilon because they thought 'kei' meant happiness and 'lon' meant strength. They got it half right, but I remember an elder telling me that 'kei' truly meant new." He shrugged. "Seemed like a good name and helped me to remember happiness instead of harboring anger."

"I didn't name a son after you." Old Keilon smiled, feeling a little lighter. "Their mothers named them before I could."

"And what about your daughter?" His eyes brightened. "They told us her name, that had to have been your choice."

"Yes," Old Keilon said as he looked down. "But that's an explanation for another time."

Sorner rolled the spare die and placed it in front of his brother. "You're rolling for a five."

The first Keilon repeated the action and placed a die in front of Sorner. "You're rolling for a three."

After a quick nod they began to shake their cups, rolling over and over again trying to match the number they were given. Then finally, Sorner reached for the stick and slapped his brother's arm.

"It seems I am still quite skilled at this game." His eyes remained a bright green. "Best of out five?"

"Best out of fifty."

The fast paced game they had invented as children continued until they suddenly noticed that Cav and the newer Keilon were watching from the kitchen doorway with confused expressions. It was then decided that the ancestors would teach the ones that came after them in hopes that more than horror stories would live on after them.

Cav found the game especially joyful, where the reigning Keilon just couldn't seem to roll fast enough. The original Keilon had never seen the game played with anyone other than just his brother, and hearing the genuine laughter constantly spill from Cav seemed to make him forget the terrors he had spent the day reliving.

Soon, Sorner had gotten the idea to make it a tournament of sorts. Pinned against each other were those who seemed to always win, Cav against Sorner. On the other side of the table the men of the same name stared at each other, green eyes lightly lined with pink lightning.

"Maybe you two shouldn't go against one another." Sorner glanced back and forth at their equally stern faces. "Or perhaps just warn us when you're about to kill each other."

"Uncle Keilon would never kill anyone!" Cav demanded. "And neither would Uncle K."

"Cav." Sorner smiled when he noticed his brother's eyes turn to amethyst. "You are so well named."

The games continued on for another hour until Cav ultimately won against Old Keilon in the final matches. No one dared to mention how slowly the ancestor had been rolling as if to let the child win.

When their guests left Sorner pulled out a bottle of wine and set a glass in front of his brother.

"Do you remember what we talked about after that last game so many years ago?" Sorner asked while swirling his wine. "What ultimately led me to summon Brennit for help?" He met his brother's azure streaked eyes. "And what made you decide to exile us?"

"The destroyed written history."

"Yes, because you said you wanted to start our cursed kingdom fresh and that the next one would only be able to break the curse if they had no idea what they were." Sorner stared into the crimson liquid. "That was a good decision in the long run."

"What?" he whispered in disbelief.

"Look at Dylah, tenacious wild little thing, and that new Keilon, good strong king, especially take note of Cav, the result of the love you never thought would be possible for the chaotic soul." Sorner smiled. "I'm saying that after all this time I agree with your decision to destroy the texts." He tapped his finger against the table. "There's just still something I'm confused about."

"The overall lack of history altogether?" The first Keilon grinned. "That took some work."

"We were sent letters that were archived into a loose history but I've scoured Fellowrock for anything about your reign and other than the stags on the banners and the fairytale everyone seems to know, there is absolutely nothing, Keilon." Sorner took a quick sip. "Not even the trees whisper your stories. It is baffling and almost admirable how you ripped yourself from existence."

"I commanded them all to forget, and made a pretty extensive deal with the Seers." He calmly took a drink. "I loved one of them."

"The other?" Sorner's eyes lit up.

"Isella." He sighed saying the name he had tried to forget. "My daughter's real mother."

At the Fellowrock castle, Keilon was trying to get an overly excited Cav into bed.

"Can't I stay up until my parents get home?" he begged. "Please?!"

"We have no idea when that will be, and I certainly won't be able to stay awake that long so the answer is no."

Cav glanced out the window then back at his uncle. "Should be soon."

"Do you want to discuss battle tactics until then?" Keilon threw a blanket over his nephew as he outstretched his legs on the bed and crossed his arms. "Let's start with flanking and battalion placements."

Within fifteen minutes Cav was asleep. Keilon tiptoed

out of the room, proud that the trick he used to use on Dylah still had the same effect so many years later. He then paused to think of the adult his sister had become, but brushed off the thought knowing that Cav would most likely grow to be more like his father.

Keilon was tired, but couldn't bring himself to sleep. It wasn't that he had a lot on his mind, something within him had been restless since the sun began to set. He paced the halls of the fifth floor, and then it hit him, the last time he felt this way.

He raced down the stairs remembering the fear he felt when their battalions were separated on that snowy mountain in Gomdea. The battle that took so many lives, nearly took Arkon, and rattled Dylah.

Keilon was pacing circles around the kitchen, deep in his worry, when the castle doors slowly opened and his predecessor tiptoed in.

"What are you doing here?" Keilon appeared in the foyer with arms crossed.

"The house is out of wine." Old Keilon continued to progress towards the kitchen.

"You're stealing wine from the castle?"

"Yes." He smirked. "I thought that was implied."

Keilon watched quietly as the ghost grabbed a bottle of wine, then decided to grab a backup just in case.

"How much do you need?" Keilon huffed.

Old Keilon turned to him ready to fire back something smart then he noticed the cloudiness of his eyes and the stiff energy of the room. "What's wrong?"

Keilon wanted to push the insinuation away but with his predecessor around the unsteady feeling in his soul seemed to feel a little calmer. "I'm not sure."

"Have you considered getting your son to help you solve the root of your worries?" Old Keilon felt the common stubbornness within his prodigy and knew the answer would be no.

"No." Keilon shook his head. "It's late and it's probably nothing."

The first Keilon pulled out a chair at the table then sat across from it, hinting that the king should take a seat. "I'll sit here and wait with you."

"For what?" Keilon sat reluctantly.

"For Dylah." He smiled. "That's what it is, right? You two have always been so well connected, I could tell from the beginning."

"I've never liked the idea of the two of us being looked after by a ghost."

"And you think I enjoyed listening to your teenage in-somniac ramblings?" The ghost rolled his eyes. "Give it a couple centuries and you'll be that creepy ghost."

"Can't I just let Dylah do that?" He half laughed. "I think she would be a lot better at it."

"I already looked into this," Old Keilon said. "It'll be both of you. I was the one who decided the previous chaotic soul should come back for the new one, and you are both the soul, so you'd both come back."

Keilon sat in quiet thought. "So Dycavlon didn't come back for you?"

"No, he was rather annoying." He shook his head at the thought. "Popping into my dreams with these vague mys-terious phrases, calling me 'child of chaos' never helped me much. Even in the afterlife he is a man of minimal words."

"So you made it so you and Sorner could come back to teach who came after the both of you?"

"I'm confused about that as well." His eyes went gray. "I never meddled with the matters of the soul of harmony."

The Keilons were locked in a stare full of confusion when the castle doors flung open and Dylah raced through the foyer and up the stairs. They quickly nodded to each other and followed after her.

By the time they caught up to Dylah they found her in her old bedroom, clutching her sleeping son with tears streaming down her face.

She looked at them with eyes of clouds and power.

"It's not over," she whispered. "Nevely is coming."

Chapter 44

Added Thorns

The men who shared a name waited in the hallway while Dylah quietly rocked her son. She finally emerged, her eyes dark as the night, and walked right past them down to the foyer.

"Dylah, where's Axen?" the reigning Keilon asked.

"Preparing," she answered shortly.

"You need to be more specific, what exactly did you see?" Old Keilon added his own lingering question.

"She's coming, her convoy was large, like she acquired reinforcements." Dylah shook her head. "There's so many."

"Take a breath." Keilon caught her shoulders in an effort to slow down her thoughts. "How long do you think we have?"

"Maybe a day." Dylah's black eyes met his irises that were slowly streaking with impending war. "We got what is needed for Arkon, Axen is having Delin make the treatment immediately."

Keilon nodded. "Okay, I'm going to Hightree." He

squeezed her shoulders. "You can come if you want and help us plan what is to come, or you can stay here and ready yourself."

"That sounds like the same thing!" she growled.

"It's very different, little sister," he said. "One is ensuring that your kingdom is ready on a large scale, the other is finding a trust in yourself to lead them."

"That just means you want me to stay here." She smiled. "Understood."

Keilon quickly went to Hightree to lend his support and begin planning with his allied king.

Dylah paced the foyer, checked on Cav twice, and continuously mumbled to herself. The first Keilon sat at the kitchen table, not wanting to interrupt the constant waves of panic and plotting that radiated off of her.

Soon, Navent and Sentry inched down the stairs. Navent gracefully navigated his way around the distracted queen and stood in the kitchen.

"We heard bits and pieces from the top of the stairs," Navent said. "Our mother is coming?"

"It seems that way." Old Keilon sighed.

"And she has reinforcements?"

"That also seems to be apparent."

Navent briefly looked at him, then at his sister. "Not entirely the news I wanted to hear in the middle of the night, but such is life."

"You are definitely from Sorner's line." The first Keilon winked.

Sentry joined them in the kitchen as they let Dylah walk through her complicated thoughts. They noticed she was winding down, but an idea came to Navent and he pulled his sister to the side to begin outlining what he thought would help the people who had so kindly taken them in.

"I thought this was over!" Dylah clenched her fists at her sides. "I hit her with that dagger, we took custody of the only doctor who could save her! How is she still alive?!"

"Don't you know our souls manage to protect our bodies?" Old Keilon stood a few steps away, wanting to help but not wanting to intrude. "We heal differently."

"She is worthy of decay." Dylah's black eyes pinned on her predecessor.

Sentry and Navent were mumbling to each other in the kitchen off to the side when finally Navent faced the pacing queen of Hightree.

"Dylah," he started slowly, "there's something I'd like to give you."

"Is now really the best time?" Old Keilon growled in her defense.

"Yes." Sentry glared at him.

Dylah sat at the small kitchen table across from Navent, her eyes were still streaked with black but she was trying her best to keep her composure.

"As you know, our father raised us after the curse was broken, and when our mother's motives turned." Navent tried his best to look at her but his eyes often drifted. "There is a bit more to the story, such as the person who helped my father rise to his title."

"Go on."

"We met our Uncle Tin when he was visiting Verinas with his son and grand army. We were still cursed but he took a few things to our father for engraving, they sparked a friendship." Navent smiled. "Every time they visited he had us brought to his tent, our mother often refused to join, but it was always a fun time."

"He let us try foods we had never tried, he had clothes made for us, he never much cared for the disparity in our sizes," Sentry said. "He and our father would often drink and joke well into the night."

"Uncle Tin truly was family." Navent's face fell. "One day he made an unscheduled visit, he was kinder than usual even though he was always quite jovial. He gave us trinkets, treasures from his country, and the morning after one of those nights where he spent drinking and joking with our father, he didn't wake up."

"I'm sorry," Dylah said with a sigh.

"Verinas held a ceremony for him." Navent swallowed the sadness he was feeling. "His son was immediately rude to those helping, he wasn't happy we attended, he even threatened us. But the military leaders all told my father that he would always have their allegiance. Before they left my father stayed up all night engraving. You see, Uncle Tin was a king, he didn't have to be so nice to people as low as we were, but he didn't care. My father engraved a rose on whatever they chose, free of cost, solely in memory of his dear friend."

"But then the curse was broken." Sentry looked down. "We watched our people descend into madness with our mother at the helm and our father remembered he had their allegiance, so he gathered his own army and we left."

"When we first arrived at that grand castle his son was away and what remained of the army welcomed us happily. Although, it did take some convincing to prove that we were in fact the same tiny people their king had loved." Navent's usual happy demeanor returned. "We were celebrated, we got to pay our respects to our uncle's resting place. It was like we were meant to be there our whole lives." He sighed. "Then word had gotten back that the new reigning king was returning, and we got the notion that we should leave." Navent shrugged. "It's not as bad as it sounds, we were traveling with a grand army, we saw so much that we never could and we were having the best time away from our terrible mother."

"But," Sentry stared into the clouds in Dylah's eyes. "About a year later we were called to help that king in a war."

"Our father gathered his men and we marched back towards that place, he felt that it was his duty to his friend to help protect his son's reign." Navent smiled. "He was a fiercely loyal man." His hand fell into his lap. "We waited outside of their kingdom, we were told to wait three days. I'm not sure why, some kind of power play or strategy." He sighed. "But three days passed and we had gotten no word. So we followed our father into their city, the people were celebrating, we assumed they had won their war. But we soon discovered that that was not the case."

"We went into the castle to investigate." Sentry saw the panic on her brother's face. "We walked up so many flights of stairs until we got to the burnt remains of a door."

"Burnt?" Dylah whispered.

"Yes, the room looked like a place of horror." Navent stared at her. "Snapped arrows, a shattered window, and there in the middle of the black marble floor, was his body."

"Our father had us stand back as he walked towards the body." Sentry gulped. "The king was young, maybe twenty-three or twenty-four but he had started his reign with tyranny. We were told he brought that same gluttonous violence to other kingdoms and that the war he started was out of jealousy. His people were happy that he had died."

Navent fiddled with the straps at his side. "This was near his body." He set a dagger on the table. "Our father took it and told us it was the dagger that was wielded to take down tyrants, he vowed to always use it for the same purpose, and he kept that word." He paused. "But he wasn't able to use it on our mother, so I took it." He slid it across the table. "And now I'd like you to have it, Dylah."

Dylah slowly reached out as a voice echoed in her head, a voice she sometimes heard on the stillest of nights, but still, it was a voice that she had pushed away for so long. *"You have so much havoc growing within you, I can see it wanting to burst and beginning to spill out of your eyes."* The words played in a loop just like they did after she had stopped the heart of her once betrothed.

She wrapped her hand around the handle of the dagger and inspected the familiar design.

"You're right," Dylah said, "this dagger was wielded to take down tyrants." Her pink eyes met Navent and Sentry's awaiting stare before they drifted over to her advisor. "And that's exactly why I used it to kill Zether, I'll continue to use it."

"You killed Zether?" Sentry gaped.

"I knew King Wrantin, he visited us often too." Dylah smiled. "He was a good man, I remember his proud laugh." She inspected the dagger again, this time without fear and echoes but with a plan. "You know, this dagger found me. I was in a battle I couldn't tear myself away from because I had the voice of a ghost in my head telling me to keep fighting." She pointed a nod at the embodiment of the voice. "I saw this dagger laying in the dirt and I knew I needed it." She tilted the blade and let the dim light reflect off of it. "And that night when I decided to kill him, I knew this dagger was meant for his final heartbeat. I remember seeing this rose on the blade, your father engraved that?" Dylah grinned at the young siblings. "Did he add the thorns after finding it?"

"Yes." Navent nodded. "And each of the added thorns represents an evil leader the dagger helped extinguish. The top one is Zether's."

"I often wonder if I was meant to kill him, a part of me never thought it was a just action." She continued to study the familiarity of the dagger and how at home it felt in her grasp. "Something told me it was what had to happen to ignite my power, that he was a terrible man incapable of change, and yes, I was protecting Axen." Dylah stared across the table at Navent and Sentry. "But now I'm starting to believe that chaos never jumps from one thing to another, it's a fire on a string, slowly burning, showing a connection as it consumes whatever it touches, but always leading down the line."

"Correct," Old Keilon finally interjected.

Dylah smiled, pink and black surging irises pinned on the blade. She calmly flipped the dagger and effortlessly caught the hilt. "Then we shall let it burn."

Chapter 45

Pretend to Sleep

Axen stood with arms crossed watching Delin mix the ingredients of what he hoped would be the final treatment. He wasn't allowing himself to worry about Nevely yet, he knew the Riloncks and all of their chaotic tendencies would come up with the beginnings of a plan in no time. Right now he needed to focus on saving his brother.

"I'm glad you brought two samples," Delin said in a tone that was closer to his usual demeanor. "One should be enough, but I'd hate for you to make that trip twice. And it never hurts to have a backup."

"Why didn't you specify more about why Dylah was needed?"

"I didn't think she'd go if I gave such a specific set of directions." Delin half smiled. "I know it's the mystery of the unknown that calls to my little sister."

"You're not wrong." Axen forced himself to remain serious even though the conversation had a casual feel to it. "How much longer do you think?"

Delin winced as he watched the bubbles grow in a beaker. "Soon, maybe five more minutes." He nodded. "You'll have to give it to him almost immediately after it's ready, I hope you're ready to run."

"His room is between the second and third decks, how fast do you think I can run up those steps?" Axen shook his head letting his exhaustion catch up to his panic.

"You're right that's quite a trek to be making." Delin furrowed his brows in thought. "I can warp it up there if you want a head start."

"What do you mean?"

"Atta taught me a while back." Delin shrugged. "She said it was something she was teaching my mother too, I'm not as good at it as she is. I can't do two people and a whole horse, but a vial should be no problem."

Axen began weighing his options, and how trustworthy his brother-in-law could be.

"You've been able to use your spells?" he finally asked. "I thought we canceled those out."

"Uh, yeah." Delin added another drop of liquid into the serum. "I figured out a way around that about two months ago."

"And you didn't tell us?!" Axen nearly shouted. "What have you been doing?!"

"Just casually checking in." Delin watched as the bubbling began to slow. "You need to go now if this is going to work."

Axen didn't have time to decide whether this was an honorable plan, nor a spare moment to begin deducing Delin's quiet trickery behind bars, he just ran up the steps towards Arkon's room.

A childhood of growing up on one of the higher floors triggered his muscle memory to kick in, remembering which stairs were the easiest to skip and which turns were the sharpest. A forgotten memory of challenging Arkon to a race up the same steps began to replay in his head, and his brother's young voice served as extra motivation.

Axen had his hand on the doorknob so fast he didn't even notice the shadow to the right of the door as it followed him in.

"Slow down!" Keilon finally said. "I know there's a lot to think about right now."

Axen ignored him as his eyes darted around. "Do you see a small vial anywhere?"

"Vial?" Keilon asked slowly.

Axen was about to let out a sigh of frustration, his fists were clenched and he was already regretting his trusting nature, then with a slight cloud of smoke it appeared at the foot of the bed.

"Help me prop him up!" Axen ordered. He ran over to the drawer of supplies and procured a syringe. "It has to go directly into his injury."

Keilon didn't answer. He stood at the side of the bed and pushed Arkon up while steadying his wobbly posture. The shock of being sat up in bed seemed to jolt Arkon into his most sentient self, rapid finger tappings, angry murmurs, and sloppy head shakes.

"I don't think now's the time to throw a fit, my friend." Keilon chuckled as Axen filled the syringe with the prepared liquid. "You can shout at me all you want soon, but for now just stay still." He placed a flat hand on top of Arkon's head to stop the silent protest.

"Okay, he'll need to stay still for a few minutes after I inject him," Axen said as he lined up his shot. "I'm not sure if there will be side effects or how long it could even take."

"Just do it." Keilon nodded. "It's going to be fine."

"Mhmm."

"See?" Keilon tapped Arkon's head. "Your brother agrees."

Axen smiled briefly and without a warning inserted the needle into the faded spot on Arkon's neck. He pushed the serum in slowly but removed the needle in an instant. He applied pressure over the injection with his thumb and began to count silently.

Arkon shook slightly, but no other reaction could be seen and he wasn't responding. They returned him to his regular flat position and collectively collapsed into the nearby chairs.

"I bet if I think about it hard enough, Dylah will bring us some coffee," Keilon whispered after too much silence had passed. "I'm sure that wouldn't be an abuse of this connection we have, right?"

"Is she handling everything okay? I just needed to do this first and I feel terrible for her to start the war planning on her own." Axen sighed. "We made a few plans on our trip home but they all revolved around hiding or protecting Cav, and if her curse would work on Cav if she held him tight enough."

"Would it?"

"She tried with the horse." Axen laughed. "It didn't work."

"Well, now you know!" Keilon shrugged. "We'll come up with some good plans, we'll beat her again no problem."

"It would just be really great if Arkon woke up so he could put out these orders."

"I'm sorry, correct me if I'm wrong," Keilon started slowly, "but I was always under the impression that you were the mastermind behind all of the tactics and planning." He raised an eyebrow. "I never thought Arkon came up with the plan to have archers jumping on rooftops."

"Well, I had to think of something to stay one step ahead of your little alley patrols." Axen smirked. "And it's much more fun to make the plans but have someone else announce them." His smirk fell. "A lot less pressure that way."

"You're tellin me!" Keilon smacked his arm. "But for what it's worth, you wore the title well, I'm almost sorry to see you lose it."

"Are you just saying that so you can continue to watch

Dylah be the most awkward queen?"

"Her wave could use some work, yes." Keilon chuckled. "But that's not it. Even when we stood on opposite sides, the way you shook my hand, the way you spoke to us, the way you carried your morals into battle, it's all very noble." He turned to him with forced green eyes to hide his own emotion underneath. "Really, Axen, you're a good king, I hope you know that."

"Thank you." Axen smacked him back. "You too, although you do hang out in a castle that's not yours far too often."

"Yeah, you wretched Rilonck."

"Those are your first words?!" Axen took quick steps to be at his brother's side. Arkon's dull hazel eyes were blinking furiously with a slight sparkle that they hadn't possessed since a snowy trip. "After this whole time you throw an insult at our ally?"

Arkon smiled slightly and began to cough. "Water," he rasped with a shaky finger pointing to the side table.

Keilon was immediately at Arkon's other side with a glass. Together with Axen, Arkon was propped up in bed. He was holding the glass on his own although his grip was a bit shaky.

"How do you feel?" Axen barely blinked, staring in disbelief at each sign of vibrant life bouncing off of his brother.

"Just clearing out the cobwebs." Arkon chuckled.

"I did see a few spiders crawl in your mouth these past few months." Keilon grinned. "Fast little creatures, couldn't stop them."

"He's kidding!" Axen blurted.

"I know." Arkon smiled, his eyes slowly rolled over to Keilon. "So the other colors finally came? The purple is odd, but it fits you." His smile grew. "I went to sleep knowing exactly what you were, Keilon."

"And have you known of the events happening throughout your nap?" Keilon asked.

Arkon sighed. "It's all a little muddled together."

"Of course," Axen started, "just rest, we can catch you up when you're up for it."

"But you have a war to plan." Arkon took another sip of water. "I mean you both do, the kings."

"You're the king." Axen gripped his brother's shoulder. "Your absence didn't change that."

"Axen, you have been running this kingdom well, I do know that." Arkon looked to Keilon and waited for him to nod. "You didn't have to do so well as an interim king, but I know Hightree is thriving."

"Thank you," Axen said slowly. "I had to for the sake of our kingdom. You think I'd just leave it to buffer while you were incapacitated?"

"You did more than enough." Arkon nodded. "And you'll continue to do so."

"As a Second, yes."

"No, brother, listen." Arkon laughed so loudly it prompted another cough. "I will not regain my title, it isn't mine anymore."

"Let's just give you a few days to get to your normal self and we'll discuss it again." Axen laughed nervously. "I don't expect you to be thinking clearly right away."

"I've spent months only thinking." Arkon's eyes seemed to widen. "Distinguishing voices, hearing worries, feeling parts of me come back." He sipped the water again. "But I did think, and the more I heard, the more I realized that I don't want to be king. My time is done, Axen."

"We'll discuss this again later." Axen stood. "I'm going to get Avalia."

Keilon waited until the door had closed before he turned back to his friend. "You couldn't have given him a minute?" He laughed. "Of all the times for you to drag out the point and you just throw it at him instead?"

"Well, do you think it's the wrong decision?" Arkon

weakly raised an eyebrow.

"Not at all, but still." Keilon grinned. "It's pretty hasty."

"Maybe I just don't want the pressure of having to make thirty three heirs." Arkon laughed and closed his eyes. "Being awake is exhausting."

Arkon lightly slept until the sound of the door woke him up. Keilon decided to wait in the hallway while the siblings reunited.

Arkon's eyes quickly landed on Avalia's rounding stomach.

"Weren't you pregnant when we left?" He smirked. "Stubborn child or expecting another?"

"I've told you quite a few times now that I was expecting number five this summer." Avalia sat beside her brother and propped her feet on the bed. "I'm so glad you're awake, otherwise I would have to name this one after you."

"Well, tell me about them," Arkon said slowly with a shifting eye towards Axen who was inching closer and closer to the door.

"Well, Frenia has started taking harp lessons," Avalia started with a wide smile. "Taron and Terner somehow fashioned a slingshot and have been aiming at birds on the first deck."

"Cute." Arkon chuckled.

"And I can't wait for Furin to finally meet you, he was born shortly after you all went to war." She pointed to her stomach. "I think this one is a girl, and we'll be naming her Iries."

Axen fell against the closed door, the weight of exhaustion, relief, and shock hitting him all at once.

"Why don't you go get some sleep?" Keilon suggested, leaning against the opposite side of the hall. "You've done enough for today and you have more to do."

"How am I supposed to sleep after all of this?" he said above a whisper. "The trip, Nevely, the treatment, and now I have to figure out how to tell Dylah that she's still the queen."

"Just close your eyes and pretend." Keilon shrugged. "Trust me, some of my best kingly decisions have come when I was just pretending to be asleep."

"I can't leave Arkon right now."

"I think you can do whatever you want." Keilon laughed. "Do I need to point out why?"

Axen sighed and returned to the room. He hugged his brother and promised repeatedly to visit first thing in the morning with Cav. Then he started walking towards the trees, he barely noticed the brooding presence matching his pace, but he welcomed it.

They passed the house nestled on the border with one light on upstairs. Their steps continued on in silence as they drew closer to the castle. The foyer was eerily quiet, each subtle creak mimicked the sound of thunder against the stillness and made them adjust their strides.

Finally, in front of the door on the fourth floor they were stopped by a barricade of sprawled out legs. Old Keilon was propped against the door, his head back, eyes closed, and arms crossed. Keilon kicked his feet to wake him.

"Oh!" He shook himself awake. "Welcome back."

"What are you doing?" Axen asked with a slight smirk. "Is Dylah okay?"

"Uh yeah." The first Keilon slowly stood. "She'll catch you up tomorrow, but she has already come up with lots of plans."

"That doesn't explain why you're crashing in front of her door." Keilon pointed fiery eyes at his predecessor.

"The young ones from Sorner's line gave her a gift," Old Keilon started, "this gift made her very excited. She was up and pacing and planning. Then after coming up here she just kept getting up again. I caught her at least four times." He sighed and shook his head. "She used the curse and slid under the door and she even punched me because she felt the need to bring you both coffee."

Keilon elbowed Axen. "See."

"But it's been long enough, I think she's finally out."

Steps were heard at the other end of the hallway, soon the shadow seemed familiar.

"Are you kidding me?!" Old Keilon growled.

"Window." Dylah laughed. "Why are you still here? You should probably get some sleep."

"We should all get some sleep," Keilon added. "We'll begin setting plans in the morning, which is just a few short hours away."

"You left a light on at the house by the way," Axen said as he began to follow Dylah into the room.

"Damnit, that means Sorner is worried." Old Keilon quickly left.

Dylah popped her head out next to Axen. "Did the treatment work?"

"Yes!" Keilon beamed. "Our friend is back with us!"

"It will take him some time to regain his strength." Axen smiled. "But he is sitting up and talking like his usual self."

"That's great!" Dylah sighed with relief. "I guess we should probably let the old guys know we'll be taking our house back once this thing with Nevely is over. I'm so happy to be the princess again." She slipped back into the room.

Axen glanced over to the other king.

"Just pretend to sleep," Keilon whispered before heading off. "We'll break the news to her in the morning."

Chapter 46

Wildly Distracting

Within the first ten minutes of gathering in the kitchen, Keilon had yawned the loudest, Dylah was already halfway through her refilled mug, and Axen watched every granule of sugar fall into his light colored coffee. Cav was oblivious as he sat scribbling in his book and kicking his legs beneath the table.

"We're visiting Arkon first then meeting with everyone?" Dylah asked.

"Yes," Keilon answered but Dylah was waiting for a response from her husband.

"Can you pass the sugar?" she asked with a raised eyebrow.

"Since when do you take sugar in your coffee?" Keilon muttered.

Axen calmly slid it over to her.

"Dear." She grinned. "I'm going to need you to say it."

"Say what?" Axen laughed.

"You know what." She leaned back in her chair and crossed her arms. "I've been setting you up for it all morning and you almost said it once then stopped yourself."

"I don't know what you're talking about."

"Say it." Dylah's eyes ignited. "Say 'of course, princess.'"

"Dylah." Keilon pinched the bridge of his nose.

"Of. Course. Princess," she insisted.

"Yeah, uh-" Axen glanced from Keilon to his wife. "I really don't think I can call you that anymore."

Dylah seemed to lose every word in existence as she looked from her husband to her brother with eyes that shifted so fast they should have made a sound.

Kunor interrupted the quiet as he stood in the doorway. "Why does Dylah look like the harbinger of melancholy?"

"She just found out that she is permanently the queen." Keilon flashed a smile at his son. "Taking it rather well."

"When we visit Uncle Arkon," Cav said, ignoring the tension in the room as he continued to scribble, "can we take the secret stairway?"

"Hightree doesn't have a secret stairway." Axen was happy for the change in subject. "But we can take the tunnel if you want to."

When the proper amount of caffeine had been inhaled the group readied themselves for a day of happy and perhaps sinister reunions.

Axen, Cav, and Keilon all left together chatting about the weather and the first signs of an approaching summer. Dylah hung back, she detached and reattached her navy and lavender cape, she fiddled with a stray wave that hung in front of her face, she sighed almost every other breath.

"Why does being the queen bother you so much, Dylah?" Kunor said from the doorway of the kitchen.

"I thought you left with them." She tucked the wave behind her ear. "We should catch up before they get too far."

"We will." Kunor took wide strides to cut her off before she could open the castle doors. "But let's talk first."

"No." Dylah crossed her arms. "Your brother has woken up from a deep sleep and there is a convoy of hatred inching closer to us with every passing second, we do not have time to talk."

"Just tell me why being the queen has you so rattled."

"Axen is a wonderful king, smart and calm, stoic but friendly, it is the perfect role for him. I swear, he was born for it." She shook her head. "But I was never meant to hold such a title and that's all I want to say about the matter."

"Okay, that's fine." Kunor smiled. "Anyway, look at this dagger Sorner gave me."

Dylah looked up, fascinated by the weapon in Kunor's hand, he raised it until it was in front of his face. Before she could catch on she seemed to be caught in his eyes of sunlight.

After his hold released Dylah growled quietly and escaped into the courtyard as he followed after her.

"I'm sorry, I had to!"

"I don't like that you're getting so good at that." She stomped towards the treeline.

"Your worries are wrong!"

Dylah planted her feet. "You can't know that."

"But I know you," he said with a grin. "Just because you are given a title doesn't mean that you will descend into what your mind calls tyrannical chaos."

"But-"

"What made him was a society of zealots who

craved every aspect of his power, I know you understand that." Kunor wrapped an arm around his aunt and
pushed her along the path. "He thrives in a place that
supports him, and as for the other half of your soul, he's
been king for a while now, do you think his power is an
issue for him?"

"Thank you," she quickly agreed with his reasoning.

"It's my purpose to be the thorn in your side that
you never pluck out."

Just as the morning was beginning to fade into
afternoon, scouts returned with new information. Plans
were beginning to occupy the thoughts of everyone in
an overly filled meeting room of Fareins and Riloncks
alike. Quiet chattering hung between those who knew
each other and those who didn't, until the doors opened
and the ones in charge took their seats at either end of
the table. Keilon and Dylah at one end, and Axen with
his newly appointed Second in Command, Kunor.

"Bahn, Brig, Kane, what did you see out there?" Keilon cut right to the point.

"It is not a traveling community like before," Bahn
started.

"She has found reinforcements." Brig nodded to his
uncle.

"We estimate she will be here by late evening," Kane
added.

"Do we fight her tonight?" Kremon asked. "Cut
them off before they get to us?"

"I think that would be preferred," Axen said with a
nervous tapping finger to the tabletop.

"You recommend we just stand in lines waiting in
the middle of nowhere?" Dylah laughed. "What advantage does that give us?"

"It protects the ones who are not fighting," he answered.

"I agree, we can't meet her in an open field." Keilon's eyes were rimmed with pink. "It is very likely that she has brought her allies from Gomdea. If that is the case then we are not safe in an open field. Remember?"

"Is Derck's army coming?" Bahn asked. "Maybe we could surround her."

"No." Keilon shook his head. "His convoy would take at least a week to get here, but I did already send word just in case."

"Our mother will waste no time once she's here." Sentry grasped the pause in conversation to speak. "Whatever we do, we need to put it in motion the second she steps off that horse."

"That's true, she's only patient the first time around." Navent rolled his eyes.

"We need to fight her in Hightree," Sorner said as he repeatedly elbowed his brother.

"No," an unfamiliar voice shook from across the table. "You are not going to use my kingdom as your battle ground when she is an enemy of Fellowrock."

"Aelof, stop," Axen whispered down the line. "An enemy of Fellowrock is an enemy of Hightree."

"Axen, who is this punchy young one?" Sorner grinned.

"This is my younger brother, Aelof, next to him is my other younger brother, Arler. They're both seventeen and would like to fight with us."

"Twins then?" Sorner laughed. "Always a delightful occurrence!"

"Different mothers." Aelof glared across the table, eyes the color of wet tree bark.

"I see." Sorner flashed a smile. "Your father had an odd manner of ambition. Hm?"

"Why do you think we should fight her in Hightree, Sorner?" Kunor asked to dull the heat.

"Oh, right!" Sorner seemed to shift out of his constant comparisons of Axen and his younger half brothers. "Keilon has a wonderful plan."

Every head at the packed table turned towards the Fellowrock king.

"Not me." The reigning Keilon sighed as he gestured towards the ancestor.

"I don't have a plan, Sorner!" Old Keilon whispered through clenched teeth.

"Yes, it's a rather old one, but you never got to use it and now would be the perfect time!" Sorner gestured to the rest of the table. "Tell them what plan you would have carried out through that final battle had we not been cursed."

Old Keilon slowly smiled as his eyes finally matched the color his prodigies had been wearing since they stepped in. "Your massive castle has a hidden stairwell."

"Oh it is such poetic justice that we finally get to carry out this plan, brother!" Sorner began to laugh hysterically.

"But why would we need to sneak into the Hightree castle?" Dylah asked, eyes pinned on her predecessor.

The first Keilon was quiet for a moment as he thought over the plan forming in his mind. "You Fareins aren't going to like this."

The meeting proceeded on with many arguments, it was apparent that the Fareins were not confident in the orchestrations of one with such an evil reputation. Dylah and Keilon were quick to back up the plan while adding in their own changes that were better suited for the safety of others. Soon enough the yelling quieted as the final holes were patched, accommodations were thought up and teams were assigned. Everyone was sent off to rest and prepare for what was coming.

With the sun sinking low Arkon, Avalia and her

children, and Cav were moved to the Fellowrock castle. With them taken care of the others would be able to focus on the task that would be approaching. Kunor paced the foyer of the castle, until a hand grabbed his elbow and led him down a hallway.

"It is imperative that I teach you something." Sorner's eyes matched the shadows they were standing in. "Part of your gift allows for a gentle passing."

"Passing?" Kunor whispered.

"Yes, as you may have guessed I am not a fighter, but I went to war to be at the sides of those who fell." Sorner nodded. "It is a final kindness to die surrounded by harmony."

Kunor thought to red snow on the mountain, the bodies strewn about and the worries he felt back before he knew what he was, along with the regrets he carried that they had died in such a way. "Teach me."

Upstairs Dylah began her instructions. "And if anything happens you take the kids, hide, and wait."

"Through the kitchens and down the basement stairwell." Chany nodded. "Don't worry, I'll get us there."

They watched as Avalia's children and Cav raced through the hallway.

"The castle will be locked down once you leave, right?" Avalia asked.

"Yes." Dylah nodded. "Chany will be in charge of anything that happens after the lockdown, but I think our plan is pretty solid so I wouldn't worry about it."

"It helps that the plan was made by someone who already attempted it once and failed." Chany laughed. "No matter how many centuries have passed since then, failure like that stings and never wants to be repeated."

"That doesn't sound too reassuring to me." Avalia laid a hand on her stomach.

"It'll be fine." Dylah flashed a smile and began

brushing through her waves to smooth them. "And it should be a fun time."

"Though I do understand the need for our safety I am a little jealous to not be going." Avalia smiled.

"Me too," Chany said. "At least my boys will have some fun though."

Dylah took a step into her old room but within a breath turned back to her sisters-in-law. "In case it doesn't go completely fine."

"Shush." Chany pointed a strong finger at Dylah. "I've seen you come back from the dead, you'll come back tonight."

"Still." Dylah watched as Cav laughed with his cousins. "Just take care of him, okay?"

"Of course." Avalia nodded. "You better finish getting ready or you'll be late to your own battle."

Dylah disappeared into the closet briefly before emerging in a sleek satin emerald long sleeved ball gown with a slit up the right leg and half of her spine exposed in the back. "But I'm not going into battle, I'm going to a ball with my husband."

"You look pretty, mama!" Cav stopped his running.

"Thanks, kiddo." Dylah ruffled his hair. "Should I wear my war eyes with it?"

"Absolutely!" Cav laughed.

When the night had finally fallen, Kremon, Dylah, and Axen peered over the edge of the first deck watching the horizon for any movement as music played loudly behind them.

"I guess we should go ahead and dance." Kremon elbowed his sister. "Queen Dylah."

She glared up at him, her eyes matching the orange jewels nestled into her silver crown. Axen grabbed her hand and led her into the dancing crowd. He wrapped his arms around her waist and laughed.

"What?" she raised an eyebrow.

"You have a dagger in the small of your back."

"I don't know why you're surprised."

"You should also be mindful of the slit on your leg, it sometimes shows the dagger sheathed to your thigh." Axen smirked as they swayed to the music. "It's also wildly distracting."

"Perhaps we shouldn't have chosen a ruse that would force you to look so damn handsome, your majesty." She grinned back with sparkling amethyst eyes.

"You do look incredible by the way." Axen pulled her in a little closer. "Unlike yourself, but still beautiful."

Dylah leaned in and gently kissed him on the cheek before whispering in his ear, "This is your sister's dress."

"Don't make this weird."

Kremon slipped beside them. "Word from the scouts, one hour."

Axen nodded slightly, balancing his own crown on his head. He continued dancing with his wife to keep up the illusion of a happy celebration and not a preemptive counter attack.

After a twirl under his arm he dipped Dylah and met her sparkling gaze of lavender. "Are you ready for this, you nightmare?"

Her eyes were pink lightning in an instant. "Born ready."

Chapter 47

Hand in Hand

Nevely raised a halting fist as her convoy approached the edge of the neighboring kingdoms. She dismounted her horse and summoned eight guards to walk with her towards the two still figures in the road.

"Get out of our way or suffer the consequences!" Nevely shouted.

"You would do that to your own children?" Navent laughed and took a step closer.

"We come offering help," Sentry added.

Nevely crossed her arms. "You were both seen helping the Riloncks as they attacked our camp. You cannot be trusted."

"We were swayed by Dylah," Navent said with a sigh in his voice. "The chaos that ripples from her is intoxicating, we've only just now forced ourselves away from her malice."

"I wish this was truly a happy reunion but this doesn't add up to me." Nevely took a slow step forward, eyes darting between her children in the night. "I need to see your worries."

"Do it," Sentry demanded.

Nevely stood staring slightly up at her daughter, she gripped Sentry's chin and forced her head to tilt downward. Her eyes went from the brightest green to the darkest shade then a steady jade as she gazed into the depths of the worries she had. "Oh my sweet Navaly, you do share the same worries I have!"

Sentry held back her sigh of relief after realizing that Kunor's erasure had truly worked.

"And me?" Navent grinned. "Do you need to check me?"

"No," Nevely said shortly. "You've always followed your sister, I know your intentions are clear if hers are."

"How true." Navent forced his grin.

"We wanted to let you know that Fellowrock is fully prepared for your arrival, one step through those trees and you will perish." Sentry funneled worry into her voice. "But Navent and I have found a weak spot."

"The Fareins." Navent pointed to the castle sparkling with party lights. "They made no effort to safeguard their kingdom, instead King Axen has decided to celebrate his coronation. What were his words again, sister?"

"'I don't care,'" Sentry huffed. "Meaning he sees you as no threat."

"But, he was stupid enough to befriend us and we grew to know that castle inside and out." Navent chuckled. "We're going to help you take it."

"If Hightree is yours it gives you a tactical advantage against Fellowrock." Sentry scowled. "Let our help be the apology you've wanted from us for so long."

"My dear children, your leaving wasn't your fault!" Nevely grabbed their hands. "It was the doing of your terrible father, he clouded your judgment, and I see that his passing has finally led you back to me."

"So now let us lead you to the revenge you so desire," Sentry spoke when she saw her younger brother begin to break.

"Revenge is not in my nature." Nevely smiled. "Only balance. Come on Navaly and Navent, show me how to attain it."

After some organizing, Nevely's forces from Verinas along with her allies from Gomdea began to walk through the quiet village in the shadows of the Hightree castle.

Each step closer amplified the music of the ball, Nevely watched the spinning silhouettes on the first desk and grinned at their temporary bliss. With pointed hand signals she sent her men to check the streets and alleys for reinforcements. Navent and Sentry stayed at their mother's side whispering the directions that would benefit her the most.

Three soldiers that had branched off felt a level of excitement away from their leader's powerful gaze. Their muffled chuckles neared closer to a humble house they were planning to ransack, but when the first soldier reached for the door he felt a chill from the knob through his thick glove. Another soldier noticed frost along the seams of the door. The last soldier placed two fingers in his mouth to signal for reinforcements, but before he could exhale he fell to the ground stiff and asleep next to his two comrades.

Other surrounding enemy forces were meeting the same end of a sleep tipped arrow before getting dragged into the shadows by a blend of allied archers in all black.

"Do you hear something?" Nevely stopped with a single halting finger in the air.

"Strays," Navent blurted. "Hightree is crawling with them."

"Fitting." Nevely rolled her eyes and continued forward.

Sentry paused for a moment to catch the flash of her beloved's smile in the shadows. Knowing he was nearby gave her a boost of strength to continue on.

"They leave their gates wide open?" Nevely laughed. "Weak."

"They're too friendly for their own good." Sentry shrugged. "It truly is a shame."

Up on the first deck the music continued with a vivacious tempo. Those in attendance shuffled about in a feverish fit of dancing, or so it seemed, because within the steps weapons were being distributed.

Axen took a moment to peer over the edge, happy to see that the citizens had followed instructions by using the ice tips he provided to keep their doors and windows secured from an invasion. He was also proud to see the blend of archers, led by his newly appointed Second in Command, taking out the enemy with precise stealth.

Dylah skipped through the crowd offering an instruction with every landing of her high heeled shoes. She knew her eyes didn't work on those from Hightree, but she felt as if they did because there was an electrified spirit to the mixed crowd of soldiers, family, nobles, and citizens. They were ready.

Axen joined his wife in a slow waltz, the softer music allowing them to take in the sounds of an approaching enemy.

"They're at the gate." Aelof stood by his older brother with his arms crossed. "Now what?"

"You and Arler need to go to the sibling hallways and make sure everyone is ready to go." Axen nodded. "You know the instructions from there."

"Why can't we stay and fight?" Aelof asked with a slight growl and glance towards Dylah.

"Hey, there's a reason why our father decided to have so many heirs." Axen laughed. "If things don't go too well tonight, you're up!" He shrugged. "Until Cav is old enough."

"Fine." He shuffled away. "I just don't understand what gave the Riloncks the right to have a say in our castle."

Dylah stepped in front of him and pointed the ancient irises up at him. "My soul made this castle!"

Aelof paid her no mind as he continued on towards his assigned mission, Arler followed without a word.

"You know he has never liked you, why do you keep giving him more reasons?" Axen smirked.

"I don't know, it's kind of fun." Dylah flashed a smile. "One last dance before chaos takes over?"

"Since when has chaos taken a break?" He laughed as he placed his hands back on her waist. "Did I blink and miss it? Will you let me know the next time the havoc pauses?"

Dylah was mid eye roll when the stomps of an approaching army were heard drawing nearer.

Nevely, Navent, and Sentry joined the party on the first deck as the music quickly cut out. The soldiers were soon behind them blocking the only exit. The partygoers shouted in a panic, Dylah clutched her face to muffle a scream as she grabbed onto her husband. Axen wrapped an arm around Dylah and took quick steps to stand between the enemy and his people.

"What is the meaning of this?!" he shouted with one hand on the hilt of his sword at his hip.

"I think you know why I've returned." Nevely crossed her arms. "You've taken something that shouldn't belong to you."

"I'm assuming you're speaking of the child who looks exactly like me and has his mother's joy nestled in his eye?" Axen laughed.

"Just tell me where he is and we'll be on our way," Nevely said calmly. With a subtle nod Navent and Sentry broke away from their mother's side and approached the king and queen.

Navent was quick to send Axen's sword sliding across the deck, while Sentry pulled Dylah away from her husband, she stood holding the queen to her front with her rapier resting across her throat.

"Please," Dylah whimpered as a tear fell down her cheek.

Nevely laughed watching the despair flood over her enemy. "Just tell us where Cav is and we'll leave you alone."

"No!" Axen managed to yell as he was being restrained by Navent.

Sentry put more force against Dylah's neck.

"Please, don't hurt him." Dylah stared at her enemy with eyes like oceans. "You must take care of my son and let him grow strong."

"He will grow strong as long as he's away from you." Her green eyes warped to nearly black.

"Dylah, don't!" Axen struggled against Navent's hold.

"He's in the room that overlooks the third deck," she said through her cascading tears. "Please just take him and leave Hightree forever."

Nevely's smile spread from ear to ear as she began to funnel her soldiers off the deck and into the castle. Navent and Sentry released their captives, Axen and Dylah immediately collapsed into each other in a flurry of sobs and anger.

When Nevely and half of her soldiers had left. Dylah straightened her posture, wiped the fake tears away and turned to the ready crowd

"Now!"

Axen grabbed Dylah's hand and ran her through the leftover crowd of enemy forces as the partygoers began throwing their stashed away smoke bombs. Axen, Dylah, and Kremon, managed to slip into the castle as the dust rose and made the soldiers fall asleep.

"Great acting, you two!" Kremon slapped a hand on Dylah's shoulder.

Axen opened the first door in the hallway and handed his brother-in-law a bow and stocked quiver of arrows. He took off his crown along with Dylah's and stashed them away for safekeeping in the same closet.

"Good luck," Dylah nodded at each of them as they adjusted their arrow tip canisters. "I'll meet you soon." She nodded to her brother, offered a quick peck to her husband, then disappeared down the hallway.

"Please be safe!" Axen called out after her.

"Of course, my king!"

Dylah gripped the skirt of her dress as she hung close

to the wall, her shoes in her other hand to ensure that her steps would fall like a phantom. She had followed the enemy soldiers to the level of the second deck but she soon heard a scuffle.

"You're a little late," Keilon said leaning against the wall of the hallway, unconscious soldiers strewn about the floor.

"You were supposed to meet me two floors down!" Dylah fired back.

"I may have lost count of which floor I was on." He shrugged then glanced at his sister. "Do we need to stop by your suite? Or are you confident you won't trip on your own skirt?"

"We don't have time," Dylah groaned. "How far ahead is she?"

"It's tough to tell, they've split up into smaller groups."

"And the kids?"

"Navent and Sentry are still with her, yes." Keilon grinned. "Which makes your job a lot easier."

The siblings nodded with an understanding that only their shared soul could convey. They continued down the dark corridors of the castle they once only dreamed of. A group of five soldiers shuffled ahead of them, their heads were on a swivel looking for any threat but paying no attention to the one quietly approaching.

Keilon dragged the straggler away with a tight hold on his neck, but during his attempt to drag another they were caught. Dylah held a shoe by the heel and knocked a soldier on the back of the head with it as Keilon shoved two others, making them knock their skulls together in a satisfying sound that sent them both into a slumber. He grabbed the remaining soldier by the collar and held him captive.

"Do you want this one, little sister? I already handled three and you only had one." Keilon laughed as the soldier tried his best to get away.

Dylah quickly scanned the soldier and forced her eyes to fog over. "Sleep."

As they progressed up two more floors, they used punches, kicks, and commanding vision to defeat twelve more soldiers, until the hallway split.

"You go right then meet back up with the others." Dylah stared down the dark hall ahead. "She's not too far ahead." She pointed electric eyes at her brother. "I got this."

"Don't take too long," Keilon commanded before vanishing down the dark hallway.

Dylah had gone the whole fight without a dagger in her hand, but the challenge of wearing a dress and using fancy shoes as a weapon was thrilling to her. It reassured her that she was always meant to be a fighter, with or without weapons she was a fitting vessel of chaos. She stood at the bottom of a stairway with a steep incline, at the top she saw Nevely, Navent, Sentry, and two other soldiers slip into the darkness. In the middle of the staircase was a group of five soldiers. Dylah knew she wouldn't have a shot at Nevely unless she eliminated her backup here and now.

When the soldiers were at the top of the stairs, meaning that Nevely was far ahead, Dylah whistled sharply and smiled when they immediately started running after her. Dylah probably should have ran, instead she studied the threat approaching, which ones she would need to take out first and which ones might give her the most trouble. With a plan in mind she started taking backwards steps as the whites of their eyes drew closer.

Pink irises narrowed as they picked their first target followed by a smack and a thud as the soldier and the shoe that hit him fell to the floor. Dylah continued running backwards, firing another shoe at the weaker of those remaining. With her hands now free she gripped the hem of her skirt and raced down a hall, three soldiers not far behind.

She wanted to laugh as her advantage approached. With enemy fingertips grazing at her shoulders, Dylah slid along the ground, enacting her curse to avoid slamming against a closed door. After successfully sliding beneath the door she returned to her normal size as the three in pursuit pounded against the other side, struggling to find the knob in their haste.

Dylah retrieved her daggers from the small of her back and her right thigh. She slid the blades together producing a shrill warning sound as the door finally opened. They stood in a staunch line blocking the only exit. Their shoulders straightened, their fists clenched, it was clear that these were Gomdeans. Two held elongated thin daggers, one had a blow dart.

Dylah flipped her daggers in the air and caught the hilts. "Ready?"

One progressed to her right, her bare foot met his diaphragm causing him to double over as he tried to catch his breath. Another came at her from the left, his dagger careening towards her face, she blocked it by crossing her own daggers, her knee hit his stomach but he only stumbled back a few steps. She huffed at his persistence, the ringing of clashing blades echoed around the small dark room as she blocked each of his slashes. When enough space was between them she lunged forward cracking his nose with her right elbow leading to a stab below his shoulder in the same motion. As he shouted in pain she slid his dagger away. The other soldier had gained his composure and shuffled towards her, she wanted to roll her eyes at all the openings she had to defeat his poor stance.

First he tried to punch her, but Dylah had anticipated the hit well before his fist moved forward. He drew his dagger and started batting at her own blades, she kept her grip loose because his strikes were landing like butterflies. From the corner of her eye she saw that the third man had received some sort of signal from the injured soldier, he was readying his blow dart, packing it with a feathered dart that Dylah knew was laced with a powerful serum.

Seeing that his help was ready, the fighting soldier began landing heavier hits, Dylah was still easily blocking them but her mind started to turn thinking of how she could avoid slipping into a barren existence like Arkon. She heard the man deeply inhale, triggering her to jump on the other soldier's back just as the dart left the blow gun. She successfully moved the man into the trajectory of the dart and after he fell to the ground asleep she smiled wickedly at the remaining soldier.

"Heathen!" he spat at her.

"Nightmare," she corrected with a crazed grin.

He took another dart out of a satchel at his hip, Dylah ripped the blowgun from his hand and snapped it in half. The soldier snarled at the destruction of his weapon, he put the dart between his knuckles and held his fists up ready to inject the serum by a different method. Dylah evaded each hit, narrowly avoiding a dart to the face but with his arm outstretched in front of her she forced his elbow to bend while manipulating his fist towards his chest, he too fell to the ground asleep.

Dylah looked around at her handiwork, sheathed the dagger on her thigh, grabbed the hem of the dress and left, heading past the two unconscious soldiers from earlier as she proceeded towards her main objective.

Axen and Kremon ran back up the steps after securing each of the lower exits with both ice and shock arrows. Aelof and Arler were waiting with a line of over two dozen siblings. It was imperative that the siblings stayed behind, because they knew that the soldiers would come this way, and the panic of the siblings would only enforce the ruse that they had been unprepared. Judging by the slightly frazzled state of the younger sisters and muffled laughs of the brothers, it was apparent that the trick had worked.

"Any sign yet?" Axen asked nearly out of breath.

"Nothing. The woman and her soldiers already walked by, they didn't threaten us at all, just mean faces." Aelof huffed. "What do you propose we do now?"

"Ah, come on!" Kremon nudged the fuming Farein. "They're wandering around in the dark, surely that takes a bit of time."

A shadow approached from the end of the hall as if it had followed them. Axen and Kremon positioned themselves in front of the others ready for whoever was coming.

"Just me." Keilon laughed. He had a thin gash along his jaw below eyes still glowing with power. "No old guys yet?"

"No, where's Dylah?" Axen asked, trying to look past his ally.

"Don't worry about her, she's having fun." He grinned. "Probably passed down this way not too long ago."

"He's right," Aelof added. "About four minutes after the soldiers."

A clamour of creaking and grinding rose from the stairway as the three middle steps opened, revealing a hidden hinged door.

"Hello, Fareins!" Sorner poked his head out. "Ready to escape your own home?"

Old Keilon pulled himself out of the opening. "See, it's just a stairway that runs completely parallel to the others, it exits in the garden."

"How have I never known about this?" Axen asked, peering down into the darkness as Sorner helped the children and teens down into the stairway.

"And how did you know about it?" Keilon pointed a raised eyebrow at his predecessor.

The first Keilon shrugged. "We were always looking for places to hide away, ya know. Privacy. You know how teens in love can be."

"Oh." Keilon laughed. "Oh," he said again as his smile fell with the realization of the word 'we.'

Arler double checked his sheet of paper, ensuring that each sibling had been taken down to the stairwell, from the youngest brother of about seven all the way up to he and Aelof. They slipped down into the darkness, followed by Kremon.

"Come on." Sorner gestured. "We need to leave!"

"Where's Dylah?" Axen asked again.

"I thought she'd be here by now." Keilon sighed.

"I'll go." Axen took a few steps forward.

"No." Old Keilon held his arm out to stop the king. "You don't know the way back and you need to get those kids out of here as quickly as possible. I'll go."

"He makes a wildly intuitive point." Sorner chuckled. "And we could use some back up, I don't expect these Hight-ree children to be armed. But Dylah is more than capable of protecting herself."

"Just make sure she gets back." Axen glared at the ancestor. "And soon."

"Or we'll kill you." Keilon's eyes ignited. "Slowly."

"Understood."

Old Keilon was given instructions on where Dylah should be, along with many other threats if she did not make it back. He progressed up the next set of stairs until he heard shouting, then he bolted.

Dylah had been trailing Nevely for two floors. She made it past her many younger in-laws with no problem, and from the end of the hall she watched as Nevely, Navent, Sentry, and the two remaining soldiers slipped into a room that over-looked the third deck. She crept closer and muffled a laugh at the fake sign they had placed on the door with her son's name on it.

Nevely's shrill scream served as Dylah's signal to enter.

"My children!" Nevely snarled looking at her two soldiers on the ground while Navent and Sentry stood strong with smirks blocking the door as it opened. "You!" Nevely narrowed her eyes as Dylah entered.

"Good work." She nodded at Sentry and Navent. "Wait for me in the hall, you don't need to be with this dreadful woman a moment longer."

The siblings seemed to slouch with relief, they didn't offer their mother a second glance as they followed their protector's instructions.

Nevely crossed her arms. "I see, this was all a trick?"

"You got it." Dylah grinned. "Chaos and trickery go hand in hand, I'm surprised you didn't catch on sooner."

"My nature doesn't allow me to see the wayward spirals of your existence."

"And yet, the other half of your soul along with your predecessor, contributed to this plan." Dylah took a step closer, the engraving on her dagger catching the light. "So maybe just admit that your nature has absolutely nothing to do with your wicked ways."

"Are you going to kill me?" Nevely's eyes darkened but her expression remained stiff.

"Not now." Dylah sheathed the dagger on her thigh. "No, the plan is to lock you in this grand castle, we've nearly emptied the kitchens and sealed every exit." She laughed. "We'll give you a day or two to decide your next step, and then we'll battle and you will lose."

"You seem a little too sure about that." Nevely pointed to her cheek. "You know our abilities to carry on despite injury, this scar you gave me is now nothing more than a faint line. The slash in my stomach has also healed. You might be stronger than me, but it should be apparent that that fact alone doesn't guarantee that you'll stop me."

"I think it tilts the odds a little more in my favor." Her eyes flashed with amaranth.

"And what of your brother? Delin?" Malice filled Nevely's grin. "Broad yet weak, easily swayed, barely a Rilonck to be feared." She chuckled. "One trip into his mind and I could have him ripping you apart. He was just the pawn I needed, I'd love to use him again. You must see him as such a disgrace."

"And do you feel the same way about your children? You swayed them against yourself and now we claim them as our own." Dylah gritted her teeth. "Without your daughter's help I wouldn't have given you that scar."

"Keep them," she huffed. "You are an unfit mother and they are unfit children."

"One more thing before I go, I'm assuming you didn't notice, so I'll explain the trickery." Dylah took backwards steps and twisted the doorknob, but the door didn't open. "We switched the knob around, making the lock on the outside. I hope your soldiers find you." She enacted her curse and slid beneath the door.

"Did you kill her?" Old Keilon asked before the other two could say a word.

"You know that wasn't part of the plan." Dylah laughed. "Why are you here?"

"We apparently took too long." Sentry sighed. "The others have left already, the old guy is going to show us the way out."

"Dylah, if I might add," Navent started, "this emerald ensemble is rather becoming on you."

"Don't get used to it." She shook her head with a light laugh as they headed down the hallway. Her bare feet planted as she looked back at them. "And you two are alright?"

"Yes," Navent said with a nod of certainty. "Better than we've been in ages."

"Good." She nodded. "And what about you, youngin?"

"I refuse to answer to that, youngblood."

The siblings muttered to each other with praises and consolation until Old Keilon flipped open the stairs revealing the exit.

"Come on." He nodded to his prodigy after the two younger ones had jumped down.

"I have one more thing left to do."

"No," the first Keilon demanded. "You need to leave with us."

Dylah glanced at her surroundings and counted the steps. "I know where this is now, I'll be able to find my way out."

"Don't."

"If it goes awry we can talk about it in the afterlife, okay?" She flashed a smile as her right foot slid back, readying for an escape.

It was easy to see that she had already made up her mind. "Fine."

She raced down the hall before the word had entirely left his mouth. The phrases from an evil woman rang in her mind as she descended deeper and deeper into the Hightree castle.

In the foyer of the Fellowrock castle Axen, Keilon, Kunor, and Sorner watched as the crowd of Fareins sorted themselves.

"Are you sure there are enough rooms?" Axen asked with a sigh.

"If they don't mind doubling or tripling up." Keilon laughed. "Only temporary! We'll have that witch ousted within the week when Derck's army gets here."

"If needed, we can house a few within our own borrowed walls." Sorner forced a pained smile. "Preferably the tidy and quiet ones."

The castle doors swung open, and when they were expecting to see four people they only saw two.

"How did you two get here on your own?" Sorner glanced over them. "Where's my brother and where is Dylah?"

"Sorry," Navent said softly. "We were all set to leave together, but Dylah said she had one last thing to do. The old guy showed us the way out then went back for her."

"Come on, Sorner," Axen said, taking strong steps towards the door. "You need to show me that secret passageway. We need to get my wife out of there."

"Absolutely understood, my Farein friend." Sorner followed.

Before they could reach the handle, the door opened again as Old Keilon entered, his hands immediately went up when he felt all the eyes in the room land on him.

"She's coming, but just know that I had nothing to do with this."

He moved aside as Dylah entered, her hand gripping Delin's elbow.

"I know," she sighed. "I'm surprised too."

Chapter 48

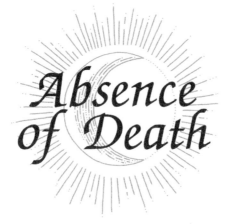

Absence of Death

Keilon pulled his sister away from their brother.

"I would like to discuss this privately," he whispered through clenched teeth.

"Yeah, I knew a lecture would be coming," Dylah answered quickly. "I just couldn't leave him to become a weapon against us again."

"How considerate of your discombobulated soul." Sorner laughed with an elbow into his brother's ribs.

"You couldn't have discussed this first?" The king was gripping the bridge of his nose.

"Brother, please tell me how the hell I'm supposed to call a meeting in the middle of my rash decisions." Dylah groaned.

"So you admit that it was a-"

"Rash decision?!" She cut him off. "Yes, that's exactly how I labeled it." She grabbed Delin's arm and dragged him towards the stairs. "So unless you plan on sneaking him into the castle we've just boarded up, let's start discussing how to deal with him and perhaps even use him." Her eyes electrified. "I regret nothing."

Keilon let out a short sharp huff instead of releasing the essay building in his mind detailing every aspect of his disappointment.

"Come on, Keilon!" Dylah shouted from the third step. "You too, enemy king!" She pointed at Axen. "And damnit, old guys, get up here!"

"I do not think I want to," Sorner whispered.

"Look at her." Old Keilon pushed him towards the steps. "You absolutely have no choice."

Dylah turned, still pulling her brother up the steps.

"Thank you," Delin whispered.

"Shut up," she whispered back, "you've said that twelve times already."

The discussion concerning the conditions of Delin's capture was brief because Dylah wasn't looking for arguments, only solutions. But when that conclusion was reached she did lose one final disagreement and reluctantly let someone else escort Delin to his temporary cell.

"Could you loosen your grip just a little bit?" Delin grimaced.

"No." Keilon gripped tighter on his youngest brother's arm. "I'm sure you realize that had it been me left in that situation I would have left you there."

"Okay."

Keilon planted his feet and turned to him. "Okay?!" He clenched his teeth. "That's all you have to say after everything you've done and the extra danger you put our sister in?"

"I'm not in the best position to argue with you, Keilon."

"Just say it." Embers sizzled in his eyes. "We're already in the thick of preparing for war and this night has been entirely too complicated for you to just draw out whatever it is you want to say." He met his youngest brother's staunch gaze.

"I'm sure you've been eloquently wording your rebuttal since Dylah swung those cell doors open."

Delin sighed. "You would've done it too."

"I think you're a little too confident in my level of forgiveness."

"And I think you forget that I'm the one who knows just how much of a soul you share with her, you knew what she did before she even did it and you agreed." Delin looked at the ground. "Not to mention, you're my parent too."

Keilon pushed his brother forward when he realized the answers he wanted to give would soften the anger he wanted to keep.

Delin was shoved into the records room and wildly threatened against using any ounce of magic. The door was slammed and locked only to be unlocked five minutes later so Keilon could toss a blanket and pillow at his prisoner brother's face. Followed by a softer slam and quick lock.

Down the hall Dylah had changed into one of Axen's shirts and a pair of pajama shorts, she laid on the bed gently running her fingers through Cav's hair as he slept.

When Axen quietly shut the door after making sure Delin was securely locked in the records room he noticed Dylah's glance had warped to gray.

"I understand, ya know." He shrugged. "Entirely not surprised at all. Of course you went back for him."

"Are you saying that I no longer surprise you?" Dylah smirked. "Perhaps we've been together for far too long."

"You're telling me." He laughed as he fell on the bed next to her and laid a hand on her face. "Then again, even forever wouldn't be long enough."

Amber light drenched the open fields of Hightree as the ancestors watched from their borrowed porch. They seemed to be in awe that the sun could rise after such a night.

"Are you proud of your lineage for concocting such a solid plan against those sinister actions?" Sorner kept steady jade eyes on the vast castle.

"Very," Old Keilon said with a wide smile before elbowing his brother. "And what opinions do you have about those in your line?"

Sorner turned to meet his brother's grin with a flat expression. "She's obviously a fluke, a product of her surroundings not her soul."

"Like me?"

"Same equation, vastly different answers." Sorner finally smiled but it didn't last long. "There is something I wish to make clear for you, brother."

"Here we go."

"I know this resurrection business is awfully twisty to the mind, and I see the gears that turn in your eyes." Sorner fell back with a sigh against the exterior of the house. "Life is always deserved. Do you understand? The breath you hold in your lungs has a purpose."

"This isn't my first time coming back." He chuckled.

"I know, and that's why I need to give you these words." Sorner took a deep breath. "Redemption can still be found in the absence of death."

"Elaborate."

"Keilon, you're not expendable." He looked into his brother's graying green eyes. "You have a history that gushes with crimson, but you don't have to die a hero's death to wipe that all away. You can redeem yourself and continue living the honorable life you've found."

"We may just have to see things differently." The first Keilon kept his voice proud.

"I know what you're thinking, and yes I do agree."

"Sorner, stop taking the scenic route to the point you're trying to make."

"Well I'm sorry but the point is rather complicated and sometimes you lose the meanings I wish to convey."

They stared each other down in a stalemate of blinks, until finally Old Keilon conceded.

"You disagree with me because you're thinking of it too deeply all at once." Sorner started. "Yes, singularly your life holds great value, you are equal to every living thing, but what is wrapping around your heart right now is the well being of your youngbloods."

"Yes," the whisper slipped out.

"And I agree with you," Sorner said with a sharp nod. "As their predecessor, those children of chaos are under your protection, as are those they love. Dylah, Keilon, Cav, Axen, the whole lot. Should the situation arise you know that you-"

"Of course I would."

It had been three days since the Fellowrock castle was packed full of Fareins. As the throng of various shades of brunette drifted around the foyer, the remaining Rilonck siblings stood huddled in a hidden corner of the kitchen quietly sipping coffee.

"There's just too many of them," Bahn grumbled.

"Remember when we thought our parents were crazy for having the six of us?" Kremon laughed before his face fell. "Nevermind, I'm about to have my fifth kid, they weren't crazy."

"How could they even come up with that many names starting with the same letter?" Keilon added. "The thought of that gives me a headache."

"They're my in-laws and I could probably only name seven of them." Kremon shook his head. "What about you, Dylah?"

"Twelve, maybe fifteen, but I'm the queen, I should know all of them." She took a slow drink.

"Everywhere I look, those damn brown eyes are looking back," Bahn huffed.

"We must be patient," Keilon began to say until a mixture of steps approached and the four siblings briefly fell silent to avoid being detected. "They are allies and family."

"I hid in a box last night to avoid them." Dylah shrugged.

"I am so jealous of your gift," Kremon said with a sigh.

The familiar squeak of the castle doors made the four collectively hold their breath.

"Hey!" the hardly recognizable stern voice of Axen shouted, causing the cacophony of chatter to cease. "You can't just overrun this castle, we are guests here!"

"We didn't come here willingly," Aelof said too loudly.

Aloria made a sound of disgust. "Shut up, Aelof."

"Has anyone seen a single Rilonck?" Axen forced a slightly calmer voice hoping for answers.

"They got coffee then left." Aluna pointed towards the kitchen door.

"No, they didn't!" Annavy rolled her eyes at her sister.

"I haven't seen them for three days!" Arvet, the youngest brother of them all, shouted. "I think they're gone."

"This was useless." Axen reluctantly headed towards the stairs, his hand pulling Cav along as he was distracted by small observations that hadn't happened yet to each of his aunts and uncles.

"That was close," Kremon whispered.

"We should get out of here." Bahn took a step forward.

"No." Keilon pushed him back. "We aren't hiding from Axen, we're hiding from every other Farein, and they're still all out there in the foyer of my castle."

"I vote we go out the windows." Dylah muffled a laugh.

After two soft steps they hadn't heard, hazel eyes blinked at the statuesque Riloncks.

"Arler," Dylah started, "you didn't see anything. We weren't here, got it?"

The young man slowly nodded along with her as he took half a step backwards.

"Arler, what's taking so long?!"

"Damnit, we're caught," Dylah groaned.

"What makes you say that?" Keilon whispered.

"Where there's an Arler, there's an," Dylah pointed to the doorway, "Aelof."

And as if he had heard his own name, Aelof appeared in the kitchen.

"Unbelievable," he huffed as soon as he caught sight of the Riloncks. "I can't wait to explain this to my brother."

"We're having a meeting." Bahn narrowed his eyes.

"Yes, a meeting." Kremon caught the hint. "About very important matters."

"Like what?" Aelof scoffed.

"Boot tread," Bahn said with a voice so gravelly and serious that it demanded to be believed.

"Yes." Kremon smiled. "We are discussing if the grooves should be deeper."

"Care to offer any thoughts on the matter?" Keilon asked. "We'd love all opinions on such a pressing subject."

Aelof shook his head and pulled his brother along as he left.

"Boot tread?!" Dylah had a hand clasped to her mouth to keep the hysterical laughter from spilling.

"None of you were offering any other suggestions!" Bahn crossed his arms, with an inkling of a smile.

"Yes," the four sets of eyes shifted over to the figure in the doorway. "Hilarious, Riloncks," Axen smirked. "If you're done hiding, Nevely has finally demanded a meeting, it's in an hour."

Half an hour flew by, kings prepared by picturing every point of disaster that could take place. Ancestors were called, armor was snapped and buckled into place. An extra cup of coffee was gulped by the commander who was carrying more daggers than necessary as she entrusted the care of her son to a multitude of guards and a slew of sisters-in-law.

"We should wait at the treeline." Axen crossed his arms.

"No, we'll make her wait." Dylah grinned. "That's always been the Rilonck tactic."

"Has it?" Sorner laughed. "I've never been late for anything."

"How close is Derck?" Kremon asked.

"Still two days out," Bahn grumbled.

"At all costs we must delay the fighting until our reinforcements arrive," Keilon demanded.

"We can take em!" Brig nodded at his father.

"Are you sure about that?" Sentry snickered.

"Don't talk to my brother like that." Kane stepped towards her.

"Don't talk to my sister like that." Navent was quick to join the conversation.

"Are you ready, youngblood?" Old Keilon asked over the constant noise.

"It's offensive that you even have to ask." She grinned.

"Stop!"

The crowd overwhelmed by the unknown hushed in an instant as their eyes of various colors pinned on the source of the command.

"Take a breath!" Kunor stood in front of the Fellowrock castle doors. "We are about to stand in front of someone so overcome with the idea of harmony that she can't even see how evil she's become. We absolutely do not need to bicker amongst ourselves."

"Are you proud?" The first Keilon elbowed his brother.

"My heart is bursting." Sorner sniffled and wiped a lone tear from his cheek.

"We are not waiting!" Kunor pointed at Dylah. "We will be arriving promptly, ready to make a plan that will appease the enemy yet benefit us." He nodded at his father. "If that doesn't sit right with anybody, stay behind!"

"You heard him." Keilon gestured towards the doors. "Let's go formally declare war."

Those fighting for chaos and the correct definition of peace stomped through the forest towards an evil adorned with strawberry blonde hair. The one with the fastest pace was Dylah, with Axen close behind. He took quick steps to catch up to her, he laced his fingers into hers, after a brief shock of discovering that she wasn't already gripping a dagger.

Her magenta eyes snapped up to him, her grip was tight, her posture rigid, but half a second succumbed to the calm within his hazel irises caused hers to sparkle with joy.

"You're perfect." She grinned.

"You're a perfect nightmare." He smirked back.

Chapter 49

The Very Definition

Anger had altered the vision of the group approaching the enemy occupied land of Hightree. Each step past the still recovering charred trees was a reminder of the crimes they planned to avenge and the atrocities they knew needed to be prevented. The lovely woman adorned in shimmering pale pink looked more like a target and the grand castle behind her begged to be taken back.

"Hello, my dear traitorous children," Nevely said too sweetly. "Navaly and Navent."

"Her name is Sentry!" Navent shouted with his arm around his frozen sister.

Where the rest of the group had stopped, giving themselves distance from the enemies, Dylah stood a few steps in front of her.

"I'm so sorry, Nevely, those are not your children anymore." Dylah grinned. "It seems the unfit mother has found her own unfit children."

"That's fine." Nevely looked past her at the waiting

crowd. "I'd like to fight in this land that was so kindly handed to me."

"That's a tough call," Axen said as he pretended to agonize over the situation at hand. "We accept."

"Are you sure?" Keilon asked for added effect.

"Yes, we'll discuss the disadvantages later," Axen added quietly with a scowl.

Within their stern nods they traded a wink, they had been hoping for a battle on Hightree soil.

"I rather enjoy your grand castle." Nevely crossed her arms. "After you've been defeated, I think I'll keep it."

"It's hilarious that you still think you can win against us." Dylah laughed.

"Oh I am highly aware that I have no chance." A grin twisted on her too lovely face. "That's why I've called for the help of those who have actually beaten you. I'm sure you recognized the Gomdeans right away."

"Truly a pleasure to see them again," Kremon muttered.

"No, it's not." Bahn wrapped his arm around his scarred son.

"Please," Kunor said as he stepped forward. "Let's not delve into past horrors, only what is to be settled."

"You." Nevely's eyes brightened as her pearly teeth shone through rosy lips. "My counterpart."

"I'm afraid you and I are not the same despite our shared attributes." Kunor took a slow breath to keep his composure within her vindictive gaze.

Nevely seemed to glide forward, darkened eyes pinned on the young prince who held her same soul. "Then perhaps I should just kill you and take it all for myself," she scoffed. "If you were truly a vessel of harmony you wouldn't feel so at peace after receiving only a portion of a soul."

"I feel honored to be given what was allotted to me," Kunor fired back. "Our nature has never known greed."

"Undeserving is what you should feel," Nevely snarled. "Such a disgrace to see you surrounded by those crazed by chaos."

"Watch the way you speak to my son!" Keilon shouted. "It just might be you who hands your portion over to him."

"And will my death be coming at your hand, your highness?" Her face remained unnervingly calm. "That's a desire that comes naturally to you, yes? Violence is merely an itch you must scratch."

"A desire? Yes, after all you've done, your blood dripping from my blade would suffice." Keilon smiled. "But you should feel undeserving of such a manner of death."

Old Keilon lightly patted the king's shoulder. "Be careful," he whispered. "It's easy to slip into the darkness our soul holds."

"Abominations," Nevely sneered. "All of you."

"I think it's the opportune time for me to introduce myself." Sorner sauntered past the sounds of grinding teeth until he was looking down on his own prodigy. "I am your predecessor, and you are nothing like what I intended for my legacy."

"It doesn't matter what you wanted." Nevely grinned. "It chose me, I am rightfully the soul of harmony."

"No no no." Sorner snapped his fingers in her face. "You are not harmony! Not one bit, your presence spews sadness and injury." He shivered. "I despise it."

"Funny." She laughed. "I had dreamed of meeting you, I devoured every story about you, your voice hung in my dreams." Nevely looked him up and down. "I'm underwhelmed. You're not a proud carrier, you're weak and soft. Everything I loathe." Her grin widened. "Like a harmless little rabbit."

Sorner's mouth fell open in shock. "I do not like you."

"Mutual." She rolled her eyes. "How are you even here?"

"We would like to start in five days," Keilon butted in.

"Three." She countered.

"Four." Dylah pulled Sorner back so she could face the enemy.

"Twenty-seven!" Sorner shouted the first number that came to mind as he was being pushed back.

"We demand at least four," Axen added.

"Be grateful I'm giving you three," Nevely snickered.

"We accept your three days." Keilon forced ignited eyes to hide his elation that their reinforcements would be arriving on time.

"Keilon the first, you sure do fall short of your legends as well." Nevely pointed her glare at the ancestor. "I grew up having nightmares of your bloody reign, I feared seeing the silhouette of the silver stag in the shadows." She chuckled. "Now you've lost your antlers and are merely a nanny to your prodigies who are just as weak."

"I don't think you're the best person to judge my reign." The first Keilon smiled.

"Aren't you all the least bit disappointed?" Nevely scanned the crowd on either side of him. "A lame excuse for the precedents of havoc you all serve."

"You can't let her talk about you like that," Sorner whispered through clenched teeth. "She's absolutely dreadful."

"I'm not going to berate her with words, that accomplishes nothing." Old Keilon laughed. "Best to let her figure out the truth on her own."

"No," Sorner insisted. "Words are the best weapons, brother! You have to."

"Weapons are the best weapons."

"Call her something awful!" Sorner's eyes darkened as his mind raced. "Call her a cat."

"I'm not going to call her a cat."

"You're right, that's not fair." He sighed. "Cats are immaculate creatures."

"Enough!" Nevely finally shouted over the noise of various discussions. "Harmony calls me to align the askew, and Dylah, you are a knot of magnificent proportions."

"Am I?!" Dylah crossed her arms and did all she could to suppress her grin.

"Absolutely, and therefore I do not trust you to wage a fair war."

"I'm not the one who set a forest on fire to kidnap a child, Nevely."

Nevely's eyes darkened as they settled on the magenta pointed at her. "I need some assurances that you won't be staging another trick like your so-called coronation ball."

"What are you proposing?" Keilon asked.

"I would like to exchange prisoners." Nevely grinned. "Until the sunrise of our agreed upon day."

"And who are you wanting?" Dylah raised an eyebrow.

"I think it's fair that the king returns to his castle." Nevely batted her eyes at Axen. "What a tragedy that you are forced to camp within the trees."

"I happen to like these trees and all that lies within them," Axen said with a proud smile.

"So you won't be coming with me?" Nevely nearly sang.

Dylah held up a hand to halt every rebuttal she knew was coming. Her head tilted slightly as she smirked at the enemy. "Absolutely not."

"Do you even have someone of similar importance on your side?" The first Keilon growled. "Your motives are disgustingly questionable."

"You had two wives, right?" Nevely laughed.

"Yes, and I hated them equally."

"The answer is no." Dylah gritted her teeth. The drive within her heart radiated down to her feet, and soon her eyes of war and lightning were in the face of violent peace. "You think I'd let you take the person I hold most dear? You think you could offer anyone who compares to him? You could give me an army, a kingdom, a mountain, or even your heart on a silver platter and I wouldn't offer up anyone to you, and certainly not my husband."

"It seems I have offended you." Nevely studied her own fingernails. "How surprising."

Dylah could feel the tension behind her, the other piece

of her soul, the one who carried it before them, along with the one who had her heart, she knew they were holding their breaths. But as their quiet panic demanded she remain calm, the chaos within her commanded something different.

The delicate silk that had been resting against Nevely's collarbone was now crumpled up in Dylah's right fist, the elegant strawberry curls were tangled up in her left.

"Let me make one thing especially clear to you." Dylah pulled Nevely's head so that she could see the line of frozen bystanders behind them. "None of those men should scare you, your children who you have wronged so severely, they shouldn't scare you either. They won't be the ones coming for you, they'll fight against you with everything they have, but your life won't be taken by any of them."

"Unhand me you slithering sorry excuse for a-"

"Oh just shut up." Dylah pulled the collar of her dress and forced the misaligned soul of harmony to look into her surging pink eyes. "None of them are going to do a damn thing to bring you down, but me, I will do everything to be rid of the evil you possess." Her bared teeth curved into a maniacal grin. "So as you rest in the castle I gave you I hope you fear the death I'm bringing to you. Because it will be me, I'm coming for you."

"You only prove the very definition I've assigned to you!"

"Good." The word rattled out of Dylah's mouth. "You expect violence and havoc from me? You'll get it. The name Nevely will live on as another book added to a stack of words I will surely forget, and as an added thorn to the rose so beautifully engraved on my blade." She released the bundle of curls to retrieve the precious dagger from the sheath on her thigh. "A blatant reminder that the most beautiful things in life still cut deep enough to draw blood."

Chapter 50

Flickering

Derck and his army arrived a full day sooner than expected. The Rilonck siblings watched with tilted heads as their shyest brother headed lines upon lines of marching men. His numbers were greater than Keilon and Axen had planned on, and after the three kings met, it was evident that they were confident in victory being an easy thing to grasp.

As the streets bustled with ignited morale and readied vengeance, there was a trio lurking the shadows trying to follow the distinct paths of chaos that were calling out to them. The king who sought protection over his family, he could almost taste the blood he was willing to spill to keep his kingdom from harm. Keilon's chaos was different, it didn't stem from injuries and a craving for war, what his soul demanded the most was freedom. To ease his worries he weaved through the crowd past his brothers whose eyes resembled the spring leaves, instead searching for the brother with eyes as brown and sturdy as the bark.

"Why so worried?" Axen asked before taking a drink of a wine made in the sand countries that he wished had stayed in the sand countries. "Did you have the wine?"

"Yes, vile."

They glanced over at Derck who gulped his country's wine with a smile.

"Are we sure that's Derck?" Axen laughed. "I do not remember him being like that."

"It's odd but beneficial." Keilon nodded.

"You know you can change your eyes, right?" He elbowed him. "You're looking pretty stormy, Keilon."

Keilon shook his head until his eyes were commanded to their natural piercing jade. "He has the numbers, yes, but are we so sure that Nevely doesn't?"

"We can never be sure." Axen shrugged. "It's always a gamble."

"What safeguards have you planned to protect Fellowrock?" The question came out almost too gruff and Keilon tried to backtrack. "We are keeping those most vulnerable here, I just can't rest until I know we've done all we can."

"Extra archers with cavern tips if needed, my siblings will know how to seal the doorways with ice tips, and everyone will be given a multitude of backup plans and escape routes."

"I feel as if I'm betraying my own damn soul by funneling so much useless worry into these things I cannot control." Keilon pinched the bridge of his nose as he sighed.

"I don't know, that sounds pretty chaotic to me." Axen smirked. "And if you haven't noticed, there are two others missing from this jubilee."

The ancestor had slipped through the crowd with the ease of a ghost. He crunched against the twigs as he stared up into the canopy that had always been his home. The first to be named Keilon had seen the trees in every shade, in every season, and through countless battering storms. His chaos was like the leaves, ever changing, where he had once itched for any form of violence, he now yearned for something more satisfying, something loud and strong yet purposeful. He craved a family.

He arrived at the empty clearing, the memories of his youth running past his cloudy eyes.

"She's still here, isn't she?"

Old Keilon whipped his head in the direction of the voice only to soften at the sight of his brother leaning against a tree, also envisioning the memories.

"I never truly believed that Enfy died," he managed to say. "Maybe physically, but not spiritually."

"I saw you break that day, the moment you ran into that burning hut you became someone else," Sorner whispered. "I knew we would never be the same after losing her."

"I know."

"Why did you come here?" He tilted his head trying to read his brother's motives.

"Why did you?" The question was ricocheted back with an unintended growl.

"That is a fair question, and there are a few reasons." Sorner smiled. "First and foremost, those newcomers are loud and their wine could melt mountains." His smile fell as his eyes settled on the gap between the trees. "But mostly because the thought of war only thrusts the memories forward. I remember her teaching me how to ease a soul's passing, I remember her advice like it was given to me just minutes ago. How cruel life is to grant us the ability to remember."

"Life is cruel, but memories are a blessing." The first Keilon leaned next to his brother. "Because you remember her you were able to teach your prodigy the same things. Because we remember her, a piece of Enfy always lives." He paused to take a deep breath. "And when our time came, it was a good thing that people remembered us in any capacity."

"And when we die again I'm sure future generations will

be rather confused by the misaligned conglomerated legends of past and present." Sorner grinned. "I hope we've made her proud this time around."

"I think she was still pretty proud of us regardless."

"Do you think they've noticed our disappearance?" Sorner sighed. "Perhaps we should head back."

"You can, there's somewhere else I'd like to revisit before it all starts."

"Keilon, you cannot wallow in the past." Sorner glanced down at the grass. "It is dreadfully murky and it doesn't serve you one bit to compare yourself to the person you no longer are."

"It serves me more than you think." He stared off. "I'm sorry we didn't get to finish writing the history."

"Perhaps we're not done here, brother."

Dylah leaned on the railing of the balcony as she stared off into the forest ahead. War was approaching, and because of what she was, the idea of clashing crowds was soothing in a way she couldn't explain. Dylah's chaos nestled into her in its purest form. She yearned for the things that made heart race, she thrived off of the sips that sent her blood racing through her veins and her clenched fists always craved the impact of a jaw.

Still, there was something impeccably human about the one who held an ancient soul, she feared for those she loved, she'd do anything to protect her son and husband, she'd throw herself in front of any blade to save her brothers. Because even though her soul was a scrambled mess of changing colors her life would mean nothing if she couldn't see the same faces everyday or walk beneath the familiar branches that had always protected her.

She didn't come here to center herself, but to visualize the fight ahead, ways she could use her power, techniques of her new skill, it all came to her in a flurry of images. The double doors behind her lightly squeaked as they opened.

Dylah turned expecting to see Axen, they often came to this spot to reminisce about the nights that changed their lives, instead she saw the one who came before her.

"Do you mind if I step away from the railing?" she laughed.

"I didn't think anyone would be out here." Old Keilon raised an eyebrow over gray shocked eyes. "Why in the world would you be here?"

"I like this balcony, it has a great view and some fond memories." She shrugged. "Why are you here?"

"I used to hide a bottle up here for when I needed to breathe and think." He leaned on the railing next to her. "It is a nice view but how can you stand to be here? If I can't look at the pond, how can you see your place of death as a happy location?"

"This isn't my place of death, it's yours." She peered over the edge and pointed to the courtyard below. "That's where I died."

"Dylah."

"This is where the curse was broken."

"Oh, that was something I never thought would be possible."

"It almost wasn't. I was so stubborn, I had exactly what I wanted in front of me, but I refused it and the colors drained from my eyes once again." She laughed lightly. "But there was this little flicker in my eyes. I felt it, Axen saw it. We both tried to ignore it and the big meaning it held. He came here to distance himself from me, then I came here to scream at the trees. Because of that quick flicker he put it all together, and someone finally professed their love for the chaotic soul, and that same chaotic soul was finally able to say it back." Dylah turned to her predecessor but could tell he didn't have the words, so she continued. "Then we learned so much, I found out the truth about myself, and you came back. My soul was tested because we were both fighting for it. And again on this balcony my life shifted, and my eyes flickered shut. Axen says he saw them flash to amethyst, and I know why. I saw every happy moment before they closed."

"Death has an odd way of pushing you to the other side." In that moment his eyes matched the color of the water that had claimed his life once before.

"So if you're wondering why I still find joy in this particular place it's because even before this truth came to light, and you came back once again, I had found peace here. The beautiful outweighed the horrific." She sighed with a relief he didn't understand. "Because of this place my purpose was sealed, and although sometimes I question it, I know that the twists and turns my soul demands are all part of the plan for my life. My eyes have to keep flickering."

Silence stood between them, Dylah was about to leave but halfway through her turn towards the door she was stopped.

"I came out here because there's something that I just can't get out of my head."

"Past life troubles, huh?" She laughed once.

"Yes."

"Who was it? One of your wives? A brother? And why now?"

"It's you."

There was a pause, followed by her hysterical laughter.

"And why is that so funny?" The first Keilon crossed his arms.

"I'm sorry," Dylah said through broken laughter. "Are you saying that I'm haunting you?!"

"In a way."

She steadied herself. "Well then we are truly even."

"Sure."

"What does ghost-Dylah say? Am I an ominous ghost or sort of annoying like you?"

He brushed off the sly insult. "More like a memory on repeat."

"Oh."

"It's what you said to me up here that night, you were right." He spoke softly. "You don't have my soul, you killed it and made it your own."

"I think I was wrong." Dylah shrugged with her hand on the doorknob.

"How can you say that?" He shook his head. "We are not the same."

"Yes we are, youngblood." She flashed a smile at him before pushing through the doors.

Old Keilon was taken aback by her use of the nickname. He pondered the claim for a few seconds before following her down the hallway.

"You need an explanation?" She laughed as he caught up to her.

"That would be nice, yes."

Dylah planted her feet and looked up at him. "I'm going to say something pretty insightful, so just, prepare yourself."

"I think I'll be okay." He rolled his eyes.

"It is most definitely a shared soul, it was never just yours and never only mine." She held up a halting finger when he tried to argue. "Dycavlon had it first, and he used it to build kingdoms, not necessarily to rule. So when you got it you already had that sense of conquest but you added the strength you needed and the power. My brother and I have both used what you gave us, but we're expanding on it." She took a deep breath to align the thoughts. "I don't think we're meant to understand our imprint just yet."

"That's a nice theory," he said as he began to follow her once again. "I just don't buy it."

"Why else would I decide to be dual wielding?" She flashed a smile. "You yourself said it wasn't a coincidence." Dylah turned away from him as she began descending down the steps. "I'm not saying you and I are exactly the same, but I'm not blind to what you gave me for the sake of not being able to give it to yourself."

"I think we will have to agree to disagree."

"We should start getting ready for what's coming." She pointed a grin at him. "Mayhem and clashing of silver. Should be fun!"

"Your chaos is different." He couldn't hide his proud grin.

"Mine is the strongest, that's why." She let her eyes sparkle. "Your prodigies request your presence, meet us in an hour?"

"It would not benefit either of you to kill me now."

"You still think that's what we want?" She shook her head. "Even after all this time? Just trust us."

The hour passed as the anxiety built. The first Keilon walked through the crowd eyeing the ones he had come to trust. It had been an odd thing to see the fruits of his bloodline come to life but looking around at what his descendants had built and accomplished made his heavily stained soul feel a little lighter.

Across the crowd he watched the one named after him scowl at the other half of his soul. Dylah held the empty wine glass in front of her brother's face to prove she had truly gulped every drop of the beverage many were too scared to sip. Then he watched as his prodigies shared a stone faced nod before departing from the crowd.

The time had come and he still couldn't put together what they would be needing from him. Dylah had become a friend, and oddly enough, his guardian. Perhaps she would be asking for a favor and how would he be able to say no to the pleading eyes he had given to her. Keilon was still a mountain against him, but lately the stone had begun chipping away. The king shone with pride and only wavered when it came to his family, especially his son and sister. Maybe it was him who would be needing his assistance.

It was in a room on the second story that was only used for storage, within two steps he noticed Sorner's lanky shadow standing alongside the overwhelming double presence of chaos.

"Hello, brother." Sorner grinned as a light was switched on illuminating stacks of various armor and weapons.

"What's going on here?" His eyes began to spark with flames.

Dylah stepped forward, she grabbed his wrists in an effort to tell him it would all be okay but she could feel the tension of his clenched fists.

"I need you to take a breath, okay?" She spoke slowly. "We know you, we need your help, you are our family."

The first Keilon looked to his brother for reassurance.

"Really." Keilon put a hand on his predecessor's back. "This is simply a sign of gratitude."

"Your effort has been great and these young ones can't ignore that." Sorner smiled.

Dylah flipped open a box and paused for a moment as she stared down at its contents. Finally she reached down and clutched the item to her chest. She turned to her predecessor and handed him the tightly folded bundle of leather.

"No." The former soul of havoc shook his head. "I can't." He stared at the crossed sheaths in his hands. "You don't know what you're doing."

"I think it's a grand idea," Sorner said proudly. "I saw you before the rage took over the stag, you were magnificent."

"But always incredibly lethal." The words were full of gravel. "You agreed with this decision?!" He pinned dark eyes on his brother. "After all the history we dug up?"

"You're not the terrible thing you think you are," Dylah insisted. "Not anymore."

"We could use someone with your unique skills," Keilon added.

Old Keilon stood in unnatural silence, the words had been ripped from his throat as memories of past carnage rippled through his mind.

"Please." Dylah handed him two thin swords from the corner of the room. "Be the silver stag again."

"For all the right reasons." The king nodded with eyes of

lightning.

"I can never be just the silver stag." He sighed. "You are missing the most important part of that title, my antlers were never just silver."

"Then I guess you have a choice to make." Dylah stared up at him. "If you buckle those swords to your back you are the one who decides just how much crimson will drip from them."

"Will you fight for honor or for yourself?" Keilon raised an eyebrow.

The ghost avoided all other eyes as he buckled the familiar apparatus to his back. He felt the glide of one sword nestling into its sheath, followed by the other. His eyes pulsated with pink as he took a deep breath and met Dylah's proud smile.

The silver stag had returned.

Chapter 51

Predictable Chaos

The sky hung above the trees in a blissful array of bright starlight. The kingdoms below were still as the quiet breaths of those sleeping rose up to join the gentle breezes that danced against the branches. But within the Fellowrock castle a pair of eyes remained open, her irises swirling with brooding storm clouds.

Through the panic of the unknown she nestled her ear against the most steady sound. A low drumming of calm and safety, the rhythm that had carried her at her weakest and at her strongest. It was easy to ignore the ancient calling of her soul when the love she had for him was stronger than centuries of a widely misunderstood magical presence. Dylah leaned into Axen, she needed the structure his love gave to her, he had the power to calm the tumultuous abyss within herself and there was nowhere else she'd rather be in that moment than resting alongside his unwavering peace. For tonight she would plan to the tune of his heartbeat, with the echoes of their resting son's quiet snores, because soon the sun would rise calling for the deafening clash of havoc and harmony.

Boots fell into line as sunlight peeked over the horizon, weapons were checked and mantras were muttered, they were ready. The commander carrying eleven daggers found herself forcing her feet to walk slower, Dylah felt the resolution coming but she was impatient for it.

"His words are still bothering you, huh?" Axen asked as he counted the arrows in his quiver. "Try not to think about it too much."

"I just wish I knew what it meant." Her gray streaked eyes pointed back to the castle where her son would still be sleeping.

"I think it means exactly what he said." Axen smirked. "You'll know when you see her," he repeated the groggy premonition Cav had left them with while the sky was still dark.

"What's left to know?" Dylah rolled her eyes but they quickly lit on fire. "What is he doing here?"

"Oh." Axen stared off at the source of her anger. "We've decided he should be an enemy consultant of sorts. He knows them."

"And Keilon trusts him?"

"Keilon's idea, but with a lot of convincing from Sorner." Axen shrugged. "Why does this surprise you? You're the one who rescued him."

"I know," she sighed. "I just thought we'd be keeping him far away from all of this. I'd hate to give him another chance to betray us."

"He'll be under constant watch, but I don't think we need to worry about him." He smiled. "I think Delin finally understands true harmony."

"And if he doesn't?"

"We'll be finding that out soon enough."

Within a few minutes of their planned charge Bahn and his two sons emerged from the thick forest.

"The bastards," Bahn muttered.

"So I see you've found something good!" Kremon grinned.

"They've staged a line of twelve men at the very edge of the treeline," Brig growled with the ferocity of his father.

"It looks like they're planning to take out our commanders first," Kane added.

"Oh really?" Keilon laughed as he turned to the person on his right. "Sound like fun to you?"

"Actually," Dylah said as she drew her two longest daggers, "sounds a little bit boring."

After ignoring most of the instructions given to her by her brother, shrugging off the concerns of her predecessor, and a quick kiss from the man she would always fight to return to, Dylah stood on a branch waiting for the opportune moment. She jumped a branch closer, a smile spread on her face, what an honor it was to spill the first blood in such a large scale battle. She now stood directly above the soldier at the center of the line of twelve men. Her eyes ignited as they squinted, studying each soldier, her mind made a list of who to take out first, who would be the most likely to run for reinforcements, and who would put up the most fight.

Dylah delicately laid her feet on the lower branch, she took two pointed steps before enacting her curse. She ventured out to the very tip of the most outstretched twiglike branch. She jumped, feeling the freedom flow through her veins as she returned to her usual size just in time to grab the strongest soldier by the neck and force him to the ground. Shrunken again and hiding in the grass she waited until their degree of panicked confusion reached an entertaining level.

When the time was right she gripped a dagger, snapped to her usual size just long enough to take down a man, but instead managed to incapacitate two. Again among the blades of grass she smiled to herself.

"One quarter down," she whispered, eyeing her next target. She jumped from the grass and landed on an enemy's back, letting her blade find the dip of his collarbone. "One third."

The remaining eight men looked at her with wide eyes. She wore all black, her leggings dotted with the protruding hilts of the many daggers she carried. The leather bodice armor gave hints that she was a seasoned soldier, but as they met her blazing amaranth eyes the legends they had heard finally matched the face in front of them.

Dylah took advantage of their shock, she threw a dagger into the necks of the two with the tightest grips on their curved swords. "Half," she couldn't help but laugh.

As far as soldiers went, Gomdeans were not among the strongest, though they were the most persistent. The remaining six stood in two tight lines, the first in each line quickly charged towards her. She allowed them to get close enough to see the sweat beads streaking down their foreheads and just when they thought they had her, she became thin air as they ran right through her presence. She appeared again right where they had seen her, but another two of their comrades laid with their faces in the dirt.

"Two thirds." She winked.

The last four began to burn with a rage that could only be explained as a weak attitude towards being beaten by a woman. With two on each side of her they crept closer, their foreign curses rolling across the flattened grass with each step they took towards her. One last time she threw a dagger, this time putting a spin on it as it flew towards the tallest of the four's stomach.

"And that's three fourths!" Of all the exposed pearly teeth, hers were the only ones encased by upturned lips. With only three left she drew her dual daggers, they were a bit longer than her regular throwing daggers with a point so sharp it satisfied the most demanding parts of her soul. A soldier on the left took too wide of a step towards her, but he was too slow to realize his mistake.

A huddled group of men watched from a few trees over.

"Now can I go help?!" Old Keilon had one hand gripping the right hilt on his back.

"Why would you need to?" Navent pointed. "She only has two- correction, one left."

"We can go back to the castle now, yes?" Sorner looked at the reigning kings. "She'll take care of the rest, yes?"

"You can go, some of us want to fight." Keilon flashed a smile at his ancestor before catching the last flip and pierce of Dylah's dagger.

But just as they were ready to welcome her back to the lines and get the real battle started she vanished. Axen's eyes darted along the ground, she was nowhere to be seen. Keilon also became visibly worried as the others watching began to look towards any possibility.

"I wouldn't stand too close to the edge if I were you," her voice came from behind them. "They were a diversion, they have catapults waiting to fire."

"Bastards," Bahn growled once more coupled with an echo from his sons.

"And at what point during that little scuffle did you real- ize that?" Old Keilon chuckled.

"Oh." Dylah laughed. "I knew before I even jumped down."

"One of these days you should probably consider calm- ing down, little sister." Keilon laughed at the blank expres- sion on their predecessor's face.

"Don't count on it, she'll stay wild," Axen added.

"I'm glad you're still okay with that." Dylah grinned.

"So now what?" Navent asked. "It's us against massive catapults!"

"Yes, I haven't a single clue on how we could possibly avoid those apparatuses of death." Sorner shook his head.

"Easy." Dylah shrugged and pointed her eyes to her hus- band. "You're up, enemy prince."

Axen smirked. "You know you can't really call me that anymore." As he adjusted the dial of his canister he instinctively muttered back, "of course, princess."

The forces of Gomdea and Verinas stood behind four catapults aimed towards the trees they were told to loathe. Word had returned that the legend they had been warned of had done exactly what they thought she would, and now knowing just how predictable chaos could be they rose their cheers to a swift victory.

Then a mixture of ice and fire rained down from the sky as another legend took the reins, the man with a flowing emerald cape and a firm grasp on all the elements within his bow.

The steam was thick as the enemy scrambled to see what would come next, in rapid succession each of the catapults were struck and quickly collapsed in a symphony of splintering wood. The soldiers banded together to form lines as they expected a ground attack after their only advantage had been depleted before their very eyes. But another fate was coming from the sky. First there was a burst followed by piles of enemies sleeping soundly against the dirt.

"Skilled enough to never miss," Sorner announced, staring at the ghost of a man he once knew. "Kind enough to understand the value of mercy."

"It's not entirely their fight." Axen nodded across the line to Kunor who was helping to execute the next steps.

"You have made your ancestral kings incredibly proud." Sorner half bowed before journeying to the middle of the conglomeration to the man he had chosen to babysit. "Any other tactical elements we should be made aware of?"

"They've been known to bury chains in the dirt," Delin answered. "So we shouldn't lead with horses."

"The chains can't be that long, right?" Dylah interrupted. "We should attack from the sides."

"And how would we manage that?" Keilon laughed. "We don't have the cover of the trees to sneak up on them."

Dylah stared at the enemy lines, she thought of the battle that left them scarred when the same enemy had the upper hand. "We surround them and give them no opportunity to escape."

"Like they did to us?" Keilon asked. "Don't you think they would be prepared to counter their own tactic?"

"No, because we don't just use their tactic." Dylah grinned. "We're going to add a bit of a twist."

Chapter 52

The Concept of War

In a matter of minutes the mixed forces of Fellowrock, Hightree, and the sand countries had broken into three groups that were balanced by skill and weapons. The plan had fallen into place in a beautiful manner that satisfied the souls who served both calm and calamity.

The attack would proceed in four phases. Each phase would prove to weaken the enemy further until a certain victory would be achieved. The first group stood parallel to the treeline facing the enemy straight on. They marched forward in a regal display as the enemy began to anticipate their next step.

A whistle flew from the right and the marching steps turned into a shouting sprint. The blended forces ran, the enemy tightened their grips on their swords, but small groups on either edge of the lines seemed to be kneeling in the dirt. Their hands dug into the loosened earth and gripped the metal links of their secret weapon. Their eyes glanced at the charging soldiers, ready to trip them and give their forces an immediate advantage. Just five more steps closer and they could unearth the chain.

Fingers tightened, arms ready to pull the metal advantage from the ground and unleash it on the clueless barbarians. When the progressing soldiers had only a step to go the chain emerged with an eruption of dust and dirt, but surprisingly no thrown bodies.

The once sprinting forces had frozen within a step of their certain loss and instead stopped in front of the raised chain with weapons drawn. Behind the first line of grinning soldiers who had snatched the upper hand in an instant was a line of archers who fired a dose of dreams with each arrow they shot into the nearby enemy.

With another great portion of the Gomdean forces asleep the allied forces could finally gain ground on the kingdom that was rightfully theirs. The leftover soldiers of Gomdea along with the spare soldiers from Verinas scrambled to assemble any counter. They dispersed into the sides of the villages to wait out the advancing lines. They stood flat against the bricks of the unfamiliar houses hoping to conceal their locations. But the progressing stomps soon stopped and the battle grew to be frighteningly quiet.

Then a sound rose that sent shivers down the spines of those whose camp was once attacked by the Riloncks.

Wolves. Their howls rose from every side, though the enemy knew the ruse all too well they also realized that this meant their troubles were only beginning. It wasn't just a sound, it was a signal.

The stomps of marching echoed again, but not from the front where they had been standing, instead these stomps approached from behind the hiding enemies' backs. They were being pushed to the center of the town by flanks of blended soldiers, their first line only a row of pointed spears.

A few Gomdeans were growing visibly angry after being outsmarted once again, these were the same ones that came prepared with a weapon that would guarantee them a win. Blow darts met the lips that concealed their clenched teeth as they readied to send a dose of barren existence into any approaching enemy. What they didn't count on was someone standing on the rooftops of his own kingdom. Axen ensured that every soldier with a blow dart would be met with what they deserved, a special arrow tip that injected both a sleeping potion and a paralytic.

The green cape and his archers were always one rooftop between the approaching forces of their allied kingdoms and their enemies. He commanded with timed whistles, sending any spare archer down into the busy streets to retrieve the blow darts before they fell into another enemy's hands.

The Gomdeans cursed the legend above them, stories of his arrows had been drifting over every mug of ale since their last battle less than a year ago. They fled closer to the center hoping that when they finally met the ground forces face to face they could retake their advantages.

Upon reaching the center streets it was discovered that what started with singing wolves only led them to a stag of silver. He smiled at the first to advance him and calmly unsheathed the crossed swords on his back.

Many from Verinas ran at the sight of the living nightmare from their childhood ghost stories. But when they reveled in the sight of an empty alley the true nightmare appeared as if from thin air.

"Before we start," Dylah began to say, "I'll let you rethink your options."

"We can take you out over the stag any day!"

"Oh so you've already made up your mind?" She flipped her daggers with the same calmness as her predecessor. "That was the wrong choice, my friends."

"Really?" a soldier spat. "You think we're scared of-"

Dylah pointed gray eyes at the group. "Go home."

She leaned against the wall to let them mindlessly shuffle past.

"That took out at least fifteen of them right away!" Axen said as he jumped down from a roof. "Not bad, I'll see if we can funnel more this way."

"This is incredibly boring."

"But extremely helpful!" He met her scowl with a quick peck before returning to the rooftops.

Dylah waited as more Verinas soldiers tried to escape down the alley, she met each group with a command that took them far away from a war they didn't start. But then another group tried to venture down the seemingly empty alley, and after making herself known she knew that her power wouldn't work on any of the fourteen Gomdeans.

Their eyes met hers as she quickly tried to make a plan, she started by throwing daggers, but when one missed she was thrown out of her element. She never missed.

The enemy knew that her shell had been cracked and they planned to take advantage of her brief moment of weakness. They charged slowly towards her, low curses falling with each step. Dylah drew her dueling daggers and pointed them in front of her as she took backwards steps, a flurry of thoughts in her head as she glanced up at the empty rooftops.

They were within two steps from where the alley would meet another side street, still no sign of reinforcements for the queen. The soldier closest to her laughed and shook his head with pity, to which she responded with a quick smirk before vanishing.

At the intersection of the alley and the street the enemy was met with a wall of Hightree archers who quickly offered them a shock with their electric arrows.

"Ya know, you really can't let us fight all your battles, Aunt Dylah." Kunor laughed.

"I am forever grateful," she said sarcastically as she reappeared. "This alley is dead now, we need to move on."

"If I were you, I'd move to the center of town." Kunor slowly smiled as he gestured for his archers to move. "He could use your help."

Old Keilon was gripping his swords in front of an ornate fountain in the center of the town.

"Four on your left!" Sorner shouted from a nearby rooftop as he let his legs dangle.

The stag rolled his eyes as more soldiers progressed. He had seen their same expression hundreds of times, mouth open with an angry shout, brows in a line, a slight twinkle of fear in their eyes. In a matter of seconds they joined the others on the ground.

"Splendid!"

"Shut up, Sorner!"

"I don't think you want me to do that." Sorner crossed his arms. "Two on your right."

Old Keilon took both down with a single swipe. "I did just fine without you on many occasions!"

"Did you though?" Sorner shrugged. "Prodigy on your left."

"You two bicker like a couple of old men." Dylah assessed the scattered soldiers. "Good job following instructions, I am pretty surprised."

"We are old men!" Sorner jumped down from the roof to meet them. "It's not my fault I'm so beautiful for a three hundred and something year old."

"Your rules are boring but I am complying." The ghost scanned the crowd of injured but breathing men at his feet. "So I no longer need Sorner to watch over me."

"I'm offended." The other ghost crossed his arms.

"It looks like there aren't many left," Dylah said with confusion. "We could break into the castle any minute."

"It did get too quiet suddenly." The first Keilon matched her stormy eyes.

A green cape approached through a nearby alley. "Are you all wondering why it all just stopped?"

"Yes! It's very odd and I hate it." Sorner scrunched his face. "Actually, I adore the silence, but its presence is rather questionable at this moment."

"Well," Axen started with a grand smile, "if you all will step out of the way for a moment, you'll see why."

"Where's Keilon?" Dylah asked with a raised eyebrow.

"Tend to the injured!" an unfamiliar voice called out as a crowd of Verinas soldiers rushed to the streets. They knelt down in a nearly simultaneous manner to care for their ailing comrades. "Carry them off if needed!" the voice shouted again.

Dylah stepped forward and was perplexed that the enemy took no note of her presence. She watched as the last few trickled from the same street until the only two walking forward were the man shouting commands, and the man who was ordering them.

"Now tell them to disarm the Gomdeans." Keilon smiled with his arm around the Verinas commander.

"Disarm the Gomdeans!" the commander yelled.

"You're a great leader." The king laughed. "Now insult Nevely."

"Nevely is mud!" the commander growled.

"Agreed." Keilon pushed him forward. "We're almost done here."

"Are you having fun?" Dylah fell into step with him.

"Yes."

"So while I was following the plan of just telling them all to leave, you were doing what?"

"I was collecting them." He flashed a smile.

"Chaotic genius."

"Oh, I like that." Keilon shook the captive commander. "Tell them that I'm a chaotic genius."

"And what is your name?" the man asked in a monotone.

Keilon thought for a moment then whispered in his thrall's ear with a grin.

"Attention!" the commander shouted. "Keilon the second but greater is a chaotic genius!"

"Are you proud of yourself?" Dylah punched his arm.

"Incredibly."

Keilon continued giving the commander his orders and the streets of Hightree grew emptier with his every shout.

"Brother, you must be proud of your youngbloods." Sorner gestured to where Keilon and Dylah were walking side by side, along with their prisoner.

"Greater," the first Keilon mumbled.

"You did a good job stopping them here," Axen said to change the subject.

"Slowing them," the stag corrected. "Stopping them is a little bloodier."

"But now they'll return home to the people who love them without sacrificing their lives for a cause that wasn't theirs to begin with." The king flipped his bow onto his back.

"That's a strange way to look at war." An eyebrow arched over slightly clouded green eyes.

"My brother once told me I didn't understand the concept of war." Axen shrugged.

"Your exceptionality isn't in your view of war." Sorner smiled. "It's in your understanding of compassion."

"I have a feeling I'm not the first one wearing a green cape you've said that to."

"The similarities still stun me." Sorner sighed. "But still, you differ from him and though similar, you have risen above your ancestors. I hope you realize that."

Keilon and Dylah joined them after commanding the remaining soldiers to run as fast as they could towards the mountains.

"Everyone ready to win our castle back?" Dylah beamed. "Well, after we find the rest of us?"

"I left Delin in the care of Kremon." Sorner nodded. "He was trying to offer information but his vernacular did not match my rather ancient mind. The advancements in weapons you've made is jarring."

"It doesn't matter who he's left with," Keilon added. "He's been threatened wildly for any attempt at betrayal."

"Oh has he?" Old Keilon crossed his arms. "Did you threaten the kidnapping arsonist wildly? Good call, your majesty Keilon the Greater."

"You were right." Keilon elbowed Dylah. "He wasn't happy about that."

"No no." Old Keilon forced a smile. "I of course want my prodigies to surpass me."

"Which was rather easy." Keilon laughed and took a step closer to him. "It's not that you're not great at what you do, you're just less than me."

"That's rather harsh!" Sorner scowled.

The first to be named Keilon began to laugh. "Holding such a grudge is a strong Rilonck trait." He turned to his brother. "I actually said the exact same thing to him when I came back the first time. And I bet he has just been waiting for the perfect moment to say it back."

"Correct." Keilon smiled too proudly.

"I don't remember that." Dylah raised an eyebrow.

"You were recovering from having your blood drained," Axen quickly added.

"It is very evident you all needed the soul of harmony." Sorner shook his head. "Come on chaotic ones, there's more fight ahead."

It seemed that with every street they passed they collected more of their brethren. Kremon proved to be a reliable keeper for Delin, Navent had somehow joined the ruffian group of Bahn and his sons, and Kunor didn't seem to notice the others as he and Sentry fell into step with them.

"And we're sure they're all gone?" Dylah asked as she headed the group.

"We didn't see any from the rooftops," Kunor answered.

"The Greater commanded them all to leave, remember?" Old Keilon laughed.

"We saw none hiding in the dark corners," Bahn added.

"Are you a little sad that the fighting ended so fast?" Axen laughed. "You nightmare."

"No." Dylah drew both of her daggers from the sheaths on her thighs. "I think the fight is just starting."

"Is she looking at the same empty street I see?" Kremon laughed.

"Sh!" Delin snapped over the mumbling.

The group stopped and began looking for any incoming threat, except Dylah who kept walking with a tight grip on her weapons.

Of the three that felt the need to go after her, Old Keilon was the fastest.

"And what exactly is your plan here, youngblood?" he asked once he caught up to her. "You have no idea what there is, just that there is something."

"That's good enough for me."

He grabbed her shoulder, and with the other hand motioned for those following to halt. "Let me go first."

"You'd like that, wouldn't you?" Dylah pointed the tip of her dagger at him. "I'm going first."

"You're a mother and a queen!"

"Yeah? And you're a ghost."

"But so are you!"

She shook herself away. "Keep arguing with me, I don't think you'll find our similarities as entertaining as I do."

He followed her after a brief growl.

Just before reaching the castle gate a throng of Gomdeans formed three lines of ten soldiers. The first line pointed spears with jagged tips at them.

Almost simultaneously, the predecessor and his prodigy stood with their right blade pointed out and their left close to their side. Their eyes alight with raging magenta above a slight smile.

Dylah glanced over to the ghost and laughed. "And you think it's not a shared soul."

The kings soon joined them on either side, Keilon with a sword he hadn't gotten to use all day, and Axen with the bow that was essentially an extension of himself. The others lined up with them, soon there were four bows drawn and various blades pointed.

"Do you think they'll charge first?" Kunor asked. "Do you think that would be better?"

"Yes." Keilon laughed, then he whistled.

Derck's soldiers flooded in from either side of them. The quietest Rilonck walked proudly to join the line of his family.

"I will never get used to you in a position of power, Derck," Kremon snickered.

"I honestly forgot you were here," Bahn added.

"He sneaks up on you just like Junia." Old Keilon laughed. "Have I not mentioned that I know your mother particularly well?"

"If you're all done," Derck cleared his throat. "I would like to charge."

"On your signal then." Dylah slid her daggers together. "Let's go!"

But just as their numbers increased, so did the enemy's, with a surprise amount flanking to support the initial thirty.

"Where did they come from?" Bahn huffed. "We checked everywhere!"

Dylah's eyes darted around the enemy as they moved in distracting ways. She sheathed her daggers to confer with her second oldest brother. "Your guys will fight long enough for us to sneak into the castle?"

"As long as you need." Derck smiled. "Is that where you think the rest are hiding?"

"Yes, I don't expect Nevely to be alone."

"Consider us to be a fitting distraction then."

Dylah didn't answer, instead as Derck was shouting orders she whispered a number in each of the main group's ears. They wouldn't all be able to sneak away at the same time, and it couldn't be ignored that some of them were subject to extra attention.

The enemy charged first but it didn't stop the plan. Dylah was one of the first to clash with the Gomdean forces, if only to let her presence grab the attention away from the first to slip away, Brig and Kane. The stag was also a heavy target and he reveled in the amount of grimaces that came his way, as it let his brother and Kunor inch their way into the gates. The kings spread themselves out through the clashing crowd, Keilon with his blackened irises and Axen with his arrows that made men fall to ground as stiff statues.

As Derck commanded his forces to swarm even closer, Sentry and Navent wove through the crowd, hoods on their heads to hide the telling tint of their hair. Then Kremon walked out with such ease he even carried a tune through a misplaced whistle, his arm hooked with Delin. Bahn didn't leave when he was supposed to, instead he let his fist meet a few extra jaws before realizing his mistake. Axen withdrew while still firing arrows at every worrisome looking soldier. Keilon walked the wrong direction just to give his younger brother an approving proud shoulder squeeze, it meant that he needed to throw a few more elbows and slashes to escape but he felt it was necessary.

"After you, youngblood," the first Keilon shouted over the crowd as he watched her fend off a progressing soldier with a single dagger.

"No, I insist, after you, old man." She tossed the dagger to her left hand to hit the soldier with a right hook which made her grin.

"You gave me the last number." He glared. "I'm number thirteen, I'm the last to leave!"

"Yes, but I skipped a number when I got to Bahn." Dylah flashed him a smile. "Which makes you number twelve and me thirteen."

He huffed, grabbed the next soldier that was running towards her and slammed him to the ground. "Let's go."

"You first."

He grabbed his right sword, pushed her back long enough to slash through the stomachs of everyone progressing, then grabbed her wrist and pulled her out.

"I don't think that was completely necessary." Dylah crossed her arms as soon as they were out of the fight that didn't seem to miss them.

"You're the one who gave me the swords again." His eyes seemed to darken. "That's what I do with the swords."

"Just because you have the swords doesn't mean you're the same-"

"I am the same person." He shook his head as he walked closer to the congregated group. "Your perception of change is laughable."

She followed him and grabbed his arm. "We're not done here!"

"You wanted the stag, you got the stag!" He glared down at her, eyes full of embers and blushing power. "I don't see the problem."

"Hey!" Sorner quickly arrived to pull them apart. "We're concocting a plan, come join us."

"You think that the past few months just erases centuries of history?" Old Keilon pushed his brother aside. "You think that handing me these weapons with a specific set of rules would fix me?"

"Yes," Dylah nearly shouted. "Because you don't have the power anymore, I do. You're simply a lost naive person in need of direction."

"Dylah." Sorner put a hand on her shoulder. "I think we're all getting a little too excited here."

"No, she's right." Old Keilon chuckled. "I'm just a lost wandering ghost, right?"

"Then what does that make me, brother?" Sorner let his eyes warp to a worrisome shade.

The first Keilon tried to brush them both off to join the others but Dylah realized her errors and pulled him away.

"I'm just saying that back then you could blame that bloodlust on the soul, I understand because it calls to me too." She shook her head. "I just don't want to fight that version of you again."

"Because I'd win again, right?" He grinned.

"Yes, you would probably win." Dylah laughed.

"Here's the plan," Keilon said after the group was finally complete. "We enter two at a time just to assess the threat."

"No," Dylah demanded. "We go in now, we know the threat, it's Nevely and an assortment of soldiers. We don't need a plan of attack, we just need to attack. We're wasting time out here!"

"You're being too hasty," Axen insisted. "We all want to take her out and we can only do that if we have a good plan. Please, just take a minute here to breathe."

A sigh of defeat floated through the group when they watched her burning magenta eyes turn away as she drew her daggers.

"I'm sorry, but we have to do this now." There was no changing her mind.

Dylah entered the dark castle foyer first despite the chorus of whispered objections behind her. Her head swiveled left to right as the others finally caught up.

"Where are they?!" She gripped her daggers even tighter.

"Don't let the silence get in your head," Keilon whispered. "Be patient."

"This is why we needed a plan," Bahn growled.

"Sh." Sorner held up a finger. "Footsteps."

"Are you sure that wasn't just me walking up to you?" Navent whispered.

"Quiet!" Old Keilon said too loudly.

"We need to split into two groups," Axen suggested. "We're stronger in numbers but we have a lot of space to cover."

"I agree," Dylah started. "Stay close to someone just in case because you never know what tricks this witch could ha-"

The shrill sound of dropping steel rattled the ears of everyone in the foyer. They scrambled to find the source of the commotion but realized too quickly that it was utterly pointless.

Dylah pounded on the walls of the metal box that had seemed to magically form around her. Her mind fired images of where these sturdy walls could have come from, had they dropped from the ceiling or risen from the floor?

"Axen!" she tried to yell but the only response was her own echo bouncing around her.

"Dylah!" The call bounced around a similar box that contained the two allied kings.

"It's no use," Keilon crossed his arms. "This is Nevely's game now."

"We have to try!" Axen said through a panicked sigh.

Another metal enclosure held both souls of harmony and the children of the enemy.

"Well at least we have a good mix of skill between us," Kunor whispered.

"Why would our mother trap us like this?" Sentry felt around one of the walls for any opening.

"Do you really think we're all trapped or is it just us?" Navent asked through rapid shallow breaths.

"As vindictive as your mother is I do believe she understands balance," Sorner started, "though in a much more domineering way. In short, yes, I do conclude that we are all trapped."

The boxed in group closest to the door contained a huddle of three growling scouts and one archer laughing nervously.

"Surely this is a joke, right?" Kremon asked.

"What a cowardly tactic to trap us!" Brig punched the wall.

"The second these walls move I'm charging that witch!" Kane added with the same ferocity.

"You two really take after your grumpy father."

"Cowardly witch!" Bahn shook his fist at nothing in particular.

One box remained of the split apart group.

"So," the first Keilon sheathed his left sword. "Am I still scum?"

"Always." Delin crossed his arms.

Chapter 53

Faceless Hands

Dylah stood with her arms crossed tightly and her foot tapping nonstop. It was difficult to determine how long she had been trapped in the metal box, and without any outside noise she didn't know if the others had met the same predicament. It didn't take long for her to figure out that her pounding and shouting were useless, all she needed to do was wait.

The stillness was nearly damning for her as her mind whirled with the angry words she had said in a hasty moment and the reins she pulled away from everyone else that caught them in the confines of harmony's grasp. She worried what might be happening to those she couldn't protect, and yet her son's words echoed once again. *"You'll know when you see her."* He had to have been talking about Nevely, but it sickened Dylah to know that Cav could be given images of the evil woman who had taken him from everything he knew.

The front wall rattled up, but only slightly, leaving a small gap where dim light flooded in.

"I'm not falling for that!" Dylah shouted.

"And why not?" a singsong voice floated through the stillness.

"I have a feeling you have an even tighter space planned for me if I roll out of here through that tiny gap."

Nevely didn't answer, instead Dylah heard the footsteps of what she assumed were four men told to wait and take the moment to capture her at her weakest. Then the front wall raised all the way up. Dylah took a slow mindful step out of her temporary prison, she took note of the emptiness in front of her then saw the other four similar boxes behind her own.

"Everyone else is paired up just how we planned." The too sweet voice came from an unseen step. "But you, you're all alone."

"But I have you," she answered with a laugh as she took a single step up the nearby stairwell.

"By the time you catch me you will realize that you have lost." Nevely laughed back. "I imagine you will also be grieving."

"You do know that the forces you left outside are all on their way home, right?"

"Yes, I expected that." The voice seemed closer. "How many did the stag kill?"

"None."

"None?!" Nevely stepped down enough to be in Dylah's view but still far out of reach. "And I bet you think that was very big of him? You think you've erased the history he damned us with? You think you did the impossible and changed him, you ignorant woman."

"I don't think he's the soul you should be worried about."

"I'm not worried about you," Nevely chimed as she turned and took a step up. "By the time you get to me you'll be ready for death."

"Not the most ominous thing to say to someone who has already died."

"See you soon." The last syllable hung in the air for far too long as the lovely woman disappeared into the grand castle.

Dylah paused to glance back at those still trapped then followed with a tight grip on her daggers and the power of her soul growing with every step.

In the foyer two more boxes opened.

"Oh I do so enjoy seeing your faces!" Sorner stretched his arms out as he looked at the other four who had been set free. "Although, scowling doesn't seem appropriate."

"Your cheeriness in the situation is unsettling," Bahn replied, his sons on either side of him to extend the image of his anger.

"I appreciate it." Kremon shrugged. "So who's left in these things?"

"My brother," Sorner answered. "Your brother," he pointed at Kunor. "And two of your brothers." He nodded at Bahn and Kremon.

Navent elbowed Sentry. "Your brother is still right here."

"We need to make a plan," Bahn said louder than necessary. "Which one do you think Dylah is in?"

"She's not in one." Kunor sighed as he pointed to an opened box. "The four of us should go after her. And you four should stay here to keep watch of any movement and to tell the others who is where and how much time has passed in between."

"And why should we stay?" Kremon raised an eyebrow. "I live in this castle, no one knows it better than me."

"He's lying, it's so obvious!" Sorner muffled a laugh.

"You're right." Kremon half smiled. "It's been years and I still get lost daily."

"Fine." Bahn huffed. "We'll wait."

Noises came from above them.

"I think that's our cue." Navent pulled his sister forward, who in turn pulled Kunor.

"Right." Sorner nodded to the remaining four. "It seems we will be proceeding up the steps towards the horrors, please send my brother as soon as possible. I am not fit to protect my grandchildren of many degrees."

"Come on, Sorner." Sentry laughed from the second step. "We'll protect you."

"She really takes after my wife." Sorner laughed. "But still, I beg you, send my brother as soon as you can."

Kremon waited in the foyer as Bahn directed his sons to scope out the now quiet battlefield. He let his eyes dart between the two closed boxes and started a gamble on which would open first. When the sound of sliding metal finally echoed, Kremon sighed realizing he had lost his own bet.

"Where are the others?" Delin nearly shouted as he distanced himself from his cellmate.

"Dylah got out first, you should probably take Axen up after her." Kremon pointed to the stairs.

"I wasn't locked with Axen."

"Up these steps?" Old Keilon used one of his swords to point.

"Yes." Kremon muffled a laugh. "Delin, you can wait here if you want."

"No, he's coming with me," the ghost demanded. "Just in case he decides to be the villain again."

"And I'm going with him for the same reason." Delin huffed as they scowled at each other.

"You're only about ten minutes after Sorner, Kunor, Navent, and Sentry." Kremon shook his head. "I don't know how long Dylah has been out. You two need to go."

Neither of the men felt the need to answer before they set off up the stairs towards the separate plans they were cooking in their heads.

Dylah was down to her last opponent at the end of a long hallway. She let her dagger meet his thigh before twirling it up to pierce the divet of his collarbone. When he fell to the ground with the four others she took a moment to catch her breath.

This was the third group she had the privilege to meet in the seemingly empty castle, there was no sign of those she held most dear, or the woman she loathed.

"Dyyylaaah," a voice chimed from the nearby stairwell.

"How many more are you sending before you finally give up?!" Dylah shouted back.

A quaint chuckle answered her.

Dylah contemplated if she should continue on into the unknown or go back to try and find backup. Her soul took over as she raced up the next set of steps.

"Dyyylaaah," Nevely sang again. "See you soon."

With the clamour of confusion falling to a near whisper those that remained together after the sudden separations clung to each other to keep pressing forward. Had this been only a decade prior no one would believe that the kings of Hightree and Fellowrock were each other's greatest ally.

"Are we sure Kremon was right about the pairings?" Axen whispered as his boots rolled through the hallways of his own castle. "Who do you think is with Dylah now?"

"Dylah is alone but she's fine." Keilon's eyes shone through the darkness. "I can feel it."

"Well, that's convenient." He stopped to peer into an opened door. "I'm sure we'll be running into Kunor's group soon enough, maybe even Delin and the old guy. Kremon made it sound like they were set free not too long before us."

"Good. We're so close to finishing this," Keilon said with a nod. "We rid this castle of those intrusive weeds and we can go back to normal."

"The halls seem too quiet, do you think they ran?"

"If they're smart they would have never come at all."

The kings kicked open every door as they ascended up three floors, all the while never running into another soul. This would have been concerning but the castle was silent except for a few laughs they had recognized to be Sorner's nervous chuckle from a few floors below.

"Something's not right here." Keilon shook his head.

"Is it Dylah?"

"No, I feel nothing, it's all too calm, too quiet, too dark."

"We greatly outnumbered them on the field, maybe they really are just too scared."

"I understand that weakness exists but it is a thing I will never accept until I see it with my own eyes," Keilon growled. "Until every room is deemed empty the enemy is still here."

"I will gladly scour every corner of this architectural wonder for as long as it takes." A phrase popped into his head and it triggered a smirk. "You wretched Rilonck."

"You damn Fareins are all the same." Keilon finally grinned.

They progressed further up, each door they opened always followed a held breath and readied weapons. The sibling hallway was a dismal scene, empty rooms with scattered toys, signs of a happy life that had been turned upside down less than a week ago.

"The entrance to the secret stairway is at the end of this hall, remember?" Axen whispered. "But I'm assuming you'd like to keep trudging forward."

"Don't you find it odd that out of all the twisting hallways this damn castle has that we haven't run into anybody else, friend or foe?" Keilon was thinking out loud. "Why is that?" He shook his head. "If they're all looking for us and we're all looking for them, shouldn't we have met already?" He let out a sigh. "And if anyone is ahead of us and winning, where are the injured soldiers? We haven't seen a single sign of injury or fight."

Axen didn't answer, he only stepped over the scattered clothes of a teenage sister's room to peer out the window onto the new dark night below. "Outside is calm too."

Keilon was soon looking out too. "Looks like a storm is moving in. You think they're scared of some thunder?"

"I think the lightning scared them first."

Past a room with a rich history and the flood of memories it held, up another set of stairs, and into another seemingly endless hallway the kings began to grow weary.

Something stood out to them, in all of the darkness and low rolling thunder, there was a light towards the end of the hall. After walking with no goal for so long it acted like a beacon to them.

They proceeded with caution yet they arrived at the door with a quiet quickness. Keilon clutched the hilt of his sword and Axen had his bow ready to fire. With a slight kick the door squeaked open. First the king of the trees followed by the archer with a new crown. The room was nearly empty as most were in such a uselessly large structure, a few boxes in the corners, nothing out of the ordinary.

"Should we check the closet just in case?" Axen asked as he lightly pulled at his bowstring.

"I see you're already prepared to put an arrow into whatever stray cat will pop out."

"I go to the trouble of making all these tips that preserve human life and you assume I'd shoot a cat?!" Axen shook his head.

Keilon pointed eyes streaked with a light amethyst and it matched the mood he was exuding. The eyes stayed lit only for a moment after the lights went out and the kings were left in darkness.

A clang echoed as Keilon's sword was torn from his grip.

Then a skidding sound as Axen's bow was slid away.

"Ax-" Keilon tried to shout before the feeling of a leather glove covered his mouth. In the havoc he heard the murmurings from across the room and knew his found brother was in the same predicament.

It was dark but the actions happened in a concise planned manner. Each king was muted in the pitch black room, they could feel hands pressing their legs down and their arms against the wall behind them. It was apparent that the enemy had a great advantage over them, as they heard a whispered foreign language they each began to panic for the other somewhere across the room.

Then, silence.

Keilon began to struggle, successfully knocking his knee into an unknown body. He smiled in the darkness when he heard a thud and a string of words he knew were curses he didn't understand.

The only hope Axen had in his situation was the far off gleam of Keilon's pink eyes. Knowing that the soul of chaos was in full force was a reminder that they had an advantage.

But the eyes disappeared all too quickly followed by a groan so filled with pain that it sounded animalistic.

Axen struggled against the faceless hands that weighed him down, his brother was injured and he would not be held hostage.

There was a shadow of a laugh within the unfamiliar syllables one of the captors was speaking. Axen didn't need to know the language to understand that they had no intention of letting him go.

Keilon was blinded by the pain, even if he were standing below a noon sun on a summer's day, we would still be unable to piece together his surroundings. He clutched his side, the hands had left him in a quiet stomping of disappearing steps, it was over and he needed to get to Axen.

First a laugh shook the too quiet room, followed by a word in a language he knew but spoken by a sinister voice.

"Archer." Misplaced snickers rose from every dark corner of the room.

Keilon dragged himself towards the word.

A blunt crack bounced from the floor to the ceiling, followed by a howl of sheer volume escaping through pressurized teeth.

Keilon pulled himself even faster.

The pain crawled down Axen's arm like a needle stitching into his skin with a thread of flames. He took rapid shallow breaths to stay alert in a situation he couldn't quite understand in the darkness.

The lights were turned on illuminating an empty room. Axen stared in horror, pressing his throbbing arm to his chest as he followed the trail of blood to the allied king that laid at his feet.

"You've been stabbed!"

"It's above the hip," Keilon managed to say. "I can keep going."

Keilon studied Axen, his olive skin was nearly white, blood collected on the floor and stained his emerald cape. But when he realized the injury dealt to the king he couldn't begin to align the right words to say.

Noticing the look of shock on Keilon's face, Axen finally took the time to locate the source of his immense pain. The bones in his hand screamed out as if they had been splintered, but that didn't explain the blood.

"No," the former archer said above a whisper.

The adrenaline of the moment wore off as Axen stared down at his right hand layered in a flood of blood pouring from where his index and middle finger used to be.

"Stay with me, okay?" Keilon knelt next to him and tore a strip from Axen's cape. "We'll get you bandaged up then we have to keep moving."

"W-why?"

"They knew exactly how to gang up on us, who knows what they could do to the others."

Axen finally looked away from his missing appendages when Keilon began wrapping his hand. "You're hurt too."

"Yeah, but it's not deep, they only did this to me so they could hurt you." Keilon knotted the sloppy bandage around Axen's wrist. "I just wish I knew where everyone else is."

Axen's eyes scanned the ground. "I wish I knew where my fingers were." He half laughed, teetering on the edge of hysteria. "Did they take them?"

"I'm sure they needed a trophy to prove that they took

out the famed archer." Keilon stood with a hand pressed against his side. "They'll realize the mistake soon enough."

"What am I supposed to do now?" Axen was taking quick panicked breaths. "I've only ever been an archer."

"No, you have always been so much more." Keilon put a hand on his shoulder. "This doesn't change a thing."

Keilon helped Axen up, they exited the room of horrors with a dagger clutched in each of their free hands. Their once laxed vigilance was now at an all time high along with their panic for the safety of the ones they held most dear. At the end of the hall two large figures appeared, the kings held their breath ready for another fight until the shadow of dual hilts became familiar.

"What happened?!" the first Keilon asked as he ran towards them. "Delin! Hurry!"

"Who did this?!" Delin shuffled behind.

"They caught us in the dark," Keilon said through a sigh. "Have you seen the others?"

"Not a single soul," his predecessor answered.

"Someone needs to find Dylah," Axen demanded. "If they knew exactly how to get the better of us they'll do much worse to her."

"And by someone we mean you." Keilon pointed dim magenta eyes at the stag. "She's nearby, I can feel it."

"Of course." Old Keilon nodded.

"Tell her that her husband and brother are hurt," Delin added. "It'll make her fight harder."

"Understood."

Chapter 54

Rise

After the ghost disappeared down the hallway Delin helped to lead his brother and Axen to a place he had already deemed safe. It was a stale room on a floor below that contained three plainly made beds and little other furniture. They took comfort that it was simply four walls, no attached closet.

"You both need to rest," Delin ordered as he dug into a bag draped over his shoulder. "I have something for the pain."

"Delin, please look at me," Keilon said as he intentionally blocked the doorway.

"There's no need to force the truth out of me." Delin shrugged. "I know I joined the wrong side initially, I understand my grave mistakes."

"Yeah, why were you dumb enough to do that?" Axen asked with a light laugh to disrupt the tension between the brothers.

Delin pointed his eyes down into his bag. "For so long I knew what science to use to combat magic. I fixed the curse with enzymes, I split Dylah's soul with Keilon so neither of them became too strong for their own good." He finally pulled out a small bottle of pills. "Even when I did use my spells it was always backed with the knowledge I already possessed." He handed two pills to Axen and one to Keilon. "Then I finally found something that neither science nor magic could solve."

"Dylah," Axen said with a sigh of grief.

"Yes." Delin's gaze returned to the floor. "The number of times I had no answers for her after so many losses was heartbreaking and mind numbing. I searched for anything I could, only to see her lose another, then another. So when an answer finally came I had to grasp it." He shook his head. "I know the terrible things I said under that woman's control, but I do love seeing my sister as a mother, I wanted her to have that joy again. I wanted you to have that joy again. Axen, I watched you both walk through life hiding your grief and living like your lives weren't being repeatedly shattered by loss. I adore my nephew and I wanted to help him have a sibling because my little sister was my best friend growing up."

"She knows," Keilon added. "It's not like she's particularly okay with the situation but she understands you and what you're drawn to."

"Keilon, you should really lay down before those pills kick in." Delin quickly noticed the fire light in his brother's eyes. "It's not like you'll fall asleep, you just might feel a little dizzy."

A little while passed as the medicine kicked in and helped the kings withstand the pain of their injuries. Delin gave Axen a proper hand wrap after applying a salve to the rough open wounds where his fingers used to be. He did a similar procedure for Keilon, all with very little conversation. Delin was finally about to say something when Keilon's eyes went wide.

"Something's off." He stood and walked towards the door. "Wait here."

"No, you should stay," Delin demanded.

"I just want to check it out, I don't understand, it feels incredibly odd." Keilon didn't wait for any other objections as he walked down the hall.

"What were you going to say?" Axen asked. "I recognize the look, you used to get it while we were building things and writing nonsensical formulas."

"Side effects of an ever spinning mind I suppose."

"Delin, just say it."

He looked at his brother-in-law then sighed. "I'm glad I found you."

"I'm glad you found us too, I don't know how long we could have wandered this castle in this shape."

"You misunderstand me," Delin said with a smile. "She seems happy and challenged and safe with you."

Through the exhaustion and pain Axen was thrown back to a night so many years ago when he was the keeper of a fugitive princess and Delin was briefly a prisoner of Hightree.

"I'll never stop doing that favor for you." Axen smiled. "Although she is a bit of a nightmare at times, I'll always protect the princess you handed to me in that tunnel."

"Good." Delin laughed. "I knew exactly what I was doing."

"I'm sure you did." Axen shook his head as he laughed. He closed his eyes and rested his head against the wall trying to find any bit of calm in the havoc of the night.

"Here's the thing though," Delin said slowly as Keilon's footsteps approached. "I have another favor to ask."

Dylah stood by the doorway, Nevely's slight shadow along with more than enough guards blocked the only other exit of the grand ballroom. One thing was certain, there would be a fight, and it would be now. She had been chasing the dreadful light laugh for far too long, Dylah was ready to end it. Black and amaranth eyes scanned the far off soldiers, they carried no worrisome weapons, but somehow that was even more concerning. As if her fears had been heard, the door behind her opened offering a beacon of hope.

"Your timing is impeccable." She laughed with relief.

"You could have done it on your own, youngblood." Old Keilon looked across the pale marble floor. "Or at least taken a few of them out along the way."

"And you're still going to help me after those terrible things I said to you?" Dylah shook her head. "We were caught up in the fighting, I didn't mean any of it."

"Focus."

"Are the others coming?" she whispered and looked up to him with pleading eyes. "Are they okay?"

"Not a single scratch on them." He grinned. "But I think it's down to you and I for this, no worries." His head tilted in the direction of danger, signaling her to follow him to the center of the ballroom.

"You wretched excuse for a sacred soul!" Nevely's growl rolled over the marble floor. "How dare you try to fight in the name of support!" Her eight guards followed her through the room and quickly made a semicircle around Dylah and Old Keilon.

"And do you look down on your own predecessor?" he asked with a raised eyebrow.

Nevely took slow steps until she was a small distance away from them. "I used to hold Sorner to the highest level of admiration, but his legends have fallen flat, he is not what we remember him as." She grinned. "But you, Keilon, your legends don't hold a candle to what you truly were capable of."

"Were?" He chuckled.

"A sword in each hand." Nevely narrowed her eyes. "The legend lives."

"Don't listen to her," Dylah whispered. "Let that ghost

stay beneath the water."

"Silver stag." Nevely laughed. "Welcome back. I await the crimson that will drip from your antlers."

Dylah outstretched a dagger to stop Nevely's slow steps. "Whatever you think you're doing just know that it won't work."

"I have to say, I admire your drive to keep the order." Nevely's grin widened as she looked through Dylah to the ancestor. "The way you handed out punishments, your commitment to your own rules, I aspire to be that powerful."

"I see that you have that drive." He kept his eyes pinned on her. "Quite the following you have." He gestured to the encircled soldiers.

"It's not nearly enough," she huffed. "I need them crawling at my feet, doing any little thing I ask. I want their fear."

"You think their fear gives you power?!" Dylah forced her gaze to break Nevely's stare. "You want a tarnished history and a life of blood and regret like he had?"

"Absolutely." Nevely's eyes darkened. "As long as I hold the power I care not about their views. If only I could ascend to that level of hierarchy."

"Let me teach you then." His voice gained a rumbling pridefulness. He sheathed his left sword on his back as a malicious grin grew on his face, an echo of a bloodthirsty past.

"What?!" Dylah clenched her teeth.

"It's perfect." He looked down on his prodigy with eyes of darkness, grabbed her with one arm and forced her to face her adversary and his new ally. "If you kill her then I can have my soul back." He leaned into Dylah. "You did so blatantly point out that the only thing I'm missing is the power of my eyes, so I think I'll be taking it now."

"Let me go!" Dylah's arms were trapped in his hold but she fought as hard as she could trying to get into a position that would grant her a safe escape.

He sheathed his other sword, ripped the dagger from her grasp, then gripped her throat in one hand. He held her captive against himself ensuring she would remain immobile by pointing the engraved blade at her stomach. "Shrink. I dare you. Try to escape, use that dreadful curse against me. You may think your freedom would be guaranteed but you'll only make this easier for us." The point of the blade pressed against the leather on her stomach. "I am always the villain, it's hilarious that you thought I wouldn't be. And yet, it's almost sad that you fell right into the trap." He shook his head with a light chuckle. "How did you ever think you could beat me?"

Nevely's eyes darkened as her grin gleamed with satisfaction. "I knew I was never meant to be her counterpart of balance, perhaps it was always meant to be you and I."

"We will do great things, conquer every weak land we come across and spill the blood of anyone who goes against us. This is the true power meant for our souls, peace is nothing but a childish dream." The first Keilon spoke lowly as his grip on Dylah's throat tightened. "But we need to get rid of this one first, then I'll oust the unworthy holder of my great name."

Dylah tried to shout but no sound could escape her constricted airway. She tried to wiggle away but with each small movement the dagger pressed deeper against her.

"And how do I know that I can trust you?" Nevely's eyes dimmed. "You've been living with these pathetic Riloncks for so long, yet you turn on them so easily?"

"I was too hasty during my first revival." He shrugged. "Jumped straight to the evil plan, so I figured this time I'd let it simmer while I gained their trust. I was worried when that delicate little brother of mine showed up, but I'm sure he'll be just as easy to get rid of this time around." The vibrations of his hearty laugh shook her already trembling limbs. "This one even gave me her house, can you believe that?"

"Pathetic." Nevely eyed Dylah with disgust. "Let's get this over with."

"It'll be quick, you useless prodigy," he whispered over

her with an evil chuckle. "Just like last time. Remember?"

"Actually, it won't be." Nevely raised a hand giving her men the signal to load their blow guns. "You know what they're using, don't you, Dylah?" She took a step forward standing too close to Dylah's face. "Just one dart has the power to make you float in the darkness, imagine what eight will do. One is a mercy, but each additional dose of the serum will throw you into a frenzy of hallucinations and hypersensitive pain, the pin prick of a needle would make you beg for death, but you won't even be able to scream. Do you understand?" She slowly ran her fingers down along Dylah's jaw. "You'll be able to hear your death approaching. You'll know the exact moment he starts sinking that blade into your wretched heart, it will feel like it's lasting your entire lifetime. It is truly the death that you deserve."

A tear slid down Dylah's face until it crashed against the fingers gripping her throat. She had no way out, she was surrounded by evil with no signs of help coming.

Old Keilon loosened his grip slightly. "Any last words?"

"Drown," she managed to mutter.

"I thought you'd offer something a little more insightful. Though, I guess I've suffered through far too much of your babbling these past few months of lying in wait." He shrugged with a light laugh. "Carry on, Nevely. Wait, how many of those darts do they have?"

"Just the one, but it should be more than enough."

"For a scrawny thing like her, yes, it should be plenty." He laughed. "But come on, you and I both know she's been able to fight against other odd circumstances. I would just like some reassurance that she'll truly be incapacitated so I can completely kill her this time. I need my power back and if you're not going to take this seriously then I don't think I can help you."

"Each man has one dart." Nevely sighed with grinding annoyance. "We didn't have enough time to make an abundance of serum, but trust me, eight will be enough."

"Well go on, the sooner the better," he said with a grin. "I have big plans."

"You're quite the hasty one." She raised an eyebrow looking him up and down.

"Make sure they take a good deep breath first so they fly fast enough to really plunge deep, or else the injection might take longer." Old Keilon narrowed his eyes. "And I'd rather they just get your action out of the way first so I can go ahead and stab her. It's long overdue."

Dylah squirmed and tried to scream.

He squeezed her throat and leaned over her. "It's not my fault you decided to waste your final words." His eyes shifted to Nevely. "Do it."

Nevely laughed as she raised her fist ready to signal her men. She met Dylah's deep blue eyes and couldn't help but stay locked on them as her fist fell.

Dylah braced herself, ready to feel each sting of the darts that would deliver her death sentence. She wasn't preparing herself for the pain of death, instead she pictured the ones she was being torn away from. Their eyes, their smiles, their embrace, the nicknames they gave her, princess, nightmare, mama. But soon after the sound of the darts being sent into the air, the hand released from her throat to instead wrap around her as she was spun away from the incoming danger.

The silver stag stood facing away from the enemy semicircle, he was hunched over, five darts sticking out of his back and three in his legs. His eyes felt heavy and a ringing pierced his eardrums, but he couldn't succumb to the serum just yet.

"Stay down, youngblood. You're not safe yet." He quickly unsheathed his left sword and although every movement of his joints felt like grinding stone he still kept a hold on Dylah. He slashed through half of the semicircle before switching arms and taking care of the other half, blood spewed from the throats of the enemy before they could even react to the quick trickery of the ghost.

Then his sword fell to the ground, followed by his knees.

Dylah finally noticed the dagger that had been slipped into her hand during the quick transition. She glanced at a fuming Nevely, but before she could take care of the harmonious evil, she helped her predecessor lay softly on the floor. She progressed towards Nevely, a dagger in each hand and her teeth bared in a rage.

Nevely's smug demeanor turned to fear before she sprinted out of the room.

Dylah wanted to chase her, but something within her told her she needed to stay a few moments longer.

She crashed to the ground and smacked at his face. "Wake up!" She shook him. "Why did you do that?! Why do something so stupid?!"

His eyes flickered open revealing only green. "That was their only dose, that was her only advantage." His eyes closed. "Go get her." Old Keilon's voice fell to a forced whisper. "Rise."

"No! Wake up!" Her bottom lip quivered as she watched his skin begin to go pale. "You can't go yet! Damnit, why did you do that? You're not done!"

"My purpose," he said through a broken sigh, "is done."

Dylah shook him again, but slow breaths were the only signs of life the silver stag could muster.

Chapter 55

No Purer Form

Dylah sprinted through the empty halls, every so often a stray enemy would try to stop her but she slashed as she ran. There had to be someone else, there had to be someone to watch over the fallen legend, but the longer she ran the more she began to believe that she was the last one standing.

"Dylah!" Keilon shouted from the end of a hallway.

The closer she got she could see he was slightly pale, he was gripping his side and taking odd breaths.

"You're hurt!"

"It's nothing." He held her shoulders. "We told the old guy to tell you, did you not find each other? What's going on? I have had the weirdest feeling."

"He tricked Nevely and now he won't wake up," she said through a shaky breath. "Is Delin with you? Does he have more antidotes?"

"Dylah, I need you to take a breath." Keilon began to lead her down the hallway. "I'm not the only one they hurt, and his injury is far worse."

"Who?"

"They snuck up on us."

"Who is injured, Keilon?!"

"It's Axen." He stopped and made her look at him. "They cut off two of his fingers on his right hand."

"But, he's an archer." Dylah saw the light on at the end of the hall and ran as fast as she could. She bolted into the door and the first thing her panicked glance settled on was his hazel eyes.

"I know this looks pretty bad, but I'm okay." He smiled. "Just a couple of chopped off fingers, it's not a spear to the chest and a dozen arrows like the last time I fought on my own home soil."

Dylah didn't answer as she took slow steps towards the bed he was propped up on. She put a hand on each side of his face and kissed him as if she hadn't seen him in a decade. He held her face in a similar fashion with his left hand. When she finally pulled away she rested her forehead against his.

"I almost lost you," she whispered.

"No, this wouldn't have killed me." Axen laughed until he met her stormy eyes. "Wait. What happened to you?"

She kissed him again, then turned to Delin. "Did you bring any antidotes?"

"I have all of the ingredients for it, yes." Delin answered. "It was a good call that you brought back more than one root."

"Is that going to be enough?!" she nearly shouted. "He was shot with eight darts."

"Eight?!"

"Who?" Axen asked. "Why so many?"

"You need to make the antidote, this is not how he dies!" Dylah's eyes filled with tears and her hands began to shake. "I promised him a much better life than this."

"He saved you, didn't he?" Delin asked. "He promised me he would, I begged him to."

"He did but he did it in the worst way possible and now

he's lying in comatosed agony because I was too cowardly to read through his ruse." Dylah shook her head.

"Look who I found!" Keilon entered the tense room, Kunor soon followed, then Sentry and Navent.

Dylah's eyes went wide, she ran to the door before the next person could enter.

"I see you missed me a fearsome amount," Sorner chuckled as he wrapped around her tight embrace. "Is everyone alright?"

"No."

He studied her deep blue eyes and knew what she was trying to tell him. Sorner pulled her into him and pressed her head to his chest. "I knew he would do something dangerous."

"We can save him, there's still a chance."

"Dylah, take a few breaths to understand why he did what he did." He squeezed her tighter. "It's you, you gave us the chances we didn't know we would get again, you let him live separate from his past. Do you understand the weight you took off of his shoulders?"

She pushed away from him and pulled him into the room where everyone was waiting.

"Delin, get the ingredients ready!"

"Dylah, this isn't over yet," Keilon said. "There are others left to save."

"What?!"

"It's true," Axen added. "We're heading there now, Delin knows where Nevely is hiding them, we imagine she'll meet us there when we free them."

"So that's it then?" Dylah shook her head.

"We're not giving up on him." Delin took a step towards her. "I know that must be awfully hard to believe coming from me, but I have every intention of saving the man who saved you." He sighed. "But right now there is a room full of helpless and scared prisoners with no one to save them, we have to prioritize that."

436

"You all aren't helping her one bit." Sorner grabbed her hand and pulled her out to the hall.

"Don't you want Kunor for this too?"

"No, my dear, this is just for you." He glanced back and forth before entering a room and immediately locked the door. "Dylah, my heart is shattering, but I need you to understand the vastness of this situation."

"You don't have to mourn! He's still alive!"

"Stop." He held her face in his hands. "Breathe. The others are right, we're not done here, there is still something you need to do."

"I can't," she whispered.

"Listen, youngblood, when we were children all we ever learned about was the greatness our souls held. We also learned that we were meant to surpass our predecessors. Allinay was a marvelous first soul of harmony, but me, I was better. You see, the souls don't just pick a vessel to live in, they pick one where they know they will thrive and continue to grow." He shook her to keep her attention. "I already see Kunor taking those steps ahead of me. But you, you were born greater, do you understand? You were always meant to stand up and scream. The storm you were born in raged harder than his storm. Your eyes ignite with a brighter spark. Your head stays level far better than his ever did."

"Stop talking about him like he's dead!"

"Sometimes terrible things happen just to provide us another step towards our potential. You are the one who makes the choice to stay on level ground or climb up." His eyes brightened. "I know you understand that, you and I wouldn't be standing as tall as we could if not for the steps you took." He dug into his pocket and handed her a small smoothed stone. "He also told me to give you this."

"He told you?" She studied the flecks in the stone. "What is this?"

"How did he put it, it was a phrase that sounded rather morbid in the moment but perhaps makes more sense now."

He smiled when he remembered. "He wanted you to know that his bones weren't there anymore."

Dylah stared at the rock. She remembered the confessions by a terrible pond, the story that had been buried beneath its ripples, the tyrant whose soul became just as murky as the water he weaponized. The amount of change that had happened since that conversation and the true gentle nature of the forest's most commanding beast told her exactly what she had to do.

She slid the rock into her pocket.

"Dylah." Sorner nodded to her. "Whatever your plan is, just know, you're going to take that next step tonight."

"I know." She grinned, standing in the doorway as the castle shook with thunder.

The rest remained congregated in the empty room. Delin added another layer to Axen's wraps as the other king grinded his teeth in the corner thinking of his own next steps.

The door flew open as Dylah marched into the room. "This is what's going to happen!"

"We're listening." Navent had an immediate smile.

"Delin, how many prisoners are there and what state would they be in?" She pointed surging eyes at him.

"Seven, unless she's picked up another through her travels," he answered. "They are rather weak."

"And you know where she's kept them?"

"Yes, they're below in the cellar."

She quickly counted those in the room. "Okay, you'll all go, if the rest are still waiting in the foyer then you'll have more backup."

"And you?" Keilon asked. "Will you be going?"

"She's not," Axen answered before she could.

"Nevely's fight is only against me." Dylah crossed her arms. "I can't lose any of you." She paused for a moment. "And if she's too busy going after me then you're free to rescue whoever."

"I'm going with her," Sorner added. "I am useless in a fight but I can watch over my brother until he can be helped. I understand he is not the priority here but I would like to ensure his safety."

"Good." Delin nodded. "I'll meet you as soon as I can gather some supplies."

"Then it's settled," Keilon said. "Let's get a move on."

They soon began to shuffle around, preparing themselves, checking their weapons and each other for any fragility. Axen removed the canister that he used to change the tips of his arrows, he divided the remaining arrows he had with Kunor and Navent.

"Here," Dylah said as she unsheathed a dagger. "It's my favorite one."

Axen smiled. "I never thought there would come a time when neither of us were archers."

"You can still be an archer." She held onto him. "I know you and you always find a way."

"I already have some ideas." He wrapped an arm around her and kissed her forehead. "But first we're going to survive the night, then we're going to take some time to just be a family. Then I'll figure out a way to be an archer with eight fingers."

"I'll bring you eight of their fingers."

"That won't actually help me much, you nightmare."

"Okay, but just remember that I did offer to do so." She laughed.

"I need you to promise me something." His voice wavered slightly. "You have to come back."

"So do you." She studied his pale complexion. "In one piece."

"Dylah?" Keilon said from across the room. "I just need a moment."

She promised to come right back, then walked over to her brother.

"I'm going with you," he demanded.

"No."

"Dylah, please." Keilon shook his head. "That woman is merciless, let me be there."

"Let's say I die again," she started, "the whole soul goes to you. You need to stay safe for that sole reason, you have a responsibility to the calamity we didn't ask for."

"So what if I fight her and you're the portion that stays safe?"

"How about I fight her, you don't, we both live and let the split soul thrive separately the way it was probably intended to?" She smirked. "I'm going to win, big brother, I promise."

"I know you will, kiddo."

She looked up at him and suddenly her fingers tapped nervously against her thigh. "You always knew that we shared something, right?"

"Yes, from the first moment I saw you that stormy night there has been a connection." Keilon pulled her in. "Easy to ignore yet painfully obvious."

"Good." Dylah waited a moment then began to walk away.

Keilon grabbed her wrist. "If she catches you, you know what you have to do right?" A slight smile spread.

"I have been extensively trained for this." She grinned back. "I will always try to escape."

They all trickled out to the hallway to wait for the next stage. Although they were already given the chance to finish their hopeful words and promises, Axen and Dylah stayed in the room hoping the others wouldn't notice.

They clung to each other in a way that only Axen and Dylah could. Their grips strengthened by the memories of love and heartache. They stood in a tight embrace that could remain speechless because the love they shared had conquered rivalries, curses, and loss but now stood on a mountain of found joy. Even standing in the midst of an unknown approaching danger, they couldn't help but realize everything their love had given to them since they were just two enemies thrown into a treasonous agreement.

"Ready?" Axen finally asked.

"Not yet."

"That's fine with me."

"Probably not fine with them, though." She laughed.

"This is our castle, they can wait a bit longer." He smirked.

"I guess being the queen isn't so bad."

"One last thing, okay?" He pressed her head into his shoulder and rested his chin against her waves. "Because I know your head is spinning. Just trust the little wise boy we created, okay? You'll know when you see her."

"Wait just a minute." Dylah looked up at him. "That sleepy little kiddo did not specify who would know, he might have been talking about you."

"Most of his premonitions involve you for some reason." He raised an eyebrow. "Which is absolutely unfair because the kid looks just like me."

"Not entirely." She pointed amethyst eyes up to him.

"Footsteps approaching!" Keilon shouted through the doorway.

They didn't need to say a word, they fell against each other with a kiss that paused the time they didn't have left. A kiss that demanded safety and return. A kiss that extended past the simple definitions of chaos and harmony because there was no purer form of balance than their love.

"Please be safe." Dylah smiled.

"Please come back."

"Deal." She nodded. "Then I say we meet up for sunrise coffee in the lilac field."

"Let's wait and see," he paused as thunder rolled outside. "I think a storm is moving in."

"Good." She smiled as they walked towards the hall. "That means that chaos is on our side."

Chapter 56

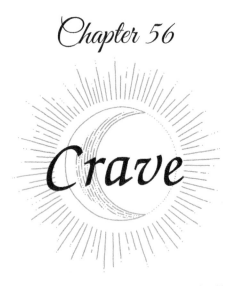

Crave

Dylah led Sorner through the vacant halls, occasionally the echo of softly treading enemy boots sounded nearby followed by low rolling thunder, but they waited them out. Right now there was only one goal in mind, getting back to the grand room where the stag laid in a painful paused existence.

"The double doors at the end of the hall," Dylah whispered as she pointed.

Sorner nodded and quickened his pace. He reached for the handles but the door only slightly shook.

"I locked him in." She half smiled. "I couldn't leave him like that without any regard to his safety."

Sorner pulled her in and kissed the top of her head. "You sweet darling!" His smile fell. "So have you got the key?"

"Didn't use a key." She flashed a smile then seemed to disappear.

On the other side of the door, Dylah scanned the empty

dimly lit room. She turned again to the door and pulled out the daggers she had shoved in to disable the handles.

Sorner walked in with an amazed look on his face. "You know, I lived with that curse for decades and I never thought to do half of the things you use it for."

"Well, it's not a curse to me. My brother spent my entire childhood teaching me that what I thought made me weak made me strong." She grabbed his wrist and led him towards the center of the room. "And it was your brother who taught me how to use it as a part of myself and not something against myself."

"That sounds like him." Sorner stared down at his sleeping brother as he slowly knelt beside him.

"Watch out for the darts." Dylah pointed to the pile of eight feather needles to the side of her predecessor. "They may still have some of the serum on them."

"Dylah, how long did you stay here with him?" He looked at her with wide glistening eyes. "The doors, the darts, you didn't have to do that much for a man living his third life. A man who had his mind made up weeks ago that he would die for you."

"Yeah, well I decided months ago that he would live an actual life this time around." Dylah slightly smiled. "And I'm the queen here, so I win."

"Remind me of the order of events once more." Sorner was beginning to show signs of his nerves. "The items will just appear for me?"

"According to Delin's plan, yes." She nodded. "He'll send it after he takes the others to the prisoners. Delin thinks he can actually use what he has to make two doses to start with, which most likely won't wake him up immediately. He can also make other forms of treatments to help any residual effects. Remember that I can go get another root or any other ingredients as early as tomorrow."

"Focus, youngblood." He smiled up at her. "Go take your next step."

Dylah paused for a moment. "But what if I can't?"

Sorner's laugh echoed around the empty room. "What a silly question!" He nudged his sleeping brother. "Did you hear that? What if she can't? Preposterous question!"

"So if it's just that simple then tell me what exactly is my next step? Hm?"

"Oh I have no idea, and he wouldn't have a clue either." Sorner shrugged. "But you're doing yourself no favors waiting in this dreary room and doubting yourself. So go."

"I just-"

"No talking, just leaving."

Dylah started taking steps away. "I'm going to lock you in again, just in case." She grabbed the sword next to the first Keilon and walked to the double doors. After the blade was maneuvered into the handles in a way that would prevent them from opening she waved to Sorner one last time before disappearing.

The moment she left a strong burst of thunder shook the grand room.

"I've been told that you can hear what's happening around you, brother." Sorner paused as the sky shook again. "I bet your heart is bursting."

The rest of the group had successfully made their way down to the foyer where Kremon, Bahn, Brig, and Kane were waiting.

"Derck's army has scared the others away," Kremon said after seeing the question on Keilon's face. "They are now staged throughout the town and along the treeline."

"Good." Keilon nodded. "We have just one thing left to do."

"I see that we're missing a few." Bahn raised an eyebrow. "Did they kill each other again?"

"Again?" Navent whispered to his sister.

"We'll explain on the way." Axen urged them on. "Our timing is important."

"That is a pretty thick bandage!" Kremon rushed to walk with him.

"They cut off my fingers and stabbed Keilon."

"Oh is that all?" Kremon shook his head.

As the group continued on towards the basement, Keilon noticed that Kunor had fallen behind.

"Come on, it's not safe to walk by yourself."

Kunor's eyes were dark as they darted around. "Don't you feel that?"

"I've felt very odd since walking into this place." Keilon tried to push him forward but he wasn't budging. "I can feel Dylah too and it's taking every bit of my sanity to ignore it."

"There's a shift happening."

"What kind of shift?" Keilon asked over the sound of rumbling skies.

Kunor took a deep breath. "I have to go."

"What? No." Keilon grabbed his arm and pulled him a step towards him. "We need to catch up to the others."

"Every step I take away from where I should be going is incredibly painful."

"And where is that?"

The sky shook again giving them their answer.

Kunor took a step away. "You understand, right?"

"I'm afraid I do."

Kunor smiled with relief. "Take a breath, father, your kids are coming back."

"I'll breathe again when you're both in front of me." Keilon quickly wrapped his arms around his son then pushed him towards the staircase. "So you better go fast."

Kunor flashed vibrant green eyes back at his father whose own eyes were a swirl of blue clouds. Then he turned with an immediate sprint towards his aunt.

It took everything Keilon had to not follow his son. He forced himself into a fog in an effort to successfully join the others. It wasn't his own emotions he was ignoring, he could feel her fear and rage twisted into a ball of perseverance. He tried to channel her same drive, but it was obvious to him that his chaos was different, it thrived on being a protector.

His strides gained more purpose as he soon found himself at the head of the group. They stopped just outside the door to the cellars.

"It will be the fourth door," Delin whispered. "I'll make sure you get in, then I'll go retrieve the ingredients needed."

Keilon pointed the hilt of a dagger to Delin. "Take this."

"No, you said I can't have a weapon." He shrugged. "I'll be fine."

Keilon put the hilt in his hand. "We might not be on the best terms with you right now, but don't be mistaken, we are in no way ready to mourn you."

"Understood." Delin faintly smiled.

"Not to mention," Keilon started with a growing grin, "you were always awful at learning combat and any of us could disarm you with very little effort."

"Easily!" Brig added.

"With our eyes closed." Kane crossed his arms.

"Without a second thought." Sentry raised an eyebrow.

"You better watch yourself, big guy," Navent grumbled.

"Congratulations, Riloncks." Axen laughed. "You've really imprinted on the youth."

Keilon opened the door and they crept as quietly as they could down the musty steps to the cellar. They held their breaths as they passed each door until they stood in front of the fourth door with their weapons drawn.

As the door slowly opened they put their weapons away.

Axen stared at the huddled group in front of them, two women stood guarding the prisoners, but they looked relieved as they gestured for them to come to the aid of the helpless captives.

"Delin," Axen said as he turned to his smiling brother-in-law, "I wish you would have been more clear about this situation."

Dylah was growing tired of outrunning the shouts from a language she didn't understand. Still, it was concerning to never know how many she had left to fight, the empty halls were constantly filled with a faceless threat and it disrupted the soul that drove her every step. Not to mention, the vibrations of constant worry that echoed from the other vessel of chaos.

Her fist twisted around her daggers as the shadows appeared at the end of the hall. First there were only four, she took three steps forward, then suddenly, ten more appeared. Her teeth grinded against each other as her mind began to rapidly fire a plan of action. Then, the lovely embodiment of evil stepped forward.

"Were you scared, Dylah?" Nevely asked calmly. "Did you think you saw your death again?"

"I thought I saw a challenge."

"You'll still get your challenge." Nevely crossed her arms. "I'll be leaving you four, then perhaps you'll run into the others later. Or maybe even more than you think." She gestured and the soldiers began to disappear around the corner once again. "And just a word of warning, your regular tricks won't work on these men."

Before Dylah could roll her eyes at the statement, four soldiers charged towards her, two with curved swords, the other two wielding knives with blades shorter than her own daggers. The first sword began its downward swipe towards her neck, but she stepped to the side and let the toe of her boot meet the point of the swordsman's extended elbow. It cracked, he yelped, Dylah grabbed the sword, shrank, dropped the sword, and popped back up as her normal self wearing a grand smile. The other swordsman was thwarted just as easily, but the remaining knife wielders seemed too calm.

The points of her blades couldn't seem to meet their targets, the enemy moved with a sharp quickness that was hard to follow. A boot hit her stomach and she stumbled back a few steps to catch her breath, but her shoulders were pushed until she was slammed against the wall. She smirked before snapping to her quickest method of escape, but she didn't realize that the other was crouched and anticipating the advantage her cursed size would give them.

Small rays of the hallway's dim light flooded into her temporary enclosure, it seemed to be woven like a basket, but the sides were extremely thin. As her two captors began to argue in a string of gritty syllables she thought through her options and cursed herself for brushing off her nemesis' warning.

Dylah looked through the cross hatching pattern to surmise her opponents positions. She waited until the moment the woven cup was lifted, then she rolled in the opposite direction while returning to her usual size. Her boot forced one man's neck against the wall as she pointed a dagger at the other.

The strange man stared up at her against the shine of her blade, he smiled and cupped his hands together.

"Catch," he whispered, then clapped his hands with a grimace. "Kill."

Dylah should have been scared, instead her blood boiled.

She walked away as their blood spewed onto the ground. Her teeth grinded as her eyes darted around looking for the next enemy, they thought they could use her advantage as theirs and she would make them see just how strong she was without her favorite trick. She'd make them realize that when backed into a corner, with no way out, she would be at her strongest, because when all else fails, chaos would always crave the dripping of crimson.

Chapter 57

Mildly Tortured

It didn't take Kunor very long to realize that he probably shouldn't have gone alone. He had been in this castle hundreds of times, but rarely alone and never with such stress on his shoulders. Still, he felt pulled by a force he didn't understand and each time the walls shook with thunder the pull only strengthened.

Between the rumbling bouts of thunder there were echoes of various sounds, a soft voice, a laugh, and a scuffle. Kunor thought he might be imagining all of it, that the labyrinth of stone and privilege had finally claimed his mind.

"This way!" a voice came from behind him as a hand wrapped around his arm.

His head snapped up to the person dragging him along. "Delin?"

"There's a few behind me, but I have to get to Sorner."

They went down another hallway and soon knocked on a door, Kunor deflated, he didn't know just how close he had been.

After a few moments of the door shaking it opened to reveal a flustered ancestor. "For such a small little thing she really did secure this lock."

Delin walked past Sorner to the fallen ghost at the center of the room.

"It may look like he's dead," Sorner said, "he's just breathing very sparingly. I check often." His focus snapped to the wide-eyed prodigy frozen in the doorway. "Helping our counterparts is a terrifying business, trust me."

"I just don't understand what help I can be to her, and why does she need the help and not my father?" Kunor shook his head. "I'm not the right person for this responsibility!"

"Another dramatic youngblood to deal with?" Sorner scoffed. "Kunor, you are the balance, and I think a part of you has always known that. Now go be the final pebble that tilts the scale in her favor, you'll know what to do."

Kunor nodded along with a nervous gulp.

Sorner glanced back at his brother. "And you have my word that you will feel no better relief than when you have successfully brought calm to their ever spinning minds."

The sky shook once more as Kunor slowly smiled and let himself succumb to the pull of balance.

Dylah had easily slashed through two progressing soldiers, though one sliced the length of her thigh on his way down. She brushed off the pain and stared down the next four, staggered like the first group, two swordsmen, two wielding knives and most likely a capture device. This time, the knife wielders ran at her first, she couldn't help but notice the flattened woven cups wedged between their fingers.

After seeing how low they were willing to sink for such an unworthy leader, Dylah wouldn't allow herself to be held back. Her boot cracked the nose of the first man, if only as a distraction for her dagger to slice from his left collar bone to the right side of his chest. She took advantage of his pain and disarmed him by relocating his knife from his hand to his inner thigh. The next wielder charged but he couldn't evade her quick enough, she had blocked his strike with her left blade as her right blade sunk into his side.

The first swordsman looked at her with wide eyes, he laid his curved sword on the ground as he tended to the worst of the injured men. Dylah was taken aback by the human response of enemies she had known to have no souls, she pondered her next move and how she would disarm with mercy in mind. Her plan went down in flames as the other swordsman put his blade to her neck as he grabbed a fistful of her hair. He pushed her against the wall, she slowly began to raise her dagger but the man shook his head with a smile as the blade drew closer to her neck. His eyes burned into her as a mist of spit sprayed from the gaps of his clenched teeth.

He studied her then shouted back to the other comrade in a phrase that sounded like a question which was answered by a word in a positive tone.

The soldier smiled, he released her hair and reached for the small axe hooked to his side. His eyes peered deep into hers as he held the axe in front of her face and whispered a single word, "Archer." Then he tilted his head back with a grand laugh.

Dylah knew exactly what he was trying to tell her, her knee met his stomach, she sliced the arm that held the sword, then she grabbed the axe from his hand. He was caught off guard just long enough to allow her time to throw him to the ground. She pressed her boot against his throat then raised the axe, the soldier spewed a myriad of pleas. His begging turned to screams the moment his right hand was severed.

Avenging her husband only fueled Dylah more. She turned the next corner and instantly let her dagger meet an unprepared soldier. The next two put up a fight, more slashes hit her legs but it wasn't anything that would distract her. They were disarmed and bleeding within minutes, but the final soldier was bigger than the rest had been. She was thrown to the ground the moment his fist met her jaw. She scrambled to rise and crossed her blades in front of her face as she inched away.

His laughter triggered her to bare her grinding teeth as her growl was lost beneath the sound of rolling thunder. He lunged, she jumped back but he caught her wrist and pulled her in, she began the motions of a downward slice but he maneuvered in such a way that led her to pierce herself in the leg.

No matter what she did, he always seemed to be one step ahead of her. After being thrown against the wall for the second time, she knew she needed a distraction.

Dylah took a wide step back, she threw two smaller daggers at his arms, paused for a moment, then stood calmly flipping a single dagger with her other hand propped on her hip.

"What are you doing?" The man raised an eyebrow.

"I'm embarrassed by how long it took me to realize that you weren't Gomdean." She flipped the dagger once more then cast her pink eyes on him before they slowly changed to a controlling gray. "Go collect your injured comrades and leave this place as fast as you can."

The man's expression fell as he mindlessly shuffled forward, but as he passed her he turned with a jerk to knock her dagger out of her hand, his foot slammed against her toe as he gripped her arms tightly.

"I'm not Gomdean, but I also only looked just below your eyes to avoid your evil tricks. You didn't even realize the failed connection." He grinned at her. "You should never put so much confidence in such a manipulative power." He lifted her just enough that only the toes beneath his boot were still on the ground. He methodically waited for her to struggle and then twisted her shoulders in one sharp motion as a crackle was heard from her ankle.

Dylah cried out in pain, she shrunk just fast enough to

get out of his hold, then thrust a dagger into his neck. She stumbled away and soon found the door that led to the third deck.

A light breeze whipped through and cooled her panicked sweats while slowing the dripping blood. She closed her eyes hoping to ignore their frantic twitching as she reeled from the events. Steps were heard approaching, Dylah gulped and turned to face them.

"End of the line, Dylah!" Nevely shouted over the rolling thunder as ten shadows lined up behind her.

Dylah braced herself on a straight arm gripping the ledge of the third deck. She couldn't begin to count the locations of pain on her body, but even in the darkness she could see the blood that peeked through each slice in her leggings. Somehow, Nevely still looked perfect. The walking embodiment of the most serene sunrise.

"I won, Dylah." She laughed.

Dylah swallowed the pain through a breath she couldn't catch, she forced her weight off of her straightened arm and stood tall even though her ankles shook.

"Not yet!"

"Give up," she huffed as she crossed her arms. "Look at you, battered and bleeding, how many times must you escape death to fulfill the needs of your terrible soul?"

"How many of your men died so you could remain intact?" Dylah asked through grinding teeth. "How many bled for the sake of your slanted harmony?"

"Some, and many more to come I imagine."

The thunder rolled louder as Nevely took a step towards her. Dylah almost smiled when the light raindrops fell, even in the moment of panic rain still made her feel a sense of peace.

"I hope you know that you didn't manage to kill my husband, you barely harmed the other half of my terrible soul, my brothers are all alive and well, your children are safe, my son is safe. What exactly did you accomplish here?"

"I killed a legend." Nevely's grin grew sinister as her delicate curls flattened against the force of the growing raindrops. "A happy accident."

"You wanted his allegiance!"

"Yes, but wearing the title of extinguishing the silver stag for good has a better ring to it, don't you think?"

The words were lost on Dylah, between the pain and the grief she couldn't fathom a plan. Instead, she watched as Nevely drew closer and closer, each step sent a flurry of thoughts that were only drowned out by deafening thunder and pounding rain. She couldn't stand watching the lovely woman inch her way closer, but instead of fighting all Dylah could do was close her eyes.

Her eyes, the place where her soul held its power, the only feature that defined her destiny. The eyes that were worn by Dycavlon and her predecessor, the same ones that gave her brother more purpose. The irises that twitched at any given change, the same irises that twitched now.

After an exhale she met the gaze beneath Nevely's furrowed brows. A bolt of lightning flashed illuminating the wall of soldiers that blocked the only exit.

"Unless you plan on jumping," Nevely said with a laugh, "you should just give up and come with us."

Dylah was left speechless, she looked down at the ground and shook her head to try to align her thoughts. Then the lightning flashed again.

Nevely raised her arm to gesture to her soldiers. "Get ready, men!"

"No!" Dylah finally found her strength. "You're still going to lose, Nevely! Because there has to be a balance and you just don't equate to me!"

Nevely scoffed as she narrowed her eyes on her nemesis, but before she could let another insult slide towards her, Dylah's eyes flashed as magnificent silver three times in rapid succession. Then a lightning strike hit close to the deck, also flashing three times.

"Your eyes," Nevely whispered.

"Yes, I know!" Dylah growled. "The dreadful eyes of my awful skewed soul, is that what you're getting at?!"

Nevely watched in awe as Dylah's eye grew with a metallic shine that flashed again before a similar flash sliced through a cloud.

"How are you doing that?" Nevely stared up at the storm clouds. "You're, the, it can't be."

"Now you choose to be a woman of few words?!" Her eyes flashed only once as a slender tendril of electricity rippled through an overhead cloud.

"You're the storm."

"Thank you."

"Don't you see it?!" Nevely took a step, her arms outstretched to the sky.

Dylah tensed as the distance between them shrank. She felt a quick tapping in her eyes, then watched as another bolt of lightning struck dangerously close.

"You think I'm calling this storm?" Dylah laughed. She let her hand slip into a sheath on her thigh.

"I do, I think somehow, your chaos has grown too strong." Nevely shook her head. "You must understand how unnatural this is, how unfair, you must give up your soul!"

Dylah drew her dagger and pointed it through the falling rain. "So what you're saying is that I have the upper hand?"

She pointed her dagger to the sky before slashing it through the air at nothing in particular. Just like she thought, seconds later lightning struck the edge of the deck, the soldiers muttered to themselves. Dylah pushed Nevely out of the way and pointed her dagger to the sky again. This time planning her slash with more precision.

Sparks rolled across the stone deck after a strike to the doorway. Three men lay singed and motionless, the remaining seven had jumped to the side before the flashes were over.

"Give up!" Dylah shouted at Nevely. "Look at you,

stricken with shock, hair a mess, disheveled to a hideous degree, yet finally your exterior matches the rot of your soul."

Nevely's eyes darkened as she looked at the churning storm clouds above them. "Dylah, you don't understand, this is too much power for one person to have!"

"Oh but Nevely, it seems as if I have your fear." Dylah smiled as she pointed her blade to the sky. "And by your standards that's all that matters." She aimed her dagger to a far off field, her eyes flashed then so did the sky.

Dylah then drew her second dagger. She held them both above her head in a crossed fashion. A proud smile filled her face, she felt charged and absolutely unstoppable. The sky rumbled above her as raindrops slid down her blades, she sliced them both through the air, the power surged through her irises as bright illuminations sparked on each side of the castle.

Dylah took two steps towards Nevely, though she was injured, in pain, and reeling, she could clearly see the next step her soul was offering. Because this wasn't just the soul at work, each lightning strike carried the strength of everyone who had ever loved her, and everyone who had ever challenged her. The clouds held the weight of her every fallen tear and the thunder echoed everything from her screams to her laughs. It was clear that this wasn't just the power of the chaotic soul, this was the power of Dylah.

She sheathed her left dagger and raised her outstretched hand to the sky, as she lowered her hand she formed a fist while the rain beat down harder and formed pellets of hail. Her grin widened as she looked again at Nevely. The emerging ability was both baffling yet felt so natural.

"Stop!" Nevely shouted as she took one step forward.

"I wouldn't get any closer if I were you." Dylah maneuvered her hand to place a wall of rain between them. "I really have no idea what I'm doing and I have a feeling you would despise a death at the hands of accidental havoc."

"You can't keep this up for much longer." Nevely smiled.

"I'll just wait."

Dylah pointed her dagger to the group of soldiers one more time as those that remained scurried to their leader's side.

"Undeserving power aside," Nevely laughed. "You are still outnumbered." She took another step closer as Dylah struggled to keep the rain between them. "If you give up we can find the balance that is meant for us, my leadership with your power would be a beautiful thing."

"You can't demand balance for the sake of tyranny!" Dylah clenched her teeth.

"And you can't live denying the need for balance!" Nevely shook her head. "Look at you, you grow paler by the second, your hands shake, I doubt you'll be able to call two more strikes before you topple over." She emerged through the wall of rain that had dissipated to only mist. "Your chaos is finicky and it is weak. What a lovely display, yet still underwhelming."

Dylah called a weak tendril of lightning to strike between them, but her nemesis was right, she didn't have the strength to keep it up much longer. She began to calculate her escape, the quickest route to reinforcements. Then, a groan rose from one of Nevely's soldiers, the confusion seemed to pause both sides as Dylah dropped any hold she still kept on the storm. Another soldier seemed to convulse before falling to the ground.

His eyes shone like sunlight from the other side of the deck and it was then that Dylah truly felt balance. It wasn't a balance that brought peace, but a balance that screamed the answers needed.

She sent a wave of torrential rain so she could sneak to his side.

"You wanted me here, right?" Kunor asked as soon as she was in front of him.

"Yes!" Dylah noticed the soldiers taking note of their location. "But we have to move!"

Dylah willed the raindrops to strengthen and when she saw their opening she grabbed Kunor's hand and made a dash towards the castle door. Within a few strides they couldn't ignore what balance was allowing to happen.

Raindrops hung suspended in the air. There was no wind, the churning of the clouds had paused, and the progressing soldiers stood frozen.

"How?!" Nevely shouted with wide eyes darting around the deck until they settled on Kunor.

"I'm doing this?!" Kunor whispered.

"Yes." Dylah squeezed his hand. "Actually we both are." As soon as she let go the storm resumed and the soldiers scrambled once more.

She pointed her dagger to the sky and pointed it at the progressing soldiers. She waited for her eyes to twitch, and at the first sign of a flash she grabbed Kunor's hand. Just as she suspected the lightning bolt stayed stationary.

"We're running," she whispered. "Don't let go until we're back in the castle."

"You're escaping?" Nevely wove through her paused brigade, she stopped once to take a dagger from a soldier's hand. "How well do you think you can call the storm inside?"

Dylah waited until Nevely was in line with the paused sparks then let go of Kunor's hand to allow the lightning to finish its strike and send the enemies to the ground. When the adversary was struggling to stand, Dylah ran down the hall.

"What's the plan?" Kunor ran after her.

Dylah pulled him into a corner. "I have no idea!" She was struggling to catch her breath. "I just couldn't do that much longer."

Kunor finally took the time to study her, though she had been soaked by the constant rain, she still had many cuts that glistened with crimson, her face was pale except the shadows that hung beneath her eyes. Stray bruises blossomed along her jawline, there was a split in her bottom lip, and he had already noticed her limp.

"You don't have to be the one to finish this." Kunor put his arm around her. "We're going to wait this out for a bit until the others can come."

"No." She shook her head. "She is one small angry woman, it shouldn't be this hard."

"Dylah." Kunor muffled a laugh. "You are also a small angry woman."

Dylah flashed a fraction of a smile. She leaned against the wall, her head completely slouched. Kunor watched as her fingers twitched with the leftover energy of the lightning she had summoned. He wanted to say anything, but she seemed to vanish, his eyes wandered down to where she was propped up against the baseboard, clutching her knees while still remaining unnervingly silent.

"We can't stay here." Kunor knelt to be a little closer to her.

"I know," she sighed. "But sometimes I just have to side with history and agree that the soul I have needed to be contained to such a pathetic form."

"Can I level with you really fast? Before the terrible lady shows back up?" Kunor's eyes darted everywhere except down to his aunt of miniscule stature and confidence. "From one youngblood to the other, I think we're supposed to be mildly tortured by what we came from and what we're capable of."

Dylah's head finally lifted as she snapped back to her usual size. "And you're okay with that?"

"Did you just see the cataclysmic things we caused? Mostly you, but still!" He laughed. "Imagine if we weren't the people we are, the dangerous things we could do wielding a power like that. Imagine if it wasn't us, what if Nevely had figured out the way to pause your storm, or think of how the old guy would have used that lightning. And I think we're supposed to recognize that, it's how we grow and use it better."

Dylah met his calm gaze with a slight head tilt. She grimaced as she pulled herself to stand. "Harmony received, let's go." She clapped her hands together.

"This way," Kunor said as he placed his arm back around her. "Delin is already with Sorner."

They moved through the empty halls staying slightly ahead of the stomps that followed them. Every so often they'd pass the strewn body of an enemy Dylah had defeated, each sighting seemed to slow her but Kunor pushed her forward with silent encouragement. But the view of the double doors deflated every ounce of air in her lungs.

Kunor pushed the door open and they were soon met with a tense shadow that quickly relaxed.

"What happened to you two?!" Keilon pulled Dylah into him and held her tightly. "What happened to her?"

"We don't have much time to explain, Nevely is right behind us." Kunor half smiled. "I told you I'd bring both of us back to you. Are you breathing now, father?"

"Not yet." Keilon looked down at Dylah as her eyes briefly pointed up at him, it was the last motion she could muster before collapsing.

Chapter 58

Ignite

Dylah awoke with ringing ears and tingling fingertips. She blinked as the light of the unfamiliar room came into focus, but covered her face as a headache began to throb behind her eyes. A hand landed on her shoulder, Dylah turned her head and peeked through her fingers to see which brother was at her side.

"Hey there, youngblood."

"Are we dead?"

"Not this time."

Dylah finally opened her eyes to see him propped up in the corner of the room. He was pale and exhaustion laid heavily beneath his eyes, his golden hair fell in a stringy disheveled mess to one side. She pulled herself up to lean against the wall with her legs outstretched in front of her. "Is Nevely gone?"

"How long do you think you were asleep?" Old Keilon laughed weakly. "You walked in just a few minutes ago." He laughed a little louder. "Then you fell, so they put you over here, you muttered a lot, shrank yourself twice, then woke up."

"Awake already?" Sorner quickly appeared. "Marvelous yet concerning."

Dylah scanned the empty room. "Where is everyone?"

"Everyone?" Sorner laughed. "You mean the three other people? They're down the hall waiting for that strawberry headed annoyance to show herself."

Dylah pushed against the heel of her only stable ankle until she was standing with the support of the wall at her back. "Which way?"

Sorner crossed his arms. "I'm not telling you and I'm not letting you leave this room."

Dylah took a shaky step forward, black and pink eyes pinned up at him. Followed by a quick smirk and an unsurprising vanishing act. She reappeared behind him. "Right or left when I go out this door?"

Sorner turned to follow her slow steps. "Well, it sure is a nice stroll you're taking to all the violence. If we walk any slower we'll be able to watch the seasons change outside the window."

She pointed pink eyes at him as thunder shook the castle.

"My apologies." Sorner flashed a look of concern to his grinning brother. "Perhaps you would like me to carry you instead?"

"Perhaps I should carry you." She raised her eyebrow and stood a little straighter.

"I find your presence so very odd." Sorner pushed her towards the door with a light hand on her shoulder. "You are the most terrifying thing yet also the most adorable."

She waited until he had pointed her in the right direction outside the door.

"How is he awake?" she finally asked.

"Well, let's not overreact, he is merely awake." Sorner

smiled. "Delin said something about perfect conditions, the darts were pulled out in time, he mentioned the serum was weaker than expected, and he got there in the desired amount of time to increase the probability. So yes, he is awake, but he'll still need a few more treatments before he's back to his regular brooding self."

"Go wait with him." Dylah began to walk past him while he stayed frozen. "This isn't your fight anymore."

Sorner grabbed her wrist. "He doesn't need my protection."

"Just go be brothers for once."

"Gladly," he said as his grip slipped down to squeeze her hand. "Thank you."

Dylah pulled away, her steps gained more speed as she willed herself to ignore the searing pain that came in waves from her ankles to her cheekbones.

"Go back to the room and wait," Keilon ordered as soon as he caught a glimpse of her.

Dylah stood between Keilon and Kunor. "Which one of you took the dagger with the rose on it?"

"Old guy took it from you and gave it to me." Kunor shrugged towards his father. "I gave it to him."

"What?" Keilon raised an eyebrow. "I don't have it."

"So we've lost the very important dagger?" Dylah sighed.

"It is possible that I handed it back to the old guy by mistake."

"Where's Delin?" Dylah looked around. "Don't tell me you misplaced him too."

"He went back to help with the rescued prisoners." Keilon relaxed for a moment. "He wouldn't have been much help anyway." He looked at his nervous son and his injured sister. "Actually, neither of you will be much help."

Dylah pointed a pink tinted glare at him, she calmly walked into the closest room and shattered the window with her dagger. She carefully reached through the shards and extended her fingers before slowly pulling her hand back in with a clenched fist. She returned to the hallway, walking with a limp but wearing a proud smile as a cloud followed behind her.

"What are you-" Keilon started but Dylah had shushed him.

She positioned the cloud against the ceiling and released the rain it held.

"Impressed?" Dylah laughed. "Now watch what your son can do." She grabbed Kunor's wrist and the drops hung suspended in the air. "And that witch didn't think I would be able to do this inside."

"You're right." Nevely's familiar chime echoed at the other end of the hall. "You've conjured a storm within a castle, is your soul not satisfied yet?"

"Where are your men, Nevely?" Dylah asked with a slight smirk.

"Your last lightning strike left me with only two, and they are gravely injured." She shook her head. "And I have taken note of the carnage within these halls."

"We freed your prisoners!" Keilon spat. "You're despicable!"

"And what do you have to say to me?" Nevely raised an eyebrow as her eyes settled on Kunor. "We share a soul and yet you have no disparaging words to throw my way? Perhaps you disagree with those who are truly your opposite, come to my side."

"Dylah, let go," Kunor whispered.

"Dylah, do not let go," Keilon demanded.

"Let go." Kunor met her stormy gaze. "Lower the cloud, I can end this."

"Don't," Keilon nearly shouted.

Dylah let go of his hand as the rain fell again, she reached her hand up and let the cloud fill the distance of the hallway between them.

Kunor walked slowly, slightly crouched, as he readied

his bow. He knew he was getting closer by the growing volume of Nevely's constant accusations of the soul he held his entire trust in. He pulled the bowstring back, still concealed within the cloud.

Nevely screamed. It was a pitch so shrill it seemed to cut into the surrounding walls, then there was a thud. Dylah dissipated the cloud.

"Kunor?!" She ran up to him with Keilon right behind her. But Kunor was still crouched, and his bow was still loaded.

Keilon's eyes darted to the end of the hall where Nevely laid face down with a dagger sticking out of her back and an ominous figure standing above her, his hands clasped over his shock stricken face.

"It's okay." Keilon put his arm around his brother's shoulders. "You did a good thing, Delin." He propped him against the wall and made his panicked darting eyes meet his commanding clouds. "Deep breaths, okay?" Delin complied. "Now go wait at the end of the hall, we'll be along shortly." Delin nodded slowly then trudged away.

"I'm so glad you didn't have that power when we were kids." Dylah half laughed.

"Is she really dead?" Keilon pulled Dylah towards him. "So many revivals have made me weary of what is possible."

"Um," Kunor said with his hands over his eyes. "I don't think you have to worry about her coming back." He slowly looked up as his eyes brightly transitioned through every shade of green before illuminating like the calmest sunbeam. "I felt it all just click into place." He let out a sigh filled with overwhelming relief. "It's all lined up now."

Keilon paired Dylah with Kunor and told them to wait with Sorner, he could tell that she could no longer ignore her many injuries. He stayed behind and confirmed that Nevely was void of breath and a heartbeat, in fact he stayed for a moment to ponder how she had ever been worthy of such a tarnished existence. He retrieved the dagger that held no malice, only justice.

He made his way back to the room. Sorner had streaks of fallen tears down his face as he shook his prodigy, Delin leaned against the wall with his arms crossed, and Dylah was propped in the corner next to their predecessor. She was folded into herself and her head rested on her knees.

"She's fine," Old Keilon said before Keilon could express any concern. "Takes a lot of energy to command the skies."

Keilon sat on the other side of her. "I believe this is yours." He held the hilt out to her.

Dylah's head slowly rose as she reached for the dagger. She studied the engraved rose and pointed to the top thorn. "You were right," her voice was low and gritty as if she were thinking out loud. "My havoc grew within me. It bursted and it spilled out of my eyes. You were so lucky to fight me at my weakest, and yet you still lost."

"Who are you talking to?" Keilon asked slowly.

"The person who first ignited the power of my soul but only through vengeance." She looked at her brother and slowly smiled. "The first thorn. Zether." She pointed to the empty space at the base of the stem. "This is where the person who ignited your soul will go."

"You shouldn't give either of them so much credit," Old Keilon said. "It's not the summer that causes the winter, it's just the natural order of life." He pointed brief glances at each of his prodigies. "Revel in the fact that you were always meant to ignite and thrive."

Chapter 59

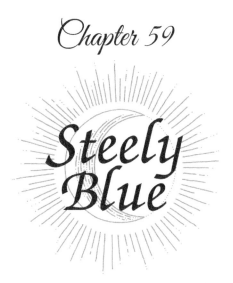

Steely Blue

After quick checks of everyone's health which included bandaging Dylah's cuts and wrapping her ankle, Keilon and Delin decided to stay with the stag and Sorner, because together they could collectively move him to a nearby room with a bed. Dylah was anxious to find her husband and return to her trees and Kunor knew he needed to be the one to give the news of Nevely's death to Navent and Sentry.

Kunor kept his arm around Dylah as she dragged her feet towards the foyer. They stopped every other floor so she could catch her breath, commanding the power of the sky had left her drained and the emotional toll of the day only emptied her more.

"Only three more floors." Kunor shook her a little. "Everyone is fine. We did it."

"I know," she said through a sigh.

They arrived at the first floor where the prisoners had been moved. Kunor stopped outside of an ornate door that was muffling a multitude of noises.

"Before we go in, you should know something about these prisoners," he said slowly. "There's a reason why my father felt compelled to aid in that woman's demise."

Dylah paused to listen. "Children?"

"Yes." He nodded. "I want you to take the time to feel the weight of who you saved them from."

"How many?"

"Seven." He pushed her a step forward. "I've been told that they're already figuring out where their parents are and where they belong."

Dylah reached for the handle on her own, the room in front of her felt like a dream. Her nephews were chasing two children along with Navent around the room, Sentry sat in a corner with a young girl who had fallen asleep, other children were laughing with Kremon. She seemed to float towards the tattered emerald cape that paced the width of a room with a slight bounce.

Axen's right arm stayed clutched to his side, but his left arm had a tight hold on a small child. From a distance it was clear that he was whispering any phrase that came to mind in an effort to keep the toddler calm, it was something that came natural to him, especially when their son was at a similar age.

When Axen turned towards Dylah she caught sight of the young girl in his arms.

The moment she saw her she knew it was their daughter.

"What's her name?" she asked before Axen could say a word.

"Rilavry." He smiled and so did the girl at the sound of her name.

"Where was she taken from?"

"They don't really know, all they know is that that woman made sure this little one had no one else left." He nodded his head towards the two women that seemed to be overjoyed by the events of the night. "Their caretakers have been able to list the other children's homelands and remember the faces of the parents they were taken from throughout each of Nevely's wars." He paused for a moment. "But I've been told that she needs a family, one that will love her and care for her. They say that she was taken two years ago, and this is the only form of family she's ever known. So I said we had been waiting for her, and we had to keep her." He glanced from Dylah's amethyst eyes to the child's eyes that were already locked on her. "Dylah, I knew when I saw her."

Dylah took the small girl into her arms and ran a hand through her silky straight obsidian hair. The moment slowed as Rilavry looked into Dylah's eyes. The color was one that Dylah was all too familiar with, gray and stormy yet steely blue, the same color that she saw in the mirror everytime the weight of her losses was too much for her to bear. Looking now at the innocent face in front of her she knew that all of her past sadness had a purpose, it had brought her to their daughter.

"I'm sure you have a lot to update me on." Axen scanned her. "And I have so many questions."

"But let's just go back to Fellowrock." She funneled every last bit of her energy into the grand smile she wore and the grip she had on the daughter who rested her head on her shoulder. "We need to see the trees."

"Trees," Rilavry repeated in a soft whisper.

"I knew you were a Rilonck." Dylah kissed her forehead as she began walking towards the door. "So many trees, you can run through them and climb them, and lilacs, so many lilacs. And uncles, you have so many uncles, and a brother, he will be the best big brother."

"Slow down." Axen wrapped an arm around them. "Let her start with trees."

They stopped to talk to the two women who had guarded the children. Between the four of them a shower of gratitude was poured. The women pointed out how quick

Rilavry had been to cling to both of them, and one of them reached into a basket and handed Axen a small bottle with a single stone in it.

"Amethyst?" he asked as his eyes went from the stone to irises of a similar color.

"She was holding it when Nevely took her," the caretaker said solemnly. "You're both holding the only two things that survived that attack."

"I need to ask," Axen started. "Were you two caring for our son when he was taken?"

The women whispered to each other in their known language. "Yes, we adored his eyes," one finally answered. "He'll be excited to see Rilavry again, they were nearly inseparable while he was in our care."

They offered their thanks once again, then set off back towards the treeline. An elated silence hung over them as they noticed that the young girl had fallen asleep with her head lulled on Dylah's shoulder. Of all the things fate had handed to Axen and Dylah, it couldn't be ignored that their children were always meant to be theirs.

Chapter 60

History of Forgiveness

Keilon walked up the steps of the Hightree castle, he couldn't believe the horrors that had taken place within the same halls only a week prior. The sunlight poured in through the occasionally spaced windows with a brightness that finally felt justified. Still, there was a sadness in the air. This was the longest Keilon had gone without seeing his sister, other than during the war against Hightree years ago.

He held his breath and knocked on the door of the king and queen's suite.

Her eyes were embers the second the door opened. "I told you ten days."

"It's been a week, is that not enough?" He smiled as he studied his sister. Slight signs of exhaustion lined her eyes, her hair was in a loose ponytail that had draped over her shoulder, and she was wearing an oversized shirt with misaligned buttons.

"We really want Rilavry to have time to adjust to just

us before introducing her to all of the family." Dylah stepped into the hall and closed the door. "Is everything okay?"

"Yeah, the old guy is walking, he has a cane. It's pretty funny, but he's walking."

"Oh, that's great!" Her eyes lit up. "And you took that news as an excuse to come see me? Very transparent, big brother." She opened the door. "It's a mess, but come on."

Within two steps Keilon was shocked by the state of the suite. The kitchen alone was a disaster, every cabinet was open and all of the contents were lined up on the floor.

"You were warned." She laughed. "The daughter has a very unique set of interests."

"I see that." Keilon stared at the young girl sitting on the only empty space of the kitchen floor staring at two mugs. "How old is she?"

"The caretakers gave us a timeline of how old she was when she was taken, and they've had her for about two years, so we think she'll be three in the next few months."

"Uncle Keilon!" Cav ran from across the room, leaping over piles of dishes. "Have you met my sister?!"

"Not officially," he said with a hand ruffling Cav's fawn colored hair. "Do you like being a big brother?"

"Yeah!" Cav grinned.

Dylah walked away the moment Rilavry began showing signs of distress towards her organization methods.

"Can I let you in on a little secret?" Keilon leaned in slightly and whispered to his nephew.

"I love secrets," Cav whispered back.

"Being a big brother is the best job you'll ever have."

"Mama said you'd say something like that." Cav grabbed his hand and pulled him over to the kitchen where Dylah and Rilavry were on the floor.

Rilavry was muttering a string of syllables while pointing to two mugs that seemed to be nearly identical.

"She's arranging by size and can't pick which one is bigger." Cav shrugged. "We had the same problem yesterday with dad's pencils."

"How did you help her solve it?" Keilon asked just before Dylah took one of the mugs and smashed it on the floor.

"Like that." Cav laughed.

Rilavry looked up and stared at the new stranger in the room. Her crystal eyes met his and he willed them to be amethyst. The girl was shocked. She stood and shuffled through the maze of dishes she had created and stood at Keilon's feet pointing up to him.

"What is she doing?" Keilon asked slowly.

Rilavry pointed to her eyes then to his, then back to her eyes, then over to Dylah, then covered one eye before pointing at Cav.

"You're right, we have the same eyes."

"Rilavry," the young girl said with a smile of approval then returned to her organizing.

"She likes to say her name." Cav shrugged.

The door to the suite opened and Axen walked in carrying a large box. He was almost unrecognizable without the common green cape. On his right hand was a pseudo glove that covered his palm and gaps where two fingers used to be.

"Okay, look at this!" He walked right past Keilon as if he was only focused on his daughter. "There are exactly one hundred and each one is a very different size." Axen held up various wooden blocks as Rilavry looked with wide eyes. He set the box down in the living room area and Dylah was quickly sitting cross legged on the floor gesturing for Rilavry to spare the contents of their kitchen.

"Kunor tells me each displaced Farein is finally all settled back into their old rooms," Keilon said when Axen returned to the kitchen.

"Yes, everything seems to be returning to normal." He smiled. "Any progress on the ghost?"

"After the last injection he's walking again."

"That's good." Axen seemed to be looking at nothing in particular. "I'd like to propose something to you, but in a more official manner."

"That's somewhat worrisome."

Axen smiled as he watched the slightly panicked grin spread on his wife's face as their daughter dumped the contents of the box onto the floor. "I've just been thinking a lot about what I want to leave behind for my family."

"Me too." Keilon nodded. "Would you like to schedule such a discussion?"

"How much longer is Derck here?"

"I think he said he was leaving in about two weeks," he responded slowly. "Do you need his input too?"

"No, let's keep our victory celebration going until he leaves, then we can work on this next step." Axen turned and looked at him, his hazel eyes also lined with exhaustion, but with the common shine of determination. "It has to start with us."

"I'm intrigued already." Keilon scanned the disastrous looking suite and turned to leave. "I'll check back in in a few days."

"You lasted a whole day longer than I thought you would." Axen smirked. "She fits right in, doesn't she?"

Keilon glanced over at his sister. He was taken back to the distant past when she claimed she'd make a terrible mother. "More of a Rilonck than a Farein, but yes, she's a great addition."

Three steps into the hall and Dylah was again at his side.

"You're pretty fast for someone who broke an ankle and summoned a storm a week ago." Keilon stopped and looked down at her.

"It wasn't that broken." Dylah rolled her eyes. "I'll add that you were stabbed a week ago and you seem fine." She raised an eyebrow. "You should know by now that our precious souls seem to help us heal a little faster."

"Yes, the ghost did mention that about twelve times."

"It feels lighter doesn't it? The soul." Dylah smiled. "I think he's finally come to terms with everything."

"It does feel lighter." Keilon met her amethyst gaze that seemed to sparkle a little more than usual. "But it's not because of him, it's you who isn't carrying the weight anymore. You recognize that, right? You've come to terms with your past pain, you're happier now because you have that little girl."

"Oh."

"You really shouldn't give that guy so much credit." Keilon laughed. "You've done more than he ever did."

"So have you." She turned to leave. "Keilon the Greater."

Inside the house nestled on the border a stalemate was happening.

"Just do it!" Sorner grinned even though his teeth were clenched and his usually perfect top knot bun leaned a little to the left. "I am intrigued and amazed and absolutely entranced by what you can do that I never could."

"I could only do it during the battle because of what Dylah was doing," Kunor muttered, almost scared of the usually calm man's agitation.

"But you have the full soul now, Dylah doesn't even have a full soul!"

"But she's Dylah."

"Youngblood, do it or I will shake my fist at you or perhaps even cry!" Sorner crossed his arms. "Probably cry, most likely cry."

"Definitely cry!" the other ancestor yelled from the kitchen table.

"Fine, throw it." Kunor sighed.

Sorner's grin turned genuine but twisted with so much joy it was almost more unsettling than his odd anger from before. He tossed a small ball into the air.

Kunor watched it intently before closing his fists tightly. The ball seemed to pause midair for a few short seconds before continuing its descent.

"Incredible!" Sorner clapped his hands together. "Okay,

you can go."

"What?" Kunor's eyes went wide. "That's it?!"

"Yes, you've done what I asked of you, so you're free to leave." Sorner walked past him and into the kitchen. "Have a nice day."

Kunor followed him and took note of the scattered papers on the table, all flipped over to hide the details of a forgotten past.

The first Keilon was refilling his coffee.

"Brother, I do so wish you'd stop forgetting your cane." Sorner tried to hand it to him.

"Who said I forgot it?" He took slow steps towards the table with a close eye on the swashing black coffee within the mug.

"You stubborn old beast." Sorner twirled the cane to give it some form of purpose. "Did you see? Kunor did the thing!"

"What thing?" Old Keilon fell into his chair and stared at his brother's quiet prodigy.

"The pausing thing, of course!" He used the cane to point at his brother. "A marvelous feat!" Sorner slouched slightly. "We are insignificant now."

"We were insignificant the moment our prodigies were born."

"I'm sorry," Kunor said as he sat at the table, "but have you seen the banners?"

"The kid has a point." Sorner twirled the cane once more.

The front door opened and soon another was sitting at the kitchen table, his blonde hair a little disheveled and his hands tightly laced on the tabletop.

"I don't need another treatment until next week." Old Keilon raised an eyebrow. "What's going on?"

"I just don't know what to do here anymore." Delin sighed. "So I'm just wandering around the kingdom."

"We can go for a walk if you want," Kunor suggested with a kind smile and calm jade eyes.

The first Keilon stood, grabbed the cane from his brother and gestured to the door, Delin followed.

"Sorner," Kunor whispered to get his attention and pointed to his own head. "You're a little lopsided."

"I have been called many odd names in my years, but never lopsided." Sorner tilted his head back and laughed.

"No, it's your hair."

Sorner's hands flew to his head. "Damn." He began to realign his ever so perfect bun. "I'm afraid you've siphoned more harmony from me than originally thought. One way or another I've turned into a mess."

"How much wine did you two drink last night?" Kunor grinned.

"Buckets."

"There's your answer."

Delin shuffled out to the deck first and immediately leaned on the railing with his face in his hands.

"You can't escape the guilt, huh?" the ghost asked once he was sure that the others didn't follow. "You did so much good, but you will never believe that it outweighs the bad."

"Yes."

"And even though they've all gone back to normal, they seem to have forgotten the pain of what you did, but you, you never will."

"I should have died during that battle," Delin whispered. "Life offers no justice."

"Sure it does." The ghost smiled. "You simply just weren't meant to die in that moment. I know, there are many things I don't believe I should have lived through. Dying is a mercy, living with our mistakes is justice."

"How do you carry it?"

"I don't." He looked off into the trees. "I think it carries me. It's almost like every step I take is uphill and the guilt I feel determines how steep the incline is." He took a deep breath and paused. "When I first came back that climb was nearly vertical, even now it's an incline but it's manageable and I feel it getting flatter. You'll get there soon."

"How can you be so sure?"

"I killed my father, two brothers, countless elders, and hordes of my own citizens." He shrugged with a kind half smile. "You kidnapped your nephew and burned some trees."

"I killed Nevely." Delin stared back.

"But she tried to kill so many people that you love." Old Keilon tried to help him rationalize. "Imagine what might have happened if she had been successful."

"I don't think I can begin to imagine that. I never did anything bad when I was younger." Delin slumped. "I always had my nose in a book, I tended to Dylah's constant scrapes and bruises, the worst thing I did was hand her over to the enemy she longed for." He shook his head. "But I don't even feel like the same person anymore. I'm tainted, like one side of me is still the light and calm Delin, but the other side was left in the oven for far too long and is burnt beyond recognition. I think I'll always feel this way."

"Lean away from it. It's awful, but ignore it." The first Keilon gulped and seemed almost scared. "If you learn to live with that dark version, you will only get deeper into the darkness." His eyes met Delin's. "Trust me."

"I see that my family has a history of forgiveness." Delin's hands began to fidget. "The person who abused my brother and killed our parents is still granted permission to visit her grandchildren under strict rules, and you murdered our sister and yet we lean on you the most. But me, I don't think I'm worthy of such forgiveness. It doesn't feel justified."

"And you think I feel worthy of the forgiveness they've shown me? The forgiveness my brother has?" Old Keilon laughed if only to cover his worry. "Forgiveness is something that is hard to give and even harder to receive. Because to them we're their brother, their friend, their whatever, but we know our truest selves, and we will never think we deserve a lighter load."

Delin tried to formulate any answer but the deck doors soon opened.

"Interesting conversation?" Keilon asked as he stood by his youngest brother.

"Not really," the first keeper of the name replied. "Just admiring the weather."

"Oh." The king chuckled. "Dylah will be introducing Rilavry to the family tomorrow night."

"I knew she wouldn't wait the ten days." Old Keilon laughed. "So you finally met the kid? I thought you'd give up after two days."

"I had very important matters to discuss with both her and Axen."

"No you didn't." The stag grinned. "You just couldn't stay away. The other piece of my soul called to you and you couldn't help but answer it."

"Is your soul really so great after what Dylah did with it?" Keilon smirked. "I never heard a single legend about you calling a storm."

"So tomorrow night?" The ancestor breezed past the comment. "At the castle?"

"Actually, she wants it to be here."

"Where should I go while this is happening?" Delin muttered.

"You should come to this house." Keilon laughed. "Where we will all be welcoming our niece."

"My granddaughter technically." Old Keilon shrugged with a smile. "Yours too though, right?"

"By default." The king rolled his eyes before focusing on his slumped brother. Delin had always been shy, but never as quiet as he had been in the past week. He was never the most muscular and never thin, but lately he had seemed to be withering away a little at a time, his shirt hung loosely around his neck.

Delin caught his brother's worried look, he had seen it too many times to count. It brought him back to each time they tested if Dylah had been cured. Keilon would stand frozen on the white line with the same look on his face. Now, the look was only amplified by the storms within his irises.

"I'm going to go for a walk." Delin took a step off the deck and noticed that Keilon had taken a step forward as well. "I would like to go alone."

Keilon didn't want to listen, he tried to follow his brother but he was pulled back by a hand on his shoulder.

"Give him some time." Old Keilon gestured towards the house. "Let's talk about a few things."

"What things?"

"I'm not sure." He shrugged and slowly walked towards the door. "I've been alive too long, I'm losing my ghostliness."

"You say that like it's a bad thing." Keilon laughed as he walked into the house to begin planning the celebration to come.

Chapter 61

Most Certainly

"They're coming, right?" Kremon asked over the sound of his twin sons wrestling. "The kids will start to get restless soon."

"Soon?" Sorner asked with a raised eyebrow. "You consider this feral behavior calm?"

"Yes." Kremon laughed.

"Really," Bahn spoke up, "who taught Dylah it was okay to be this late? It is incredibly rude."

"She is allowing you all to meet her daughter days before she intended, so maybe give her some leniency." Sorner took a step back when the twins' scuffle had creeped closer to him. "Perhaps the same leniency you give to these two."

"Eh, don't worry about them." Kremon shrugged. "Bahn and I were the same way and we turned out just fine."

"Damnit, Dylah!" Bahn smacked the table. "I'm so bored!"

"I see." The ancestor offered a weak smile in reply.

Sorner slipped into the living room where most of the others were waiting. Avalia with her two other children and growing belly, she was chatting with Chany, along with Arkon close by in a wheelchair in a discussion with Derck. Kunor sat with his hand tightly gripping Sentry's. Navent was exchanging jokes with Brig and Kane, they were promising to show him their favorite hunting grounds now that everything had been settled. And sitting on the third step of the staircase was the shadow of Delin, he had reluctantly joined but had shown no effort of participation.

Sorner floated through the clouds of conversation out to the deck where men of the same name soaked up the quiet calm of the forest. He stood still enough to not be noticed, it seemed they were deep into their conversation.

"I have a lot of respect for your mother, considering, but I think she was wrong about one thing." Old Keilon laughed at the king's instant glare. "You shouldn't have been named after me, you should've been named after Dycavlon and Dylah should've had a form of my name."

"Go ahead and explain," Keilon said through a sigh.

"I've spent an eternity with Dycavlon and you two are quite similar, you'll enjoy his stoic company."

"I'm going to take that as a compliment."

"Neither of my prodigies were given my name," Sorner said to announce himself. "Though I'm told my name lived on as a surname, and I'm not sure that I like that."

"Why? Whole families carrying your name sounds like a great honor." The first Keilon turned to his brother. "Your name would never really die that way."

"I suppose, but I've always cherished the thought that names match the soul they are given to." Sorner sighed. "And, not to be too boastful, but not many are graced with a soul such as mine."

The first Keilon looked again at the man that had been named after him, the same man who was the first to hold any piece of the chaotic soul after centuries of lying dormant. He thought about how much of an honor it was that the king that handled such hardship, had conquered the impossible, and so much more was wearing his own name. He was about to vocalize his pride through a snarky remark, but soon small feet raced up the steps of the deck.

"We're here!" Cav raised his arms up as if he had won a great victory.

"I see you and no one else." Old Keilon laughed. "Did you leave them?"

"They're coming," Axen said as he joined them on the deck. "We meant to be here two hours ago."

"What took so long for you to head this way?" Keilon asked.

"I guess I should rephrase that." Axen laughed. "We have been on our way here for two hours."

"My sister is easily distracted." Cav giggled.

Through the leftover glow of the setting sun they saw two silhouettes walking hand in hand through the trees, at an incredibly slow pace. After a bit of waiting, Dylah and Rilavry finally walked up the steps to the house that Axen had built.

Rilavry stared with wide eyes up at the tall men, she was clutching an enormous stack of leaves.

"Did she find a favorite?" Axen asked.

"She found a lot of favorites." Dylah laughed.

Rilavry stared at Keilon, the only one she recognized. When his eyes flashed to the amethyst she so loved she handed him a leaf. Then she handed one to her brother, her father, and her mother. She stepped away from Dylah to look at the ancestors, her steely blue eyes drifting from Sorner to Old Keilon many times before she handed them each a leaf.

Sorner knelt down to express his gratitude and adoration to the small girl, but her instant growl and bared teeth made him stand up with a step back. "That is most certainly Dylah's daughter!"

The first Keilon couldn't help but laugh at his brother's

fear towards such a small girl, and he soon met the girl's icy stare. The color nearly took his breath away. The same color he had seen in his own eyes when the despair and worry of his past was too much to carry. Seeing it linger in irises above a slowly growing grin that crept closer to him made him feel lighter.

Rilavry stood in front of him with a grand smile, she pointed at her eyes then at his while mumbling insistent syllables. He tilted his head in confusion.

"She liked your eyes," Dylah whispered. "Change them back to lavender."

The stag complied with a nod and pointed eyes that didn't need to be forced down at the girl with an ever growing smile. After a few unblinking seconds, Rilavry handed him another leaf before returning to her mother's side.

"Rilavry!" the girl giggled.

Those on the deck made their way into the house where the rest of the family was awaiting the promised celebration. Their collective elation frightened Rilavry who growled against her father's shoulder for fifteen minutes until the crowd calmed and separated into different rooms.

First, Rilavry was introduced to her doting aunts, both were handed leaves, she giggled when Avalia tried to braid her hair.

"She's perfect, Dylah." Chany gave her a quick hug. "I am always available to watch her at a moment's notice." She smiled with all of her teeth.

"Under one condition," Dylah started, "you have to be prepared to take over the life lessons when I'm just not ready to." She slowly smiled. "Ya know, the stuff that might cause me to have an existential crisis."

"Of course, but I expect you to be far braver than your brother was at raising a strong willed girl." Chany winked.

Rilavry was soon perplexed by the wheels on Arkon's chair and even allowed him to hold her while he showed her how he rolled about, he was also given a leaf. Derck had very little to say as usual, but it was enough to be granted a leaf. Brig and Kane made brief introductions that were rewarded with smaller leaves. She was the most interested with Navent and demanded to hold his hand for a solid minute before handing him three leaves and walking away.

They entered the kitchen in the middle of an argument between two generations of Rilonck twins. Bahn and Kremon were shouting at one another, Bahn's brows were tightly scrunched together while Kremon laughed through his anger. Taron and Terner were still rolling around the floor in a scuffle that seemed to have no beginning or end. The men went silent when they caught sight of their sister with the young girl in her arms, the boys paid no attention.

Dylah set Rilavry down and let her walk towards the others. She could tell that the girl was studying the eyes of the tall blonde men, the twins' scuffle came too close to her and she growled so loud it made the fight stop. Rilavry pointed her stare back up to Bahn and Kremon, she picked a large leaf from her collection, ripped it in down the middle and gave them each a half, she repeated the action with a smaller leaf for the boys.

"Well she is adorable, Dylah." Kremon laughed. "Frenia couldn't stay awake, but we'll let them meet tomorrow, she's very excited to have a cousin that's a girl."

"I would like that." Dylah nodded with a smile. "I also need Avalia to teach me how to do her hair. I have no idea." She handed her daughter over to Axen who had been waiting by the door. She walked back over to Kremon and grabbed the collar of his shirt to bring his face closer to her line of sight. "And if your children tell my daughter my secrets before I have a chance to, I'll break your arm again, just like when we were kids."

Kremon grinned. "Understood." He pulled away from her and straightened his shirt. "Motherhood suits you, Dylah."

She laughed as she took a step towards the door. "That

was actually a threat from the queen."

The celebration carried on into the night with stories exchanged and drinks passed around. Cav had fallen asleep on one of the couches, Sorner was asleep on the other. Axen was lost in conversation with Navent. Dylah paced the deck with Rilavry lulled against her shoulder. The party had been fun for her, but so much newness made her crave the strength of the forest, which was evident to her soul, as two others joined her.

Keilon leaned against the railing, the first Keilon propped himself against the side of the house.

"Dylah," the ghost whispered, "I couldn't help but notice her eyes."

"Familiar to you too, huh?" she whispered back. "That's how I knew she was mine."

"What are you talking about?" Keilon asked quietly.

"You might not know, your eyes are still pretty new." The stag glanced over at the king. "But in our saddest moments our eyes fill with despair and worry, they are an odd mix of blue and gray. Sea and steel, just like Rilavry's eyes."

"Oh." Keilon looked at his sleeping niece.

"Life can be so cruel, until we look at our children and see our own eyes looking back." The ghost sighed thinking of the similar eyes his daughter had worn, along with the sparks that flew from the irises he was surrounded by.

Keilon glanced over at Dylah, while thinking of the ever-changing shades of green his son had acquired.

Dylah thought of Cav and held Rilavry a little tighter.

Axen tiptoed out the door. "Hey, it's getting late, we should head back." He smiled when he noticed their daughter had fallen asleep. "We should also really take advantage of her sleeping."

"I'll start walking now." Dylah laughed at his quick agreement as he slipped back into the house to get Cav. She turned towards the ghost. "We'll catch up soon, I have a few questions for you." She turned to her brother. "I'm assuming you'll be stopping by first thing in the morning, please bring coffee."

"You got it, little sister."

Dylah took a step down towards the forest before turning back. "Will you bring Delin too? He wouldn't go near us tonight, and we wouldn't have our daughter if not for him."

Keilon nodded before she walked away, Axen soon followed clutching their sleeping son.

"History will remember them." Old Keilon smiled as they watched the two silhouettes meet near the glow of the treeline. "They'll remember you too, but ya know, mostly the love story."

"All because a Farein loved a Rilonck."

Tandem laughter was heard approaching and Keilon whipped his head towards the sound. He covered his mouth to hide his smile when he saw his son approaching, clutching Sentry's hand.

"Did you two have fun?" Old Keilon chuckled.

"Uh, yes." Kunor stammered. "We just decided to go for a walk while we waited for Axen and Dylah to get here with the kids. Hope we weren't gone too long."

"They've already made the rounds and headed back." Keilon raised an eyebrow. "You really lost track of time."

"Perhaps he didn't lose it, maybe he controlled it." The first Keilon began laughing. "Or maybe he's just young and in love."

Chapter 62

Severely Uneven

Dylah paced the suite waiting for a knock at the door. Cav was drawing in his usual morning notebook, Rilavry had her own notebook of abstract scribbles in an attempt to copy her brother.

The door shook and Dylah opened it with instant disappointment.

"I didn't bring coffee and Delin kind of disappeared one story down." Keilon took a step into the suite, knowing that Dylah would contain her emotions around her children.

"Damnit," she whispered. "You should see what Cav is drawing, you might need to consider a few things." Dylah watched as he walked towards the table and stared down at the papers.

"He's drawing flowers?" Keilon looked up in time to see his sister slip out the door. He let out a sigh of defeat as he took a seat between his niece and nephew. "Okay kiddos, let's discuss the importance of not escaping."

Dylah didn't feel too guilty after sneaking away, she knew Axen would be back any minute and there was no one else she would trust to watch their children. She had other matters pressing her mind and between the worries and adjusting to a new child, she was barely sleeping. It was clear to her that if she had any amount of energy to handle a situation, she had to snatch the opportunity.

When she arrived a story below her own suite she walked with extra stealth and enacted her power at every door to peek in. She saw a ladies' tea that seemed to be pushed by awkward conversation, another room held a handful of Farein siblings in the middle of a math lesson, most rooms were empty, except the last one, a small closet.

Delin didn't want to disturb his sister's new happy life with the weight of his actions, and when they passed a closet he took the advantage to disappear. He decided to wait in the darkness until he knew his brother had given up on finding him, afterwards he would take the long way back to the castle or perhaps wander far away.

"Delin," Dylah said, blocking the only entrance and exit after appearing from nowhere.

"Dylah." He sighed. "You shouldn't be here."

"Jammed into a dark closet? Yeah, you shouldn't be here either, prince of Fellowrock." She pulled on his wrist. "Come on."

He hadn't considered that Dylah would be the one to seek him out, and he was powerless to her commands. He followed her up a few stories, tiptoeing past her own suite, and finally stopping outside a room that overlooked the third deck. She pushed him inside and pointed to the bed.

"What are we doing here, Dylah?" he muttered as his eyes wandered around the stale room.

She sat next to him. "I just wanted to remind you of your first crime." She took a deep breath. "Your treason against our brother, when you sought out the enemy and asked him to do a favor. When you damned me to miniscule stature and furniture based imprisonment."

"I never need reminding."

"I know." Dylah smiled but it quickly fell as her hand slid over to grasp his. "The life I have now is because you looked past the scope of right and wrong in favor of someone else's happiness. My happiness."

"It was also quite careless." Delin seemed to sink into himself.

"Maybe." She shrugged. "But who am I to judge carelessness?" After a few moments of thinking she squeezed his rigid hand. "The kingdoms wouldn't be thriving if not for the deal you made. I wouldn't have my husband, or my children if not for the favors you asked Axen to do."

"I took Cav."

"Did you injure Aloria?" Dylah asked bluntly.

"No, a soldier did before I could stop him." He gulped.

"Did you set fire to the trees?"

"No, Nevely ordered her soldiers to do that, I begged her not to."

Dylah let go of his hand. "Why did you inject me when I finally had Cav back?"

Delin rested his face in his hands. "I can't put the blame on anything but myself."

"I've seen what the serum can do, I know you gave me a very diluted amount." She sighed. "I just want to know why."

"Because you were still my sister, Dylah."

"Then why did you fight so hard for her?" She tried to hold back the tears that began to blur her vision.

"Nevely had helped to erase my worries far too frequently, and an odd thing happened when she snatched a worry she would replace it with a desire." His voice began to waver. "And for so long I had a desire to help her achieve her goals. It wasn't until I was captured by my own family that the seeds she planted in my mind began to fade, that the weight of what I did for her hit me in full force."

"Did it lift after you killed her?"

"No, it only made it worse."

"Do you feel the blade in your hand in the dead of night? Feel the way it glided towards their death? Hear the muted sounds from that singular moment? Does your heart race thinking of how you stopped theirs?" she whispered. "Do you hear their voice on the stillest nights?"

"Yes."

"Years later and he still haunts me. They all do." She shook away the images of battles past and recent. "How did you know where the children were being kept?"

"Spells." He shrugged. "Simply a fly on the wall."

"You spent a lot of time with them when you traveled with Nevely?"

"It started because I wanted to stay with Cav, but he's such a friendly kid and he made friends with all of them." A slight smile formed on his face. "Especially that little girl with black hair."

Dylah stood. "Come see them together, please." She took a step towards the door. "You don't have to stay long, you aren't obligated to say a single word. We'll start slow until we're back to normal."

"You think normal is possible?" He stood but seemed weak with a slouched posture.

"No, I think a lot of what happened will always remain." She crossed her arms. "But maybe we shouldn't strive for the normal that existed before I was ever brought to this room. The past shouldn't repeat just to strengthen the present, I think carrying on in a way that will satisfy our needs is our own responsibility."

Delin saw the familiar pleading gleam in her eyes, the look he saw far too often when they were just kids, he couldn't think of any other argument. He was again left following her in silence until she opened her suite to him. He stayed back a few steps as she checked on her children at the table and exchanged a silent argument of glances with Keilon. Finally, Keilon stood and retreated to a different room where Axen was working on his own plans.

Delin inched a little closer, trying not to draw too much attention.

"Hi, Uncle Delin," Cav said without lifting his pencil from the paper.

The young girl turned towards his direction with an immediate smile after recognizing him. She jumped from her seat and hurried over to him, her head pointed straight up to see him.

"She remembers you." Cav laughed.

"Rilavry." Delin knelt down and smiled. He moved his hands together while saying a quick chant that produced a single yellow flower.

"What do you know about her past?" Dylah asked. "Anything?"

"Her native language is one that not many know," he said quietly. "I scoured the camp for any other information and there was some. But I really only know the meaning of one word. Did they give you the stone that they found with her after the raids?"

"Yes," Dylah answered with a sigh.

"I know the word for amethyst." A smile grew on his face and for a fleeting moment he was the Delin she had always known. "It's rilavry."

The two kings waited in a nearby room in slightly stiff silence.

"How long should we wait?" Axen asked.

"Just a little longer." Keilon listened through the door. "They need this." He glanced over at what Axen was working on. "Designing new fingers?"

"Not yet." Axen laughed. "Something else."

"Does it have anything to do with what you'll be asking me once Derck leaves?"

"Not at all."

"You got a lot of things going on, kids, plans, maybe you

should take a break." Keilon insisted.

"You always had kids and plans, did you ever take a break?" Axen tried not to laugh when his brother-in-law struggled to form an answer. "That's what I thought."

"So I get no hints about what I should expect?"

"It's a sword," Axen said as he transcribed a formula. "But with a few twists."

"No, I meant about the other plans you have going on." Keilon chuckled.

Axen set his pencil down and turned towards him. "Dylah doesn't know about it yet, like I said, it's something that has to start with us."

Keilon couldn't think of an answer, and he wasn't sure that he liked that his sister was being left in the dark. When a soft knock came to the door, he almost let out a sigh of relief. He opened it to see the mismatched stare of his nephew.

"Mama told me to tell you that Uncle Delin is waiting in the hall." Cav grinned. "She also said that you owe her coffee."

"Of course." Keilon nodded to Axen before joining his two youngest siblings in the hallway.

Dylah was waiting just outside the door, her expression could have been exhaustion but Keilon knew it was grief. Delin leaned against the opposite wall a few doors away.

"He'll never be the same, will he?" She stared down at her feet.

"No, I don't think he will." He squeezed her shoulder. "But that doesn't mean that he'll always be this way."

Dylah nodded with a quiet sniffle. Keilon glanced over at Delin, his head was also hung and his eyes closed tightly.

"How many times did you go to Delin instead of me?" Keilon wrapped an arm around her. "A lot of times, right? Especially when you were around thirteen?" He shook her a little. "Bet you didn't know that I knew about that, kiddo."

"You were kind of a jerk back then," she struggled to get the insult out through her quiet sobbing. "I trusted him. He helped me." She paused to wipe away her collection of quickly growing tears. "Broken bones and broken hearts, he was always who I went to."

"Well." Keilon took a step away from her. "It sounds like your relationship is severely uneven and perhaps maybe now it's your turn to figure out how to help him."

Chapter 63

Chaos Has Settled

Another week had passed and Sorner couldn't help but be proud of the resiliency his bloodline had kept for centuries. Even as he walked past recovering trees he felt inclined to breathe in the scent of the forest, it was all too familiar to him, it reminded him of strength. He spent the morning in the Hightree gardens with Kunor, he helped his efforts to fine tune his ability only slightly. It was possible that Kunor could have achieved full control of pausing time had it not been for Sorner's soliloquy of pride after every minor success.

Sorner wandered the forest unintentionally, he had seen a rabbit at the treeline and followed it for an undetermined amount of time. When the small creature finally found its home, the past soul of harmony was disheartened by the location it had brought him to. With a sigh he turned away from the empty plot of land that held so many memories of his youth and headed back towards his temporary home.

The first Keilon stared into the ripples of his mug as

the dark liquid cascaded with a constant flow of steam. His thoughts left him as flashes of smoke and water flooded his mind. Digging into the past had proven to be a necessary torture.

"How much coffee have you had?" Sorner asked from the doorway as he watched his brother fill his mug. "My goodness that was the last in the pot!"

"Couldn't sleep." He shrugged and sat back at the table by piles of paper.

"You don't have to push yourself to finish these if it's killing you."

"I'm just a little stuck on some names." He sighed. "I'm trying to remember each one but for a while there were just so many and I wasn't always in a clear state of mind."

"Maybe it's okay if you don't remember each one, I know that doesn't sound fair, but maybe that only further highlights the wrongdoings." Sorner tried to talk louder than his brother's scribbling. "I have some worries."

"Just some?" Old Keilon laughed. "Congratulations."

"I want to take you far away from this place."

The pen stopped abruptly. Eyes that usually shone with a constant hint of magenta were a stark green. His breath even came to a halt.

"Keilon? Brother?" Sorner wiggled the table. "Did you hear me?"

"You want to leave?" he asked just above a whisper.

"Yes. You can't stay here." Sorner's eyes darkened. "The trees will always be home, and we can visit often, but if we stay much longer the memories that constantly fill the breeze will choke you."

"I can't."

"Yes you can! You can do whatever you want!" Sorner slowly grinned. "We are tethered to nothing!"

"No." He shook his head and let it fall into his hands. "My first life was filled with whatever I pleased, how many died because of that freedom?"

"But-"

"Then my second life, what a disgrace. I killed my own prodigy."

"She doesn't seem to mind." Sorner half laughed. "You can't punish yourself forever."

"Where did you go when you died?" The first Keilon brought his head up, his eyes were an obviously forced green. "Were you there with your predecessor?"

"Yes, odd, it was just Allinay and myself walking through a forest stuck in a perpetual sunrise. It always felt like the beginning of a summer's day."

"I was in a forest stuck in twilight."

"Our souls bear so much poetry it's stifling." Sorner smiled as if the images were in front of him. "Allinay was a delightful companion, she constantly held lovely insightful conversations. I felt like I was there for forever and only a moment all at the same time."

"Dycavlon is not a talker. It felt like an eternity." His eyes briefly flashed with fire before settling to a stormy gray. "But then Junia came."

"Oh yes, the mother of your prodigies, the grandmother of mine." Sorner thought for a moment. "How is that possible? Why was she granted access to that plane?"

"I think it's because she finally brought the chaotic soul back, and in turn replaced the soul of harmony too."

"Odd but understandable. Just you, Dycavlon the original chaos wielder, and Junia."

"And Dylah."

"What?"

"We died at the same time, we fell back into that forest at the same time." His face returned to his hands.

"And that's why she has found forgiveness with you?" Sorner began tapping the table. "Some sort of afterlife resolution?"

"I woke up first and -"

"She has no idea you were there."

"Exactly." He nervously tapped the pen against the paper to the same rhythm as Sorner's fingers. "It hit me all at once, what I had done. The life I stole from her, the place I was damning her to, all of it. So I waited. I sat there with her and planned what I would say when she woke up to the news of being dead, but then Dycavlon showed up." He gulped. "Then something weird happened, I wasn't letting him get any closer to her. I pushed him back, I told him she was my responsibility, that I wasn't allowing him to influence her in the slightest. I dropped to my knees and held her as if she was my own child, I begged Dycavlon to send her back and to undo what I had done. But he wasn't hearing it, he gestured to a clearing where Junia was standing. He pointed to the pain I put on that mother's face and told me I had done too much to forgive this time, then he pulled Dylah out of my arms and pushed me away from her. It was the most he's ever said to me. I told him at least I was trying to be a teacher. But all he did was point to the potential in her that I had snuffed out."

There was a pause of silent voices but still constant tapping.

"And what else?" Sorner leaned closer with an insistent grin. "There's more, isn't there? Come on now, tell me what happened after she left the afterlife."

"I visited."

"Sporadically?"

"Often."

"The kid?"

"I watched him grow up more than I watched my own children."

"So you can't leave." Sorner sighed. "I understand."

"It's not just them. It's that I have this duty to the past versions of myself, to the past you, to Teyle's past self, to the lives I took, to the lives I created and didn't care for, to the people who carry our last name and wear our green eyes." He folded his arms and rested his head on the table. "I will be spending the remainder of this final life making sure that my past missteps are understood and won't be repeated by another."

"I'll stay too."

"No!" Old Keilon propped his head back up. "You have nothing to answer for, you lived an honorable life, you should treat this time as a reward for that!"

"You're right, my life was lovely, filled with love, I am yet to see another being more beautiful than my own four children." He paused to remember their faces. "But don't forget that I spent two thirds of my life as a miniscule thing, and not to mention, separated from my remaining siblings. We didn't get to see each other grow old, so as long as we're doing that this time around, I'll be happy."

Old Keilon was about to say something when the front door opened and a set of small footsteps ran towards the kitchen.

Cav stopped just shy of the table as the brothers scrambled to stack and cover the papers.

"We're going to go throw stuff over the courtyard wall!" Cav struggled to say through his staggered breathing. "Wanna come?!"

"Who is we?" Sorner asked as the door opened again and soon Dylah walked into the kitchen with Rilavry on her hip, the small child pointing to every object in sight.

"Are they coming?" Dylah asked.

"Throwing things over the wall?" the first Keilon asked with a slight laugh.

"Yes." She sighed. "Someone woke up with a lot of energy, someone's father is also very busy today, while the same someone's mother is absolutely exhausted because of another certain someone. So someone's mother suggested the first string of words to come to mind, and yes we will be throwing things over the courtyard wall." Her eyes settled on the mug on the table and briefly flashed pink. "Is there coffee?"

"Not a drop." Sorner laughed at her immediate flash of fire. "It's his fault."

"Cav, I need you to do me a favor!" She smiled and set Rilavry down. "I want you to take your sister upstairs and just show her the door of your old room. Okay? Just the door. But also, go very slowly."

"Because she likes to look at everything?" Cav asked as he grabbed his sister's hand.

"Yes, that's why." Dylah nodded.

As soon as her children were out of the kitchen she smacked the back of her predecessor's head.

"What was that for?" The question was his only reaction.

"Why aren't you sleeping again?!" She fell into the chair with an immediate slouch.

"Why aren't you?" he asked with a raised eyebrow above a cocky grin.

"The daughter has a newfound fascination with the moon." Dylah yawned. "She wants to watch it until it goes away. It's like she's sworn some sort of oath to the thing, perpetually on guard for the glowing circle in the sky."

"Why don't we take the kids and you stay here and sleep?" Sorner asked as Dylah propped herself up on a wobbly elbow. "I think I must insist."

"No, it's okay." She smiled with her eyes closed. "I love her so much."

"You know, you demanded time to catch up, and yet I haven't seen you since Rilavry's party." Old Keilon pointed a look at his brother. "See, Sorner will keep the kids entertained."

"Has it really been that long?" she asked through another yawn. "Seems like only a few days."

"Perhaps because you've only slept a few nights?" He laughed and could tell that even with her eyes closed she had rolled them. "You said you had to ask me a few things."

"Uh, yes." Her eyes opened and her posture straightened. "Now what?"

"I'm not sure I understand the question."

"The question is simple." Dylah smiled. "Now what?"

"Elaborate," he said slowly.

"The souls have all matured, I myself have surpassed you, your brother is alive, Fellowrock is thriving, the curse cannot come back, the history is almost replaced, so now what?" She laced her fingers on the table. "What will you do now that chaos has settled?"

The stag was at a loss for words, he didn't feel it was the right time to repeat the reasoning he had given to Sorner. "No idea, any suggestions?"

"Liar." She crossed her arms. "You're telling me that you've given this absolutely no thought?"

"I honestly thought I'd be dead again by now." Between her bluntness and exhaustion it was hard to tell what her motives were. "And I'm not even halfway done with the history."

"So you're staying?" Dylah asked with forced green eyes.

"Are you asking for your house back?"

"No." She returned to her slumped posture as another yawn interrupted her own words. "A lot of change has been happening, I just don't want to be blindsided by something else. I've gotten too accustomed to the presence of ghosts, it would be a pity to lose it now."

Sorner stepped back into the kitchen holding Rilavry out at arm's length while Cav followed close behind. "Dylah, I regret to inform you that your daughter bit me twice."

Dylah covered her mouth in apparent shock, but in reality to cover her grin. "Yes, we're working on that." She stood and held her daughter tightly. "But here's the thing, we like her wild."

"Understood." Sorner nodded. "I just think it would benefit you to lay down some manners now instead of later."

Dylah smiled. "I heard you've been helping Kunor with his time pausing."

"Yes, quite the shift in conversation though."

The sunlight that had been pouring in through the windows darkened, Dylah held Rilavry with one arm as she held her palm up to Sorner. "I've been practicing too." She outstretched her hand as bursts of electricity circled her fingers. "Just thought I'd let you know before you decided to say anything else."

Sorner's eyes went wide. "The child may stay wild."

Dylah lowered her hand as the sunlight returned. "Great, then let's go to the courtyard." Cav let out a cheer as he followed his mother and sister into the forest.

"Well." Sorner crossed his arms tightly. "I bet your h-"

"Yes." The first Keilon stood to follow them. "It's bursting."

Chapter 64

The Six

The day lasted longer than initially planned. After a few other Riloncks noticed their game of tossing things over the wall it turned into a tournament of sorts. Bahn's sons took it too seriously and at one point one of Kremon's sons was seen flying over the wall. Rilavry soon added "wall" to her very limited vocabulary which was celebrated extensively. The games continued as the sun sank closer to the horizon, Delin even joined with a smile that seemed almost genuine. Kings and ancestors held lively conversations, children chased each other around trees and up the walls, all while laughs rose into the air following jokes they had already heard. Glances were passed around from the three who held a power and the two that had held it in another life, their subtle nods agreed that this is what a true balance of chaos and harmony felt like.

After tucking Cav in, and then tucking Rilavry in for the third time and letting her babble herself to sleep, Dylah wandered the dark suite to soak in the quiet night. There was stillness for once and she never felt so at home in the absence of constant mayhem.

Axen was already asleep and Dylah decided to pour herself a glass of wine and watch the stars from the first deck. Beneath the bottle of wine there was a folded note. She read it three times before putting her boots back on and quietly slipping out the door.

The forest at night was always peaceful but Dylah was annoyed that her brother had called a meeting in such an odd way, especially after spending most of the day with him. Yet, the possibilities thrilled her. She entered the castle foyer and rolled her eyes as soon as she saw Keilon sitting at the small kitchen table.

"Okay, I'm here." She fell into the chair across from him. "What do you need?"

"What do I need?" He laughed. "You're the one who called the meeting."

"Have you lost it?"

"Did you write this note and leave it on my desk?" He held up a slip of paper.

"No." She held up her own note. "Did you write this one and leave it under a bottle of wine?"

"I did," Delin said from the doorway.

"Why?" Keilon asked.

"I need a pretty big favor."

Dylah stood and walked to the counter, she seemed to be frozen for a moment. "How big of a favor, exactly?" She reached for the cabinet of mugs then retracted her hand. "Wine or coffee?"

Delin walked over to her and reached into a tall cupboard, he pulled out a dark bottle of wine and maneuvered the stems of three glasses between his fingers. He sat at the table and poured them each a glass as Dylah sat back down. They sat quietly for a moment, waiting for someone to speak.

"I know that it seems as if we have moved past what I did," Delin started, "but I will never forgive myself for the pain I caused and the destruction I enabled."

"Let me go get Kunor and he can help you," Keilon said.

"I see Kunor five times a day." Delin's head pointed down. "It's all too much to accept. He takes the worry away, then I see one of you, I see the trees, I have a single thought and it all comes back."

"So what exactly are you needing from us?" Dylah stared into her swirling glass.

"Before I ask, I just want to be upfront that this is a rather selfish request."

"Go on." Keilon crossed his arms.

"I want to leave." Delin finally looked up and let his misty gaze dart between his brother and sister. "But I want to leave a different person."

"What do you mean?"

"He wants us to zap his memory." Dylah took a sip. "He wants us to help him forget the terrible things he's done and then he just wants to walk out of here."

"Yes."

"If you don't remember everything then why would you still need to leave?" Keilon shook his head.

"Because, my ignorance would just burden you over time."

"Let's say we decide to do it," Keilon said through a sigh. "When would you want to leave?"

"Tonight."

"No." Dylah set her glass down. "I've been trying so hard to get you back and you just decide to abandon us to walk around without a care?" She closed her eyes. "That's not fair. I understand the reasons behind your missteps, I'm moving on from them because even Cav still smiles when he sees you."

"He's a child, Dylah, forgiveness comes easily to him now, but one day he'll begin to understand." Delin's words began to gain volume. "And I want to leave before it's too late, before he sees me as the villain I truly am."

"You've really given this some thought, huh?" Keilon pointed forced green eyes at him. "You really want to leave."

"More than anything."

"How much would you want us to take?" Dylah asked with a quick worried glance to Keilon. "Would you still want to remember us?"

"I don't want to lose my family, you're all I've ever known." Delin shook his head with a weight they couldn't begin to understand. "But I think that maybe I deserve to."

Dylah took a large gulp of her wine. "I'll do it." She nodded at him. "Under one condition."

"Just hold on a minute." Keilon glared at her. "We need to discuss this."

"What's the condition?" Delin asked.

"You don't leave tonight." Dylah smiled politely. "You leave tomorrow, you're not going to just disappear, you have siblings and friends to say goodbye to."

"I can do that." Delin breathed a sigh of relief.

"So." Keilon crossed his arms and finally looked at his youngest brother. "What would you like to do for your last day?"

Delin thought for a moment. "I want to go back to the days before it all got so complicated." He sighed. "When our world was still so small. Before cures and resurrections. I just want the six of us together again."

"The Riloncks." Keilon smiled. "Done."

"Lucky you." Dylah grinned with the glass of wine to her lips. "Derck is still here for a few more days."

Delin spent the next day slowly drifting around the two kingdoms, he knew the memories would only last until the night but he still wanted to take it all in one last time. He visited the ancestors under the ruse of dropping off a few extra doses of the antidote treatment even though the stag was already cured. He stopped by Kremon's suite to watch his nephews wrestle while his niece followed Avalia as she clutched her young son and her flowing skirts stretched around her growing stomach.

Next he listened as Cav explained his vague predictions, then he helped Rilavry line up a few boxes of different sizes. His final conversation with Axen was brief, they talked about formulas and nothing more. Delin had begged Dylah to keep his parting a secret and the normalcy of his final conversations gave him the most calm.

He excused himself after their conversation hit a lull and offered a promise to see them the next day, which he knew needed to be a necessary lie.

Four steps down the hall and the door opened behind him.

"Delin," Axen called after him.

"I'll bring you that other formula tomorrow," Delin replied with a smile. "It's somewhere in all of my notes."

"I don't expect it to be tomorrow." Axen shut the door and took a few steps towards him. "But when you've come up with the solution, I'll be waiting for it. I'll keep my eyes on the trees for a ribbon of any color."

"Lavender?" He grinned, while fighting the lump in his throat at the veiled farewell.

"Whatever you think will catch my eye." Axen took slow steps back to his suite. "I am forever grateful for the favors you asked me to do." He turned to look at Delin one last time. "For the change you made to the times."

After an afternoon of short meetings and disguised goodbyes, Delin joined three of his older brothers in a meeting room on the fourth story of the Fellowrock castle. Bahn and Kremon were arguing over something insignificant and Keilon struggled to make any conversation. An hour had passed before Derck and Dylah finally joined their siblings.

"Okay," Bahn spoke before Keilon could get a welcoming word out. "I kept this damn secret all day, even while you were making the most awkward conversation with my boys.

Do you know how hard it was to not smack you?! What are you thinking?! You're leaving?!"

"Yes." Delin nodded. "And I will be forgetting all of you."

"It's true." Dylah glanced at Keilon. "I'll be clearing his mind in two hours."

"Two hours?" Kremon slumped. "And you're okay with this?" He pointed the question at Keilon.

"Yes." Keilon pinched the bridge of his nose. "Well, no. But I've come to understand his side and I do believe it is what is best for him."

"To forget us?!" Bahn crossed his arms. "Will he remember that he's a Rilonck? That he's the one who cured the curse?"

"No," Dylah answered. "He will be made to think he is an entirely different person."

"And the six of us?" Kremon's eyes darted to each of his siblings. "We're the six Riloncks! You can't erase one of the Riloncks! What will history say?"

"History will still say that there were six Riloncks," Derck spoke up. "History will remember that Delin Rilonck created the enzyme cure that medically broke the curse. But we have to let our brother be free from his pain."

Something about Derck's unusually proud voice made them start to realize that there was no turning back. Instead, they passed around mugs of beer and began reciting memories from their youth.

"Always scribbling in a book!" Bahn laughed after downing one full mug. "Oh the dangers you avoided because your head was down in a book!"

"Dangers? Like what?" Delin asked with a slight smile. "I obviously didn't notice."

"Like that one day when Bahn set up a stupid obstacle course." Kremon elbowed his twin brother. "And Dylah tried to kill him."

"That wasn't my fault!" Dylah demanded.

"I remember that day." Keilon chuckled into his own

mug. "I had to pull her off of you like she was a feral badger."

"I barely remember that," Bahn growled.

"You dug the trap hole too deep for me to get out." Dylah pointed fire streaked eyes at him. "Then you told me that our parents found me in a basket by the pond."

"Oh, yes, I do remember that." Bahn laughed loudly. "Hilarious."

"Jokes were never your strong suit." Kremon shook his head.

"But really, Delin." Bahn looked over to their quiet brother. "You avoided every single trap I set up, you just kept writing everything down."

"Oh. You thought I was writing." Delin laughed to himself. "I did almost fall into the first trap, but then I realized that the next trap was exactly ten steps ahead, then the next one too."

"You were counting?!" Bahn's eyes went wide.

"Yeah, and mapping just in case I had to go back the same way." Delin shrugged.

The night continued on with short stories that always segued into a different story with a similar memory. Like how the memory of a nine year old Delin messing up a spell and accidentally lighting his bed on fire but also freezing it at the same time reminded them about the time their mother had unintentionally caused a snow storm in the castle foyer. Soon enough the mugs were empty, and an extra hour past what they had planned slipped by.

First Derck said his goodbyes, they were whispered and brief but ended with a kind smile. Then Kremon told a series of jokes, none of which truly made any sense, but it was the effort that Delin appreciated from his funniest brother, they parted with a quick embrace of understanding. Bahn approached the goodbye more gently than expected, he mumbled his pride and promised to remember him enough for the both of them. Finally, the only two left were Keilon and Dylah.

Keilon wanted to call the whole thing off, but there was an energy coming from the other piece of his soul that let him know that they had to let their brother go. It would be for the best in the long run, because really, Delin hadn't been the same since Nevely arrived and there seemed to be nothing else that would ease his mind or eliminate his guilt.

After a decisive breath Keilon wrapped his arms around his youngest brother, the kid he watched grow up to be the savior of their kingdom, but he had told him this all before. Delin hugged him back and whispered his own thanks and appreciation, including a brief reminder that Keilon had been the parent they all needed.

"You didn't have to do that for us, Keilon," Delin said as his eyes watered with the tears he had been holding back. "I hope you see the change that was made at your hands."

"I'm sorry that you have to forget the change that was made at yours." Keilon tried his best to remain strong. "But please know that I never will." With that, Keilon left the room with a final stormy blue stare back at his brother.

"Well, I guess it's time then." Delin sighed and looked at his sister with a slight smile. "I'll miss you, Dylah."

"I'll miss you too," she said calmly.

"Can we just leave it at that then?" Delin gulped. "I feel as if we've already said it all before, and if I dive into just how much we've meant to each other over the years I'll back out."

"I agree." Dylah looked deep into Delin's eyes. "But can I tell you how much I loved growing up with you just a door away?"

"I loved each time you barged in." He laughed slightly. "It was great having a little sister."

Dylah took a slow deep breath to keep her composure. "Are you ready?"

"I'm sorry that I have to forget you."

"I'm sorry that it's come to this too." She blinked the tears away. "Before I do this, I just want you to know that I understand, and I forgive you. You've helped me far more than you've ever hurt me and everyone is entitled to terrible decisions."

"Thank you." Delin let his eyes fill with tears.

"And I'm sorry for this."

"What?"

Dylah's eyes warped to dulling storm clouds. "Delin, you have been living with our brother in the sand countries for almost three years now. You love it there but you hate the wine. You're studying the different plants and how they are able to grow through the sand. You've come back for a visit and it's been fun, you got to meet your new niece, Rilavry, but you'll be leaving tomorrow with Derck."

"It's a long trip," Delin answered in a monotone.

"It is a very long trip." Dylah held his gaze. "We'll miss you, Delin, do you know that? I've rarely spent any time away from you in my whole life."

"I'll miss you too," he replied. "Please visit."

"I'll try." She gulped. "We'll all come."

"Yes, bring the brothers," he said as he nodded. "Keilon, Kremon, and Bahn, and the nephews and nieces, and Axen, please bring Axen too. Bring everybody."

"Yes, all of us." She smiled. "Can you tell me what it is you want from the life you've been leading?"

"Happiness."

"Love?" she asked. "You've never really let yourself settle down."

"That would be nice."

Dylah smiled. "Well then, Delin, now that you live so far away from us and have no need to constantly worry and check on us, I want you to prioritize your own happiness. And if that means finding love, then I hope that happens for you."

"I should go pack if I'm leaving tomorrow."

"Derck already did that for you." She thought for a moment. "Okay I need to try something." Her eyes fell to their natural state of green and gray as her hold on him fell. "Delin, where are you going tomorrow?"

"I'm heading back to the sand countries, I've lived there for the past three years." Delin chuckled. "Did you hit your head?" He caught sight of a window. "Wow, it's late! I should get some sleep before the journey, it's so far to travel!"

"I think that's a great idea, this has been a lovely visit." She led him to the hallway feeling overly proud of herself until she saw the other four brothers staring back at them with worried glances.

"My brothers!" Delin shouted. "It's been a fun trip, I hope you visit soon!"

"What?!" Kremon glanced from Delin to Dylah.

"Oh Kremon! Always the jokester!" Delin laughed as he walked down the hall. "See you all in the morning before Derck and I head back!"

The remaining three brothers pointed stares at Derck and Dylah.

"Dylah, what did you do?!" Keilon pinched the bridge of his nose.

"I did what you told me to do," she answered with a smile. "I figured out how to help him."

"And you helped?" Bahn growled at Derck.

"Yes." He nodded as a proud grin grew. "The sand countries could really use someone with his capabilities."

"I wasn't going to let us lose a brother." Dylah laughed as she began walking away. "I died for one whole day and you all lost your minds."

Chapter 65

Wine or Whiskey

It had been three days since Keilon watched two of his brothers ride away. Though there was a joy in seeing Delin as his usual but edited self, there was still a sadness watching them sink into the horizon. Keilon didn't know whether it was his soul or just his parental instincts that told him there were only a few changes left before he could take a breath.

The steps of the Hightree castle seemed steeper than before. Maybe it was the weight of the unknown, maybe it was the excitement of the mystery. Either way Keilon was ready to meet whatever was coming.

He waited outside of Axen's office for an amount of time that seemed too long. The wait only made him worry about the proposal he would be receiving, Axen had given very little clues but made it clear that this decision bore a lot of weight.

"Sorry," Axen said as he walked towards him from the end of the hall. "Rilavry has been fascinated with the pins I use for my cape." He laughed. "Took me longer than needed to find a matching set."

"No worries, let's get started."

"Actually." Axen's eyes darted back and forth. "I want this conversation to be on neutral ground. Would you mind going to the tunnel?"

The kings of Hightree and Fellowrock walked with very little small talk, except a few gushing remarks about Rilavry and Cav.

They descended under the river and walked past each torch until a prominent white line appeared.

"Please stand on your own side." Axen gestured towards Fellowrock.

"Will you be explaining soon?" Keilon stood over the line with a huff of impatience.

"I just want us to remember the division of the past." He pointed down to the line. "The border your kingdom had to fear. I want you to remember that the people of Hightree were taught to fear your people, that we taunted you every morning with arrows, that we snuck over your border to mock you and escaped when we knew you couldn't follow."

"Why bring that up now?" Keilon interrupted to stop the string of uncomfortable reminders.

"We've spent a lot of time digging up a dark past for our ancestors, but we've neglected that we also come from a dark past." Axen took a deep breath to support his next statements. "We were divided for centuries by eye color, by height, by a treeline, and I just don't want that to be what resonates about us."

"I'm on your side, what are you proposing?"

"You'd still be the leader of Fellowrock, and I'd still run Hightree, but," Axen paused and met Keilon's stormy eyes with a look of determination. "We would be merged into the same kingdom."

"You're saying you want one kingdom with two regions?" Keilon asked slowly.

"Yes." Axen finally let out a breath. "What are your ini-

514

tial thoughts?"

"I have no thoughts." Keilon laughed. "I am completely dumbfounded."

"I know it's a lot to take in," Axen said. "But I've been thinking about it for a while now and I'll give you some time too."

"I appreciate that."

"Do you think you could let me know in a week? Something of this scale would need to be started as soon as possible."

Keilon thought for a moment. "Yes, let me think it all over."

"I'm not quite sure how two kings should even come to an agreement of this size, or disagreement." Axen began to think again. "I would understand if you didn't agree, it wouldn't change a thing between our kingdoms. And it wouldn't disrupt our great friendship. I'm just a little lost on how we should approach the answer. You've been a king for a lot longer than I have."

"That is very true." Keilon chuckled over his own racing thoughts. "How about this, if I bring you wine, it's a no, if I bring you whiskey, it means we can start planning."

"Then either way I look forward to sharing a drink with you."

The kings shook hands before walking off in opposite directions. Axen forced his mind to pause the issue he had proposed and flipped to thinking of designs. Keilon could only think of the proposal. He stepped out of the tunnel and soon found himself walking up to his own office in a daze. He sat down at the old desk and let his fingers graze the markings of the king who had come before him.

His father had now been gone for longer than Keilon had actually known him, and yet Fren's gruff voice still hung in his mind as he stared at the scratches. *"Keilon, when you're king make sure you don't worry as much as I do. This poor desk just can't take much more stress."* The words were always followed by a booming laugh.

In an effort to determine how King Fren would react to the news of Fellowrock merging with Hightree, Keilon slipped into a frenzy of memories from his youth. Thinking of a time when he was just a kid and not a king seemed so foreign, and he found it odd that his foremost thoughts went to his brothers, the personalities of their youth that helped them grow into the men they had become. He wondered if he still held his own youth the way they did.

Soon enough he was pondering his insomniatic tendencies in his teen years. If only his mother had told him the true reason for the ghost in his dreams. He wondered what his life might look like if his mother hadn't been so cryptic about what she gave to her oldest and youngest children. He was so lost in his thoughts that he didn't even hear his own door creak open.

"There was such an odd energy coming from this castle that I thought you and Dylah were trying to kill each other." The stag grinned. "So I came to watch."

"Well it's just me so you can go." Keilon sighed. "Nothing of interest is happening here."

"And that's why your eyes are swirling with different colors after every blink?" He laughed. "That makes perfect sense."

"It's really none of your business."

"I think you underestimate my ability to keep a secret." The ghost dropped his voice to a whisper, "I'm the only one who knows the true reason behind the kingdom's motto."

"Is it because it's somehow about you?" Keilon groaned and gripped the bridge of his nose.

"Maybe."

Keilon sighed and tried to ignore the weight of his predecessors insisting stare. "I have a decision to make and I am processing."

"Decision about what?"

"It doesn't concern you."

"I can just go ask Dylah, she'll tell me." The first Keilon crossed his arms and leaned back in his chair waiting for his prodigy to budge.

"Dylah doesn't know." The king rubbed his temples.

"Oh." Old Keilon straightened his posture a little. "That's new."

Keilon thought for a moment of how to present the situation while still keeping it a secret. "Back before the curse, when you were trying to take over Hightree, did you truly believe it would be better for Fellowrock?"

"Yes." The ancestor nodded. "If Fellowrock had more land that wasn't forest we could expand in ways we'd never known before. And also, if we had that grand castle we could be seen as a threat. Taking over Hightree was my biggest goal but it was obviously the beginning of my downfall."

"Right," Keilon muttered as he tapped at the markings on the desk.

The first to carry the name thought over the king's question. "Wait!" He smacked the desktop as he stood and pointed a finger at his prodigy. "You are not conquering Hightree!"

"That's not what I'm doing!" Keilon rolled his eyes.

"You said that Dylah didn't know, and you specifically asked me about it!" He shook his head. "It sounds like you're trying to take your sister's kingdom!" His teeth clenched along with his fists. "You think I'd let you sever the bond I gave you both over such a pointless conquest?!"

"Stop." Keilon crossed his arms. "This was Axen's idea."

"What?" The first Keilon sat back down. "Is he surrendering his title?"

"No." Keilon laughed at the ghost's confusion.

"So you're not conquering Hightree, and Axen isn't giving you Hightree, this makes no sense, there's no other options."

"There is one other option and it is what I am considering." He thought for a moment. "Wine or whiskey?"

"Depends on the type of wine." The stag shrugged. "And

also depends on the type of whiskey. What do you have?"

"Do we merge Fellowrock and Hightree or keep our kingdoms separate?"

"What?!" The ghost's eyes were a stark green from the shock. "Why would you be asking about wine and whiskey when that is the decision at hand?! That's what you're considering?!"

"I have to keep this secret from my brothers and sister, I do not have any other past kings to lean on," he said as he tapped on the markings his father had made. "So if you would like the chance to actually be of some use to me, now is the time to take it."

"Alright, youngblood." Old Keilon's eyes sparked with magenta as he relaxed in thought. "So neither kingdom would have absolute power?"

"We would still be Hightree and Fellowrock but under the title of one unified kingdom with two regions."

"Axen's idea?" The ghost laughed. "I like it. He's much more like Brennit than he will probably ever realize."

Keilon sighed. "I'm not sure that I like it."

"What's holding you back?"

Keilon stood from his seat and began to pace the office. A part of him wanted to be having this conversation with someone else, but he couldn't ignore that he needed the guidance of his predecessor.

"Had this been presented to me a year ago, I wouldn't have walked away without an answer. I wouldn't be promising a bottle of whiskey to celebrate or a bottle of wine to ease the pain of a no." He looked everywhere around the room except at the man who had given him his name and soul. "But now that I have what I have, now that I know what I know, and I have seen what I have seen-"

"Stop repeating yourself." Old Keilon laughed. "Just say it."

"Expansion is dangerous for the chaotic soul." Keilon looked out his window down at the courtyard.

"I see," he answered slowly. "So your only apprehension is the history of one terrible ancestor?"

"Not just you." He shook his head. "I saw what it did to Dylah, what she could have become." A breath caught in his throat. "And me, because when victory was on the table I promised my sister to a terrible man for my own gain. That was the soul at work, right? I can't believe I did that."

"Have a seat, let's get a few things straight."

Keilon returned to his seat, slightly offended by the command, but there was a level of trust between them that he could not understand. "Go on."

"You are not your sister, and as you have made it very clear, you are definitely not me. As for your own decisions, did they hold any lasting effects? I don't see how you could ever see yourself in such a dark light." The stag stared into the storm clouds of his prodigy's eyes. "We may be linked by the same soul, we may share similarities, you may have gotten some tendencies from me, you have my eyes, you have my name, but you are not weighed down by what came before you. Do you understand? Do not take on that burden, it will drown you."

"So I'm supposed to just agree to something that could potentially unleash a bloodthirsty side of me?" Keilon's face fell into his hands. "What if I'm damning my own people? What if I take us right back into isolation and constant struggling?"

"Again, you're referencing what I did, something that was done well before your existence was even considered."

"If I'm a good king it's because I have always prioritized Fellowrock's future, I have spent my entire life digging us out of the past."

"You're a good king because you craved freedom." The stag grinned. "You grew up being told to stay behind the trees and your soul wouldn't accept being caged. You wanted the same thing for your family, your friends, your people, and anyone who followed. That had very little to do with me and everything to do with you."

"It wasn't just me who got us out of isolation, it was mostly Delin."

"See, you're humble! That's something you obviously didn't get from me!"

"I think I have to say no." Keilon sighed. "There's just too much to consider."

"Stop." The first Keilon pointed eyes mixed with hints of blue. "There might have been havoc hewn into your heritage but it's your responsibility to rise above that." He leaned back and crossed his arms with a proud smile as he watched the sparks of pink ignite in his prodigy's eyes. "So what are you going to do, youngblood?"

Keilon held up a halting finger, he briefly left the office and returned with a bottle of wine and two glasses. Just before the stag could ask him why he had arrived at such a decision, Keilon opened the bottom drawer and pulled out a different bottle and two smaller glasses. He gave himself and his predecessor a glass of wine and a glass of whiskey.

"Let's discuss the pros and cons." Keilon clinked both of his own glasses together.

The ghost was a little shocked that he was being included, but he was honored by the trust his prodigy had in him. He clinked his own glasses together in a similar fashion before igniting the discussion.

Dylah was sneaking away from the Hightree castle, she had been feeling a weird pull on her soul for hours but she couldn't find an opportunity to check on her brother. Finally, Axen was able to distract both kids long enough for her to blow a kiss as she slipped away.

Even without the odd pull on her soul, the day had felt heavy yet exciting in a way she didn't understand. Axen apologized extensively for the things he couldn't explain to her yet, but she took comfort in his honesty. When she told him that she needed to check on Keilon he urged her to go as soon as she could and finally divulged the extent of the situation.

The house on the border had a single light on upstairs, the breeze swept through the branches with a slight chill, the courtyard was still and the castle seemed too quiet. As Dylah ascended the steps to the fifth story the sounds of laughter grew.

Only a few doors away from her brother's office and the hysterical laughter seemed to be double sided. Dylah quickly made a list of which brother could be with him, Derck and Delin had gone, Kremon was at the Hightree castle, Bahn only seemed to laugh once a year, and it sounded nothing like Kunor.

She pushed the door open with a clenched fist ready for any threat.

"Yes! Exactly like that!" Keilon pointed at her as soon as the door opened. "But she was probably eight at the time, that old soldier had no idea what to do when a little girl gave him a command."

"I would have paid to see that!" The first Keilon matched the thunderous laughter.

"What's going on here?" she asked as she studied the empty bottles and partially full mismatched glasses on the desk.

"Your brother had planned this lengthy discussion." The stag took a sip from his wine glass, though the liquid inside didn't look like wine. "But we reached a solution rather quickly."

"But still had too much left to drink." Keilon stared at the contents of his own wine glass. "You're right, these do not mix well."

"All the more reason to drink it quickly!" Old Keilon raised his glass briefly before he and the king tilted their heads back to down the remaining mixture of wine and whiskey.

Dylah fell into the empty seat next to their predecessor.

"He tends to talk about my childhood when he's been drinking, how much has he told you?"

"Quite a bit!"

"You were the cutest kid." Keilon grinned.

"But probably not too cute after she broke Kremon's arm right?" Old Keilon chuckled. "That sounded terrifying."

"Absolutely terrifying." Keilon stared into his empty glass. "Teenage girls are the worst, I don't know how I survived her adolescence."

"I should probably catch up." Dylah laughed. "Pour me a glass."

"You got it, kiddo." Keilon reached into a low drawer and was surprised to find another bottle there, he refilled each of their glasses before raising his own. "To history."

"To the future," the ghost replied.

"To balance," Dylah added.

"To the queen of Hightree." Her brother laughed.

"To the king of Fellowrock." She rolled her eyes.

"To the silver stag," Keilon said with a slight smile.

"To the youngbloods," the predecessor said as their eyes slowly ignited with amaranth. "May you continue to rise above me."

"Unmatched." Dylah nodded to her brother.

"Unbroken," Keilon answered.

They brought their glasses together before taking a drink.

The first Keilon never truly understood why his soul had been split between two vessels, he longed for someone else to shoulder the burden with him but never dreamed it could be done. Now seeing it in front of him, their love, trust, and connection, it all made sense, this was always the way it was supposed to be.

Chapter 66

Known as Death

It had been three mornings since the sound of her childrens' laughter felt like a hammer on her brain, but Dylah didn't mind the small consequence after having the opportunity to let her soul rest with its other pieces for a single night. She barely remembered stumbling out of the office after her brother fell asleep at his desk and the stag had fallen to the floor to briefly rest his eyes while mumbling slurred syllables of a forgotten language.

That night felt like a shift to their new normal. Dylah had been brainstorming ways to use the predecessor as an active member of Fellowrock. Perhaps he could be a commander, she remembered a brief conversation where he stated that he enjoyed mapping, maybe he'd be of some use in a more logical way.

Her pen tapped on a blank page as her son and daughter scribbled furiously on their own papers, a morning routine that would probably always remain. She was halfway through a sip of coffee when Cav dropped his pencil in frustration.

"I don't know what this means," he grumbled.

"Maybe you should take a break then, kiddo." Dylah smiled to hide her instant worry. "You can always revisit it later."

"I don't know." He sighed. "It's really different."

"Would a walk help?" Dylah gestured in the direction of the treeline.

"Trees!" Rilavry laughed.

"I don't know," Cav repeated before continuing his sketches.

Dylah had never seen him in such a way, and she could only think of vague ways to explain the behavior to Axen before she had to leave for a training session in Fellowrock. She was in awe of her son's gift, she appreciated the piece of her mother that he carried, and she had known he was special the moment she knew of his existence. But as she walked towards Fellowrock, she couldn't help but notice the ripple in her own optimism that his worry over the unknown had caused.

It had been three mornings since the first to be named Keilon woke up on the floor of his prodigy's office with the worst headache he had had in centuries. But after the hangover passed he found an ignited purpose to finish what he had started so he could continue to be an advisor to the fawns of Fellowrock, the prodigies he was so proud of.

His motivation quickly waned as the topics of his writing grew darker with each word he scribbled onto the paper. The words grew with rage, their bite seemed to spring off the page and clamp around his heart.

"Where are we at now?" Sorner asked, trying to ignore the worrisome lines beneath his brother's eyes.

"After I exiled you." Old Keilon gripped the pen a little tighter. "Not many survived the grief and regret I carried."

"Take a break, I beg of you, just take a break."

"If I stop then I'll never finish." The stag closed his eyes for a moment and let the images of those begging for their lives fill his sight. "I have to get it done."

Sorner's face fell into his hands as he began to weep. "I should have begged you to let me stay. I should have ran back to you. I should have been a better brother after Enfy's passing. I should have taken the fall for Hekar's death. I should have done my part and prevented the buckets of chaos. I failed you."

Old Keilon reached across the table and held his brother's arm. "Stop, we have no idea what that would have changed. It may have even created a bloodier history."

Sorner attempted to form many words but couldn't get further than their first syllables.

"It's terrible I know, the trees of our kingdom have only grown so tall because I fed the soil with countless bodies." Old Keilon sighed. "But the more I see the thriving kingdoms now, the more I realize that I had to be that villain. My crimes are in no way justified, but would we still have our strong prodigies if I had been benevolent? If I hadn't erased the history and let them grow knowing what they were, would they be so level headed with their power? I have to write this, because it is important in a way we may never understand, because one day our prodigies will have their own prodigies of peace and power and I owe them the truth."

"Then I shall sit here and watch you wither away from the weight of your choices," Sorner mumbled. "And it will also kill me in the process."

The first Keilon gulped away his brother's sadness as he went on to describe the trio of rebellious thieves that thought they could oust him in his sleep. He explained that two of the assailants were brothers and the other was their cousin, but all three fell after one swipe of the stag's left sword. A simple comma separated the words 'they bled out' and 'I went back to sleep.'

Sorner was now entering a state of harmonious panic.

He had snatched a blank sheet of paper and was furiously scribbling a sketch of a rabbit. He took a deep breath with each petal on a tulip he drew. Where he had found lightness, a cloud of grief covered the other half of the table.

"Would it ease you at all to know that my forgiveness started within the last second you were in front of me?" Sorner sniffled.

"My own guilt began well before that moment."

"I never knew how truly blessed we were to be exiled." Sorner hung his head. "We had so many problems to solve, but we were safe and protected, we thrived." He shook his head. "I felt how much you suffered, I really did, but how was I to know you carried so much?"

"I think I'll stop for the day." He stood and pushed his chair in.

The deck doors opened with an excitement that almost scared the two ancient men.

"Come with me!" Cav shouted as he entered the kitchen. "We have to go now!" He was struggling to catch his breath, and moments later his father followed after him.

"Sorry about that." Axen came to an abrupt stop with a hand on his son's shoulder. "He said we had to go then just ran here, I don't know what he knows!"

"Child." Sorner stood and took a step towards the mismatched eyes. "What have you seen?"

"I have to show Uncle K something!" Cav grinned. "I was looking at my grandma's book and a voice told me where to go!"

"Junia's voice?" Axen asked.

"No." Cav shook his head. "They said they made a deal with the water. I don't know what that means." He grabbed the ghost's hand. "Come on! I have to show you!"

Old Keilon shared worried glances with his brother and Axen, he was confused and terrified by what forces could have spoken to the boy he so adored.

Cav trudged through the forest pulling the stag's hand.

Sorner and Axen followed quietly. They took sharp turns that didn't seem to make sense until they reached a tree with an energy around it that felt welcoming.

Axen studied the surroundings, Fellowrock's geography often confused him but something about this specific area felt familiar. Then he saw it, just behind the tree was the purple glow of the lilac field. "Cav," he said with a raised eyebrow. "Where are we?"

"Here!" Cav smiled and finally let the ghost free.

The young child stood at the base of the tree and put a flat hand on its trunk. Within a moment a small compartment opened above the boy's head.

Axen stepped forward and stared with wide eyes at the stack of aged papers within the tree. He picked up the top one and recognized the familiar handwriting of Queen Junia. He scanned it and the more he read, the more he couldn't help but smile.

"Here." Axen handed the stack to Old Keilon. "These are about you."

"What?" He slowly took the papers.

"They're very important!" Cav laughed.

It took a few long seconds for the stag's eyes to settle on the writing.

It was always the seers' plan to bring back the chaotic soul. I know, it sounds silly, but one of our own loved him dearly and we had to take her words to heart. For they could have broken the curse but he never allowed himself to vocalize what was in his heart for the safety of those he could harm outside the borders.

"What does it say, brother?" Sorner asked.

"I can't believe this," he whispered.

We began trying to bring him back a century after his death. It allowed enough time for Fellowrock to heal, and forget. But just like his legends claimed, he was a stubborn soul to catch. Many tried and they all failed. A few claimed that they were successful but found the soul to be reluctant and fleeting. But I, Junia Rilonck, finally figured out the riddle behind the chaotic soul. Not only did he want his prodigy to grow up ignorant to their power, he also didn't want to place that full burden on another.

And that's precisely why I named two of my children after the chaotic souls. I got my Keilon so easily, really, I was shocked how easily I got him after reading these accounts of constant failures. He arrived through the strongest blizzard Fellowrock had ever seen, I instantly knew what he was. But I could tell after trying again with my second born that the soul was terrified of returning in full force to the trees. Then my sixth child, my daughter, arrived in a grand storm with specks of lavender in her eyes. The first part of my plan had been successful.

The first Keilon took a moment to process the motives of a woman he thought he knew so well in the afterlife. But still, questions remained.

Before his death, the silver stag wanted to find a way to come back to teach the person who followed him. A truly noble offer, but most were skeptical given the gruesome nature of his reign. And maybe that is why their attempts failed. They wanted their child to have the power without the knowledge of who it came from, they tried to eliminate his ability to return altogether. I was instructed to tell my daughter that her eyes were simply a gift and nothing more. But, I chose to not repeat the mistakes of my own ancestors. I looked into the future and saw the way my daughter and son arrived at the conclusion, I watched as they surpassed him through their own ignorance. So I put it all in motion.

The field beyond this tree used to be a hidden corner of Fellowrock, where the seers hid after discovering that they could not be persuaded by the chaotic soul's eyes. But they still welcomed him to their tents, I'm told he spent his older years mapping out Fellowrock just trying to find this place. By the time I became queen the magic around this field had faded and it was just an empty space. I had already given birth to a portion of the soul, I just needed to prove my commitment to get the remaining piece.

Together, my son and I planted this field of lilacs. I watched them grow but after her birth they stopped, almost stunted. The lilacs today are the same ones that grew until she entered the world. That is how I knew he would come back for my children. But the sign was clearer than I intended. See, a flower pausing its growth is very obviously chaos, but maintaining its beauty? That's harmony.

I tweaked the first Keilon's request. We wouldn't just need someone to teach our new chaotic souls, we'd also need the soul of harmony.

His breath came to an abrupt stop as he stared at Sorner. His second chance with his brother was welcomed but he never understood how it happened.

After compiling a few accounts from Hightree and Verinas I knew that the brothers' split was among the most tragic things to happen because of the curse. Had Keilon not lost Sorner perhaps our history wouldn't be drowned in blood. The order to exile so many was both evil and merciful and history may never see it that way. No, this was not my original plan, but you see, I had five sons. I know the bond that brothers have.

With the soul split, Keilon will have two chances to return and make amends with his past. These may be high hopes, but I have to try. Moreso, if the chaotic soul is split then the soul of harmony is split too. It may take a while but the last soul will gain the power in their eyes once the first Keilon acknowledges his wrongdoings, owns the blood he spilled, and has a will to carry on in a new life with joy.

If this happens, the souls will be complete and Sorner may return through an eclipse.

To history he was known as death, but my hope is that the future sees him for who he truly is. Therefore, if the person reading this has been a witness to such an event, let it be known that if the souls of chaos and harmony are at their strongest and working together in peace, then we, the seers the only ones who remember the true history of Fellowrock, acknowledge that Keilon Rilonck, the first of his name, will be absolved of his past.

Old Keilon held the bundle of papers to his chest and breathed a sigh of relief. For the first time in all of his lives the weight of murky water no longer filled his lungs. He could finally breathe deeper than ever, he was a tall man but he no longer felt dwarfed by regret and grief. He closed his eyes tightly just to feel it all and behind his eyelids he saw a pink burst of lightning as if he had been reborn in that moment.

"Brother?" Sorner put his hand on his shoulder. "Say something."

The stag smiled with his eyes still closed, and when he finally opened them they were an amethyst that sparkled brighter than ever. "We can do it now. Sorner, we can leave." He looked up into the canopy of the forest. "I'm free."

Chapter 67

On a Mountain

The papers had been passed from Axen to Sorner and back many times as the first Keilon laughed while he watched Cav climb a tree. They found that the papers listed the history they needed, which meant that the stag no longer had an obligation to write it. He loved where Fellowrock was at, he adored how well his prodigies were thriving, but Sorner was right, they needed to leave. The history had been something he owed to the people he wronged and to the people that would come after him. But freedom was something he owed to the young version of himself from three hundred years ago, to the man he could have been during his first life.

"So I'll be telling my prodigy tonight," Sorner said while pouring a celebratory glass of wine. "When will you be informing yours?"

"I'm trying not to think about it." He took the bottle from Sorner but realized he wouldn't be able to stomach the taste with everything on his mind. "Though I'm almost positive one won't need to be told."

Sorner's eyes went wide as he stared at the doorway behind his brother. "I think you are right about that."

Old Keilon turned to meet her eyes of flame. "Youngbl-"

"Oh did I arrive too early?" Dylah's arms were crossed tightly and her left foot tapped at a concerning speed. "If I had been just two minutes later would you have still been here? Hm?"

"I lived with giants for decades," Sorner whispered. "She dwarfs them all with that stare. I'll go find Kunor."

"Would you like a glass of wine?" Old Keilon asked slowly as she began taking steps towards him. "May I ask what weapons you brought?"

"I didn't bring any." She leaned against the counter with her head pointed down. "For your safety."

"Ya know, I actually kind of thought you'd be happy for me."

"Cav told me. Then Axen explained." Her head finally tilted up to look at him. "I didn't think I'd be the last to know."

"You're not!" He laughed. "Keilon doesn't know yet, and Kunor will be finding out very soon."

"Was any thought given to this?" She sighed. "Or have we bored you already?"

"Dylah, please, you have to understand that I need to leave." The first Keilon shook his head. "I can't stay here, this place was never meant for me."

"The chaotic soul is most at home within the trees! That's a fact!" She forced the volume of her voice if only to push her sadness away.

"I'm not the chaotic soul anymore."

"What about your prodigies? You're going to abandon us?"

"C'mon, youngblood." He half smiled. "You're stronger than I ever was."

"What about Cav?!" A tear slid down her cheek. "He

adores you! You helped him grow his gift, he leaned on you so much after all of that kidnapping trauma. Now you just leave him?"

"I've talked to the kid extensively." Old Keilon leaned against the counter with arms crossed. "He's even given me a few warnings about my journey."

"You leave in two days? That's what Axen said." She took a few steps towards the door while shaking her head. "I'll try to see you before then."

He took a wide step and grabbed her arm. "Let's get a few things straight right now." He watched as she changed her bluish gray eyes to green in a single blink. "I have failed you more times than I have helped you. Your favorite childhood fairytale was a lie because of me. I trapped you in these trees. I am the reason you felt compelled to keep a terrible curse. I gave you nightmares as a child. I gave you nightmares as an adult. I killed you." He leaned over her with a dark glare. "I have moved past who I once was, but don't ignore it just because of these last few months."

"That doesn't mean you have to run away from all of us."

"Oh, I see." He slowly chuckled. "Got a little attached, did we?"

"I just don't see the benefit in you leaving right now." She crossed her arms.

"I get it. I know exactly what you're thinking and you are absolutely wrong." He waited until she was just about to answer then he cut her off. "You've associated me with your successes and I must say, that is ridiculous."

"Oh please, elaborate!"

"The power in your eyes." Old Keilon pointed at her face then to his. "You learned that from me." He raised an eyebrow. "That fun little curse trick you can do, you only took that because of who again?" He grinned. "Oh right, because of me!" He laughed as her eyes lit up with fire. "And the lightning, I'd like to imagine that was all because you thought your dear predecessor laid down his life for you, am I right?"

"Contributed slightly."

"That's a yes!" His grin widened. "But what you need to understand is that you did that all on your own, I was merely a witness."

"Flipping from ominous to joking doesn't suit you very well." She nearly smiled. "It's actually rather childish."

"Well you did say I was about twenty-six, right?" He held back a laugh. "So that makes me younger than you, your majesty."

Dylah softened after taking the time to study his forced smile and soon she let another tear fall. "You're scared to leave."

"Terrified." He took a seat at the table. "Since the curse was placed I dreamed of leaving and traveling so far away."

"You always wanted to escape," she whispered with a sudden realization.

"Yes." He chuckled. "I did leave before the curse, I fought in a lot of wars, too many to count really. And I met Teyle a few times while she was away studying. But I never really got to take any of it in. Plus most of it was all boring flatlands and marshes, I'd like to climb a mountain this time. A real mountain, not the constant hills I once thought were mountains."

"That first time on top of a mountain after breaking the curse was something I'll never forget." She smiled. "And not just because it was the moment my eyes changed."

"I'd like to stand on a mountain again."

"Again?" Dylah raised an eyebrow. "But you just said-"

"I know what I said." The first Keilon met her confused stare with ignited magenta. "I've seen the top of a mountain once before, I saw it with these same eyes. It sparked life into me just like it sparked a purpose in you." He smiled. "Because I looked down on that foreign terrain, I saw the way the yellow grass danced in the wind. I felt so full of rage but the oddest thing was how small I felt."

"What?"

"I am simply saying that I saw it with my own eyes but

during a time when they did not belong to me." He laughed as he watched her mind spin. "Again, I also felt quite small."

"You saw it through me?"

"Yes, Dylah." His grin widened into a full smile. "I've known you since my first life. And maybe that's why it's so hard for us to say goodbye."

"Your first life?" She shook her head. "How is that even possible?"

"Long story for another time, I trusted a seer, that's all you really need to know." He shrugged. "You pulled that spear out so fast! Did you even feel the pain? It was awful and there was so much blood!"

"You felt that?"

"Yes," he said through a constant chuckle, "centuries before you ever did."

"I think I've always known you too." She sighed. "I have memories that I know never happened to me and I always swore I was a king."

"There's something else about that vision I had." He glanced at her briefly then let his eyes wander down to his fidgeting hands. "It wasn't just the mountain, there were other images too, and sounds. I could hear your name but it was all a little distorted, almost like I had heard it under water. I thought your name was Dylidah."

"Dylidah?" She half laughed. "That's still a pretty name."

"I thought so too." He slowly smiled. "It was my daughter's name."

Dylah's eyes were fire in an instant. "You named your daughter after me and yet you still killed me in your second life?!"

"Sorry, youngblood." He pointed to himself with a proud smile. "I've been absolved of my past so that was a different guy."

Dylah calmly stood from her seat, poured two glasses of wine without saying a word, then returned to the table with more tear streaks than before.

"Can I be completely honest with you about something then?" She watched as she swirled the wine in her glass. "I didn't think you were all that bad the first time around, well, at the beginning. You were a good teacher and I trusted you. It was actually pretty painful to realize the other motives you had." Her finger tapped nervously on the glass. "I think a part of me always knew you were family, and what hurt the most about that revival was that I failed. We could have had this sooner."

"Oh I can beat that bout of honesty." He grinned when she looked up with a look of shock. "I knew the moment you gave up on me."

"You did not." She rolled her eyes. "I was so sneaky."

"Please, I invented sneaky." He rolled his eyes back. "Now before you argue, just remember that I can always tell when you're forcing the color of your eyes."

"That day in the woods?"

"That's the one."

"Damnit." Dylah took a drink. "I'm actually a little confused about something."

"I really can't explain that vision I had so many years ago." Old Keilon shrugged. "I was given a really awful drink and I saw it all play out from my own eyes but they were actually yours somehow."

"No, it's not about that." She sighed. "The letters said that my mother was giving you two chances. So that means that she lied to me in that twilight forest." Her eyes swirled with clouds as she stared at the crimson liquid. "She didn't want me to be like Dycavlon either."

"You're right." He smiled. "She didn't want you to be like any of your predecessors, not even your brother. She just wanted you to be Dylah."

The door slammed open once more and heavy stomps approached with an abrupt stop in front of the ancestor.

"You're leaving?!" Keilon asked with crossed arms and eyes aflame.

Old Keilon sighed. "Would you like to join us for some wine and honesty?" He stood slowly and took a single step towards the counter. "I have some stories to share about you as a wild little teenager."

"He held me by the ankle out of a fourth story window once." Dylah laughed.

"You weighed nothing." Keilon smiled. "I could have done that for days." He thought for a moment. "I still can."

"He very much enjoyed pacing the halls." The first Keilon shook his head. "Walked through me several times no matter how hard I tried to get his attention."

"I knew you were there." Keilon took the glass of wine from his predecessor. "I simply just ignored you."

"You mean to tell me that I spent nights trying to chase your presence through those halls and you knew I was there?"

"Yes." Keilon grinned. "I found you rather annoying."

"I'm just grateful that I barely remember the nightmares you gave me as a child." Dylah took a drink.

"Ah yes, but I still remember the terror your little screams gave me." Keilon rolled his eyes.

"You don't even remember all of the ones I gave you as an adult." Old Keilon chuckled.

"What's that supposed to mean?" She glared as her wine glass hovered in front of her mouth. "I was having them almost every night after my eyes changed."

He took a drink as his laughs persisted. "I'm almost sorry to tell you this."

"What?" she growled.

"I tried to visit you before your eyes actually changed." Old Keilon slowly grinned. "We felt the color in your eyes come back and I thought it was time, but, well. You were cursed and the soul felt so damn condensed, I tried but I couldn't quite talk to you." His grin spread into a smile. "Then you really started to panic."

She thought for a moment. "Are you talking about when

I was in Hightree? After I was reunited with Axen and the colors came back, no that doesn't seem right. I would have remembered that." She shook her head. "I had one nightmare, but it was about Delin."

"Right, about that." He laughed. "Remember the night in the jail cells, who did you think I was at first?"

"Delin." Dylah slumped at the realization as her predecessor laughed into his wine glass.

"At least with him roaming the world he can't do stuff like that anymore," Keilon added.

"How did you even find out he was leaving?" Dylah asked with a raised eyebrow.

"Well, I was working in my office when I heard this wailing coming from the foyer," Keilon answered. "I ran to see who was mortally injured, but instead I found Kunor trying to console Sorner."

The door opened one more time as Kunor pushed Sorner into the house, Sorner was still quietly crying as he cradled a rabbit to his chest.

"He's fine." Kunor let out a deep breath. "It was a little rough there for a bit, but then we found the rabbit and that seemed to really help."

"He's a precious friend and harmonious protector of the forest." Sorner sniffled. "And I love him."

"Do we need to pack him a bag so he can join us on our journey?" The first Keilon covered his smile.

"How dare you!" Sorner's eyes went dark. "I would never steal him away from everything he's ever known and loved." His eyes softened as he looked at his brother. "I'm going to go set this friend down outside."

They waited in silence for Sorner to take a seat at the table, they waited a bit longer for him to compose himself once again. Glasses were poured for the souls of harmony but still no words were passed around.

"What will you do with the house? It was a dream to live within these walls. Once upon another lifetime Brennit always joked about building our house on the border." Sorner's smile softened at the memory. "It's truly lovely, would be a shame to leave it empty."

"I don't know yet," Dylah said through a sigh. "Maybe Kunor and Sentry could make some use of it."

Kunor's eyes went wide and shifted between Dylah who was grinning and his father who was not. "Um no, I don't think that is necessary at this point in time."

"Good answer." Keilon smiled.

The embodiment of balance sat at the table sharing a drink and avoiding what was coming. They talked of the weather, of weapons, and the ancestors explained the syllabic meanings of each of their names. When the wine was gone they went their separate ways, but only because it wasn't truly goodbye yet.

Chapter 68

Always

Dylah narrowed her eyes to funnel every bit of focus and precision she had into the tips of her fingers. She had tried and failed too many times already and she wasn't going to let this break her. After a deep breath she began again, all while reminding herself that she was a commander, a queen, a storm, a fighter. She refused to give up now.

A knock came to the door of their suite and Cav answered quickly, because he already knew who it was.

"Hey, kid." Old Keilon grinned. "I was hoping we could walk around the garden again today."

"Because you're leaving for a really long time?" Cav asked with a smile.

"Yes," he answered slowly. "And you're still okay with that?"

"Yeah." Cav shrugged.

A familiar groan echoed from the living area, followed by a soft giggle.

"Everything okay here?" The first Keilon asked as he

stepped further into the suite.

"Mama is trying to braid my sister's hair." Cav laughed. "She's not very good at it."

"I see that." He chuckled.

The suite door opened again as Axen walked in reading a paper. "Okay, Avalia wrote down the instructions and even added a few pictures."

"I really almost had it this time," Dylah said through a rumbling sigh. "But halfway through I realized most of her hair wasn't actually in the braid."

"I've seen you braid your own hair, is it really that different?" Axen regretted the question the moment he saw embers in her eyes.

"If you two don't mind, I'm going to take the kid for a little while." Old Keilon tried not to laugh at their panicked frustration.

Dylah looked up at him. "Now?" she whispered. "Are you sure?"

"There is no other time."

"Better get going then." Axen smiled with a nod towards the door.

The ghost and the kid raced down the many steps of the castle, they paused to knock on the door of Avalia and Kremon's suite, but ran off laughing before they could answer. Finally they arrived at the gardens that rested behind the castle. Old Keilon listened intently as Cav rattled off the names of each flower they passed. Of all the things that had ignited his final life, the boy with mismatched eyes was at the top of the list.

"Do you like being a big brother?" he asked as Cav skipped along the edge of a raised planter.

"Yeah! But sometimes she growls at me." Cav laughed. "Do you have a little sister?"

"Two," he answered with a forced smile.

"Any brothers?"

"Four." If it had been just a week prior, the answer would

have felt like a stab to his heart. Now that he felt at peace with a past that felt separate from who he truly was, he could remember his brothers' lives, and not the deaths he sent them to.

"Oh, mama has five." Cav jumped down from the planter. "Dad has eighteen."

"Is that all?" Old Keilon laughed at the child's calm deliverance of such a strange fact.

They walked a little further, Cav led the way with a prideful energy that had obviously been passed down to him from both of his parents.

"So Cav, I'll be leaving tomorrow," he finally said. "Are you still okay with that?"

"Yeah!" Cav smiled. "It'll be fun for you and the funny one."

"What did you see?"

"Mountains!"

"Exciting! Anything else?"

Cav thought for a moment. "That's for you to see."

"That's fair." They turned to head back towards the castle, it shocked the stag to feel small fingers grab on to his. "Cav, how long do you think we've known each other?"

Cav laughed. "Always?"

"You're right." He squeezed his hand. "I'm sorry for the nightmares, purely a misunderstanding."

"That's okay." Cav smiled up at him. "I'm sorry for lying."

"What?" Old Keilon stopped walking and looked at the boy with a confused look of shock. "I don't believe you'd ever tell a lie."

"Remember that one day when you noticed that your mug had moved a little bit?"

"Yes."

"And you asked me if I drank any of your coffee?"

"You did, huh?" He laughed and continued walking.

"Mama never lets me try hers and she's always drinking it so I wanted to try it!" Cav huffed.

"Well, what did you think?"

"Disgusting."

They walked for a little longer, it was evident that neither of them were in a hurry to get back.

"Before we part ways, is there anything else you'd like to ask me?" Old Keilon forced a laugh. "It may be a very long time before we see each other again."

Cav thought for a moment. "How are you my uncle? You're not my mama's brother, and I don't think you're my dad's brother either."

"Hate to break it to you but I'm actually not your uncle." He grinned. "I'm your great great great great great great great great grandfather. Give or take a few greats."

Cav tilted his head before bursting with laughter. "You're funny!"

"Just ask your mother!" He laughed with him, and soon the door to the suite came into sight. "Well, do you think they braided her hair yet?"

"They did." Cav smiled. "But they'll have to do it again."

"Your mama has a gift that belongs to the forest, do you know that? Well you should also know that your gift brought your ancestors to that very forest, because they could see the potential when a certain leader just wanted to stay in this big castle he had built." He knelt to be at Cav's level. "Cav, you are a seer, and that is a very special thing to be. You're the child of the people who broke a curse. One day you'll be the king, and you'll be a great one because you have been surrounded by strong and just leaders. But most importantly, you are Cav Farein, named for the joy you constantly exude, and that is a very special name to carry."

"My mama is about to open the door." Cav pointed at the suite.

"Understood." Old Keilon smiled. "I've really loved our time together, Cav."

"Me too." He grinned back with all of his teeth before reaching his arms around the ghost's neck.

The door opened and Dylah smiled at the display she had come across, but felt guilty that her interruption took her son's attention away from the ancestor's goodbye.

"It's okay," he whispered to her. "A few seconds longer and I would have called off the whole trip."

"Sorner is here waiting for you." She gestured for him to come inside.

Sorner was sitting on the couch, Axen and Rilavry sat in a chair facing him. Sorner was holding his arms out to Rilavry, but the young girl only scowled back.

"Are you ready to go?" Old Keilon asked.

Sorner whipped his head in the direction of his brother's voice and immediately pinned his eyes on Cav. "Child, come here, I would like to hold you if only to absorb a brief amount of your young blissfulness."

"He's been like this for about twenty minutes," Axen whispered towards them.

"I said my farewells to my prodigy and then stupidly visited the grave of my former lover so excuse me if I'm a little sensitive at the moment!" Sorner clutched a stuffed animal that he had found lying on the ground.

"I see you got the braids in," the first Keilon decided to change the subject.

"Yeah!" Dylah smiled with amethyst eyes that were pointed at her daughter. "Adorable."

Rilavry met her mother's gaze and pulled the bands on each of her braids before shaking her hair free.

"That is definitely your daughter." The stag elbowed her. "I'll see you tomorrow then?"

"Tomorrow." She nodded.

"Tomorrow!" Sorner's face fell into his hands as his sobs intensified.

"He forgets that this journey was his idea." Old Keilon helped his brother up, he paused to shake Axen's hand, then to ruffle Rilavry's loose obsidian hair, before saying another farewell to Cav.

The Rilonck brothers from centuries before left the Hightree castle they had once fought to take, they barely spoke with each step towards the final night in their borrowed home. Tomorrow would prove to be exhausting, the first leg of their journey into the unknown, and the severing of a trio bound together by a single soul.

Chapter 69

Shoulder to Shoulder

The morning came unfathomably fast after a night that seemed to drag on. The brothers had packed up the last of their few belongings and shared a silent cup of coffee. They were excited to venture out, but sometimes change demands very little reaction to give it the strength to move forward. Soon enough, they were staring at the courtyard walls, allowing time for the stag to ready himself for one last farewell.

Bahn and his sons situated them with two horses, though Bahn said they wouldn't be missed he also hinted that they were good steeds that would carry them for years. Sorner had named his within minutes, and a few moments later had named his brother's horse as well.

They walked through the forest towards the mountains slowly taking in the sight of endless trees. Old Keilon hoped there wouldn't be another forest like Fellowrock in the wide world because he had always known that his kingdom was special.

Two silhouettes blocked their path, which made the stag's heart sink.

"Sorner, do you mind waiting a few steps ahead?" The first Keilon asked as he watched his strongest prodigy tightly cross her arms.

"I get it." Sorner grinned and began to lead their horses away. "A single goodbye has the power to shred the heart over and over again for centuries."

Old Keilon smiled and turned to his prodigies with bright lavender eyes. "Hey there, youngbl-"

"Stop it." Dylah glared, her eyes aflame.

"Stop what?" He laughed.

"You're forcing the color of your eyes," she huffed. "Stop it."

"Fine." He let the deep blue shade shine through his irises. "Now stop forcing yours."

She sighed and met his solemn stare with the same shade of despair.

"You too, your majesty." The first Keilon grinned as he looked at the man who wore the same name.

"I long for a time when I could hide my own emotions." Keilon slumped a little and within a blink his eyes matched that of his sister's.

"You promise to visit?" Dylah asked with a tinge of anger to hide the sadness that resonated in her voice. "Or will your prodigies have to hunt you down from time to time?"

"I'll visit." Old Keilon nodded. "Though the hunt sounds like more fun."

"It wouldn't kill you to write a few letters," Keilon added.

"It might." He winked.

"I want you to take this," Dylah said as she handed him a small but heavy bag. She waited for him to take it and stare at the assortment of rocks. "It's so you can leave your bones everywhere you go."

"Quite the sentiment." He stared at the rocks from the

pond that held so many of Fellowrock's secrets. The stag thought for a moment about what he was leaving behind, he briefly considered staying, then an idea came to him. He turned towards Sorner. "We can't leave yet! I have to do one more thing!"

"Sure, will it be quick?" Sorner shouted back.

"I'm going to go jump in the pond!"

"Have you gone mad?!" Sorner raced after his brother and his two prodigies.

"For the first time in so many lifetimes I finally feel sane, brother." Old Keilon laughed with relief as he walked towards the site of countless nightmares and terrors. The place where his horrors began. The place that quenched his bloodthirsty soul, the place that became a home to vengeance and merciless killings, and the place where his restless violence was finally put to an end.

Keilon and Dylah followed silently, but both of them could feel a lightness within themselves, a change in something so deep in the core of their souls they knew it could only come from the person who gave them their power.

They arrived at the pond, it was nearly noon and sunlight reflected across the water. Dylah stood a little closer to her brother after a toad jumped several feet away from them. The first of his name kicked his boots off.

"Brother, please think this through." Sorner panicked. "We have made too much progress to fall into ruin now."

"I'm not trying to fall into ruin." The first Keilon took slow backwards steps towards the water. He extended his arms, closed his eyes, and fell back into the calm ripples.

Surviving the water was not something that came naturally to the predecessor of chaos. He had spent so much of his childhood fighting against the depths, throughout his adolescence he stared up through the distorted sunlight and considered sinking to the bottom. This water became his weapon in his adulthood, and now, in his third life it washed away the pain of the past.

He closed his eyes as he floated and felt the weak waves carry him as the sunlight spread over him. For centuries he dreamed of true freedom, he wondered what the price of it would be, and who would stand in his way. Though the price had been steep and the wait lengthy, he finally knew who had stood in his way the whole time. It wasn't rival kings, or vengeful soldiers, not even the ones who came after him, the only one who had held him back from feeling true peace was himself.

He plugged his nose and dove beneath the ripples to let the water wash away the last of his fears. He lingered under the surface for a while longer, he waited until his lungs wanted to burst. Finally he emerged with a breath to start yet another life, and immediately met Sorner's worried gaze treading water next to him.

"You know the last time you went under for that long you told me a man was trying to call you to the other side, child of chaos," Sorner huffed. "But do you feel better now?"

"Yes." He wiped droplets of water from his amethyst eyes. "Let's leave."

As they walked towards the treeline, Dylah fought the urge to laugh at how childlike her predecessor seemed. He stomped through the forest almost completely soaked, his laugh shook the branches they passed and almost sent the horses running. She thought back to when he had first arrived for the second time, after he helped them rescue Cav and she fought to keep him around. She looked at them again, and for the first time they didn't seem like ancestors brought back by tricky magic, now they were two young brothers setting out to see what the world would give them.

"This is it!" he said as turned to face his prodigies at the treeline. "Wait, you two look awfully dressed up."

They were both wearing navy capes that seemed a little cleaner and stiff, Dylah's was lined with lavender while Keilon's was lined with black.

"I have some business to attend to soon," Keilon said.

"I'll be giving my decision."

"Good." The first Keilon nodded. "And you, young-blood?"

"I always look like this." She grinned. "A new cape is warranted after a large battle."

"Sure," he answered with a smile.

Keilon stepped forward first, he shook the stag's hand and offered him parting words that hung heavy with the same sentimentality he carried for each of his siblings.

"Continue to be greater." Old Keilon put a hand on the king's shoulder.

"That won't be too hard." Keilon met him with a quick embrace before waiting off to the side for his sister.

"Arizmia is a really lovely place, and it is just over that mountain," Dylah rambled, "or if you decide to go through the valley look for a path to the left, it's an incredible view. Stay away from all mushrooms, some regions have some that are deadly and that's not how the first Keilon dies." She took a deep breath to continue her ramblings.

"Your chaos is different." He grinned.

"That's because mine is the best."

He took a deep breath and wrapped his arms around her. "Everything I have is because of you."

"Everything I have is because of you," she repeated his own words. "Well, most of it."

There was an understanding that hung between them in that moment that told them that nothing else needed to be said. He took slow steps away from the strongest friendship he had ever known to join his brother.

"See ya around, youngblood."

"See ya around, old man."

She kept her feet planted to watch the ancestors begin their journey. Keilon was soon at her side with a hand on her shoulder.

"I have to go get a bottle from the castle before I head to Hightree, care to join me?"

"Wine or whiskey?" Dylah asked with a wide smile.

"That's not for you to know just yet."

They turned to head towards the castle just as their predecessor decided he needed to look back at his prodigies one last time. He studied their strides, a king and his second in command, a queen and her many special gifts. And as they walked through a sunbeam that pierced through the canopy of the forest he finally realized what was so different about their new capes.

The silver gleam of antlers hung on both of their backs, spreading from shoulder to shoulder. He thought about calling out after them, but instead soaked in the image that gave his lifelong title a new meaning.

"We are wasting precious sunlight, brother." Sorner nearly shouted.

"I'm coming," he sighed and turned to follow his brother.

"I know that time is not something you can grasp because of your frazzled little soul, but it is rather important to me," Sorner said sternly. "So I would just like to make that clear right now."

"You're a thorn in my side, you know that right?"

Sorner breathed in the fresh air of the unknown. "And yet you still don't pluck me out."

Chapter 70

Trees and Lilacs

Dylah collected her children from Avalia's suite in the early evening. The day had been heavy but the sadness lifted when she held the hands of her son and daughter. With so much of the past left behind she walked towards her suite with an excitement of what could come next. She had spent an hour of the day practicing her lightning strikes in an abandoned field. Dylah was getting stronger than ever before and the possibilities were dancing at her electric fingertips.

After opening the door of their suite, Cav and Rilavry ran in towards their father who was just as excited to see them after his own long day. They carried on their normal evening routine, not wanting to vocalize the other's hardships in front of their young children. When dinner was over, and Rilavry had been put back in bed twice. They sat at the couch hand in hand collecting their breaths.

"How are you holding up?" Axen asked. "And don't lie, I saw that lightning from my office window."

"Great sadness is only a reaction to the loss of great joy." She forced a weak smile. "What about you? Did today go how you expected?"

"My first prototype of the sword could use some tweaks, but it's better than I expected."

"And are you still excited to see yourself as anything other than an archer?" Her smile became genuine.

"I'll be an archer again one day, but there's something about the sword that is rather thrilling." He laughed. "I think you're rubbing off on me, nightmare."

"Well it's about time, enemy prince." She placed a quick peck on his cheek.

"Enemy king," he corrected with a laugh.

"And the meeting with Keilon?" Dylah asked slowly. "How did that go?"

Axen stood and walked to the kitchen. "Well, let's just say it's been a long day for both of us." He pulled out two glasses. "I could use a drink, what about you?"

"Depends on what you're offering." She smiled as she watched the familiar smirk grow.

Axen held up a bottle. "Whiskey."

"Then yes, it seems we have a lot to celebrate." She wrapped her arms around him as he rested his chin on her waves. "And you'll need to start planning."

"What do we call it?" he asked as he held her close. "The new kingdom, it needs a name, I don't even know where to start."

"You'll think of it." Dylah looked up at him to give him a quick kiss. "You always do."

She grabbed her glass of whiskey and they offered up cheers to the future for generations to come. They sat at their couch and stayed up chatting about every benefit the merging of the two kingdoms could offer them. Dylah finally kicked her boots off, she showed off her new cape and teared up a little when explaining how Keilon had come up with the idea to put the antlers on their backs.

After another glass they laid on the couch, Dylah rested her head on his chest and soaked in the feeling of endless possibilities for a bright future. A smile grew as she thought of the lost boy she met so long ago and the things he had accomplished through his curiosity. Because hazel eyes had fallen in love with the sight of lavender, their kingdoms would be changed for the better.

The sound of his heartbeat had almost lulled her to sleep when a small silhouette shuffled towards her. Dylah maneuvered herself out of Axen's hold without waking him up. She held Rilavry close and walked to the window so she could check on the moon.

"Trees." Rilavry smiled at the window. "Go?"

"It's late, maybe we can go tomorrow," Dylah whispered with a wide smile. "Trees and anything else you want to see."

"Flowers." Rilavry met her mother's bright gaze.

"Flowers? How about some lilacs?"

"Yes!" The child's excitement bounced around the room. "Trees and lilacs!"

Dylah squeezed her daughter a little tighter. "Trees and lilacs." She kissed her forehead. "Of course, princess."

The End

The saga will conclude with "Through the Treeline" Book Four

Malice Made from Memory

The history is finally told in the
Through the Treeline prequel

Havoc
Hewn
into
Heritage

About The Author

Tuesday Simon

 Tuesday Simon has always been a storyteller and is overjoyed to share her stories with the world. The wild imagination of her youth never went away and has only grown through her life experiences. Tuesday is happily married to the most handsome man in the world, Jake. He has answered approximately one million questions concerning plot holes, battle strategies, and character theories throughout the drafting of this series and never seems to mind. They lived in Hawaii for a couple years before settling down in Colorado, except they sold that house after a year and have once again settled down for good (probably). Together they enjoy obsessing over many fandoms, doting on their two dogs and a cat, and sipping scotch. Tuesday knew the moment she saw him nine years ago that their life together would be full of fun, and boy was she right.

There are many things that shaped Tuesday into the super cool person she is today, such as the time she watched her grandma punch a shoe thief in the face. Her family is large and loud and she is inspired by each and every one of them. After her paternal grandmother's passing she was tasked with being the family's historian. She currently holds centuries worth of family trees and plans to continue digging until she proves she's related to the most fearsome vikings.

Tuesday hopes that through reading her books, the readers

learn that there is power within their souls, that what makes them weak makes them strong, and that they should absolutely stay wild.